13 Voices (by Fanny Ferris of Black Horse l

Bradford, Leeds and Huddersfel'
tell your tales and tell them well,
there's thirteen voices whispering still
in Bradford Leeds and Huddersfel'

Over the tops the wind blows ill
and whistles down the grey stone valley,
it darkens when it meets the mill
and weaves with evil in the alley

Yorkshire flagstones marked with chalk,
hopscotch, skipping, hear the clapping,
girls at play plan lives at work,
never knowing what will happen.......

She remembers childhood simple treasures,
a kali-sprinkled liquorice,
roaming moors, collecting heathers,
dropping stones to make a wish

Evil threw him to the streets,
madness whipped him into sinning,
crouching behind him horror waits,
twas horror, horror, sent him spinning,

Life's warp and weft brings them together,
he kills her hope! (Her hope is dead.)
No wish come true, no lucky heather,
a twisted kiss to the back of the head.....

She hides there, mattress over her,
a horror-sprinkled geo-cache,
waiting for her next discoverer,
waiting to turn to dust and ash.

Yorkshire flagstones marked with chalk,
by shaking hands, a dead-life mapping,
grown men falter, hear them weeping,
as they survey his terrible work.

In death she dreams a ghost-life gone,
the joyful song of the busy thrush,
her eyes' light fades and fixes on
the purple jewels of the bilberry bush......

Oh Keighley, Bingley, Heaton Hill
there's thirteen voices whispering still
of Bradford, Leeds and Huddersfel',
Of Hull and Halifax and hell,

Horror sent him spinning, spinning,
watch him! Catch him! Spinning, spinning,
girls at play are spinning, spinning,
the dark satanic mills are spinning,

Keighley, Bingley, Heaton Hill,
there's thirteen voices whispering still,
of Bradford, Leeds and Huddersfel',
Of Hull and Halifax and hell.

By Black Horse Fairy

For Ashley Cartwright AKA Archie Blackwell
(of The 'Mighty' Black Horse Fairy)

CONTENTS

- The Yorkshire Ripper (A Prologue)
1. Love on the Rocks
2. Genesis of a Serial Killer
3. Northern Moses
4. Irish Annie
5. Olive
6. Silsden
7. Wilomena (Wilma)
8. Emily
9. Marcella
10. Irene
11. Leeds (Horsforth – Hidden History)
12. Tina
13. Jayne
14. Maureen
15. Scottish Jean
    Interview with a Serial Killer 1&2
16. Marilyn
17. Yvonne
18. Elena (Helen)
    Pen Pal 1 & 2
19. Eva (Vera/Mary)
    Interview with a Serial Killer 3&4
20. Ann
    Pen Pal 3
21. Jo
22. Audio Red Herring
    Interview with a Serial Killer 5
23. Babs
    Wearmouth Suicide Attempt
24. Flush out the Ripper, Privately Financed Policing
25. Ilkley (Hidden History)
    Interview with a Serial Killer 6,7,8 & 9
    Drink Driver
26. Margo
27. Uphadya
28. Leeds (Hidden History)
29. Theresa
30. Jackie
31. Ava
32. Hammerton Anarchy

33. Dewsbury Police Station
34. Sheffield
35. 6 Garden Lane
36. Dewsbury Police Station Revisited
37. Peter the Confessor
38. Do It Yourself (DIY) Gimp Attire
39. Dewsbury and the Magistrates Court
40. HMP Armley
41. HMP Parkhurst
42. Peter meets James
43. Peter Meets Keith
44. Broadmoor Hospital (Chapter 44)
45. Peter Meets Paul (Chapter 45)
46. Peter Meets Ian (Chapter 46)
47. Broadmoor Routine (Chapter 47)
48. Yorkshire Ripper created 1967CE expired 2001CE
49. The Devils Accomplice
    Sonia Maree (McCann) Newlands
50. Peter Meets Patrick
51. Regina versus Coonan
    References

THE YORKSHIRE RIPPER (A Prologue)

March 1981 CE eight previous interviews Peter's tryst with God becomes public, the good Lord sent Peter a message that now was to reveal the motivation behind the murderous mission.

The Gospel according to Peter

Sunday the 2nd of June 1946 CE, Kathleen Frances Sutcliffe (nee Coonan) and John William Sutcliffe are blessed with the birth of their first born, a boy who was to leave an indelible stain on the landscape of northern England. A Gemini in the Zodiac, a celestial co-ordinate system. A map of destiny but was Peter's destiny pre-ordained by another force? An Ancient Greek, attempt at mapping the heavens. A circle of animals, the circle of life. The beast inside, a mythological hybrid of man and beast, a lone wolf, damaged goods, but all this was yet to come.

The happy couple name their son Peter William. A man who was to end up with a mission, a modern-day seer a prophet, with supernatural insight into the future or a sadistic necrophilia murderer? But all this was yet to come, however the truth behind the Yorkshire Ripper merges with the myth, reality merges with fantasy and sanity merges with insanity. A twilight world on the margins of society, a twilight county disjointed/detached from Mother England, the West Riding of Yorkshire.

Old Testament, New Testament to the Postmodern Testament, a binary assessment of man's communication with God. Black and white. Good and evil. Wrong and right. A deregulated bible contorted and distorted by all that is low and base in the world. Throughout the bible there is reference of God speaking to various men, surprisingly Peter felt that his name had been added to this illustrious list.

Adam, Eve, Noah, Abram, Abraham, Ibrahim, Isaac, Jacob, Joseph, Moses, Gideon, Samuel, David, Elijah, and Isaiah, all on the right side of white western history. This group of people were auspicious company in which to be held. Trailblazers, history makers, history changers, important figures religiously and politically. Peter William Sutcliffe/Coonan, AKA the Yorkshire Ripper, 'Spring Heeled Jack', 'our kid', believed they were his peers, his predecessors, passing on the baton of truth honesty and virtue to him to pursue, prolong and persist in. Unfortunately, Peter William Sutcliffe was on the wrong side of history.

Peter was to become a vessel, a tool for the Lord to work. Peter's mission was to be built on Adam's original argument at the beginning of history, for Eve was the real wrongdoer and was therefore responsible for the predicament of man and society in general. Peter unlike Adam remained honourable and did not besmirch, sully or slander God unlike his religious forbear. Peter remained steadfastly loyal to God. Peter was to give his freedom, a true sacrifice unlike the play acting of Abraham, AKA Abram. For everybody knew that woman was in league with the serpent, the devil and as such could not, should not be trusted. Peter was to become a dark Angel doing the much-needed dirty work that no one wanted to do, no one wanted to sully their reputation, no one wanted to soil, spoil, smear, denigrate, degrade, discredit his character. It was a prize he had thrust upon him and a price he was more than willing to pay.

Paradise, circa 3761 BCE, 'The Garden of Eden', original sin and the fall of man. The tree of knowledge and the tree of life, forbidden fruit, the serpent, punishment and expulsion. The beginning of the end. Eve, the mother of creation, largely overlooked, the misogyny of the Bible? The misogyny of the Yorkshire Ripper.

Peter often pondered his fortune that Eve ate from the 'Tree of Knowledge' and not the 'Tree of Life', for it would have been quite difficult if not impossible to kill the whores if they were immortal. The critical path of creation linked to his critical path of killing, for God had the foresight to make man mortal. Culpable and responsible for their wrongdoing, their sins. More importantly the sins of womankind.

Peter's tale was to take on biblical type proportions not unlike his forebear Noah, of the ark fame. Both men would have films made about their deeds. Noah, born 2705 BCE, was the great, great, great, great, great, great, great grandson of Adam and Eve. He was the last of the antediluvian patriarchs and the first patriarch of Judaism. The last of the old world, the first of the new world. Reminiscent of the world and society that Peter was born into, a child of the 1960's CE the dawn of a new age, the genesis of the Postmodern Testament and the demise of all that predates it. The death of morality, where hedonistic extremes lead to avarice, envy, wrath, sloth, gluttony, lust, and pride. A world in which its inhabitants were out of control and required domination and fear to mend their ways. A world that demanded the Yorkshire Ripper must exist.

It is the summer of 1966 CE. Peter William Sutcliffe was twenty years old. He was working alone in the Catholic section situated at the top of Bingley Cemetery digging a grave, his shovel fighting against the hard ground to cut through the solid soil. Immersed in earth his feet set in the base of the aperture some five feet sub ground level. Leaning on his shovel for a breather he heard an echoing ambiguous voice unclear, but near. Surveying his surroundings for the source of the sound Peter looked around alas there was no one in sight. Intrigued unhinged he emerged from the bowels of the earth and proceeded to walk up the steep slope. Peter walked to his right and to the top of the hill but still no one appeared. He heard the voice again indistinguishable words on top of words a super imposed tapestry of chatter. As he walked forward the source of the noise was directly in front of him emanating from the head of a gravestone, (a white stone cross with a black metal miniature Christ in the crucifix pose positioned to the centre of the cross), on the crest of the hill, just short of the wooded perimeter.

The gravestone was that of a Polish man Bronislaw Zapolski. This day was to resonate with Peter and leave an ineradicable mark upon his psyche, the details of which were slightly blurred with the passage of time. But the basis of the events and the details of the day stood the test of time. Fifteen years after the event Peter would incorrectly recollect "*I remember the name on the grave to this day. It was a man called Zipolski. Stanislaw Zipolski*". Peter's grave digging career concluded in November 1967 CE. The fact that Peter remembered emphasises the indelible significance this moment had on his life and ultimately the life of others.

Peter walked warily towards the gravestone enthralled by the noise, he compared and contrasted the graves in front of him, trying to discern the direction of the voice, a message from the grave. Staring blankly at the white gravestone, transfixed because of the voice, Peter retreated slowly down the slope at a loss as to what was occurring. His gaze still on the headstone, confused disorientated but excited and privileged. Peter read 'Jejo' on the tombstone and assumed this to be the Polish for Jesus. Jesus was talking to Peter through the grave of Bronislaw. Peter continued to withdraw from the headstone walking backwards towards the path. Jesus said to Peter *"We be the echo"*. The heavens opened as it began to rain. Peter then walked to the top of the slope encompassing the valley, he surveyed the valley and its surroundings as he did so he contemplated heaven and earth and the insignificance of mankind. Throughout he felt an increased sense of self-importance his being resonated with significance, substance and magnitude. He felt fantastic flushed by the fact that God had chosen Peter William Sutcliffe to hear his words. It was so real, yet unreal in quality, so wonderful, what it lacked in context and content the delivery stirred something deep within. Peter told no one he had been selected, after all if it was meant for everyone to hear then they would hear it. Peter told no one he had been chosen and he was now a tool of God's will, he was important. Still unsure of the messages meanings mystified and confused as to why he had been chosen Peter continued with his daily life. Why me he thought and continued to look for reasons, but none was forthcoming. He could not get this episode out of his head. Peter had joined an exclusive club; Peter could talk to God and God had spoken to Peter. Just as God had spoken to Noah.

It was 2225 BCE, (Before Common Era) when God told Noah of his imminent plan to flood the world, *"I am going to put an end to all people, for the earth is filled with violence because of them. I am surely going to destroy both them and the earth"*. Noah a God-fearing man built an ark as commanded by God in preparation for the oncoming storm. 2105 BCE, Noah's Ark, the day of judgement, deluge, and dove, olive leaf and rainbow, wine-drinker and drunkard. Peter's God shared similar sentiments to that of Noah's, however the target of the violence was very definitely female. For Noah a flood of rainwater for Peter the flood of blood.

And so, it continued, enter another member of the heavenly conversationalists. Abraham, also known as Abram (Noah's great, great, great, great, great, great, great, great grandson and the 'second' patriarch of Judaism) was born 1813 BCE, in the city of Ur in Babylon, present day Iraq. Abraham was originally called Abram (which translated to High father). There are interesting Bible stories in relation to Abram/Abraham and his interesting and radical view on life. Shades and reflections of Peter's singular interpretation/misinterpretation of his destiny. Echoes of his fore runners, clearing a pathway for Peter's deeds. *"We be the echo"*.

One such story is that Abraham's father Terach traded in idols. A young Abraham headstrong and strongly independent was incensed by this aspect of his father's life. For Abraham believed that there was only one true God and was upset that his father was perpetuating the unabashed blasphemy of these false idols. Terach left Abraham alone in his shop and Abraham acted upon his affront at the idols. In a rage he smashed all but one of the idols to pieces with a hammer. He left the largest idol intact and placed the hammer in its hand.

A staged crime scene for maximum effect, the weapon of choice a hammer, Ripperesque. But Abraham was soon apprehended unlike his successor. Peter would run wild and free, like Abram/Abraham he would lose one title for another, seemingly shedding his mortality and transcending into the seemingly supernatural mystique of the Yorkshire Ripper.

Abraham was a progenitor, a precursor a prototype, a forerunner a forebear, the original friend of God. Peter repeated reinvigorated these traits, a nostalgic revivalist with a deadly spin.

Sure enough, Terach returned and was devastated by the chaos and destruction that greeted him, not to mention the financial loss. *"Abraham how has this happened?"* Terach asked.

"The idols got into a fight, and the big one smashed all the other ones".
"Don't be ridiculous. These idols have no life or power. They can't do anything".
"Then why do you worship them?"

We live in a land where sex, money and horror are the new Gods, the false idols of society. Peter set out to smash and destroy these 'idols'. Did he model himself on Abraham and the false idols? A little bit of truth helps sell the biggest of lies. Both men had a seemingly baron marriage, but God was to intervene in the case of Abraham. Peter and Sonia's failed pregnancies, miscarriages, a pale imitation of his predecessor but God was to intervene in a very different way, for Peter was to leave twenty-three children without a mother. Abraham became the father of Israel, Peter became the 'father' of English serial killers. Peter desecrated the process of murder.

Circa 1728 BCE Hagar Abraham's house maid bore Abraham a son, Ishmael. The relationship between Hagar and Sarai (Abraham's wife) understandably strained soured irreconcilably in 1714 BCE when Sarai gave birth to Isaac, a miracle from God, for at the time of his birth Sarai was ninety years old and Abram was ninety-nine years old. It was in this year that God changed Abram's name to Abraham (which translated to father of the multitude); he also changed Sarai's name to Sarah. Peter changed his name from Sutcliffe to Coonan. The tabloids, not God changed Peter's name to the 'Yorkshire Ripper'. Distant echoes, unmitigated endorsement? Or was God the instigator? The Yorkshire Ripper was not born, he was created by an act of God.

Three Angels visited Abraham he offered them his hospitality, eventually the group walked and talked and looked out from the crest of the hill, overseeing the cities of the plain, Sodom, Gomorrah, Adnah, Belah and Zeboim the Angels told Abraham that God was to unleash his divine judgement and destroy the cities. Abraham pleaded that the cities be saved and begged God to spare them, especially Soddam (where his nephew was living). Abraham implored God, explaining that if ten righteous men were found in the city, it was worthy of being saved. God agreed to Abraham's plea. Agreeing to send two of his Angels to Sodom to assess and ascertain how many 'righteous men', if any were living in the city. So therefore, God instructed two of Abraham's three visitors to travel into Sodom, where Lot Abraham's nephew played host to them. A rabble assembled outside Lot's house and demanded that Lot give his guests up to the men of the city, Lot refused and a near riot ensued. This confirmed Gods concerns and Abraham's fears. The Angel's failed in their bid to find ten righteous men and the inevitable happened. The cities were to be devoured in fire and brimstone and the wrath of the Lord. The Angels attempted to save Lot and his family from the destruction and devastation.

Unapologetic sinners, Sodom and Gomorrah symbols of vice, corruption and immorality, twin cities of sin. Leeds, Bradford, Huddersfield, Halifax and Manchester cities descending into similar debauchery, was Sutcliffe a precursor to a similar fate for these cities. Some of the cities would burn, not too long after Peter's mission was curtailed, the streets would burn, like the Biblical apocalypse the Chapeltown (Leeds) 1981 CE (Common Era) riot and the Moss Side (Manchester) 1981 CE riot. Burngreave (Sheffield) 1981CE, not to mention heightened civil unrest in the town centres' of Halifax and Huddersfield 1981 CE.

1677 BCE and God decided to put Abraham to the test he commanded Abraham to sacrifice Isaac to show his faith. Abraham walked for three days with Isaac and their servants, the group reached their destination and Abraham and Isaac walked on alone up to the summit of the mount. Abraham was delaying hoping for a reprieve, waiting for God to intervene, but there was nothing. Slowly he bound Isaac and placed him on the altar and pulled out a blade, with which he was going to kill Isaac. Isaac lay defenceless, unaware and over trusting he had been tricked into submission and the role of victim. Abraham stepped forward knife raised prepared to murder his son, his flesh and blood when an Angel of God intervened and stopped Abraham at the last minute, with the words, *"now I know you fear God"*.

Similar actions, similar commands, different outcomes. Peter didn't dilly dally about, he struck hard and fast. Stun and kill, divine retribution. He once openly questioned God in the act but was brought to heel, in fear of God's wrath. Peter then toed the line and continued his mission prompted by the word of God.

A latter-day saint, a northern Moses for the Postmodern Testament. For the Postmodern Testament is not set in the Middle East, the cradle of civilisation but the working class North of England post industrial revolution, mid industrial decline, the slow death of the manufacturing North and the even slower death of male dominance therein. William Blake's, new Jerusalem, Peter William's dark satanic mills.

1804 CE and William Blake's poem 'Jerusalem' foretold his coming, a modern day seer a prophet of the dislocation of society instigated by Margaret Thatcher's conviction politics, Peter the prophet had seen his homeland debased, degraded, tainted and tarnished by the self-righteous politics of greed and envy and his mission was to stop this; for Peter was a prophet and not for profit. He was on the cusp of two worlds, two paradigms, a crossover, an anachronism, a left over, a misguided deranged force for good in an irretrievable world of evil, a sadistic necrophiliac killer. Unbalanced, unhinged and unshackled.

Peter a lapsed Roman Catholic, retired altar-server thought why me, why not somebody more worthy, why have I been selected? Why did God select Peter for this divine mission? The rhetoric reassured him, the messages reassured him, and God reassured him. Peter was reassured, the women of northern England were not.

The voice was a constant throughout the subsequent twenty-eight years advising and reassuring. Like a naked flame to the blue touch paper his 'mission' was reignited. It was his divine mission, God had ordered him to kill prostitutes - clean up the streets, God had told him to get rid of prostitutes because they were the scum of the earth. Peter William Sutcliffe became a tool of God's will. Peter saw the words Wehvy and Ecko and the message on the gravestone. Jesus was speaking directly to him, Peter felt privileged to hear him and often returned to the gravestone in the vain hope of God/Jesus communicating with him through the crucifix statue on the grave. Peter was not to hear the voice again at this location.

Your mission Peter, should you decide to accept it, is to rid the streets of prostitutes. As always, should you or any of your force be caught or killed, God will disavow any knowledge of your actions. This tape will self-destruct in five seconds. Good luck, Peter.

Rings a plenty, (Peter's pockets were always full of gold rings he'd procured from the hands of the bodies he buried). Bingley folklore would tell of his grave robbing and a morbid fascination for the dead, Peter wasn't squeamish when it came to death. Talking skulls and frightened schoolgirls true or false, truth or dare; why let the truth get in the way of a good story. An apprenticeship of macabre, ghoulish beginning formulating the hatred and despair of a lost soul.

The history books were to tell that from 1975 CE up to 1980 CE Peter actively pursued his mission. Not including the false dawn of 1969 CE, the dry runs, the clumsy attempts to kick start his/their mission. Throughout the years on occasions Peter sometimes doubted his mission, this upset and disheartened him for a day or maybe two; especially despondent when he'd read the newspapers when he had supposedly killed an innocent victim. However, this doubt was soon dispelled, the messages continued and convinced him that they were prostitutes, they advised him when he was down in the dumps; God didn't make mistakes, but the newspapers did. Then there was the new five pounds note fiasco, he'd read the newspaper report about it being traced back to the Midland Bank in Shipley, but God intervened with a miracle and ensured Peter escaped discovery. An undefeatable team, an irresistible force for good.

Urges and hallucinations affectations the police are incapable, unable to contemplate whilst the discerning doctors do. High on a hill not too far away, bordering his two favourite hunting grounds, High Royds Hospital, Menston. Now that would make the ideal retirement home. God still talks to Peter, Peter still listens to God attentively, in God we trust.

The messages filtered through to Peter, like a Thatcherite trickle-down effect, the champagne fountain of mislead Monetarism. Wide and varied manifestations of misunderstood misogynistic mayhem. Mixed messages, misinterpreted signals, words, voices encouraging him to do God's will; cajoling him, encouraging him to kill. Steering him clear of depression - the black dog, despicable a silent killer, cured by a Holy Trinity antidepressant, ironically cured to become a silent killer. Since 1966 CE Peter had had hundreds of messages; Peter recalled in his slight Yorkshire voice *"When I have been on this sequence of kills I have heard, 'God giveth and God taketh life' and 'God works in mysterious* ways' and odd comments as normal conversation to kill and wipe out all the people called scum who cannot justify themselves in society". But Peter had fought the good fight, he had struggled with his conscience, he had questioned the voices, "I have tried to fight it. I have been frightened of it. I have been unsuccessful, and I wondered whether it was God when I killed an innocent person".

The bible said that 'For the mind that is set on the flesh is hostile to God, for it does not submit to God's law; indeed, it cannot'.

'For the word of God is living and active, sharper than any two-edged sword, piercing to the division of soul and of spirit, of joints and of marrow, and discerning the thoughts and intentions of the heart'.

The Yorkshire Ripper his acts of nihilism and hatred reveal nothing about himself or the world he inhabited, but also reveal everything.

Here is the story of the Yorkshire Ripper, the beast of Bingley.

Chapter 1
Love on the Rocks

A jump forwards or backwards in time and this is the time, the time for action. External events impact on Peter his sweet sixties (1960's CE) love affair is on the rocks and will/may lead to innocent women getting rocks thrust into their heads. A primitive early attempt at the ultimate kill, unfortunately Peter was to obtain a lot more experience.

1969 CE the Beatles, the Rolling Stones, swinging London, Vietnam, all a far cry from Frizinghall Bradford, all a far cry from the Northern Lights. Sonia Szurma Peter's 'steady' girlfriend had been a little unsteady of late and had been seen with the Italian Stallion. An ice cream salesman with a fondness for fast cars and Peter's girlfriend. He and Sonia were seen sharing giggles in a white sports car. This fast driving Romeo impressing Sonia with his show-off antics; driving around with the top down on his sports car, Sonia laughing as the wind caught and blew the silk scarf wrapped around her neck. The blatant unscrupulous couple were seen around Cottingley, no Cottingley Fairy Tale but gritty northern fact. Peter was made aware of the situation, by his over eager younger brother and was thrown into a dilemma as to how to deal with his rival for the affections of Sonia - what should he do?

Thursday 7th August, 1969CE the Beatles (with their trademarked dropped T), Apple Records, the Garden of Eden, forbidden fruit from The Tree of Life, a flash back to The Sacred Heart Church which is on Nethermoor View, Bingley BD16. Then a flashback to his not too distant past. A flashback to his religious family and possibly an explanation as to why he had been chosen.

Spare rib, women's lib, burn your bra, flesh of my flesh, bone of my bones, naked & unashamed untainted, original sin created, female serpent, seductive serpent, sinful seductive serpent...Sonia. The fall of man became the fall of Peter? Sonia, Italian stallion, sports car, duplicity and betrayal. Peter couldn't Adam and Eve it! The Italian Job (Paramount Pictures), 'Getta Bloomin' Move On', the Self Preservation Society. Inundated with input from God and others, cascading, invading and degrading, Peter was dazed and confused. A Head full of nonsense, heart all at sea, Peter was in turmoil. Peter turned to God, the Lord is vengeful against his foes; he rages against his enemies. Peter knew what he had to do. Leaving work early asking workmates to cover, Peter was to have it out with Sonia, Peter confronted Sonia, Sonia was unrepentant, resentful, Sonia would do what Sonia wanted, if Peter didn't like it, that was Peter's problem. Peter knew what he had to do.

Out of his brain as he drove down Lumb Lane, unable to restrain himself, Sonia had stirred the beast inside, resentful and angry and out for revenge. Peter felt cheated and wanted to level the score, Peter was angry. Driving down Manningham Lane, he noticed a woman that tickled his fancy, he pulled over and enquired as to whether or not she was 'doing business', the answer was in the affirmative. Peter opened the front passenger door and in she hopped. The price was right at five pounds, but Peter only had £10, they would go back to her place, where she explained that she had change. It seemed like a good idea at the time whilst his dander was up, but his anger had begun to subside, to diminish. Was he acting through diminished responsibility?

They arrived at her flat, Peter began to panic, he wanted to back out of the transaction, what a coarse & vulgar person she was, he didn't want anything to do with her, but he didn't want to lose face. The woman then decided that she too had made a mistake and she didn't have the fiver change in her flat after all. However, she had a big Alsatian dog that made him feel even more uncomfortable, if that could be. Taking control of the situation, she said there would be change at the petrol station nearby where they had first met. He agreed, desperate to get out of the flat, desperate to get away from the Alsatian. The pair exited the flat and Peter drove her to the garage. Peter sat in the car perturbed and disturbed, wanting his money and wanting this nightmare to end. Whilst she entered the garage with his £10 note, he waited, she stayed in the garage, he continued to wait, and she stayed in the garage. Through the windows of the petrol station he could make out the woman seemingly talking to two men. He continued to wait, one of the two men left the garage and approached his Morris 1000 car, and he continued to wait. Hoping that the man would disappear, hoping that he could disappear, and hoping his ordeal would end. Then the woman left the garage she was arm in arm with the second man from the garage, the woman left the garage with his £10 note. The first man banged on the Morris 1000's roof, he taunted and threatened Peter with a wrench, fight or flight thought Peter, his foot hit the accelerator as he sped away from his indiscretion. Has he drove away he was sure he heard the woman and the second man laughing. Anger welled internally, ignited anger welled eternally. My Lord is vengeful against his foes; he rages against his enemies. Peter decided to sleep on his predicament, things would look/seem different in the morning, God would guide him, and God would send a message. In God we trust.

Friday 8th August 1969 CE Peter returned to his work as a labourer at the Water Board to find out he was in hot water. In his self-imposed absence caused by Sonia's indiscretions his absence was brought to the attention of the water works director when some Water Board operatives had nearly drowned, this 'near miss' was deemed Peter's fault for going AWOL (Absent With Out Leave). The director told Peter he had no option but to demote him from his current position within the Water Board. This poured salt on the open wound of his probable break up with Sonia and his humiliation at the hands of the prostitute and her friends. Peter took to drinking in the pubs and clubs of the red-light district of Bradford in the hope of crossing paths with the confidence trickster prostitute, he could then cross swords with the bitch and take out his anger at that Italian bastard on her, he'd show them, he would teach them all a lesson that they wouldn't forget in a hurry.

Saturday 30th August 1969 CE, Peter was having a drink in The Perseverance Public House 161 Lumb Lane, Bradford, West Yorkshire. BD8, when he spotted the prostitute who'd fleeced him a few weeks previously. Peter decided to offer a solution, Peter decided to offer the olive branch, Peter walked up to her and spoke to her *"I haven't forgotten about the tenner, why don't you give me it back and we'll forget all about it"*. A hysterical shriek emitted from her red gloss lips, the harpies red gloss lips, the hussy's red gloss lips. This brought their conversation to the attention of the captive assembled audience. Like a football team, playing away from home, it was time to batten down the hatches to adopt the siege mentality. In the Perseverance he showed his perseverance, however the result was flawed. He'd played the scenario through in his head a hundred times previously, this was not the way it was meant to happen. But before he knew, it seemed the entire pub was laughing, laughing along with her, all laughing at Peter. His pale features reddened with embarrassment, he flushed further with anger. He had tried to be the bigger man, he had tried and failed. He stormed out of the pub angry, a red mist blinding his way, a red gloss mist. My Lord is vengeful against his foes; he rages against his enemies. Peter stormed out of the pub, his tail firmly between his legs, that bitch would pay and she'd pay in more than money. And so it began, an upstart twenty-three-year-old would leave his mark in more ways than one.

Chapter 2
Genesis of a Serial Killer

Saturday the 13th September 1969 CE, 18:45 hours. Peter Sutcliffe was out with Trevor Birdsall, the two friends were parked up in Trevor's Austin minivan, on Saint Pauls Road, in the Manningham area of Bradford (BD8). They had been cruising the red-light district in search of the woman who'd ripped Peter off. They were sat chatting having just finished fish and chips, the greasy newspaper still in their laps, good Northern cuisine, fine dining in every respect, when Peter's attention was drawn to a lone woman outside staggering around drunk. Peter assessed the situation, the middle aged woman was walking slowly on the pavement, unsteady on her feet due to drink, her attention focusing on passing cars, she was alone in the red-light district, Peter knew the tell-tale signs, and this was his chance to even the score. It all starts here, his debut. Peter jumped from the vehicle oblivious to everything but the woman. Mission vision submerged his being as Peter followed the woman up Saint Paul's Road.

Peter walked briskly up Saint Paul's Road the terraced houses with their small secluded gardens enclosed the road and enhanced the security offered by the open street. Peter soon caught up with the woman, he fell into step with her, holding back, walking a few steps behind her, he had his hands in his jacket pocket, his right hand was holding a sock, within the sock was a stone, he juggled it's weight in his pocket as he walked behind her. He also weighed up the situation looking for an opportunity to attack. The woman was close to her destination a house just off the main road, she turned right into the garden, expecting the stranger to pass by, he didn't he also turned into the garden. She turned to face her fears, to face the stranger and was astonished to see the fresh faced twenty-something year old, with a shock of black hair, his facial features bordered, highlighted and emphasised by an immature growth of facial hair, a fledgling beard on this fledgling attacker, she recognised the face, she'd seen it on a number of occasions, usually shouting abuse from the open windows of a kerb crawling car. His childish actions had become an irritation to the women on the streets; slowing up, pulling in and winding down the window, feigning interest, asking *"How much for business?"* Offering derogatory responses of deflated prices, childish laughter emitting from the car at the expense of the unimpressed street girls. His familiar taunting, abusing, cat calling on and around the Manningham streets was a source of much annoyance to the 'working girls' of Bradford.

Peter the big man in front of his friends and from the safety of his car, now felt vulnerable. Deep down, he was out of his depth an insecure naughty schoolboy. *"What the fuck do you want?"* she questioned turning the tables on Peter, *"Nowt, I just wondered if yer looking fur business?"* he stammered in his soft squeaky voice.

"Piss off before I get me fella to batter yer!" She lied, through gritted teeth. Her boyfriend was in Armley prison at Her Majesty's pleasure. Peter grabbed the open end of the sock with his right hand, which was still in in his jacket pocket, he pulled it out of his pocket and held it down to the side of his leg, the weight of the stone made it drop vertically, the one size black sock that was going to give this bitch one hell of a shock.

"It's not a laundrette love". She joked. But Peter wasn't laughing.
"All mouth and no trousers, all sock and no cock!" She mocked.
"You dirty old buer!" He screamed, raising his right hand and forearm above his shoulder, he brought his arm forward the sock striking the woman a glancing blow to the crown of her head, as she stumbled back to avoid the full force of the blow, the alcohol numbed the pain of the blow, but not enough. Peter panicked at his actions he couldn't believe he'd actually done it. The woman screamed and raised her hands to protect her head. She was expecting a second blow, but Peter was off, he ran back down Saint Paul's Road, back to the waiting car, back to safety. The woman stumbled back into the safety of her home, when she eventually recovered and later she called on a close friend to discuss the incident, the pair then went to a public phone box and contacted the police in order to report the earlier events.

Hurriedly Peter climbed into the car a little out of breath and a little flustered, Peter told Trevor to *"Drive off"*. Trevor did as he was told but was intrigued as to what his friend had been up to.

"Where have you been". Peter gathered himself and told Trevor of his little escapade.

"I followed that buer to a house and let her have it, I hit her over the head. That'll teach em, the thieving filthy whores, the stupid old cow".

Peter then took a sock from out of his pocket and turned the sock inside out to reveal a small stone. Peter opened the passenger side window and threw the stone out of the speeding vehicles window. Trevor confused, concentrated on his driving unsure whether or not to believe the babblings of his excited friend, as he drove back towards Bingley along Manningham Lane which became Keighley Road, which became Bradford Road, which became Bingley Road. Bradford became Shipley became Bingley.

Sunday 14th September 1969 CE, 57 Cornwall Road, Bingley, West Yorkshire, BD16. (The family home of Peter Sutcliffe). Two police officers interrupt the Sutcliffe household, they urgently need to speak to Peter William Sutcliffe about a reported incident of assault the previous evening. The police had visited Trevor Birdsall earlier that morning in relation to an accusation that a woman had been attacked and struck in the Manningham area of Bradford. The distraught victim had seen and managed to remember the registration of the minivan. Trevor when questioned by the police had no qualms in implicating his friend Peter and pointed the police in Peter's direction. The police established that it was Peter William Sutcliffe, who had attacked the woman.

"Yeah, I gave her a slap wit back of me hand". Peter expounded. Peter William Sutcliffe was severely rebuked and reprimanded by the two officers for his actions of the previous evening.

"You're a lucky lad, she doesn't want to press charges".

The woman in question was a known prostitute and was unwilling to press charges. The police were also quite unwilling to waste their time on investigating something so trivial. Anyway, she was on the game and probably deserved it. Peter pondered as they left, was this a sign from on high that God was smoothing the way for Peter to try again? Was God allowing Peter to fulfil his apprenticeship in the mission or was it just coincidence. He also wondered why he was being punished, was God testing his loyalty. Sonia continued to see the Italian, Peter saw Sonia on a Saturday, these meetings tended to disintegrate into abuse and vitriol. Sonia saw the Italian two or three times a week. Peter felt short changed, this intensified his inadequacies, this fed his hatred, fuelled his frustrations. He centred his resentment and hatred on prostitutes, he was Adolf Hitler, they were the Jews, he was to be the final solution, and prostitutes were hateful people and must be wiped out. The fact that she did not want to press charges in some ways reinforced his resolve, it endorsed his mission and showed that a higher force was watching over him, (Psalm 59:1) 'deliver me from mine enemies, O my God: Set me on high from them that rise up against me'. The show must go on, the mission must be continued both he and his victim knew this.

One/Zero
Bradford, Saturday 13th September 1969. (19:00 hours). *Peter was suffering from violent headaches, he was depressed and he blamed prostitutes, he hated prostitutes.*

The way this incident was brushed under the carpet, its seriousness diluted reinforced Peter's perception that he and he alone was the victim here, the sympathetic, pathetic manner it was dealt with by the police became prophetic, in Peter's world in Peter's mind *'In this body is a man whose latent genius, if unleashed, would rock the nation, whose dynamic energy would overpower those around him. Better let him sleep?'* He was a theological terrorist sleeper cell, the police were sympathetic to his moral crusade, his mission. She was asking for it and got what she deserved, rather than nip this unacceptable behaviour in the bud, their action's fertilised Peter's still susceptible mind.

Chapter 3
<u>Northern Moses</u>

Monday (night) 29th September 1969 CE, Tuesday (early morning) 30th September 1969. Peter was on the prowl again, he had work to do, he was a man on a mission, in his Morris Minor driving around Manningham. Armed with a long-bladed knife and a hammer, Peter knew he had to kill a prostitute, the voices said *"It's not good enough just attacking them. You must do the job properly. You must kill them"*. Fortunately, or unfortunately for Peter his suspicious actions were scrutinised by a 'Bobby' out on his beat. Police Constable (P.C.) Bland noticed a man sitting in a car, the engine was running but the headlights were switched off this raised P.C. Bland's suspicions. P.C. Bland decided to speak to the occupant and find out exactly what he was up to.

Peter saw the officer approach and in a fit of panic floored the accelerator pedal and sped away from the 'danger'. An all-points bulletin was transmitted and shortly the empty Morris Minor was located, lights a glow with its engine running. The officer aware of the earlier happenings decided to take a closer look. Close by he discovered a young man crouched, hidden behind a garden hedge.

"Hello, hello, hello, what's all this then". Or words to that affect came from the policeman's mouth.

"Hello officer I'd just stopt to look for me hub cap. It just flew off".

P.C. Bland held out his free hand, the other one was carrying a torch.

"Pass me the hammer lad". Peter handed it over immediately. The policeman asked, *"What's with the hammer lad"*.

"I've just used it to knock hubcap back in its seating".

"And I've just fallen off top of a Christmas tree. Why did you drive off earlier if you've got nothing to hide? I am arresting you for being in possession of an offensive weapon. You do not have to say anything, but it may harm your defence if you do not mention when questioned something which you later rely on in court. Anything you say may be given in evidence. Do you understand?"

Police Constable Bland secured the suspect's vehicle. A police van was called to collect Peter and take him to the police station for further questioning. Peter still had in his possession the long-bladed knife; he knew that he must remain calm. Whilst he was in the back of the van in transit to the police station Peter knew he had to lose the knife. He collected his thoughts, assessing his surroundings he noticed a gap between the side of the van and the mudguard cover. Peter concealed it there and the police were none the wiser.

Now to deal with the small matter of a police interview Peter relaxed and prepared his excuses. They didn't need to know he was on a divine mission from God to rid the streets of prostitution. On your marks, get set, BANG! Another false start, when would he kick start his work. Maxwell's Silver Hammer, Helter Skelter Bradford's very own Charles Manson, cease to resist. 'Woman is the Nigger of the World' the phrase coined by Yoko Ono in an interview with Nova magazine in 1969 and was quoted on the magazine's cover. The article went on to describe women's subservience to men and male chauvinism across all cultures, it also went on to inspire John Lennon to pen lyrics for a song with the same title? But just now it summed up Peter's attitude towards the fairer sex.

The game of cat and mouse continued down at the police station, Peter continued to argue his innocence, denying any wrongdoing, denying any criminal intent. The course of this interview went well for Mr Peter William Sutcliffe, the initial charge of 'being in possession of an offensive weapon' lessened to a charge of 'going equipped to steal'. This was to be of major significance as the tale of the Yorkshire Ripper was to unfold. His mission although stalled was not over, it was not over before it had even begun it was just on hold. The time was not yet right, he was on still pause awaiting Holy orders, his fate was sealed, all would be revealed, watch this space, for within the body of Peter William Sutcliffe something sinister stirred. This was veritable kid's stuff to what he would unleash upon the unsuspecting women of northern England, a trial run an apprenticeship, the early steps of a religious mad man, a baleful black sheep guided by a crooked staff. *'The Lord is my shepherd, I shall not want...He restoreth my soul: he leadeth me in the paths of righteousness for his names sake...Yea Thou I This walk through the valley of the shadow of death, I will fear no evil: For Thou art with me; thy rod and thou staff they comfort me...Surely goodness and mercy shall follow me all the days of my life'* (Psalm twenty-three).

October of 1969 CE, Mr Peter William Sutcliffe aged 23 of Cornwall Road, Bingley appeared before Bradford Magistrates Court charged with 'going equipped for theft', as he stood in the dock Peter placed his hand on the Holy bible and said, *"I swear by almighty God that the evidence I shall give shall be the truth the whole truth and nothing but the truth"*.

Although Peter pleaded not guilty the magistrates found in favour of the police and he was found guilty and fined £25. In essence this conviction was a result and Peter took it as a sign, he would need to be more careful next time, if there was to be a next time.

After all the ball-pein hammer is the tool of choice for every would be Bradford burglar, but then again to be fair no normal person would hit another with a hammer over the head, good police work or sloppy police work, it is now history and every incident has its own context. The Yorkshire Ripper could have possibly been snuffed out at inception, however twenty-twenty hindsight vision is in small supply or non-existent. Or was it a benevolent God watching over a willing worker in Peter, steering a clear and safe passage through the minefield of moral indiscretion, like the burning bush on Mount Herob, Peter had been chosen to be a burning beacon of light in the moral darkness. As God had spoken to Moses over two-thousand years previously, God had come down from heaven to rescue the moral majority. He had picked Peter his northern Moses to carry out that task. It was not yet time for the great Exodus of the immoral miscreants, however their days were numbered.

Chapter 4
Irish Annie

November 1974 CE Anna visited her local corner shop (42 Belgrave Road, BD21 on the junction with Highfield Lane) on a regular basis, almost daily. It was just across the road from her home 62 Highfield Lane, Keighley, West Yorkshire, BD21. A modest stone built mid-terrace, through terrace Yorkshire house. The home she would buy courtesy of the actions of Peter Sutcliffe.

It was through this patronage that a very strange rendezvous was formulated. A gentleman that went by the name of Michael Gill had also begun to frequent the shop, Michael on one of his many visits left a message with the shopkeeper that he asked him to convey to Anna. 'Would she please give him the pleasure of her company for an evening meal complimented by a few drinks', Anna's initial answer was NO! However, Michael was nothing if not persistent and would not take no for an answer. Eventually Anna agreed to the 'blind date', just to appease her would be admirer. The 'date' for that is what we will refer to it as was nothing if not non-descript. Michael picked Anna up and drove the eleven miles south east to Bradford city centre, Michael was an amiable character, well-mannered, reserved, considerate and courteous. Michael explained to Anna that he lived with his elderly grandmother who wasn't in the best of health, they shared their home with several cats. Michael knew an awful lot about Anna, a fact that she found disconcerting, however his mild manner and his love of cats helped to set her at ease. She found his soft-spoken West Yorkshire twang disarming and if truth be known felt sorry for this strange disconcerting young man, they enjoyed a lovely meal served by waitresses in long black dresses. The conversation was instigated with tales of woe around Michael's grandmother, interspersed with feline fables, but always the conversation returned to Anna and revolved around her, Michael had an unhealthy knowledge of Anna's background and daily routine. When the pair had finished their meal, Michael ever the gentleman drove Anna home, ever the gentleman and chivalrous to the last, Michael refused Anna's offer of a coffee, explaining that he had to return home post haste to put his grandmother to bed, he left Anna at her doorstep without even a kiss or a peck on the cheek to conclude the evening. This evening out faded in the memory of Anna a dull, plain and boring would be suitor that she had obliged out of pity. His appearance had made little impact on her, his conversation was mundane in fact the whole evening had been a chore, she took the opportunity of the kindness of the would be suitor/benefactor to lighten the boredom and tedium by over indulging in alcohol to help pass the evening, however this also clouded her memory.

Thursday the 24th of April 1975CE and Peter had time on his hands having recently accepted and received (February 1975CE) a voluntary redundancy pay out of four hundred pounds from his former employers at Britannia Works of Anderton International, the canal side Bingley firm where he had worked nights for the past twenty months. The night work had curtailed his cravings, stifled his opportunity to facilitate his mission, still on hold from its false start some six and a half years previously. The fact that he'd married Sonia his long-term girlfriend had also reduced his cravings and promoted a more responsible side to Peter. Since his/their wedding day on 10th of August 1974 CE Sonia and Peter had lived with Sonia's parents at their three-bedroom council house in Clayton on the outskirts of Bradford. It was time to get his life on track and restore the moral standing of society, it was to this back drop that Peter enrolled on a heavy goods vehicle (HGV) driving course with APEX HGV/LGV Training Centre in Steeton a village between Keighley and Silsden, both places were to play an important part in his role (illogical) theological crusade.

On Wednesday the 4th of June 1975CE, Peter successfully obtained his HGV Class 1 driving licence. Radiant with success excited and wishing to share his good news, Peter headed along Skipton Road into nearby Keighley. He parked his car on Alice Street and made his way into the town centre to celebrate his success with a well-earned drink. Peter had seen Anna around town before and was attracted by her over friendly demeanour, unfortunately for Anna these often-encouraged inappropriate advances from menfolk of this northern enclave. Mis-reading the signs or re-writing them into an inept misinterpretation for the emotional void of mid 1970's man to misunderstand. Walking through the town hall square an elated Peter pondered his future, under the spring shadows of the cenotaph, colloquially locally known as 'old man's park'. Peter had earlier spied Anna, who was to become his quarry. The square concrete flagged area bordered by grass verges interspersed with wooden benches and decorated with flower beds and blossom trees, these flower beds were bordered to three sides by roads, North Street, Cavendish Street and Cooke Street; to the fourth side was Keighley Town Hall a prominent Yorkshire sandstone building that still portrayed a pretence of its former power. Although this was a hollow pretence, the town hall, a shadow of its former self this echoed similar sentiments in relation to the town of Keighley itself, of an identity stripped and consumed by centralization and the urban sprawl of Bradford Metropolitan District Council. 1974 CE had seen the demise of local rule and the rise of Bradford's domination over its parochial neighbours. Regional imperialism, a money saving action that reinforced the shortcomings of Keighley and directed central government money away from the indigenous Keighley population.

Peter approached Anna who was on her way home, he was unsure what his advances would yield, but buoyed by his driving success he thought 'what the hell'. He tapped Anna on her left arm to grab her attention and then asked, *"What about you take me home for a nice cuppa tea?"* Anna was taken aback by the forward nature of this stranger, but also felt flattered that this dark haired younger man had propositioned her and she turned to Peter and duly responded in a diplomatic manner, *"No and don't be so cheeky".* She then continued her short journey home thinking little or nothing more of the brief conversation. The up-beat, care free feeling from the initial altercation soon faded at the realisation that Peter seemed un-perturbed - unaware of the rebuff and had continued to follow Anna across the traffic busy North Street and up the incline that was Highfield Lane. Peter paid little attention to his brush off believing Anna was playing games, however when it became evident to Anna that she was being followed, the Irish in Anna leapt to the fore. She turned and directly challenged Peter.

"What do yer think yer doin I thought I'd told you to get lost". Finally, Peter seemed to get the message the commotion that was simmering under the surface remained between both parties, but Peter didn't want any unwarranted attention, anyway, why spoil a good day. Peter shrewdly slipped into the side streets, evaporated into the ether. Anna continued her walk home uninterrupted pondering the earlier episode she called in at the corner shop before going home. When in her dwelling she dismissed the incident and paid it no further mind. Peter was not quite so dismissive, resentment simmered as he drove away from Keighley. His celebratory mood deflated by that woman's rudeness. He drove to Cromwell Road, Bingley to inform his mum and dad of his newly acquired HGV licence. He then continued his journey 'home' to 44 Tanton Crescent, Clayton, West Yorkshire, BD14.

Saturday the 31st of May 1975CE, Anna walked into J Wild (family bakers) Confectioners Ltd café, where she also worked has a waitress. The café was located on the outskirts of the shopping centre and adjacent to the bus station, next to the stand for the 710 Laycock , the large open spaced punctuated by walk through bus shelters, open ended at one end and an access panel in the side to allow passengers to enter the bus when it arrived, sky blue painted panels to the base of the shelter up to the height of two and a half feet, on top of that toughened glass divided by dark blue metal supports attached to the dark blue flat metal roof. These bus shelters were perched on pedestrian islands surrounded by access roads frequented by predominantly red single and double decker buses; the perimeter of a wide pavement which had sections railed off to ensure safety when people queued along the pavement at the open bus stops. A hive of activity surrounded by shops, cafes, amusements and bookies the transport hub of this busy northern town was the backdrop to possibly the third meeting between Peter and Anna. Peter watched from his vantage point, under the clock tower, outside Keighley town centre post office, in the shadow of the multi-storey car park, he was killing time, awaiting an opportunity, he then saw a familiar face, it was Anna, he watched as she entered Wild's Confectioners, she walked through the take out section into the café area and took a seat. Suddenly Peter appeared in the café and plonked himself down facing Anna who was at the same table. Anna noticed Peter's dark soulless eyes, his black hair and bushy beard seemed at odds with Peter's small dainty hands and soft high-pitched voice. *"Would you like a drink?"* Peter offered. Anna seized the occasion to make her unease known, *"Not you again, how many times do I have to tell you no. If you don't leave me alone you'll regret it!"* Once again, his approach rebuffed and aware of the captive and increasingly hostile audience, Peter leapt up from the table turned on his heels and was gone as if by magic. All that was missing was a cloud of smoke, however this was partially provided by a number of onlookers who puffed on their cigarettes whilst waiting for the scene to run its course. Again, Anna was unsettled but she soon forgot the incident and regained her composure, but Peter didn't and their paths would cross for a final time in the not too distant future.

Friday night on the 4th of July 1975 CE, American Independence Day, three years short of the bicentenary, no taxation without representation, the Boston Tea Party, King George the Third and General George Washington. But we are some 3150 miles away from Boston and our once colonial cousins, and some 199 years from the inception of the United States of America, with its Bill of Rights, to protect life, liberty and the pursuit of happiness. We are in a little West Yorkshire town, by the name of Keighley, a mill town, a mill town built up around the river Aire. Mrs Anna Patricia Rogulskyj (nee Brosnan), aka Irish Annie a 34-year-old divorcee, tall, good looking with a rash of light blonde hair. Her often over familiar demeanour in her work and social life, confident and friendly had on occasions resulted in misunderstandings and misread situations amongst her male counterparts.

A warm midsummer afternoon saw Anna finish her shift at J Wild Confectioners Ltd, The Airedale Shopping Centre, 120 North Street, Keighley BD21 where she was a waitress, she went home and did her chores, hung out some washing then prepared for her evening out, for Anna was hitting the bright lights of Bradford, with some girlfriends. A similar scene that was being played out throughout the country. However, there was a fly in the ointment, Geoff 'Taff' Hughes, Anna's on off boyfriend was not enamoured by the fact that Anna was going out without him, Anna was happy with her new colour television a recent gift from Geoff, but his possessive and irrational behaviour was beginning to wear a little thin. Their argument continued as Anna continued to get ready for her planned evening on the town, it culminated with Geoff storming out, but unbeknown to Anna, he had firstly hidden all her shoes in the vain hope that this would prevent her leaving her home, an informal type of house arrest. Anna continued unimpressed and unattached, this was childish, this was kid's stuff, this was the final straw; Geoff needed to grow up or go. She eventually found her shoes hidden in the kitchen, they were on the kitchen table chairs that had been pushed under the kitchen table to obscure the shoes from immediate view. Anna thought she'd teach Geoff a lesson and decided to call on him at his North Queen Street, (BD21) address prior to going to Keighley bus station, where she was going to catch the bus over to Bradford. His house was only a small detour away from the bus station and the buses to Bradford were every ten minutes, so she called by to let him know his hide and go seek shoe game had failed miserably. Geoff was not home so Anna proceeded to the bus station and took in the pleasantness of the evening. She boarded the Bradford Bus, the 665 which was soon underway, with fellow revellers and the last of the commuters. Anna's bus journey was broken by a brief visit to see her sister in Heaton, however she was not in so Anna continued her journey catching another bus to Bradford Interchange bus station, Bridge Street, Bradford, BD1.

Her evening on the tiles began with a visit to the public bar at The Great Victoria Hotel Bridge St, Bradford, and West Yorkshire, BD1, where she met some friends and the frivolities began. Anna ended her excursion to Bradford by visiting the Capricorn Club (aka Bibby's club), 21 Cornwall Terrace, Valley Parade, Bradford, BD8.

Peter was unable to raise the Tanton Crescent crew for a night out, so he went solo. His constant interest in the seedier side of society continued to grow, his pretence at disgust was there to shroud his overzealous almost obsessive need to participate. He'd argued internally that it was fundamental to the success of his mission, know your enemy. The voice within had become clearer, more habitual, more commanding Peter had no choice other than to obey. He decided to go to Keighley for he remembered a conversation he'd overheard in his time working nights at Anderton Circlips that Keighley was rife with prostitution

Peter set off out into the Summer evening in his lime green Ford Capri GT, with the pretence of visiting his mother and father at their Bingley home, which he duly did. After the visit Peter decided to investigate first-hand if the red-light rumours that abounded were factual. Driving the short distance from Bingley to Keighley passing through Crossflatts, Sandbeds, Riddlesden and Stockbridge being welcomed into Keighley by Cox of Keighley car dealership on what was locally known as Cox's corner. Peter parked in the car park to the rear of The Eastwood Tavern, (37 Bradford Road, Keighley, BD21), a Timothy Taylor's pub; he recollected past visits with a previous girlfriend but that was what seemed like a lifetime away, his Holy instructions had not yet been fully initiated, however that was to change tonight. Nothing much doing here he thought, a couple of pints to calm the nerves then on to The Gardeners Arms, (14 Hanover Street, Keighley, BD21), he parked his car in the man-made chasm that formed the ramp access to the delivery route to shops at the Keighley shopping centre, this was to the rear of the pub. The Gardeners, yet another Timothy Taylor's pub was one of his favoured retreats when he visited Keighley. He ordered himself a pint and as ever went to the juke box where he selected The Spider and the Fly, by The Rolling Stones, again and again; this song was the B-side to (I Can't Get No) Satisfaction, their 1965CE smash hit. Not willing to draw further attention to himself Peter supped up and moved on, he walked along Hanover Street towards East Parade but before he reached the junction of the road where Hanover Street meets East Parade, he turned right and walked up the pedestrianised Low Street until he reached the junction with Market Street, on the corner of the meeting of these two streets was the Black Horse, 26-28 Low Street, Keighley, BD21.

This was not a typical Peter pub, however he had heard tales told about the Black Horse Fairy's, for this was the public house allegedly frequented by the prostitutes of the Keighley district. The deals were allegedly brokered in the public house and the deal consummated in the dimly lit open air market area to the rear of the pub, overlooked by Saint Andrew's Keighley Parish Church but otherwise away from prying eyes. Fortunately, fact does not reflect fiction and the distorted tales and rumours that abound in a small northern town are often just that, the Black Horse Fairy was one such untruth. A form of social control to ostracise women who would not conform to what was considered the social niceties of the times. Peter entered the pub by the Low Street entrance and approached the circular bar that was central to the large room. The bar was central to the pub, an intrinsic hub from which everything generated. Peter approached the bar maid and ordered a drink, he surveyed the room for likely candidates to kick start his killing spree. On this occasion he searched to no avail, no suitable candidate came to the fore. He lingered becoming an irrelevant bystander to the boisterous revelry, the rowdy, raucous rabble of the locals, prominent amongst the merry makers were numerous females, this fuelled Peter's internal fire for murder, however it also unnerved him. The open expanse of the open plan pub made him feel vulnerable

There was a late night bar upstairs called Fillies, he decided to try his luck up there and the shadowy enclaves of anonymity, a thinly veiled meat market with the backdrop of a disco beat, dimly lit expanses broken by bright coloured moving lights; nicotine smoke acted as dry ice. Peter hoped to see Irish Anna, she was a well-known woman around town, it looked like his luck wasn't in he'd have to single someone out get them alone and do the dastardly deed. The urge surged within but there were no takers for his dark good looks that would only bring bad luck. The bell for last orders rang out at 24:00 hours and the room lights were turned on has the bar staff encouraged the unsuccessful singles and the self-congratulating couples down the stairs to the propped open door and into the balmy July evening. He followed the flow of the crowds, downstairs through the rear doors and into the area that housed the open-air market. Unsure of what to do and with time on his hands and an insatiable appetite to begin his mission, for in essence Peter had prepared himself for this, what was to be the genesis of the Yorkshire Ripper, a second dawn or was it just going to be another damp squib.

Leaving the club at around 00:30 hours Saturday 5th July with two Afro-Caribbean clubbers who'd agreed to give her a lift the ten miles home. The two good Samaritans offered to escort Anna to her door and make sure that Geoff was 'going to behave', an offer Anna declined, thinking their presence may inflame the situation.

It was now circa 00:30 hours and he thought of Anna again and like a moth to a flame found himself making his way to her Highfield Lane abode he had staked out over the previous months in his failed efforts to woo her. He loitered outside her house, when the silence of the night was broken by the occasional straggler from the evening's frivolities winding their way home. Peter was a little disconcerted there was no sign of life at Irish Annie's, he decided to return to his car and call it a night. However, his intentions changed as a car engine could be heard in the near distance struggling against the gradient of Highfield Lane.

Anna arrived home circa 01:00 hours, to her humble abode in Highfield Lane, expecting to find Geoff, none of them saw the dark figure in the shadows lurking in the darkness of the night, Anna was more concerned that there was no Geoff.

The headlights approached Peter who instinctively averted his gaze, as the car passed, he saw that Irish Annie was in the rear of the car. He turned to see what would unravel. Hiding in the half light of the night, he watched as she exited the car, bid her fond farewells. Peter decided to linger longer, the car drove away and disappeared into the night, whilst the outlined figure of Anna could be seen in the near distance entering her home.

She opened the house door and felt deflated, empty like the house so she poured herself a nightcap and decided to play her favourite record Elvis Presley (the King) 'Crying In The Chapel', again and again and again.

Peter walked past the row of terrace houses, he had done this many times before, unbeknown to Anna her action's towards him had seen her fall from her pedestal Peter had plans to bring her down to earth in more ways than one. Their last insignificant encounter had resulted in Peter's unrequited attentions being combatted by an angry, perturbed and disturbed Anna heading directly for the comfort and safety of her home. She had suffered the unwanted attentions of emotionally immature men a number of times and had swiftly dismissed their misguided aspirations. Their last insignificant encounter had resulted in Peter's humiliation and therefore there was now a score that had to be settled, he heard the familiar tones of Elvis Aaron Presley from within the house.

A time delayed recreation of a similar moment shared earlier in the Gardner's Arms, shared by Peter the song was different but the sentiment was similar, Peter's 'The Spider and The Fly', to Anna's 'Crying In The Chapel'.

He tried the door handle, but it was locked, he decided to reconvene, survey the scene, take a backseat and see what fortune would unfold and where it would take him. He walked up and down the street contemplating his next move, he questioned God on what was happening and why.

Then feeling a little maudlin and a little disconcerted that Geoff, was not there, it was then that she decided to find exactly where he was and see what Geoff was up to, Geoff lived a 5-minute walk away. Downhill into the down centre, downtown to give Geoff a piece of her mind, to make up or further break up.

Then he heard the distinct noise of a door opening, he looked up from his hunch necked position but also down Highfield Lane, for he was considerably above her due to the gradient of the road. His eyes gazed towards Anna, again an outlined figure in the near distance and decided this was a sign from God, manna from heaven.

Anna hurriedly scurried down Highfield Lane unaware of the shadowy figure walking in her wake. He followed her unaware of what would transpire, he knew he had to repay this bitch, he felt inside his jacket for the handle of the hammer, it reassured him, reinvigorated him, refocused his being. Down Highfield Lane, a left turn through Rosemount Walk, a right turn onto Mornington Street, then across North Street walking towards the town centre. A left turn down Alice Street walking in the pale moonlight. Here was his opportunity he had to cover one hundred metres to her seventy-five, he had to look indiscreet, appropriate and in control, no heavy breathing, he slipped off Alice Street onto Lord Street, then a sharp right down the ginnel (an alleyway) which spat him out onto North Queen Street opposite the Fair Isle Buildings, with seconds to spare he positioned himself discreetly in an enclave of a doorway awaiting his fate. What was to be Anna's fate? Would she meander along Alice street or would she turn right onto North Queen Street like he had speculated, guesstimated, Peter held his position and his cool as Anna sealed her fate and turned right unsuspectingly onto North Queen Street and the unwanted advances of Peter. Anna's attention was captured by a silhouetted figure of a man, framed in a shadowy doorway. He spoke in a soft voiced local accent. This figure only murmured *"Do you fancy it?"*

Anna's answer was short and to the point *"Not on your life!"* She didn't give him a sideways glance, or a second thought, she had bigger fish to fry, as she headed on to Geoff's house. Anna knocked on the door, but there was no reply. Anna knocked on the door again, still there was no answer. She knocked louder, bang, bang, bang *"Come on Geoff, I know you're in there"*.

She proceeded to tap on the window, louder and louder, harder and harder, *"Geoff, let me in"*. But still silence from within, as a final act of frustration Anna removed one of her shoes, that Geoff had hidden earlier, she raised the shoe above her right shoulder and brought the heel crashing down into the living room window, but still no answer. In an act of irony witnessed from the shadows a certain Mr Sutcliffe watched on, he was soon to commit a similar action, a type of delayed synchronicity. The realisation that her action's may have been seen or heard by neighbouring properties or another third party seemed to bring her to her senses. She put her shoe back on her foot, adjusted her clothing, composed herself then strolled off home as if nothing untoward had happened. She'd decided her bed was more enticing than an argument with Geoff, or an evening in the police cells. Tunnel vision kicked in, she turned on her recently replaced heels and started to retrace her steps, (well not quite). In a world of her own she was startled to hear the shadowy figure still loitering, this time he'd positioned himself in the doorway, at the rear of the Ritz another dark enclave that shielded him from prying eyes and unwanted onlookers. *"Do you fancy it?"* Peter questioned again.

Anna said abrasively *"How many times, no!"* She then veered left, down the alleyway at the rear of the Ritz Picture House, Alice Street Keighley BD21, to avoid the attention of her would be suitor. The red brick building of the Ritz cinema looked out of place surrounded by the Yorkshire stone terraced houses, but Anna paid little concern to such insignificant trivialities, the tarmac pavement to the rear of the Ritz was easier to walk on than the cobblestones that surrounded the main thoroughfare. A decision made on a practicality, a practicality that was practically to cost Anna her life.

For every action, there is a re-action, she walked down the dark dimly lit alley, her mind muddled by alcohol and at what to do with her chaotic love life. The shadowy figure moved out of his protective alcove and began to follow her down the alley. Dark featured he seemed nondescript able to melt into the background a type of urban camouflage. Anna had almost reached the entrance of the ginnel, when the dark figures stealth mode switched off and the sadistic night worker kicked in. Peter struck. The thud of the ball-pein hammer, almost silent in the night, as steel met skin, met flesh, met bone and exploded in Anna's brain. Peter repeated this process twice more, the balled end of the hammer sinking further into Anna's skull. Unbeknown to both Anna and Peter, this unnatural happening had been overheard by an occupant from a house in Lord Street, whether it was a scream or a shout, the occupant felt unhappy and decided to investigate further. Peter in a frenzy continued in ignorance, the first blow saw her stumble forward, away from him. He readjusted his swing accordingly, the second blow, saw her crumple to her knees. Again, he readjusted, the third blow, saw her collapse. This was more like it, not the stone in socks kid's stuff, this was the real thing. Peter placed the hammer in his inside jacket pocket and pulled at her blouse, lifting it to reveal the bare-naked flesh of Anna's stomach. He pulled the knife from his back pocket and slashed at her stomach. Once, twice, thrice. *"What's all that noise, what's going on?"* Came a concerned and somewhat annoyed voice from the Lord Street doorway.

Startled and snapped back into reality Peter composed himself and composed a lie to save his skin and appease the concern of the nosey parker. *"There's nowt to worry about, get yer'sen back inside. Everything's alreight now".*

The neighbour paused *"Alreight, if yer sure".*

"Aye nowt to worry abart". Phew that was a close call, Peter would have to be a little more careful in future. He decided not to push his luck any further and, in some ways, felt a

little cheated that he had been interrupted mid flow. He fled the scene the deed done at 1:20 hours. Anna's seemingly lifeless body was found at 2:20 hours, the young man quickly raises the alarm. An ambulance appeared within minutes and Anna was taken to Airedale General Hospital, she was immediately transferred to Leeds General Infirmary and underwent a twelve hour operation, to remove splinters of skull from her brain, her condition was so bad that the last rites were given, however 'Irish Annie' would live to fight another day.

The first true casualty of Peter's crusade, for Anna would have to learn to live with her wounds for the rest of her life, the social stigma in association with the Yorkshire Ripper that came in September 1978CE, was perhaps the final nail in the coffin of her social life, scarred like her head with the crescent shaped indents caused by the hardened metal face of Peter's ball peen hammer. In essence a lost victim, trapped in time unable to continue with her fractured life.

Two/Zero
Keighley, Saturday 5th July 1975. (01:20 hours). Ground zero for his modus operandi and a new start after the false dawn, the mission starts here. An attack unintentionally initiated by Peter's workmates at Anderton Circlips, Bingley and facilitated by God. Rumours were rife amongst the tea and biscuits that there was 'a plague of prostitutes in Keighley'. Still struggling with his pathological hatred of prostitutes, this would manifest itself through piercing headaches and depression, however Peter knew this was only a passing fad, so he remained silent. Gripped by a madness, stripped to his primal instincts, primed by a guiding hand, the message continued to filter through.

Thursday the 8th of January 1981CE and the police visited Anna Rogulskyj to ask some questions in relation to her attack five and half years previously and possible connections to the suspect they were holding in custody in relation to their investigations into the Yorkshire Ripper murders. According to Annie, their enquiries centred around several names, pseudonym or alias, all of which were allegedly used by Peter William Sutcliffe AKA The Yorkshire Ripper in various degrees throughout his reign of terror. 'Peter Logan', 'Tony Jennis', 'David', 'Trevor' and finally 'Mr Gill'. Anna went pale as she struggled to remember the insignificant individual who hounded her those six plus years ago, the realisation that she'd probably shared time with her assailant sat uncomfortably on her narrow shoulders. A shiver shot down her spine as she struggled to believe the questioning officer. She tried to recall the woman she was before her path crossed that of The Yorkshire Ripper, but she just could not remember.

Anna Rogulskyj passed away in April 2008 CE at Airedale Hospital, she was seventy-five years old.

Chapter 5
Olive

Mrs Olive Smelt was forty-six years old, she was an office cleaner and lived at 11 Woodside Mount, in the Boothtown area of Halifax, (HX3 6EN). Steep banking falls away from the cobbled sets of Woodside Mount, dropping into the abyss of wilderness, reclining into the declining Dean Clough's mill complex which abutted the wasteland. The mill chimney adjacent, abutting, overlooking, witnessing all that surrounds. She lived with her husband Harry and their fifteen-year-old daughter Julie and their nine-year-old son Stephen. The couple had a third child Linda, aged twenty-five who had flown the family nest.

Olive was meeting her best friend Muriel Falkingham for their weekly girls' night out, it was a rainy Friday on 15th August 1975CE, but that did not deter Olive and Muriel who went into Halifax town centre. One of the 'watering holes' they visited was the White Horse Inn, Southgate, Halifax, HX1 1DL, where they spent the time drinking and socialising with the usual Friday night crowd. Muriel left at 22:50 hours to catch her last bus home, whilst Olive went onto the Royal Oak alone, in Clare Road, Halifax, HX1 2HX. It was there that she bumped into a couple of male friends who bought her a drink and offered to drop her off in Boothtown on their way home from the pub. It was a quiet night in the pubs and clubs of the town, a possible reason for this being the inclement weather. However, Olive Smelt or her family would not be concerned with the weather or the forecast, they would be concerned with the surgeons forecast as to whether or not Olive was going to survive.

Meanwhile another couple of friends were out in Halifax, unimpressed by the weather and the general ambience of the area they decided to try their luck in the Royal Oak.

"Let's go to't Oak, I've heard it's full of prostitutes and punters, it'll be a laugh". Peter said. Arriving in the Royal Oak about 22:30 hours Trevor and Peter had a look around at their newfound environment. It was dry warm and reasonably busy. By the time Olive arrived Peter was in full swing, he noticed her and pointed her out to Trevor.

"I bet she's on the game". The pair giggled. Peter egged on by his friend became a little bit too leery, a little bit too overfriendly. He passed Olive on her way to the toilet, he accidently bumped into her, she turned at his presence and Peter said, *"How much do you charge?"*

Olive Smelt a no-nonsense northern lass replied bluntly *"You've no chance you jumped up little bugger. Bugger off back to yer boyfriend yer Nancy Boy".*

Peter again found himself not in control, isolated alone, on his own. Outnumbered and on 'foreign' ground Peter was the butt of the joke. The locals and Olive's friends laughed as his bravado backfired. His mind flashed back to Thursday 7th August, 1969CE and the humiliation he'd had to suffer at the hands of that uncouth whore and her two henchmen. Anger intensified within his torso, he rushed to the toilet to hide his embarrassment. Safe in the toilet and behind the cubicle door Peter took deep breaths until his anger subsided, Peter then glided from the toilet to Trevor's side indignantly cursing, *"The stupid old whore"*. His ire inflamed the latent beast stirred once more, his mission must continue, every sinew and fibre longed for revenge, sanctified theological revenge upon woman kind, his antics of just less than five weeks had not satisfied his need and his greed to control and enrol corpses to his would be collection and protect society from the sinners. But this business would wait until the opportunity arose and Peter knew it would arise because God Almighty would deliver them to him.

23:30 hours, Peter and Trevor decided to end their evening and head off home, Peter was still seething as he started his lime green Ford Capri, (registration number EUA831K). Whilst Trevor made himself comfy in the passenger seat, Peter absentmindedly drove the car away from Halifax town centre, down Haley Hill and up Boothtown Road, with Akroyd Park to their left. Trevor was aware that Peter although physically sitting next to him was strangely distant. Trevor also thought that Peter's driving was not up to the usual standard. Trevor sat silent reflecting trying to put his finger on the reason why. They hadn't drunk that much. He'd been driving with Peter when they had both drunk much more. Trevor just looked forward to getting back to Bradford and getting his head down. It was as if Peter was elsewhere, he then pointed to a figure in the approaching distance walking towards them on Boothtown Road. The woman turned onto Woodside Terrace, still holding out a forlorn hope that the local fish and chip shop may still be open. *"That's that prostitute we saw earlier"*. Peter indicated and pulled into Woodside Terrace, the woman turned into Bath Place unaware of the fact she was the interest of the two onlookers. Peter pulled his Ford Capri into Bath Place and brought the car to a halt at the side of the road. Trevor saw him fumble at the side of his seat before climbing out of the car.

"I just need to have a word with this bloke". Peter explained excitedly. He then saw Peter walk to the rear of the car and disappear into the night apparently no longer interested in the woman, but with a different task in hand. Peter proceeded in what seemed an entirely different direction to Olive, he turned into a ginnel that connected Bath Place with Woodside Place and Woodside View. Peter began to run, he had an idea, if the opportunity arose. Olive meanwhile was walking on a parallel ginnel that connected Bath Place with Woodside Place, Woodside View and Woodside Crescent. Like The Lone Ranger, he hurried along, the ginnel eventually turning left onto the back road that serviced both Bath Place and Woodside Place then onto Woodside View and finally onto Woodside Crescent with the intention of cutting Olive off at the pass. He was in position, his plan was coming together he waited in the shadows, she approached, a voice from the shadows.

"The weather's letting us down, isn't it?" Peter said referring to the heavy rain that had punctuated the evening.

"Yes". Olive replied more out of decorum than interest, but the man had gone, he'd briskly disappeared into the night. She thought it and him a little strange but her main concern was for the elements and her missed fish and chips supper, she continued along the labyrinth of cobbled ginnels and forgot about the strange man and his muttering the strange man who looked like he wouldn't say boo to a goose.

Peter reappeared as if by magic he began to follow Olive down to the bottom of the alley, along the corridor of uncertainty replicated seven-fold. The symmetry of the narrow ginnels enhanced by the single set of cobbles that formed its centre, either side of which a patchwork of cobbles set so their camber diverts surface water to the central cobbles. The design had been of use that evening due to the on/off heavy downpours. The towering gable ends of the terraced houses offered some protection from the elements, but were also going to offer the protection of cover to an attacker, of an unarmed unaware innocent middle-aged woman. The darkness of the ginnel acted as a natural shield, this was compounded by the fact that no streetlamps were sited on them to alleviate the darkness. The darkness comforted Peter, whilst Olive was oblivious to the oncoming onslaught.

Peter felt in the inside of his jacket pocket and pulled out the ball pein hammer, holding it tight into his body at waist level, preparing to strike. He'd already placed the knife in the back-right hand pocket of his trousers, the handle sticking out for ease of access. He'd checked over his shoulder to ensure the coast was clear and no one was there to witness his intended actions. He then decided to take his chance, he increased his pace so he was in touching distance of Olive, the noise of their footsteps merged into one. It's now or never, he thought. Peter knew that fate was just seconds away from him and her, he started anticipating the oncoming onslaught. She reached the corner where the ginnel met the small cobbled road to the rear of Woodside Road. The time was 23:45 hours and he was upon her, he struck her two heavy blows to her head with the hammer, she collapsed at his feet, he quickly put the hammer back in his inside coat pocket and then drew the knife. Olive face down on the cobbles with Peter crouched down over her, his victim and pulled at her blouse. Revealing the marble flesh of her lower back and her bare buttocks. Murder in mind, echoes, voices, compelling, telling him clearly kill her, kill her! The mission, his actions and thoughts, his very being a weapon in a theological crusade, the mission. He slashed the knife across the flesh, once, twice, he then heard the hum of an engine and saw some headlights lighting the nearby Woodside Road. Headlights distracting, impacting on his actions, should he continue with the attack or abscond, had they witnessed the incident, he couldn't risk it and he was up and off, on his feet, the chance had gone the urge dissipated, the opportunity to finish her off gone. He ran up Woodside View along the ginnels and back to his car arriving back at 23:50 hours.

"Ey up Pete where've yer been?" Trevor spluttered surprisingly.

"I've just been talking to a reight buer". Peter replied as if nothing untoward had happened. He then started the car turned onto Boothtown Road and drove over the tops to his then home to Clayton. Trevor and Peter sat in silence throughout the journey, Trevor maintained the belief that Peter was a little quiet, a little distant on this return trip. He put it down to tiredness and looked forward to getting into his own bed, oblivious of the woman lying face down in a pool of her own blood, oblivious to the misery his friend Peter William Sutcliffe had caused and was going to cause. Peter felt detached, distant, distressed, but not at his actions, but at his inactions, his inability to dispatch this brazen hussy, his inability to complete his mission.

Wardle's of Manchester metal framed streetlights illuminated the summer night and cast shadows onto the cobble stones. A pool of Olive's blood also stained/shadowed the cobble stones. Olive grasped at her chance for survival, Peter's indecision at the car headlights enabled her to crawl further away from him, dragging her desperate limp almost unresponsive body along the pavement, finally she managed to shout for help. Her pleas for help continued until aid arrived, soon she was in her living room, the blood-soaked survivor sat shell shocked as all around failed to hide their concern for her life. Olive Smelt was rushed to Halifax Infirmary where she was transferred to Leeds General Infirmary, she underwent brain surgery and was discharged ten days later.

Three/Zero
Halifax, Friday 15th August 1975. (23:45 hours) Their eyes met in a smoked filled room, she annoyed, irritated Peter in an insignificant way. *"I took her to be a prostitute".* Peter said to Trevor *"That is the prostitute we saw in the public house".* Peter stopped the car and left Trevor with the excuse that he was just off to speak to somebody. *"I hit her on the head and scratched her buttocks".* Saved by car headlights that drew attention to his assault, Peter retreated to his vehicle and unsuspecting passenger.

Saturday the 16th August 1975CE evening time Trevor Birdsall read an article in the Telegraph and Argus (a Bradford area local paper), about a violent assault on a woman in the Boothtown area of Halifax. It caught his attention because he had been in the area at the time of the attack. A seemingly motiveless attack on a middle-aged woman, nothing was stolen, and there was no sexual assault? His mind wandered to the previous night's activities; Peter and Trevor had been drinking together in Halifax and driven home through Boothtown. Peter stopped in Boothtown and went AWOL for a quarter of an hour just before midnight, the victim had been found around midnight. Trevor finished his flight of fancy, flicking to the sports space and dismissing his stupidity, but he did think it was a strange coincidence.

Olive passed away in April 2011 CE at Huddersfield Royal Infirmary, she was eighty-two years old.

Chapter 6
Silsden

Fourteen-year-old Tracey Brown lived at Upper Hayhills Farm, (Horne Lane, Silsden, BD20) with her twin sister Mandy, two other sisters and mother Norma and their father Anthony.

It was a Wednesday night August 27th, 1975 CE, a lovely late summer evening, bright, balmy and moonlit. Tracey had been in Silsden village with her sister Mandy and two other friends. As usual the Browne twins needed to be in no later than 22:30 hours, Mandy fully aware of this had made her excuses and set off earlier than her sister ensuring she didn't have to suffer the wrath of her father, a firm but fair man. However, Tracey had hung on until around 22:00 hours and was rushing to ensure she did not break her curfew. As she walked briskly home in the footsteps of Mandy she began to wish that she had joined her sister and set off earlier. She walked on Bridge Street and turned right up Bradley Road. Unbeknown to Tracey a lone man stood by his lime green Ford Capri, looking for an opportunity, an excuse to break his duck. As the gradual gradient of Bradley Road began to steepen, the climb, the length of the day, the heat of the summer and her physical exertions began to take its toll and once more she wished she'd joined Mandy and set off earlier. With an eye on her watch and her mind on her hot aching feet she had a good mile to walk and she knew she was cutting it fine, Tracey stopped to take off her shoes and continued up the road, lined by trees and surrounded by fields. She turned to see a man walking up the road behind her but paid him little heed. Shortly the man drew level and carried on past her, it was then that he slowed to a halt allowing Tracey to catch up with him.

"Nowt much doing in Silsden is the". Enquired the stranger, in a soft Yorkshire voice.

"Not really". She replied. They began to walk together up the country lane, her newfound companion often sniffling, occasionally sneezing, suffering what he described as a summer cold. They walked in silence interspersed with snippets of conversation.

"How far have you gotta go". He asked. Gauging how long he had to attack and kill her.

"About a mile". Came her reply. Peter continued to small talk, all the time looking for the best place, the ideal moment to attack. With each step he realised that his opportunity was diminishing, however he had to choose the right moment. There had been too many false starts God would be angry at his lack of results.

"What's yer name?"
"Tracey Browne".

"I'm Tony, Tony Jennis".
"Have yer gorra boyfriend".

"Yes, he lives in Silsden". Tony had his hands seemingly embedded in the front slit pockets of his trousers. The conversation dwindled as they walked up the hill, but Tracey felt safe with the stranger. As they walked together it gave Tracey time to observe Tony's appearance a somewhat dark figure, with dark Afro (esque) tightly curled/crinkly hair, a beard and a moustache with a thin face, he looked to be in his late twenties, he was quietly spoken. He had a knitted cardigan V neck cardigan, which he wore over a blue shirt.

"Me pal normally gives us a lift, but he's in't nick for drunk driving".
"Where do you live?" asked Tracey.
"Holroyd House". He lied.

On occasions he stopped to sort out his dripping nose; he was carrying a packet of paper handkerchiefs for that purpose; or crouched down to tie the laces on his brown suede shoes. Two or three times, Tony fell behind and two or three times Tracey politely stopped and waited for him. 22:30 hours and just in the nick of time, Tracey had eventually reached her turning for home, and again Tony had dropped off the pace, she'd reached the gate to the driveway to her family home. Tracey turned to bid a fond farewell to her walking companion and thank him for his company. But she did not get the chance, the last time Tony had slowed down and pretended to tie his shoelace, he had really taken a ball-pein hammer that was stuffed down his flared dark brown trousers. Tracey arriving at the entrance to her driveway had forced the issue and Peter took the chance. He hit Tracey with all his might.

ONE. *"Arrrgh!"* (love, 15) This time he had to make it count, there was to be no interruptions, this was it. Tracey fell to her knees.
"Please don't, please stop". Pleaded Tracey.
TWO
"Arrrgh!" (love, 30)
"Black Panther". Screamed Tracey, believing she was being attacked by the notorious killer.
THREE
"Arrrgh!" (love, 40)
FOUR
"Arrrgh!" (fault)
FIVE
"Arrrgh!" (double fault 15, 40).

Tony aka Peter heard a car engine straining at the uphill drive from Silsden. Tracey was collapsed on the floor, she stumbled across the road on her knee's trying to escape her assailant, the second and third blows left her prone on the tarmac in the centre of the road. Four and Five Tracey began to fade, unable to see. Peter scooped up Tracey like a rag doll, one arm under her legs, the other on her waist, he scooped her motionless body up and dumped it over the barbwire fence that bordered Dixon Green Farm, Horne Lane, Silsden, Keighley BD20. The headlights were now visible ascending the lane, Peter composed himself and began to walk down the road towards Silsden as if nothing had happened. The car passed by and Peter began to run apace down the hill, down Horne Lane, down to Bradley Road and down to his car left parked on Skipton Road, down to Silsden. He would now go down in history; his mission had started or so he believed.

Tracey hit the hard ground with a bump she heard Tony's footsteps disappearing down the lane, she was disorientated, unsure where she was and unsure as to what had just happened. She staggered to her feet and headed towards a blurred-light blue shape in the corner of the field. Partially sighted and full of panic and in shock thoughts flooded through her mind, will Tony try and finish what he'd started? Blood flooded out of her head wound. She continued towards the blurred-light blue shape.

"Help me, help me, someone please". She clambered through the field the commotion had woken the farm hand Alec Hargreaves who lived in the light blue caravan on Dixon Green Farm, he opened the door and hurried to help her. He hurriedly escorted her to her parents' home some six hundred metres away. Norma, Tracey's mother initially thought that somebody had poured a tin of red paint over her daughters head the bleeding was so profuse. Tracey was immediately rushed to Airedale General Hospital, Skipton Road, BD20, a mere three miles away. She was hurriedly diagnosed and transferred to Chapel Allerton Hospital, Chapeltown Road, LS7 4SA. During a difficult and delicate operation that took more than four hours neurosurgeons laboured to remove a splinter of her skull that was imbedded in her brain. Tracey's recovery was nothing short of miraculous being released from hospital after a week, although still under specialist supervision and an array of medication. On Saturday the 13th of September just over a fortnight after her assault Tracey, a wig and a woman police constable escort traversed the public houses and discotheques of the district in the vain hope of identifying Tracey's assailant Tony Jennis of Holdroyd House, AKA Peter Sutcliffe of Forty two Tanton Crescent.

The group visited properties in Silsden, Steeton and Keighley; in a temperate, tee-total pub crawl. The strange and sombre nature of their visits, seemed somewhat detached from reality juxtaposed with their surroundings, like the local Salvationists from the nearby Keighley Corps who'd been selling the 'War Cry' and 'The Young Soldier' to local revellers yesterday on Friday evening. The Warp Dressers and Twisters Social Club, The Kings Arms, The Punchbowl, The Silsden Conservative Club, The Red Lion, The Robin Head, The Bridge, The Grouse; then out of Silsden and onto Steeton. The Old Star, The Goats

Head, The "Sailor's and Soldier's Club"; then out of Steeton and back home to Silsden and the comfort of her family. All their efforts were to no avail for the man who they were looking for was relaxing on holiday in mainland Europe, enjoying a welcome break. Peter paid little concern to his earlier actions and prepared to travel to Prague on a holiday visit with the Szurma's,

Four/Zero
Silsden, Wednesday 27th August 1975. (22:30 hours) Retrospectively admitted but at the time unlinked, ignored. Dark - a modern day Heathcliffe, unassuming hay fever sufferer, lonely road, Jimmy Connor's, with love beads concur that Silsden is a rural backwater with not much doing. Much A Do About Nothing, (and no prostitutes in sight); Peter doesn't want this one putting down to his handy work.

Chapter 7
Wilomena (Wilma)

A fine and clear evening on Wednesday the 29th of October 1975 CE, Wilomena (Wilma) McCann (nee Newlands) a twenty-eight-year-old mother of four, Sonia (nine), Richard (seven), Donna (six) and Angela (five). She had been separated from her Irish husband Gerry for a good two years, originally from Inverness she had moved to Leeds in 1970 CE and settled in the Chapeltown district of Leeds.

19:30 hours, Wilma left her home a council house at 65 Scott Hall Avenue, Leeds LS7 2HJ to spend a night out on the town, it was the 'big midweek' Wilma liked a drink and to socialise, it provided respite from her busy domestic schedule, a role she'd struggled to fulfil over the recent weeks due to her increased alcohol intake. However, it wasn't something she was unduly worried about, it was probably just a phase, she had a lot to deal with, Tommy her abusive boyfriend had gone A.W.O.L., after burning the family photographs in another violent row. When would he return and what mood would he be in? Domestic chaos, empty milk bottles unwashed the sour residue of curdled milk, discarded bottles and cans. Dirty plates, pots, pans and cutlery the debris of the last family meal. Unclean, untidy, lived in. Ice formed on the condensation of the windows, sparse carpets or bare floorboards were the minimalistic fashion accessory of necessity and not choice. Economically marginalised, Wilma's coping mechanisms were cigarettes and alcohol. Before she left for her big night out, Wilma drilled her troops.

"Sonya doll you're in charge of the wee bairns".

She then slipped out of the back door and walked around the perimeter of the Prince Philip Playing Fields away from prying eyes, interfering busy bodies and liberal do gooders; leaving her children to their own devices.

Your mission Peter, should you decide to accept it, is to rid the streets of prostitutes. As always, should you or any of your force be caught or killed, God will disavow any knowledge of your actions. This tape will self-destruct in five seconds. Good luck, Peter.

The forlorn figure of a young fourteen-year-old Jayne MacDonald witnessed Wilma's penultimate walk across the lush green playing fields. In a touch of irony, she would meet her death at the hands of the same man.

Into the city to forget her worries, to have fun, for after all she deserved it. A pre-planned tour of the 'mucky pubs' of Central Leeds, what they lacked in cleanliness and amenities they made up for in character and characters. These pubs were frequented by the 'ladies of the night' a lively bunch, on the game and game for a laugh, plying their trade and adding to the atmosphere, with a little fear, a lot of fun and the occasional frolic, (for a fiver of course). Other clientele of these bastions of 1970's CE Leeds boozers were the all-day drinkers, one-time social drinkers descended into the darker side of drinking. Licensing laws were less laissez faire, however if you knew the area you could always find an accommodating venue. In at opening time, queueing up to get in, knocking on the door to ensure the landlord/landlady opened up punctually. These guys would be struggling having amassed hours of solid drinking, not to mention the skinful that they'd been carrying in the bloodstream for the past ten years.

Her first port of call was the Regent Inn, 109 Kirkgate, City Centre, Leeds LS1 6DP, where she had a couple of beers and concentrated on the job in hand. A couple of beers later and a couple of whisky chasers, the Scots woman walked around to the Scotsman's Arms, 106 Kirkgate, City Centre, Leeds LS1 6DP one of her favourite city centre pubs, again she had a beer and a couple of whisky chasers.

Kirkgate Road, drab, tired, shabby, openly showing the wounds of time. Care worn, Leeds oldest street with Anglo-Saxon origins, its eighteenth-century façade a living history of historic Leeds. For the oldest street, the oldest trade prostitution. As Rudyard Kipling wrote in his 1889 CE book 'On the City Wall', 'Lalun is a member of the most ancient profession in the world'. Lalun was a Lahore, whore a courtesan, a lady of the night a Jezebel. Salt of the earth people, getting salty, acting inappropriately, immorally. The street had stood the test of time as had the exchange of money for sex. Peter in his bid to end prostitution had to participate in it, it was a downside to his mission. When you frequented the pubs on Kirkgate Road you were never far away from a slice of vice. Kirkgate Road the oldest road in Leeds, prostitution the oldest trade of humankind both intertwined both combined.

Then to the White Swan, (The Mucky Duck), 37 Call Lane, LS1, Peter the shoe entered the 'Mucky Duck' a little off his beaten track, he looked and dressed like a gentleman belying the fact he lived in a hostel in Chapeltown. He wore a big overcoat, pulling back the coat from the lapel to reveal a row of six shoes all right footed, he opened the other side to reveal a further six left footed shoes, newly liberated from Marks and Spencer.

"Interested in my wares Wilma love?"

"Nae tonight Pete". Again, she had a couple of whiskies, time was passing by she decided to move up 'town' and closer to home. Up to the Royal Oak, 29 Kirkgate, City Centre, Leeds LS2, 22:30 hours last orders was fast approaching, she would have to forgo the pleasures of the Robin Hood, 71 Vicar Lane, City Centre, Leeds, LS1, maybe tomorrow. Two whiskies later and then onto the Room at the Top, (The Shaheen Club), largely an Afro Caribbean clientele, 215-219 North Street, Sheepscar, Leeds LS2. Up the stairs, for a

bit of a boogie on the dodgy dancefloor. The Room at the Top played soul, reggae, Motown and disco. Typical tracks and floor fillers would be the likes of Barry White, Gloria Gaynor, Freda Payne, Disco Tex and the Sex-o-Lettes, Carl Douglas (Kung Fu Fighting), a drink and of course a portion of chips and curry sauce, one of her favourites to end the evening, she left at 01:00 hours on Thursday morning the 30th October, the fog had got worse and all Wilma wanted to do was get home, the sooner the better, she'd had a good night but the cold had drawn in and with no overcoat she needed to get out of the cold and get home. She staggered out into the road and waved down a passing lorry driver, he stopped to prevent knocking her down but did not agree to her request for a lift and the endless possibilities that could entail, he then continued along his journey towards the M62, he continued with his work and forgot all about Wilma.

Meanwhile close by there was another gentleman about to commence work, however this was work of a different kind, and it was God's work. Peter had drunk a couple of pints and was in a good mood, he decided to cruise the streets and see what was happening, he saw Wilma thumbing a lift at the junction of Barrack Street and Scott Hall Road and walking up the grass verge. He pulled his Ford Capri GT over and leant over and opened the passenger door.

"How far yer going?" Peter asked.
"Nae far thanks fur stappin, nice car". Said Wilma, then climbed into the passenger seat.
"Have you had a good neight art then?" Peter small talked.
Peter continued to drive down the Scott Hall Road for about two thirds of a mile, Wilma directing him to her destination.
"Are yez lookin fer business?"
"Eh?"
"Blady Hell, dae I hav'tae spell it oot!"
"No, alreight, I mean yeah".
"It'll cost yer a fever!"

Wilma directed him to turn left onto Scott Hall Avenue, and then to turn left again into a field that sloped up, Peter parked at the edge of the playing fields. The pair sat in the dark, in the front of the stationary vehicle, in a seemingly isolated area, but in truth only yards from others. The night had cooled further the fog descended, this added to the solitary sense at the scene as if detached from reality. The pleasantries passed it was down to the mechanics of the proposed procurement.

"What yer waitin fer, ger on wiy it!" Wilma then opened the passenger side door and shouted, *"I'm gannin, yer ganna tek all fackin day. Yer fackin useless!"*
"Hang on, dun't be like that".

"So ya can fackin marnage it now can yer! I'm nae ganna dae it next tae the car!"
"There in't much room in't car, can we do it on't grass?"

Wilma had seen enough, it was cold, miserable and this weirdo was annoying her. Peter thought his chance had gone, however he remained patient, it was now or never. Reaching into the back seat, he fumbled in the tool box and picked out a ball-peen hammer, he then climbed out of the car, taking off his car coat and draping it over his left arm he had the hammer in his left hand, holding it tight into his thigh. He followed Wilma and caught up to her on an incline to the edge of the playing fields. Peter used the car coat to cover the damp grass, inviting Wilma to sit on it, Wilma did so and unfastened her white flared trousers.

"Cam on then, gerrit over with!" Wilma protested.

He had tried his best to coerce this woman further up the incline and suffered a barrage of abuse and foul language. Peter was standing above Wilma who was sitting on his coat, he was higher up the incline and Wilma had her back to him.

"Don't worry. I will". The left hand that the hammer was in was quickly raised to its full height he then swung it swiftly down, like a windmill sail, stopping when it met the resistance from the top of Wilma's head. He repeated the attack with a second sickening strike. Wilma fell flat on her back, in shock, her beehive hairstyle had done little to soften the blows, now blood seeped from the open wounds. A strange gurgling moaning noise emanated from Wilma lips. Panic and euphoria flooded into Peter's body - 'what have I done?' Peter partly lifted Wilma's prone body to enable him to pull his coat from underneath her he then hurried back to the car with an idea to flee the scene. He sat in the front seat contemplating his options/actions and the possible consequences, in the distance he could see Wilma lying on the grass banking, arms flailing as if beckoning him to return? He leant back into the back seat and replaced the hammer into the toolbox. Arms flailing, were they beckoning him back, what if she got up, she'd be able to tell everybody what he'd done, the police there would be serious consequences to pay, what would Sonia say, and it was then that the penny dropped, he had to silence the witness to his atrocity, in for a penny in for a pound. He reached back into the toolbox and selected a single bladed kitchen knife, with a wooden handle, the blade was about 7" long. He climbed out of the car and rushed to Wilma and stabbed her in the neck, he then pulled her pink blouse open to reveal her naked torso, so he could see what he was doing. He then pulled her brassiere up above her breasts, then stabbed at her chest five times and then down to her stomach a further nine, until he could be sure she was dead and she was unable to reveal his actions. Aroused at his actions and in the throes of his theological mission, the necrophilia obsessed Peter took out his manhood and in a final hoorah masturbated over Wilma's lifeless corpse.

The panic subsided as his energy subsided, it was 01:30 hours on Thursday morning the 30th of October 1975. His artistic bent then came to the fore, he pulled her white pants down around her ankles, and he looped the red leather strap of her handbag around her left hand and lay the handbag beside her. During the initial knife attack he had ripped apart her pink blouse and her blue jacket. He then pulled her pink bra up to expose her naked breasts. He posed her body half through circumstance in an effort to humiliate her womanhood. He took the small white top clasp purse out of her handbag, failing to notice the personalised 'Monicker' MUMIY on it. He later threw this away in a half-hearted attempt to plant the seed that this was a robbery gone wrong. A sign of the personal tragedy, a sign of collateral damage in Peter's very personal Holy war.

A seething mass of resentment, lust and anger. This humiliation was the final straw and Pandora's Box was prised open the metaphysical genie was let out of the bottle to unleash untold vengeance on the north of England. Unwittingly, Wilomena had signed her own death sentence with her behaviour towards him. The dormant sleeper cell had awoken.

Peter then returned to the car, started it up, reversed back along the narrow road, which led onto Scott Hall Avenue, he then set off back home to Bradford, travelling West through Headingly, Horsforth, Rodley, Calverly, Eccleshill and then home to Tanton Crescent, Clayton, back to mundane normality, but things could never be the same again. He sat in his car outside the house and inspected his clothing for blood stains, he then went into the house and straight into the bathroom, where he cleaned himself up, then went straight to bed.

Thursday the 30th of October, 1975CE 05:25 hours, Sonia woke Richard and alerted him to the fact that their mum had not yet returned home, this was a first. On occasions Wilma had been unable to rise from her bed incapacitated by too much alcohol, too much of the good life, but for all her failings Wilma loved her children and cared for them as best she could.

"Mum's not come home, put some clothes on and we'll go look for her".

Sonia and Richard dressed hastily, haphazardly, throwing shoes onto bare feet and overcoats over their pyjamas or dressing gown, to protect them from the crisp cold air. The duo stole out of the back door of their home, just has their mother had done ten hours earlier, a lifetime ago; leaving Angela and Donna to the safety and security of their innocent slumber. Wilma had taught them well, she had taught them to avoid the busybody, be wary of the outsider, the stranger, the liberal do-gooder, the social workers, with their false pretence of help. They weren't here to help, they wanted to hinder, interfere, to control and preach. Creeping stealthily down the back garden through the hedge and onto the field where the dead body of their mum lay. Under the radar, undetected, unseen as if invisible. They saw a milk float, other than that the roads were empty. They turned left and hugged the borders of the playing field, and then a left turn onto a ginnel and then onto the main bus route of Scott Hall Road.

Two small silhouetted figures sat like shadows in the metal and glass framed bus shelter, hiding their faces into their coats against the whirling cold autumnal fog, waiting for their mother to return. Eventually the first bus came, but there was no Wilma, just a grumpy driver who huffed and puffed at these modern-day street urchins for wasting his time. He pulled away leaving Sonia and Richard slightly more dejected, neglected, deserted and worried. An hour passed and each time the inner feeling of uncertainty grew, their hopes raised by a bus in the distance and dashed as it revealed no Wilma. It was getting light and they were more visible, they decided to return home, anyway Angela and Donna would be stirring and they would be scared if no one was there to look after them. They retraced their earlier route still in stealth mode, hoping above hope that their mum had returned in their absence, but of course she had not.

07:41 hours, Alan Routledge a local milkman had the misfortune of finding Wilma's lifeless body - initially Alan thought she was a discarded Guy, but Paul his ten-year-old brother looked closer and ominously that it was a body. Alan ran to the nearby caretaker's bungalow bordering the car park of the Prince Philip Centre Scott Hall Avenue, Leeds, West Yorkshire LS7 2HJ and began to knock on the door. John Bauld the caretaker his morning routine interrupted by the commotion at his front door wondered what was going on. He opened the door to see a horrified and clearly distressed Alan mumbling incoherently about a dead body. John 'steeled' himself and walked purposely across his garden to the perimeter fence, he peered over the fence and witnessed the disfigured body, immediately he recognised the identity of this lost soul, the image of Wilma's blood covered mortal remains lying on her back, her clothes open and her eyes staring upwards. *"Alan phone the police".* He instructed Alan, who dialled 999 and reported to the operator that he had just found the body of a woman, with her throat cut. Margaret, John's wife on hearing the commotion pulled back her bedroom curtains and was startled by what confronted her. Margaret's eyes focussed in on Wilma and her staring eyes seemingly looking up towards the Bauld's bedroom window. John and Margaret recognised Wilma immediately, her trademark blonde hair and the fact that her kids, Sonia, Richard, Donna and Angela attended or had attended the adjacent nursery school. The fact that they had slept with the window open and heard nothing and the fact that Butch their South African ridgeback dog didn't bark, dumbfounded them. Butch always barked when strangers were nearby, it was not unusual for the couple to be raised from their slumber by the barks of Butch warning of possible danger. It was as if the murderer had supernatural powers, a cloak of invisibility/invincibility or was being watched over, protected by a higher power.

Sonia instructed Richard to go to the front gate at the top of the garden and keep a look out for mum, Richard did as he was asked. From his vantage point he could see a crowd milling around the flashing blue lights of two police cars. Richard went back in and told Sonia what was going on, the pair decided to find out what was happening first hand and put plans into place for Donna to stay with Angela, then off they went. Soon they were amongst the crowd, a policeman saw the strange couple and crouching down asked. *"Who might you two be?"*

"Sonia and Richard McCann". Replied Sonia.
"And where are you going?" He quizzed.
"Our mum hasn't come home. We're looking for her". Richard explained.
The demeanour of the policeman changed as if a strange realisation had come upon him.
"Where do you live?" He asked.
"65 Scott Hall Avenue, Leeds".
The policeman spoke into his radio.

The strange trio then walked silently back home. The policeman followed them into the house.

"Where's your dad? When did you last see your mum? Do you have a photograph of your mum?" The policeman spoke into his radio again. The policeman waited with the four children until another officer arrived, this one was not in uniform. The children were then taken to 'Beckett's Park Children's Home', Greenwood Mount, Meanwood, Leeds; the staff were expecting the children and settled them in as best they could. A time of limbo caught between the knowing and not knowing the painful truth. The plain clothes police officer returned to the fold, he sat amongst the children, then unleashed the bombshell.

"Your mum has been taken to heaven, you won't be seeing her anymore". One life ended and four lives shattered, invisible victims of an evil maniac.

9:00 hours, *'This is BBC Radio Leeds, good morning it's Thursday October 30th, 1975. Police are investigating the discovery of a woman's body on a playing field in the Chapeltown district of Leeds. The woman who has not yet been identified was found by a milkman on his early delivery round. Murder squad detectives have been called in and a press conference on the case will be held in the morning'.*

Peter went to work at Common Road Tyre Services, Oak Mills, Cliffe Hollings Lane Oakenshaw, Bradford BD12 and went about his life in a 'business as usual' manner, although this was easier said than done. He received an untimely reminder whilst watching Yorkshire Television's (YTV) Calendar News later that evening, when there was an article about the murder of a Leeds prostitute. His heart skipped and for a fleeting moment he was back on the playing field in Leeds, master of all he surveyed, master of his victim. Peter felt sick to the pit of his stomach, he was anticipating what would/could happen to him, and he half expected the police to be on their way to Tanton Crescent to arrest him. He made a considered decision to act naturally and not court interest.

As he grew into the role of the Yorkshire Ripper, his hatred grew for prostitutes, it matured and he cultivated it. He used it to justify his actions, in a twisted way he'd saved her soul from eternal damnation. Saint Peter of Bradford, he liked the sound of that, society had become corrupt with a false morality and someone would have to pay the price.

Five/One
Leeds, Thursday 30th October 1975 CE. (01:30 hours) The deed finally done, the divine mission is under way no more false starts. After his first success Peter played up his hatred of prostitutes, developing a dislike in order to justify his Holy crusade. No more panic, this is street art; as he disarranged her clothes, one of his signature traits, a trademark, a final fling a hidden insult. *"When they find them they will look as cheap as they are...I just wanted to get rid of her".* Unhinged yet unaware completely unaware, the seal was now broken and Pandora's Box was well and truly open. five pounds please, no sex please we're British. Peter wanted to do what he had in mind as soon as he could. After that it grew and grew and he became a beast. Peter continued safe in the knowledge that he was the chosen one, doing God's bidding, it was his calling and he had no issues in proceeding and God was protecting him.

Anxiety, fear that the police will be coming for him, panic stricken Cluedo nightmares disturbed his sleep. It was Mr. Peter William Sutcliffe in Prince Phillip's field, with a ball peen hammer and a knife. However, with each passing day acceptance became more common place the voices reassured him and instructed him to repeat the process. In Peter's eyes the drunken spiteful taunting from Wilma were the trigger that instigated the action that ultimately unleashed the axis of evil on a largely unsuspecting northern public, the consequences of which would be far reaching and detrimental. A very bad thing had been released and so the Yorkshire Ripper after his fledgling foot faltering steps had finally come of age.

Chapter 8
Emily

Emily Monica Jackson, (nee Wood) aged forty-two, mother of four, roofing assistant, office manager, driver labourer, administrative assistant and part time prostitute. She was a thick set woman not unattractive, an industrious soul, always on the go with an insatiable lust for life, and she lived with her husband, Sidney a father, a roofer and a volunteer part time pimp? The couple lived at 18 Back Green, Churwell, Morley, Leeds, West Yorkshire LS27. With Neil, eighteen (roofers labourer), Christopher, ten (scholar) and Angela, eight (scholar). The family motto of 'life is too short, live for today' had been adopted after the untimely death of their first born son in a terrible accident in 1971 CE, when Derek (then aged fourteen), had fallen to his death. Since his premature passing the Jackson's tended to overindulge when imbibing alcohol, their drinking, frivolities and festivities possibly lightened the darkness they felt in some small way. Their lifestyles had changed considerably of late, times were hard, the inland revenue wanted their piece of meat and the expense of Christmas had forced Emily into her new side line of freelance sex worker, with the blessing of her husband of course. Tuesday 20th of January 1976 CE, had proved another cold and windy day, although the freezing rain of late was conspicuous by its absence, this had seen the Jackson family busy in their work, roofing repairs were the order of the day. However, an afternoon storm had curtailed their work for today. Emily had a meal prepared and it was time for the children to rest, under the supervision of Neil the eldest sibling, whilst Emily and Sydney went out to play. She had put on her 'glad rags' but was also suitably attired to keep the elements at bay, she had done her brunette hair, her makeup and applied and blotted her lipstick and perfume, Coty L'Aimant with ritual panache, behind the ears, on the wrists then rub the wrists together to disperse the smell. The phone rang disrupting Emily's preparations Neil answered and passed the phone to his mum.

"Its Mrs Stone abart some work".

"I'll come round first thing and have a look". Emily explained to Mrs Stone, then told Neil he'd have some weekend work. Times were tough, but work was work and had to be taken when it was on offer. Emily sat in front of the mirror and checked her makeup for one last time. Showing her teeth, she turned to her son

"Can yer see any lippy Neil?"

Neil replied, *"No mam"*. Emily then retrieved her lighter and a cigarette from her handbag, her nicotine yellow fingers raised the lighter to the cigarette she had placed in between her recently decorated lips, she lit the cigarette and sucked/inhaled on it, then inadvertently exhaled the toxic smoke into Neil's face, who spluttered and coughed his indignation.

"Sorry love". Emily put on her white sling back shoes and left her final instructions.

"You two, (meaning Christopher and Angela) bed at half seven and behave for yer brother or I won't bring yer any crisps home". Sidney then appeared coming down the stairs.

"Are yer reight love?" The children were fed and watered and Emily and Sidney had climbed into the couples battered blue Crommer van, BNK953K, with the dodgy front bumper, with the ladder still on top, with the work worn body dents, Emily driving, Sidney the passenger. Emily turned the engine over attempting to start it, nothing; it had been temperamental for a couple of days, she turned it over again and the engine spluttered into life, she made a mental note to get it serviced tomorrow, then they set off to the bright lights of the city. Driving the five miles to her regular 'stamping ground', Emily was going out, she was going for one of her infamous, what she referred to as a 'Night on the Town', inwardly excited at the multiple possibilities that could ensue, Tuesday is the new Saturday. They arrived at the Gaiety Public House at 18:00 hours, 89-95 Roundhay Road, Leeds LS8 situated on the junction with Gathorne Terrace and bordered on the East by Bank Side Street. Emily pulled into the car park of the Gaiety, this 1972 CE super pub was the hub of the drinking community and attracted a curious and colourful cross section of the local population. Gipton Beck split the building and an archway incorporating this natural feature was built, allowing the beck to run unmolested through a culvert and under the archway. Therefore the building had two sides which were bridged by a room which housed the Vaudeville Bar, there were a further four bars, some of the bars had the capacity to house around four hundred customers, and it was a busy and popular destination.

Sidney went to the bar whilst Emily remained in the van and applied the finishing touches to her make up. She then met him at the bar where they shared conversation and their beverages, fortification for her oncoming frolics and then they parted, going their own separate ways. Emily went to the car park, where she had a brief chat with Maria Sellars, a nineteen-year-old casual acquaintance and street worker

The time was 18:55 hours, their pleasantries were cut short when Emily's attention was caught by a bushy bearded man in a Land Rover parked across the road, Emily approached the Land Rover, words were exchanged a deal was struck, five pounds for a fuck and in she got, Maria's last recollection of Emily was of her disappearing down Gledow Road in the passenger seat of a Land Rover unbeknown to her, in essence, she was embarking on her journey to the 'other side'.

Peter finished work around 19:00 and decided to take a sojourn to the city and its bright lights, he'd forgo the pleasure of the communal Bigos (Polish Hunters Soup) and exchange it for another pleasure, but somewhat less communal. Thornbury, Stanningley, Armley &

then up to Chapeltown, like a moth to a flame, or should that be a flame to a moth. Peter still in his work attire was restless, he was unable to supress the urge that welled within. Circa 21:00 hours Peter was cruising the now familiar Chapeltown, North Leeds district (sin ominous for Peter) synonymous for its links to the seedier side of life, he was driving his Ford Capri North along Roundhay Road when he saw Emily in her overcoat, she was standing prominently on the pavement occasionally edging into the road if she thought she'd caught the eye of somebody who wanted to sample her wares, her figure sheltered slightly by the red telephone boxes behind her. Peter pulled over, wound down his window and brokered a deal.

"How much?" he asked.

"Five pounds". came Emily's reply. He nodded his agreement and opened the passenger side door and gestured with a flick of his head for her to get into the passenger seat.

"I know where we can turn the car around and head towards the city centre". Emily jovially instructed Peter. He meekly obliged and headed back down Roundhay Road, the smell of her perfume in the confined space of the car upset him but he stoically continued with the task in hand.

"I usually drive". explained Emily, *"I find it quite relaxing".*
"Yes, so do I". replied Peter in his quiet Bradfordian twang.

"Turn left love and then left again...Pull over". Peter complied eventually pulling up behind some disused red brick buildings on the cobbled cul-de-sac of Enfield Terrace, off Manor Street and also off Roundhay Road. An unlit area often frequented by prostitutes and their punters, littered with discarded rubbish, overgrown with weeds, derelict. Peter pulled into Enfield Terrace, a dead end road blocked by a ten foot red house brick wall, he used the width of the cobbled road to perform a three point turn, a voice in his head warning him to take all precautions and make best endeavours to ensure a fast and hassle free flight from the forecast felony. He pulled the car up directly outside Hollingsworth and Moss Bookbinders, Manor Street Industrial Estate, Leeds, LS7, its flat roofed silhouette to his right, he was now facing towards Enfield Street.

Peter then switched the car engine off then turned the ignition key clockwise, but only so the red warning light came on. The red warning light was symbolic, he did not turn the key fully for this would not fit in with his plan.

"It won't start. I'll have to pop't bonnet. Can yer give us a hand?" Emily agreed to assist her hapless punter, nothing was too much trouble for a customer.
"Yeah love believe it or not I've got one like this at home, what do you want me to do?"

"I don't suppose you've gorra torch have yer?"
Emily then suggested *"I've got me lighter, will that do?"*

"Ey, owt's better than nowt". He then reached down the side of his car seat and felt for the hammer that he had concealed there before he set off on his journey from Bradford, he also grabbed his Phillips cross head screwdriver and placed it in his back pocket, has he climbed out of the car. Falling into her daily hands on role of roofers labourer, she proceeded to the front of the car raised her right arm and held the lighter aloft to enable Peter to see what he was doing. Peter was now standing beside her the car bonnet raised with the support arm locked in place, Peter pretended to peer into the abyss of the engine, he took two steps back, then raised his arm in a grotesque dark shadow of the light from Emily's lighter, he then brought the hammer swiftly down on the back of her head, an action he repeated. Emily fell down from the first blow onto the cobbled road, Peter quickly concealed the ball peen hammer in his inside jacket pocket, he then grabbed Emily by the wrists and dragged the incapacitated Emily across the road into a disused ginnel out of sight, out of mind.

The derelict ginnel was once covered, the charred and scorched timbers overhead all that remained of the roof after an a arson attack, it was strewn with rubbish and detritus, the flotsam and jetsam of a run-down inner city industrial landscape, secluded, a half world of lost souls, sucked into the gutter through their very existence. The area was ear-marked for demolition works, Peter was to perform his own demolition works on Emily. Enfield Terrace, off Enfield Street, off Roundhay Road, not even a mile away from Leeds city centre! He pulled open the blue, green and red checked overcoat and raised Emily's blue and white horizontal striped dress to enable him to get to his work.

Emily was slumped face down in the dirt, he pulled the Phillips screwdriver from his back pocket and proceeded to stab Emily in the back with it, this was to ensure she was dead and could not tell a soul about their encounter, it was also his duty to save her soul from her sinning ways, a nineteen seventies Doctor Van Helsing, transferred from northern Rumania to northern England. Peter stabbed Emily some thirty-two times in a concentrated seven-inch squared area. Like an avant-garde seven-inch single record picture sleeve designer Emily suffered for Peter's art. He turned Emily over onto her back and started to slash and stab again, this time in a state of mild agitation, the earlier fury had diminished, he stabbed Emily in the lower neck with the screwdriver, he pulled up her bra to reveal her breasts, he then moved down stabbing the upper chest, he then moved down again stabbing her lower stomach a further twelve times, one for each of Jesus's disciples. In total he stabbed her fifty-two times. He then saw a piece of discarded timber some three foot long by one inch wide, he went to pick it up and stumbled on her right thigh and had to stand on it to regain his balance eventually leaving a size seven Dunlop Warwick heavy ribbed wellington boot print on Emily's thigh. He pushed the timber towards her genitalia as she lay dead on the cold stone yard floor. He tossed the timber away and decided to end his attack. He composed himself then departed the seclusion of the ginnel and walked out onto the cobbled street out onto Enfield Terrace, Peter was about to get back into his car when another car it's headlights adding light to the scenario and also a possible witness to his earlier activities. Peter remained calm he tried to blend into his surrounding he saw the punter prostitute duo whom seemed wrapped up in one another. The derelict industrial area seemed somewhat out of context for Yorkshire, the red 'Manchester' house bricks that formed the backdrop to his crime seemed to unsettle him. The fact that life went on even after the untimely passing of Emily unnerved him further still. So close to capture, so close to freedom Peter opened his car door discretely hid his tools on the car floor and drove west back to Bradford, back to Clayton along Clayton Road which becomes Bradford Road, taking a right into Terrington Crest, then third left up the cul-de-sac section of Tanton Crescent, back to his in-laws at 44 Tanton Crescent, back to normality like nothing had happened. An inspection of himself and his clothes for any tell-tale signs that might make people suspicious of his earlier antics, Peter was astonished that he was as clean as a whistle. No late-night rinsing, sponging, wiping, scrubbing and cleaning for him, it was as if he was protected by an invisible force, he was invincible. For Emily, no more nights on the town, no more Bingo, no more anything.

Oblivious to his wife's demise Sidney continues to drink and make merry, until that is, the last order bell rang at the Gaiety 22:30 hours, he finished his drink then headed out to the pub car park, his blue Commer was still there, but no Emily. He gave it ten minutes and thought 'Que será', (whatever will be, will be) and ordered a taxi, he went to bed unaware of the tragedy that had befallen him, Emily and his family.

Six/Two
Leeds, Tuesday the 20th January 1976 CE. (19:30 hours) Fully focused foot to the floor throttle full on, Peter knew that it was important to his cause that the mission had to be continued. By now, Peter was obsessed with killing prostitutes. He couldn't stop himself it was like some sort of drug. Most importantly, the mission had to be continued, it was central to his core, it was his calling.

Wednesday 21st January 1976 CE, 08:10 hours a man on his way to work pulls up his car on Enfield Terrace, its free road parking close to the city centre made this part of his daily routine. He parked the vehicle almost parallel to the ginnel where Emily's body was laying he climbed out of the car, closed and locked. Making sure no valuables were left on display, after all it was not the most salubrious of areas. He was wrapped up against the miserable weather, the cold wind and rain providing a conflicting environment to the warm car he'd just vacated. Keeping his head down brow beaten by the elements he caught a glimpse of what he thought was a discarded dummy, nothing out of the ordinary he thought for this unwholesome, unhealthy and uninviting landscape. The bulldozers couldn't come fast enough, he then thought this would inadvertently cost him his free parking space, where else would he park. He took a second glance and to his horror realised that it was not a tailors dummy it was a body, it was the body of a woman, hidden in plain sight five metres into the ginnel amongst the discarded bric-a-brac and rubbish. He took a second more detailed look in order to ensure this was real, unfortunately it was. Emily's body was slumped to the right-hand side of the ginnel when viewed from Enfield Terrace, the workman's vantage point. Her soiled sling backs lay forlornly free from the bare feet they once adorned. The body lay supine, Emily's left arm down by her side, her right arm pointing sideways at a ninety degree angle to her body, her left leg was pointing straight down towards the entrance of the ginnel, whilst her right leg faced outwards towards the left hand side and open area of the ginnel with its rubbish and now blood stained concrete. All tics was encompassed under the remnants of the fire damaged roofing and the open cold rain filled sky above. Emily's fawn coloured imitation leather handbag lay open a couple of metres from her head, its contents still intact. The workman had seen enough, he rushed to the red telephone box situated at the junction of Sheepscar Street South and North Street some four hundred metres away. He dialled 999 and asked for the police.

West Indians become Afro-Caribbean, ladies of the night/good time girls become sex workers, beer and stout, become lager and alco pops. Names change, but the mechanics remain the same. Murder becomes a theological mission, a soul saving favour, a Christ lookalike do-gooder. Justification, gratification, satisfaction and fulfilment for a job well done. Peter reverted to type, the conscientious lorry driver.

Friday the 23rd of January 1976; Peter sat in a greasy spoon transport café when his attention was caught by a lurid headline' 'Ripper Hunted in Call-Girl Murders' read the headline in the Sun. National acclaim and a nickname to match. The mission was well underway.

Chapter 9
Marcella

Marcella Claxton was a twenty-year-old immigrant originally from Saint Kitts (Saint Christopher Island), an Island, in the West Indies. Her mother brought her to England at the age of ten to start a new life, a better life, it turned out to be a tough childhood, which was more survived than enjoyed.

Marcella was classed as educationally subnormal, with an IQ classification of 50, in old money that's an imbecile, (IQ rating 21 to 50), one up from an idiot (IQ rating 0 to 20); but one down from a moron (IQ rating 51 to 70). For of course this is a non-PC northern town. Marcella was an unemployed single mother of two, true pioneer of the as yet undiscovered underclass, she lived in one of the many back to back terraced houses in a street off Roundhay Road in the Chapeltown area of Leeds.

Saturday 8th May 1976 CE was a dry sunny day a spring preamble into the heatwave that was to produce Britain's hottest summer since records began. Late Saturday evening Marcella decided that to go out as was her wont, she went to The International Club, 58-62 Francis Street, Leeds. LS7 4BY, later she went onto a local Shaheen club, to relax, unwind and drink. Marcella was three months pregnant and drunk; it was Sunday morning circa 04:30 hours and Marcella decided to leave the 'party' and walk the short distance home. Marcella was walking along Spencer Place, when a white Ford Corsair pulled up and stopped, Marcella assumed the dark crinkly haired man, with a beard and moustache was a kind-hearted motorist.

Chapeltown was a mecca for immigrants from the end of World War Two, successive waves of immigrants have contributed towards the multi-cultural makeup of the area, firstly the Jews, then the Poles, then the Afro-Caribbeans, then the Pakistanis. Chapeltown's square of vice developed, it's parameter being to the north Harehill's Avenue, Roundhay Road to the east, Barrack Road to the south and Chapeltown Road to the west. The square of vice serviced the sexual needs of these first generation pioneer immigrants, mainly single men a long way from home, the housing stock in this area was big, formerly sought after houses which were ideal for multi-occupation, it was an ideal hotbed for vice, with staple police involvement relating to prostitution, assaults, woundings, missing persons, liquor licensing and sexual offences.

Peter thought here was a prostitute he could take off the street for eternity. *"Are you Babylon?"* Marcella quizzically asked. Peter looked puzzled.
"Eh!"
"The police, are you the police?" Marcella explained.
"Nah do I look like a copper?" Peter joked. Although booted and suited, in a black suit,

white shirt and tie Peter found her assumption amusing.
Marcella was tired, it had been a long day and she decided a lift would be preferable to a lonely walk home and climbed into the red upholstered front passenger seat of his car.
"How much do yer charge?"

Marcella was allegedly slow, but she was quick on the uptake when it came to an opportunity, she'd take her chances, here was an opportunity too good to be missed. She'd take this mug up to Soldiers Field, take a fiver for her troubles and disappear into the night.
"Five pounds. Do ya know where ta go?"
"Nah, I'm not from rand ere".

Marcella instructed Peter as to where to go, Peter followed Marcella's instructions he drove north up Spencer Place, taking a right at the junction onto Harehills Avenue, this road eventually merged into Roundhay Road. Just before Roundhay Road becomes Wetherby Road, he turned left into Oakwood and then right onto Park Avenue, following the road around and then turning left up West Avenue, up towards the end of the dead-end road. To the west Princess Avenue, bordered by a row of trees on the right-hand side, facing north and a double row of trees to the left-hand side, like a bold and normal print border. To the right-hand side of Princess Avenue is Soldiers Field a location that will soon be indelibly printed into Marcella Claxton's mind, with a little help from a ball peen hammer at the hand of Mr Peter William Sutcliffe. Then up to the solitude and tranquillity of Soldiers Field, LS8 1JX. A journey of some two and a half miles.

"Stop now". yelled Marcella, her inhibitions removed due to the alcohol consumed. Peter pulled the car to a halt about fifty yards shy of the end of West Avenue, he leant forward in his seat, reached into his back suit trouser pocket and found his wallet, he produced a Fiver, pressed it into Marcella's palm.

"Gerrout at car, take yer clothes off and we can do it on't grass".
Marcella took the fiver, her idea was going to plan. *"I need to take a pee".*

Marcella exited the vehicle and disappeared behind trees to the right-hand side of West View bordering Soldiers Field, a name that developed because it was an assembly place for troops in the Great War. Peter quickly followed, picking up his hammer, by now his weapon of choice from underneath the driver's seat. As he walked towards the area he had last seen Marcella, his eyes were struggling to acclimatize to the darkness, he called out, *"Where yer gone".* He stumbled over a tree root, this caused him to drop the ball –peen hammer. Marcella's voice came from the trees

"Me hope that ain't no knife".
Peter honed in on the direction of the voice and let out a false laugh.
"It's me wallet, let's get darn to it".

"No, argh!!!" came the short-lived reply from Marcella, for Peter had found his target and struck home with a blitz Krieg attack to the back of Marcella's head. One, two, three, four, five, six, seven, eight, another stumble eight and a half, and then nothing. Energy levels and the rage within had subsided. Marcella a crumpled heap on the margins of Soldiers Field. He surveyed his work and then standing above her lifeless body took out his penis and began to masturbate. His urge fulfilled and his victim dispatched, he pondered whether or not to cut her up. His knife was hidden down the side of the driver's seat back in the car, he couldn't be bothered to get it, and she wasn't worth the energy. He felt the job was done and there was no need for the knife and with that he drove off into the night.

Marcella, the supposed imbecile had played dead, Marcella the supposed imbecile would live to fight another day, or would she? Peter was unsure if he'd seen the prone figure of Marcella rise from her demise, a latter-day Lazarus, he had been over concerned with self-gratification and with making a quick exit in the hope of ensuring escape. As he drove away, this began to play on his mind, if she was alive, she could possibly identify him, what would Sonia say? He decided to return to the scene, just to make sure. To his shock, the body had gone, he got out of the car to see if there was any sign of her, but there was not. He then briefly drove around the area to see if he could see her, but this was to no avail. He decided to cut his losses and return home to Tanton Crescent. He drove into Leeds city centre, through Armley, east to Pudsey, then to Thornbury, through Bradford city centre, then up to Clayton. But first a few moments to collect himself to control the situation, a few moments of quiet reflection. What had he done? Morbid depression encompassed his very being, and he checked his attire, his appearance to see if there was a trace of his earlier actions, there was not.

Marcella staggered south in the pitch black, blood pouring from her open head wounds, Marcella's recently removed knickers were used as a makeshift bandage stemming the flow, a walk to the lights of Roundhay Road, a half a mile as the crow flies, a half a mile to ensure nobody dies. Crawling, bleeding and barely conscious across the expanse of grassland to the safe haven of civilisation, the white metalwork of Oakwood Tower, under the gaze of the gold affect owl sitting on top of the gold effect weathervane. The safe haven of urban sprawl and the sanctuary of a red telephone box, a General Post Office (GPO) kiosk number eight, designed by a Mr Bruce Martin in 1965 CE and introduced onto the streets of Britain in 1968 CE. This rectangular shaped cast iron and glass safe haven was a lifeline and ultimately a life saver, or was it? Marcella fumbled as she dialled 999.

"999 what's your emergency?"
"Ambulance me got clots coming from me head. I need ambulance".

Marcella sat on the concrete floor of the kiosk, the white light was silhouetting her dark figure making her highly visible, and this was something she did not want. The eighteen-inch red cast iron frame at the bottom of the phone box partially obscured her body. She watched with horror as the white Ford Corsair and her attacker kept driving past, circling like a shark, the ultimate predator circling its prey, up/down Roundhay Road, up/down Princes Avenue and up/down Park Avenue. Peter was concerned he wanted to finish what he'd started and needed to find Marcella.

The ambulance arrived and rushed Marcella to Leeds General Infirmary, where she needed fifty-two stitches to close the trauma to her head. She was discharged after six days but was scared to return to her own address. Although unsuccessful in his attempt on Marcella's life, Sutcliffe did claim a new victim, a silent victim, Marcella's unborn baby.

No Stephen Lawrence enquiry here, no Stephen Lawrence Charitable Trust, no institutional racism, just plain old racism. An indiscriminate attack in a world that did not care.

Seven/Two
Leeds, Sunday 9th May 1976 CE (04:00 hours) *"I hit her once on the head with the hammer, but just couldn't bring myself to hit her again. For some reason or another, I just let her walk away".*

1978CE, two years after her attack Marcella gave birth to a daughter, she called her Marcia. In a twist of fate Marcia was also to be the victim of a vicious assault, some twenty-seven and a half years later. Wednesday the 10th of December 2003 CE three men wearing balaclavas and armed with handguns called at Marcia's Savile Drive home, they kidnapped her at gunpoint. The trio drove out of the city questioning the terrified Marcia about drug dealers from Little London, an area to the north of Leeds city centre with a proliferation of 1960's CE high rise council flats. Marcia unable to answer the questions would feel the wrath of her abductors, they drove her to a secluded lane - echoes of her mother's ordeal. She was then told to get out of the car and crouch down on all fours. The assailant then shot Marcia four times, once in the thigh, once in the arm, once in the knee and once in the calf. The trio then drove off but left Marcia with some words of warning.

"You're just a stupid whore no one cares about. Your face will be all over the front of the paper tomorrow. If you tell, you're dead".

Marcia struggled to the roadside and finally managed to signal the help of a passing motorist who took her straight to hospital.

Two of the perpetrators were arrested the next day, they were later convicted for their crimes, their home addresses were, Spencer Place and Louis Street both addresses in Chapeltown. Throwbacks to earlier days when the Yorkshire Ripper stalked these very streets. No guns for Peter; ball-peen hammers, knives, screwdrivers and cord. But still death and destruction caused by man on woman.

Chapter 10
Irene

When two sevens clash, union power, punk rock, anarchy, safety pins, bunting, street parties, monarchy and mayhem. 1977CE.

Irene Richardson was a twenty-eight-year-old mother of four children an alleged divorcee, who had recently broken up with her boyfriend/fiancé/common law husband Stephen Joseph Bray, a thirty-nine-year-old labourer. Stephen was six foot tall, heavily tattooed and had a warrant out for his arrest due to the fact that he had absconded from HM prison Lancaster a category C prison, whilst on home leave officially being recorded AWOL on Monday the 1st of March 1976CE. Irene and Stephen were due to be married at the register office on Saturday the 22nd of January 1977CE, however both parties failed to attend, because both parties were still legally married. It was shortly after this missed appointment that Irene's life began to unwind and fall apart, in essence setting into motion a sequence of events that would ultimately cost Irene her life. Irene was outwardly jovial, but suffered from post-natal depression, this was compounded by her circumstances, she was in and out of work, she had been working as a chambermaid as well as a cleaner at a Young Men's Christian Association (YMCA) hostel and was looking for work, however with no fixed abode, this was proving very difficult. This also made it impossible for Irene to claim State Benefits, (then Social Security); Irene had well and truly fallen through the safety net that the State hoped to provide. Irene had been struggling to find a roof to cover her head, since Tuesday the 25th of January 1977CE sleeping rough on occasions, she had slept on friends floors and even the public lavatories but by Saturday had managed to contrive a shelter for her troubled soul a one roomed bedsit on Cowper Street in the seedy heart of Chapeltown the area infamous for vice and sleaze and synonymous with Leeds dark underbelly of crime and misrule.

To understand Irene's life, we must look further at the context of her life, a transient tour seemingly lurching from one calamity to crisis. Irene seemed to be one of life's victims Peter Sutcliffe was to confirm this on a cold winter night in a Leeds park.

Irene Richardson (nee Osbourne) and on occasions AKA Eileen was originally a Glasgow girl, born in the Possil Park district north of the river Clyde, born Friday the 23rd of April 1948CE into a large family having nine siblings (six sisters and three brothers). In 1965CE at the age of seventeen she left the family home and moved south to London, it was then she lost touch with most of her family, embracing her new life and discarding the old. She hooked up with her elder sister Helen who was living in Blackpool and moved to the north-west resort town later that year.

She met a man called John Henry Wade and they had a daughter Lorraine who was born in 1966CE, Irene 'struggled' in the role of mother and it was decided that foster care and possible adoption would be beneficial to all concerned, this included Mrs. Phillip's a Blackpool social worker who was allocated Irene's case. Irene arrived in Blackpool 1968CE and worked in domestic service, firstly as a chambermaid, and then later has a nanny. These jobs were both in the tourist industry, The Glenshee Hotel and The Clyde Hotel, she also worked in private residencies at Osbourne Road, Grasmere Road and Exchange Street. Her home address remained transient encompassing various areas and property types that Blackpool and the Golden Mile had to offer; Kirby Road, Raikes Parade, a flat at 104a Central Drive and Burlington Road.

In 1969CE Irene had a second child Alan who was born on Thursday the 30th of October 1969CE at Glenroyd Maternity Hospital, Blackpool. Irene did not disclose the identity of Alan's father, however it was believed that he was a Blackpool mechanic named Jim Brown although social workers case notes also identify a close friend by the name of Dennis, who may have been the father.

Unfortunately, she found it difficult to cope and history was repeated. Alan too was put into foster care in 1970CE and ultimately was adopted. Irene met Mr. George Richardson who was to become her husband the same year, he was working as a bar man but had diversified his skill set and was also doing some plastering work. The couple married in June 1971CE and settled into the marital home at Balmer Grove, Blackpool, FY1 5QT. Irene found work at Pontin's holiday camp. 'Welcome to Pontin's Blackpool, 'Fun, Fun, Fun", read the entrance sign to the Squire's Gate site, situated on the south shore. The stability of marriage supported Irene and the couple had two children, daughters Irene and Amanda. Although fun seemed in short supply, post-natal depression haunted Irene and was a major factor in the breakdown of her marriage to George. Irene left Blackpool and the relative constancy of her family life and fled to London, George reported Irene missing to the police in the March of 1975CE.

Irene later contacted her estranged husband, she was working at the exclusive Grosvenor House Hotel, 86-90 Park Lane, Mayfair, London W1K 7TN and living in the South Kensington area of London. George packed his bags and travelled to London in a last-ditch attempt to save the floundering marriage, setting up home in the South Kensington area. This ill-fated attempt failed and once again Irene absconded leaving no forwarding address in April 1976CE, this time there would be no re-conciliation. Irene would never see George again, but George would see Irene on one more occasion, as he identified her lifeless body on a mortuary slab in Leeds some ten months later.

1976CE saw Irene meet Steven Bray who was working as a chef in one of the resorts many hotels. The star-crossed lovers set up home together living in various London bedsits as their relationship developed.

A former seaman, (a chef in the merchant navy) and a nightclub doorman (bouncer); Stephen had a secret, a skeleton in the cupboard. He was already married and had a wife who resided in Hull. Not to be out done, Irene also had a secret, a skeleton in the cupboard. She was already and had a husband who resided in the west coast seaside resort of Blackpool. Eventually the couple moved to Leeds in October 1976CE. Irene adopted Bray's surname throughout their Leeds sojourn.

The post wedding double jilt hit Irene harder than Stephen, she was left to fend for herself on the mean streets of Chapeltown Leeds and unable to find work, Irene had little option than to live on her wits, in what was to prove the last two weeks of her life. Disenfranchised, dishevelled and down on her luck.

1976CE saw Irene meet Steven Bray who was working has a chef in one of the capitals many hotels. The star-crossed lovers set up home together living in various London bedsits as their relationship developed. Eventually the couple moved to Leeds in October 1976CE and the delights of Chapeltown a less than salubrious area where rundown bedsits housed the couple and encouraged anonymity and encouraged instability.

On the evening of her death, a dour Saturday on the 5th of February 1977 CE, Irene oblivious to her fast impending fate sat in front of a small mirror and did her shoulder length hair, put on her bangles and her imitation gold watch, she was intending to attend Tiffany's where she hoped Steve would be working the door that evening. Irene left her 1 Cowper Street, ground floor bedsit off Chapeltown Road, LS7 4DR at 23:15 hours, she had a brief conversation with Pam Barker a fellow resident of the Cowper Street rooming house, telling her she was off to Leeds city centre, to Tiffany's dance hall, located in the Merrion Centre, Leeds, LS2 8NG to confront her estranged boyfriend. She believed he'd collected her wages from the YMCA earlier that week. 23:30 hours Irene called in to see her friend Mrs Marcella Margaret Mary Walsh of Sholebrook Avenue

Monday the 24th of January 1977CE, Irene turned up at the YMCA hostel in Chapel Allerton where she worked as a cleaner. She spoke to the warden Mrs Nellie Morrison and explained she had a large bill to pay and needed some money quickly she asked if she could have an advance on her wages to cover the cost. Mrs Morrison gave Irene one pound.

Irene, in a downward spiral, her life out of control, lurched from one crisis to the next. On Wednesday the 26th of January 1977CE, Irene failed to turn up for her cleaning shift at the YMCA hostel.

Friday the 28th of January 1977CE Steve Bray calls at the YMCA hostel where Irene had recently worked and collected all monies that were due her, Steve used this money to finance his escape from the situation he had contrived to get himself into. He used the money to finance a trip to London and then later he travelled to Ireland. Unfortunately, this action plummeted Irene further into despair, desolation, dejection and misery. Irene called into the hostel, to collect her overalls and shoes. She explained she was having problems at home and had split up with Steve, she apologised for her behaviour and for letting them down by failing to turn up. She then found out about the money and left wondering what she was going to do to survive in the oncoming days. Steve's actions had unwittingly sentenced Irene to her fate. The fate of death at the hands of a maniac.

Peter arrived in Leeds around 23:15 hours and began to cruise the streets of Chapeltown, in particular, the square of vice, in his white Ford Corsair (KWT 721D), he had so far had little success. He pulled up on Nassau Place and repeatedly propositioned a woman who repelled his attentions, his last failed attempt was 23:35 hours. His frustrations were beginning to get the better of him when he circled the streets again. On nearly completing his circuit he saw a sole woman walking down the street, he pulled up on Nassau Place a cross street in the epicentre of the red-light district, just in front of the woman. The woman was Irene Richardson, the time was 23:40 hours, Irene opened the passenger door of the car and got in, and she said nothing.

Peter said, *"A might notta wanted you"*.

A desperate Irene *responded "Al show ye a gud time, ya no gonna send me away are ye? We can go tae the Soldier's Field"* The duo seemingly aware of the deal sat in silence as Peter replicated his journey of some nine months ago, he drove north up Nassau Place, taking a right at the junction onto Harehills Avenue, this road eventually merged into Roundhay Road. Just before Roundhay Road becomes Wetherby Road, he turned left into Oakwood and then right onto Park Avenue, following the road round and then turning left up West Avenue, up towards the end of the dead end road, on the left of which was Soldier's Field, LS8 1JX.

Leafless trees bordered the lonely road, to the right the rolling driveways that led to the posh houses of West Avenue to the left a small cluster of trees that surrounded the sports pavilion and the open expanse of the playing fields. Hob knobbing it within a stone's throw of the great and good of Leeds. A journey of some two and a half miles, he pulled off the road onto the grassland and stopped near the toilet block. Irene needed the toilet, she got out of the car and placed her imitation suede fur-trimmed coat on the ground and then went to use the public convenience but when she reached the entrance she found them locked. Whilst Irene was attempting to enter the public toilets, Peter reached under the driver's seat of the car and picked out his ball peen hammer and a Stanley knife, he placed them in his inside breast pocket. Outside Irene still needed to urinate, however she also needed to remove the tampon to enable her to show Peter a good time she returned to the car.

"*They're bloody locked, I'll take a pish here*". Peter opened the car door and stepped out onto the grass land. Irene removed her boots, she also took off her dark coloured coat and placed it on the grass and quickly pulled down her two pairs of knickers and her tights, crouched down and removed the tampon. Peter took the hammer out of his pocket and held it in his left hand primed to strike. Peter then hit her hard at the back of the head with the ball peen hammer, once, twice, three times. She dropped to the floor and he was on her. Her handbag lay open at this location, some of its contents had spilt out onto the floor and lay where they fell undisturbed a one pence piece, a mortice lock key, a cosmetic bag and a lipstick. Her purse remained housed in the handbag and was found with the contents of thirty-five and a half pence (two pound twenty-five pence in 2015CE terms).

He dragged her further into the night. Further away from the road he flipped her over and ripped open Irene's yellow two piece suit and her blue and white checked blouse, lifting up the garments to expose her naked flesh and started slashing, stabbing, thrusting and cutting her lower stomach three times, pulling the Stanley knife deep down into her flesh causing her intestines to spill out of her body and then he cut her throat with the Stanley knife.

Peter conducted his grotesque life sculpture by removing Irene's long brown leather boots and placing them on the back of her legs, running down from the thighs to her calves. He removed a pair of red knickers from Irene and her right sock, he then started to roll down her tights on the left leg, as he did so he tucked the knickers and the sock into the tights, and these were gathered up around the left knee. He then proceeded to gather earth and debris from the ground and tuck these into the top of the tights. He then placed Irene's right hand over her abdomen and then placed the left arm on top, in a crossing position. Peter stood back and put himself in the position of the first person who would come around the corner and see his handy work, he stood back and set a grotesque freeze frame that would remain an indelible image in the head of the unfortunate finder. Three times it took him to arrange the body of Irene Richardson to create his desired effect. Like a horror film or a T.V. producer, he dragged the body around the muddy grassland to create a horrific still shot, a macabre snap shot that would haunt the person who stumbled upon this grisly memento of what was Irene's lifeless body.

He then heard voices in the dark, this disturbed his work and unnerved him. He also saw the headlights of a car cutting through the dark winter night leaving one of the exclusive apartments on West Avenue. His parting action was to throw the dark coloured imitation suede fur trimmed coat over Irene's forlorn figure and walk to his car and drive away. As he drove away he saw the source of the voices he had heard earlier, they were emanating from two figures that sat on a bench nearby where the line of trees gave way to the tarmac of West Avenue.

Peter drove directly home, during the drive he dwelt and pondered his mission, it was all encompassing, after all he was obsessed. Murder was like a drug and he couldn't control his intrinsic need to kill. Peter stopped his journey short, he pulled up and checked his clothing before he entered number forty-four, and astonishingly there was no evidence of his earlier activity.

Eight/Three
Leeds, Saturday 5th February 1977 CE. (23:30 hours) Peter's mind was in turmoil, a battle between whether he should or should not continue to kill, continue with his mission. It was a long time since he had drunk at the well and now he had decided to quench his thirst, he was willing to submerge his very being into the crusade. His inner homing pigeon led him back to the scene of his previous misdemeanours. Back to Leeds in search of a prostitute to kill, obsessed, he couldn't stop himself. The night closed with a successful mission concluded and one less prostitute.

The soft ground behind the sports pavilion had captured a clue. Police were able to determine and identify the make and position of the tyres on the killer's vehicle. Two India Autoway tyres, an Esso 118 tyre and a Pneumant tyre (all these tyres were cross-ply). The police also obtained measurements and calculated the rear track width of the vehicle and identified twenty-six possible car types.

07:50 hours Sunday 6th February 1976 CE, John Bolton a forty-six-year-old accountant from Gledhow Road, Leeds LS7 was out for an early morning jog, when he chanced upon Irene's body. He saw Irene's body lying on the damp grass, his initial thought was that Irene had collapsed and rushed to her aid. *"What's the matter?"* He shouted his concern tangible. He was now standing over Irene's body, he bent down and swept the hair away from Irene's face, revealing the blood-stained neck and her vacant staring eyes. The realisation of what he had found hit home to John and he hurriedly ran to number ninety West Avenue where he rang the police.

On Monday the 15th of March 1976CE Stephen Joseph Bray was apprehended in London, he was arrested and interviewed about the murder of Irene Richardson, he was not linked to this crime, however he still had a debt to pay to society and was returned to HM prison Lancaster to fulfil the remainder of his sentence for theft.

Chapter 11
Leeds (Horforth, Hidden History)

Thursday the 21st of April 1977 CE Debra Marie Schlesinger was eighteen years old, she lived with her parents and her sister Karen on the Hawksworth estate in Horsforth. Debra worked in a supermarket and had been out drinking with a group of young women in Leeds city centre, has the night out came to an end Debra and her friend Pat Power caught the bus from Leeds city centre to Horsforth. The girls got off the bus at Hawksworth Broadway and began to walk the quarter of a mile home. The pair proceeded to Cragside Walk, LS5 3LX, the home of Pat. It was here that the girls parted company for what was to be the last time. Debra only had a few short minutes to live, she was to die at the hand of the strange, dark haired bearded man who was lurking in the shadows of the semi-rural idyl. An English idyll that was soon to be shattered. Debra and Pat waved their goodbyes and Debra set off on the short journey home, circa fifty metres. It was a destination she never ever reached. The stranger appeared from out of the ether, as if by sinister magic, spring heeled Jack, AKA the Yorkshire Ripper, a guest appearance in an upper crust area, a busman's holiday from the perceived lowlife filth he usually frequented.

The stranger lunged with his left hand, the knife it was holding sank into Debra's heart. Debra let out a scream. The thrust of the knife was to prove fatal, although Debra in panic rushed up the road fleeing from her assailant. Neither attacker nor attacked had realised the severity of this single blow. Her lifeblood ebbing away in a blind panic she stumbled to the Hawksworth Conservative Club, Cragside Walk, Leeds LS5 3LX. The dark-haired attacker was close on her heels, chasing his victim down wanting to complete his objective. Disquiet at a task half done unaware that he had fatally wounded his victim. There was no need Debra collapsed in the doorway of the club. Uncertain as to whether or not to intercede and finish his deed. Peter held back, this proved the right decision, soon the commotion caused resulted in a flurry of reaction. Debra's father was in the club.

The furore this escapade created tested Peter's fortitude and also his athletic prowess. Disquiet surged through his being, club members were reacting to the uproar. Peter ran into the night down-hill and disappeared without trace.

Peter was a regular visitor to Horsforth, a regular visitor to Kirkstall Forge to be precise and was familiar with the area. In fact, he had delivered some pallets there earlier in the day.

Resonance of Tracey Browne's attack. The victim did not fit the expected Yorkshire Ripper victim. The location did not fit the usual Yorkshire Ripper hunting ground. There was no hammer, no posing of the body, no stripping, no mutilation only death. But these actions may have been intended and the Yorkshire Ripper did not have to work in the confines of what the West Yorkshire Police Force expected or prescribed. Peter may have been planning to inflict these indignities on his victim but was thwarted by Debra's brave and astounding fight for life.

1992 CE, Keith Hellawell is castigated by his subject.
"Sonia thinks hav betrayed her admitting to them two attacks". (Tracey Browne and Ann Rooney) Peter bemoaned.
"But you did do them Peter. You described in detail who, what, where and when. You described things only the attacker could know".
Peter shook his head apathetic to the situation.
"What about the murder of Debra Schlesinger in Horsforth, 1977? What about the Maureen Lea attack in Leeds, 1980? We've discussed these cases in detail before, was it you?"

"Look Mr Hellawell, I trust you. If you say I've done some more, I must have, and I'll admit what you want. I don't remember". Peter felt he'd regained control, had manipulated the situation to his advantage. Keith Hallawell did not rise to the bait. Keith Hellawell kept his powder dry and reported his findings to his senior officer.

Nine/Four?
Leeds, Thursday 21st April, 1977CE.

2003 CE, there was a concern within the police service that Peter William Sutcliffe/Coonan after successfully challenging the validity of his seemingly open ended sentence, would eventually serve his term and then be eligible to appear before a parole board and be considered for release. If this was to happen the police had a plan to veto this situation by charging Sutcliffe/Coonan with 'new' murder's not previously attributed to the handy work of the Yorkshire Ripper, Debra's murder was allegedly one such crime.

Chapter 12
Tina

Patricia 'Tina' Atkinson (AKA Mitra, AKA McGee), was thirty-three years old, a divorcee, she had three daughters, Judy, Jill and Lisa who all lived with her estranged ex-husband Ramen (Ray) Mitra. Tina had fallen into the company of her boyfriend Mr Robert William Henderson. In late 1977CE, she'd made an attempt to turn her back on prostitution. As late autumn approached and the leaves dropped from the trees, she too decided to turn over a new leaf, however good intentions are often ill founded and she slipped back into old ways. Her life somewhat shipwrecked and desolate, Tina lurched from crisis to crisis, her heavy drinking had matured into alcoholism. This did little to help her out of a cycle of spiralling debt in the shape of multiple unpaid fines exasperated by her ad-hoc lifestyle. This was further emphasised by the haphazard relationship she formed with Henderson, her lover. It was with this contextual back drop that Tina fell back into prostitution, in the ultimate self-help process and before Margaret Thatcher's adoption of the free market economy, Tina launched her new business venture in the Easter of 1977CE. She lived at (Flat 3), 9 Oak Avenue, Bradford, BD8, this was where she also conducted her salacious soliciting activities, in the minimal creature comforts of her humble abode. Meagre surroundings but a marketable extra that also increased the customer experience.

Saturday the 23rd of April 1977CE, Saint George's Day, the patron Saint of England, a bright and sunny day, winter is well and truly over and spring has finally sprung. This was an ideal day for an outside activity, however Tina was not interested in anything like that, Tina fancied a drink and what Tina wanted, she generally got. Her day started circa 11:30 hours, after she had slept off the excesses of yesterday's overindulgence. She dressed in her usual and favoured attire of the day, faded blue denim jeans, a light blue denim shirt, open at the neck, as the day and drinking progressed, this would eventually be open to her midriff, if not further. These clothes looked quite impressive on her slight slim figure, she did her shoulder length dark hair. Finally, she finished the look, by putting on her matching blue sling-back denim shoes and her black leather jacket. An outgoing character who had a drink problem, she did not feel the need to hide her nocturnal activities; quite recently she'd been arrested and convicted for soliciting in the Manningham area.

So, Tina decided that an afternoons drinking was in order, in and around the red-light area of Bradford which included Lumb Lane and, Manningham Lane. An epic drink-fest by most standards, but Tina was a hardened drinker and always seemed attracted to the excesses of life. In effect this was just an ordinary afternoon, if somewhat busier, supplemented by weekend drinkers. The Manningham Lane pubs attendances were bolstered by Bradford City supporters who were entertaining Southend United at their Valley Parade home. It was to prove a successful day Bradford City taking the spoils two nil and ultimately gaining promotion out of the Fourth Division. Pre-game supporters would converge on the pubs to speculate about their team's chances and post-match revelry celebrating a victory. This event contributed to an eventful afternoon that would see Tina's lifeline expire before the day was done. The Belle Vue Hotel, 187 Manningham Lane, Bradford, BD8, with its two bars was always popular with the football fraternity and was also like a home from home for Tina. She had worked the striptease circuit, however her love for alcohol often impacted on the professional delivery of her performance. Weekends saw a twenty pence admission charge to the strippers' bar with the additional feature of a topless disc jockey. Then onto the Royal Standard, 22 Manningham Lane, Bradford, BD8. A former hotel, it evolved into a popular pub and a live music venue. It was also a one-time favourite haunt of a certain Peter William Sutcliffe and the graveyard gang, in-fact this was where Peter met Sonia Szurma way back in 1967CE on Saint Valentine's Day, Tuesday the 14th of February. The Standard was on appearance a classic old-fashioned public house its frosted windows were complimented by mahogany, leather and brass fixtures, fittings and furniture. With the classic Victorian bar taking pride of place. 'Fisherman's Cove' was the name of the principal room and the remnants of fishing nets, corks and floats added to an ambience that was enhanced by the AMI jukebox situated in the corner of the large room.

The seedy feel of the general area was promoted by a plethora of bookies shops, sex shops, and illicit drinking dens. Unsanitary café's and fast food 'restaurants' were interspersed with run down bedsits and derelict properties in ill repair. This created a cosy atmosphere for those who knew the area but unnerved strangers. Prostitutes and pimps littered the streets and ginnels and frequented the clubs and bars with their smoke-filled tap rooms, crumpled up betting slips, dodgy deals done by dodgy characters and warm beer.

Then the short walk or taxi drive to the southern end of Lumb Lane and into The Flying Dutchman 31 Lumb Lane, Bradford, BD8 owned by Samuel Webster and Son's Limited, cosy, friendly, warm hearted, wild abandonment, noisy hustle and bustle. Pool balls clattered their noise mingling with the music.

The white painted render of the West End Bar, 63 Lumb Lane, Bradford, West Yorkshire BD8, sat by the Yorkshire stone of James Drummond and Son mill, where John Sutcliffe, Peter's father worked. The textile industry an essential if endangered part of the areas life blood. The Sutcliffe's interwoven into the fabric of the area.

Then onto the Barracks Tavern, 94 Lumb Lane Manningham Bradford BD8 at the junction with St Judes Place. Past the renowned Sweet Centre cafe 110-114 Lumb Lane, Bradford, BD8.

The Perseverance Public House 161 Lumb Lane, Bradford, West Yorkshire. BD8. Audrey Naylor was the landlady and had been for thirty-one years. She was seen as a mother figure in the Lumb Lane area and the local Afro-Caribbean community took her to their hearts and kept a watchful eye on their elderly neighbour. The YOUNG LION Café written in bold black on a yellow background, its red frontage combined with clear glass windows 165 Lumb Lane, Bradford, BD8 was a vibrant social focus for the Afro-Caribbean community of Bradford. The heavy Reggae bass a soundtrack to the walk. Then onto the Yorkshire stone of The Queens Hotel, 195 Lumb Lane, Bradford, BD8. Then onto The New Inn which was situated at 77 Church Street, Manningham, BD8. It was a rough and ready pub with sparse decorations and internal facilities that were compensated by the cut price beer. As the evening progressed there were generally a couple of women decorating the entrance acting much like human door posts, an action that was repeated throughout the public houses and doorways on the lane and the surrounding area. The New Inn pub is almost opposite The Mowbray Hotel, 5 Lily Street, BD8, so it would have been rude not to include this hostelry in the pub crawl. Then onto The Junction Hotel which was situated at 115 Church Street, Manningham, BD8, with its name embossed on the front of the building at high level. Again, the warm interior and welcoming women enticing unsuspecting passers-by possibly to their personal wreck and ruin like the sirens call in the sea shanty songs of yore. Finally, a trip to The Carlisle Hotel, 86 Carlisle Road, Manningham, Bradford. BD8. 22:15 hours Tina left the pub having been refused her request for another drink, in fact she'd been asked to leave after an impromptu striptease. Clearly drunk she staggered out of the pub onto Carlisle Road, turning right and walking down Carlisle Road, then taking a left onto Ambler Street, passed Trees Street on the right and onto Church Street, she'd had a brief chat with other street girls and was talking of finishing her night out with a trip to the International night club, the 'Nash', on Lumb Lane, if it had been anyone else they'd have cautioned her to go home, but Tina's capacity for drink and her ability to hold it went before her, the girls dispersed saying their goodnights, the time was 23:15 hours, Tina was at the junction with Church Street and Saint Marys Road.

Peter was driving up Lumb Lane, Bradford in his white Ford Corsair (KWT 721D), he crossed the junction where Carlisle Road meets Marlborough Road, he continued straight on across the junction and along Church Street he following the road to the right, then came to a junction with Saint Marys Road. Peter took a right up Saint Marys Road. It was then that he saw Tina. She was evidently worse for ware and was obviously drunk, Tina's behaviour drew Peter's attention to her. She was staggering, shouting, swearing and banging her open palm on the roof of a white Mini, this was on his right on Saint Pauls Road just off the junction with Saint Marys Road and Church Street. Peter acted on instinct, he turned right off Church Street onto Saint Pauls Road. Peter heard the woman shout, *"Fuck off!"* and the white Mini sped off into the night, Peter then pulled his car up to the side of where Tina swayed, in effect taking the space vacated by the white Mini. Tina jumped straight into the passenger seat of Peter's car.

"I fucking told him where to gerroff! I've a flat we can go there".
"I live on me own".

Tina instructed Peter where to go, he drove down Saint Pauls Road to Manningham Lane, where he turned right, he then turned second left down Queens Road and then third left onto North Avenue, he then turned second left onto Oak Avenue and Tina's flat. Peter parked his car outside the somewhat dilapidated 1960's CE flat roofed flats, whilst Tina crossed the concrete flagged drawbridge style entrance that spanned the severe drop on either side, Tina opened the door and loitered in the sheltered entrance. Peter picked up a claw hammer that he had hidden under his seat, he had recently purchased this from a hardware store in Clayton, he placed it in his jackets inside pocket. He then repeated the process this time with a knife, he then dutifully followed Tina inside, in through the main doors into the communal stairwell and hallway, then downstairs and into her ground floor flat. Tina waited for Peter to catch up and guide him to her flat, once in the flat, she drew the curtains then it was down to business.

Peter entered the room, he surveyed his surroundings. In the bedroom/living room there was a three-bar electric fire, Peter noticed a RAC road map of Yorkshire pinned up like a poster, above the fire. The cheap carpet had seen better days and like the rest of the flat was in need of a good clean. It was a sparsely furnished room; a double bed was in the corner pushed against the wall. There was a double wardrobe, a dressing table with a large mirror attached, a small settee and two chairs. The flat was not particularly homely, more functional, Tina sat on the edge of the bed and took off her black leather jacket, unfastened her faded blue bell-bottomed denim jeans and was beginning to remove her light blue denim shirt to reveal a T-shirt beneath. Her back was to Peter, as Peter took off his jacket and hung it on the coat hook behind the door, he took out the claw hammer and hit Tina on the back of the head four times. His victim incapacitated fell off the edge of the bed and landed in a bundle on the floor. Peter then despatched a fifth hammer blow to Tina's head. Bright RED blood illuminated by internal electrical lights, very different from dark dim fumblings to which he had become accustomed. Pools of bright red blood were on the floor. Peter pulled the bed covers back, then he picked Tina's dead weight up and lifted Tina up by placing his arms around the top of her body and gripping/lifting her under the arm pits. He heaved her limp body up onto the bed. Tina was now positioned on the bed laying on her back, she was gurgling, gasping for life. More bright red blood soaked into the bedspread. Peter then pulled down Tina's unfastened denim jeans, followed by her white knickers, just below her bottom. The patterned jumper was hoisted, her shirt was ripped open and the T-shirt lifted to expose her stomach and chest, he also unclasped her bra and hoisted it up to reveal her breasts and then he restarted his sadistic work. A swing of the hammer, a thud of impact, then swivelling the hammer in his hand and using the claws of the hammer to stab, scuff, scrape, scratch and graze. All to the backing vocals of Tina struggling to breathe, her death rattle. Not content with this he returned to his coat and retrieved his knife, he climbed on the bed and stabbed Tina six times in the abdomen, he man-handled Tina onto her front and hacked at her back with the knife and slashed at the left hand side of her trunk. Peter dropped his trousers knelt on the bed and took his penis into his hand and began to masturbate. His urge spent, his needs met, his sick sadistic perverted desires, masked by his mission. Peter thought he'd pursue his artistic bent. Sick sculpture Peter did his best to emulate Henry Spencer Moore, his West Riding counterpart, the sculptor and artist was famous for his semi-abstract sculptures generally of the female form. Peter now had the aid of a fully lit room to master his masochistic art. He placed Tina's arms down by her sides and then pulled her jeans down to her ankles, he then yanked her tights down to her ankles, before pulling the jeans back up to just below her knee. In the struggle Tina had lost her shoe, he left her with only one shoe on and then covered the evidence, Tina with the bed sheet, a strange gurgling noise was emanating from Tina's throat, he blanked out the noise surveyed the room once more, looking for the flat keys, so he could lock Tina in and keep intruders out, a parting shot, to hinder aid and exclude assistance, his half-hearted search failed, he put on his coat and left the flat closing the door quietly behind him and disappearing into the obscurity of the night.

The keys for the flat, one yale, one mortice, were found later, the mortice key was found embroiled in the murder scene amid blood and semen stained bed sheets, in front of Tina's knees. The Yale key was found afterwards below her right knee, trapped between the body and the bed clothes. The keys helped signpost the police to another clue, the bright red size seven boot print, was the clue to unlock the mystery to the identity of this mad man?

He then drove home to Clayton. Before he entered the house he inspected himself there was blood on his jeans and on his brown Doctor Martin's, he rinsed the offending jeans in the kitchen sink as Mr & Mrs Szurma slept upstairs, as Sonia, his wife slept feet away, he rinsed the boots under the cold tap and wiped the dark staining of the blood from his boots with a sponge, returning them to their near pristine brown leather, he hung his denim jeans up to dry and then retired to bed. The evidence of his antics wiped away like Tina, his hapless victim no more blood on him or his clothes, no more bright red blood, well not until the next time. A change from his usual al fresco murdering interior homicide was a switch from his usual modus operandi. Peter returned to the daily grind and carried on regardless.

Sunday the 24th April, 1977CE, 18:30 hours Mr Robert William Henderson, rings the doorbell at Flat 3, 9 Oak Avenue, a little concerned about Tina's whereabouts. He gets no response, he subsequently knocks on the door, still no response, he then tries the door handle, and pulling down the handle he opens the door. He heralds his entrance, shouting out, *"Hello Tina, its Bob"*. He enters the flat and enters a scene of devastation, a pool of blood on the floor, the bedclothes draped awkwardly over the still figure of Tina, whose body peeped even more awkwardly from under the covers, realising Robert's worst fears. Tina's pale arm poked from the blood stained covers her face pale, her hair darkened with matted blood. In blind panic and desperation Robert ran to the flat of Mr Jack Robinson, who was the caretaker of the flats. The police were duly called and another murder enquiry was started.

Ten/Five
Bradford, Saturday 23rd April 1977 CE. (23:15 hours) Foul mouthed abusive. *"No decent woman would have been using language like that at the top of her voice"*.

Chapter 13
<u>Jayne</u>

Jayne Michelle MacDonald was a sixteen-year-old girl who lived with her parents. Wilfred and Irene and her siblings Janet (aged nineteen), Debra (aged fifteen) and Ian (aged twelve) at the family home of 77 Scott Hall Avenue, Leeds, LS7 2HL. A council house door away from Wilma McCann's former home. There was another sister, Carol (Mrs Carol Skorpen, aged thirty-three), who lived in South Africa. Jayne was working as a shop assistant in the shoe department at Grandways supermarket; a job she started in the April of 1977CE; 'serve yourself and save' was the catchphrase of the staff at 243 to 249 Roundhay Road, Oakwood, Leeds LS8 4HS. Her father worked for British Rail at Leeds City station whilst her mother worked as a waitress.

Saturday the 25th of June 1977CE Jayne washed, dried and styled her shoulder length light brown hair. She dressed to impress, her clothes emphasising her 5-foot 3-inch frame and her youthful beauty. The blue and white gingham skirt, covered by a blue and grey waist-length gabardine jacket, dark brown tights and brown and cream high heeled clog fronted shoes with brass studs around the sides. It had been a warm and pleasant sunny day that faded into a balmy sunny evening circa 18:50 hours Jayne crouched down and kissed her father Wilf who was sat in his favourite armchair. She kissed him on the forehead, *saying "Bye, I won't be late tonight dad"*.

"Where are you going?" he politely asked.
"Into town with a girlfriend".
"Enjoy yourself love and don't forget to ring if there's a change of plan".

"OK, I'll see you later". With these final words she set off for an evening of dancing and possibly a little romancing. Wilfred would later reminisce at the scent of his daughter on this final parting.

19:00 hours, Jayne walked along Scott Hall Avenue on her way to the bus stop into town and popped in to see the Bransbergs on her way into Leeds city centre. Mr Jack Bransberg, a forty-two-year-old neighbour and friend of the MacDonalds, Jack worked alongside Wilf, as a guard for British Rail. The Bransbergs were one of the few households in Scott Hall Avenue to possess a telephone, somewhat a novelty in the 1970's CE. The families were on friendly terms and Jayne would ring them on occasions if she was staying over at a girlfriends or going to be late. The Bransbergs would then pass the message on to her parents.

"Where are you for tonight Jayne?" Jack asked.
"Into town, dancing at the Astoria Ballroom and then onto a late-night disco in

Roundhay".

"*Have fun*". Jack replied as Jayne continued on her way into the city centre.

20:00 hours, Jayne and a girlfriend arrived at The Hofbrauhaus an octagon shaped annexe of the Merrion Centre 58 Wade Lane, Leeds, LS2 8NL. The city centre pub was a German themed pub, it was a replica of a Munich bierkeller, where the resident house oompah band dressed in lederhosen, like a real life incarnation of the character in the Ayingerbrau lager beer pumps of the local hostelries

It was a typical boisterous night with foot stomping hedonistic Arian anecdotes, the oompah bands musical backdrop encouraging the customers to consume copious steins of lager, their high spirits manifested in table dancing, the tables were heavily built from bulky pieces of timber, thick set to hold the numerous revellers. Draped awnings framed each of the black wrought-iron light fittings carrying nine torches interspersed with the odd ornate deer head that decorated the room, a little bit of Bavaria just off Belgrave Street.

Between the rhythmical sounds of the deep brass tuba mixed with the higher pitched clarinet, accordion and trombone. The music was interspersed by the leader of the oompah band loudly proclaiming a toast at the top of his voice *"Ein Prosit, Ein Prosit, Der Gemutlichkeit. Ein Prosit, Ein Prosit, Der Gemutlichkeit. Ein, Zwei, Drei, G'suff!"* ("A toast, a toast, the cosines, one, two, three, drink up!"). This happened seemingly like clockwork, approximately every ten minutes, once the toast was proposed the audience would respond and drink heartily. Jayne chose not to join in the drinking games and sensibly stuck to soft drinks.

Amidst the mayhem, melee, music, milieu a mass of over five hundred people added to the ambience, participating in the party atmosphere and partaking of the strange tasting German bread schwarzbrot, semmel, sesambrotchen and sonnenblumenbrot, not to forget the obligatory bratwurst.

It was from this backdrop that the group of pleasure-seeking partygoers left the Hofbrauhaus and started to drift into the city centre, fleet footed youths, ambitious, arrogant and vibrant; life revolved around them, or so they thought. The world their oyster. Their future a clam (molluscans), the broad horizons of their dreams and aspirations a fallacy, the unknown truth would see their horizons closed down snap shut like the tightly closed valves of a live clam. Glam rock, bellbottom flared trousers, Chelsea collars, platform shoes, velvet jackets, Gary Glitter, glitter balls, glitter band, disco fever and big Afro hair; with a backdrop of 'Saturday Night Fever'.

The night was still young and so were its protagonists, one of whom would stay forever young. (They shall grow not old, as we that are left grow old: Age shall not weary them, nor the years condemn. At the going down of the sun and in the morning. We will remember them). The time was 22:30 hours and Jayne was with one such group. Whilst in the Hofbrauhaus Jayne had met, danced with and made the acquaintance of Mark Jones (aged eighteen years old), his youthful good looks had caught the attention of Jayne who was attracted to him, Mark fully reciprocated Jayne's interest. With his broad shoulders, svelte physique and swept back blonde hair. The pair walked within the group from the Merrion Centre to Briggate.

"I'm starving do you fancy some chips?" Jayne asked Mark.
"OK". Agreed Mark.

It was at this point that the pair split from the main group in search of their chippy supper. When they had eventually found, procured and eaten this northern delicacy Jayne had missed her last bus home. Neither seemed to care, the irresponsibility of youth abounded as the pair whiled away the night on a wooden bench in the city centre outside the C & A (Clemens and August Brenninkmeyer, the International Dutch chain of fashion and retail stores). The continental, almost cosmopolitan connotations emphasised that Leeds was a provincial powerhouse and a leading light in more things than serial murder. They wandered along the wide expanses of Boar Lane with its wonderful Victorian architecture, evidence of former glories and financial flamboyance, historical ostentatiousness, but they didn't care about that, they were young and wrapped up in their own little world. Boar Lane becomes Duncan Street-originally Fleet Street, re-named Duncan Street after Admiral Adam Duncan in honour of his gaining an historic victory of the Dutch fleet during the Battle of Camperdown in 1797CE. They then turned left onto New York Street, then first right onto Call Lane past the Corn Exchange, its ornate circular exterior and domed roof with a clock face in pride of place at high level, ag ain a sign of the city's former Victorian splendour. The white clock face, with its short thick black hand and its longer thinner minute hand and the Roman numerals that looked down and told the pair that it was 00:15 hours. Blissfully unaware they continued without a care, then as the streets began to narrow onto the red brick built buildings that lined New York Street, then onto York Street further up the hill past the rough and ready red bricked Woodpecker public house at the junction of York Road and Burmantofts Street, (a phoenix raised from the ashes of adversity) the couple continued their care free meander up Burmantofts Street turning right onto Rigton Approach and bringing into view Mark's family home on the Ebor Gardens Council Estate.

"If me sister's in, I'll ger her to give you a lift home". Mark promised.

Jayne seemed indifferent, undecided either way, she was just going with the flow and would end up where the night would take her.

Providence played its part and as Mark's home came into view it became evident that his sister was not home, her car was absent from the roadside.

"It's alright". Jayne responded to the semi-despondent look upon Mark's face and the duo formulated a revised plan of action. They walked further up Burmantofts Street and then Beckett Street past the Fountain Head a Tetley public house, a unique two storey square building, the blue bordered cream painted Portland stone effect first story frontage that acceded to the red brick of the neighbouring terraced houses to the rear and the red brick second storey, out of place, out of time. Behind the pub towered the trio of Shakespeare Flats (Court/Grange and Towers) that act to separate Burmantofts from the bordering Harehills district. Onwards and upwards they walked passed the Florence Nightingale public house, 132 Beckett Street, Leeds, LS9 7JX then across the road and up the road a further fifty metres to Saint James Hospital, (circa a third of a mile), within the grounds of the hospital the pair found their way to the private gardens that serviced the nurses homes within the complex. It was there that the couple spent approximately three quarters of an hour laying on the manicured lawn, kissing and cuddling, caught in the moment. Eventually Mark called a halt to the proceedings.

"It's getting late I'd better get home".
"OK, I'll see you on Wednesday then?" Jayne answered.
"Yeah Wednesday will be good". Mark agreed.

The pair walked to the front gates of the hospital with its gothicesque architecture and turreted four faced clock tower the backdrop, the clock face said it was 1:35 am the ornate iron railings separating the grounds of the hospital from Beckett Street, the stone pillars separating the gates from the fence. The pair kissed their parting kiss, it was to be Jayne's last kiss. Mark walked south west down Beckett Street. To his family home, whilst Jayne continued north east up Beckett Street, to her right the high wall of Leeds Cemetery and the hospital on her left. She walked past the bright yellow AA (Automobile Association) van, with its two occupants, 'You'll feel just fine with the AA sign, it's great to feel that you belong', and paid it/them no mind. Why should she? They later recalled to police investigating the murder of Jayne Michelle MacDonald, the young lady teetering in absurdly high heeled cream/brown clog style shoes up Beckett Street, but in the moment it was just an everyday occurrence, how were they to know of the horrors that awaited. The AA, the fourth emergency service (24/7 roadside assistance, 365 days of the year), were of no real help. Jayne walked past the red bricked Florence Nightingale, the professionally hand painted sign on the building read, 'A warm and friendly welcome'. The pub was dwarfed by the fourteen-storey high rise structure of Spalding Towers.

She continued to walk Up Beckett Street where the Portland stone of The Dock Green pub, located on the junction where Beckett Street meets Stanley Road, meets Ashley Road, meets Harehills Road. (Dock Green Inn, Ashley Rd, Leeds, LS9 7AB). A former police station purchased by a brewery and subsequently opened by the actor Jack Warner who played the role of Police Constable George Dixon, stationed in the fictional 'Dock Green' a rough district of London. Unfortunately, former police stations and fictional police officers were of no real help. Jayne attempted to call a taxi from the kiosk near the Dock Green pub, she dialled the taxi number, the phone rang in the taxi office close by, but it was never answered. If only the taxi operator was not busy elsewhere, if only a private hire vehicle was free and available in the area, unfortunately circumstances had conspired and Jayne was reconciled to continue her journey on foot.

She continued to walk slowly up Harehills Road, turning left onto Bayswater Mount and into the labyrinth of terraced houses that made up this part of the city. Then right onto Gledhow Road up to the junction with Roundhay Road (A58), Jayne crossed the main road and turned left into Back Side Street, she then walked diagonally across grassland onto Gathorne Terrace, north and up to the junction with Louis Street, then left onto Louis Street for fifty metres then right onto Spencer Place, left onto Cowper Street, then right onto Chapeltown Road. The pleasant night air had seemingly transformed Leeds into a Mediterranean holiday resort, its streets awash with late night revellers, the very nature of Chapeltown guaranteed increased footfall as she walked closer to her home. A false reassurance by the more populated streets, the familiar faces and the familiar surroundings. With each step Jayne moved closer to her attacker, with each passing minute she moved closer to her fate. The busy familiar faces and places of her Chapeltown home reassured her. The coming and going the toing and froing, Fforde Grene, Potternewton park AKA Potty park, the Gaiety pub, Cliffs, Sonny's, 62's and 49's (on Spencer Place) revellers spilling into the warm north Leeds enclave of iniquity, Easterley Road, Harehills Lane, Spencer Place, the Hayfield hotel, carnival, red stripe lager, sensimilla. Ganja, Strega Blues bar and the crime ridden epicentre of red-light Chapeltown a thriving anti-community. Familiar places and once familiar faces-Marcella Claxton, Emily Jackson, Wilomena McCann and Irene Richardson, had all frequented these places, Marcella and Jayne still did.

This maize of mystery, mayhem and misadventures was the daily backdrop to Jayne's daily life, her footsteps had trodden these very streets on numerous occasions. It was part of her very fabric, woven like the textile factories, the dark satanic mills that scarred the Yorkshire landscape. Gods own county, the fabric of life was to be slashed wide open, by a knife in the hand of a maniac, Gods personal helper, Gods confidante.

The Tanton crew had been out, doing the rounds of Bradford pubs, Peter driving - Ronald and David Barker his passengers and drinking companions. Returning from their evenings excesses Peter dropped the brothers off at the junction of Terrington Crest and Tanton Crescent on the council estate that lay on the outskirts of old Clayton village, where the brothers on disembarking returned to their family home of 46 Tanton Crescent. Peter had murder in mind, he went on auto-pilot, he placed his trust in an evangelical satellite navigation system, a puppet orchestrated by God, his GPS (global positioning system) instigated by his master, Peter an unwittingly willing disciple. Sonia was working at the Sherrington Private Nursing home 13 Heaton Road, Bradford BD8, so it left Peter free to follow his personal interest of murdering women. He then drove west down Clayton Road into Bradford city centre, he drove across the city to Leeds Road, through Laisterdyke, Stanningley, Kirkstall, onto Woodhouse Road towards the city centre then north onto Chapeltown Road.

Peter drove to Leeds in his red Ford Corsair registration PHE 355G with the intention of killing a prostitute. Peter drove slowly up Chapeltown Road keeping his eyed peeled for a potential victim he noticed the Hayfield Hotel 241 Chapeltown Road, Leeds, LS7 and its distinct white exterior ensuring it stood out amongst the other buildings it was actually set back from the single storey flat roof shops that lined Chapeltown Road number 243 William Hill bookmakers, number 245 W.D. Perkins' Bakery and number 247 Wilby's, grocer/mini market, as it approached the junction with Reginald Street. It was here when he saw the petite five-foot three-inch figure of Jayne slowly strolling, sauntering towards the traffic lights and the traffic island crossing on which they were sited. She ambled pausing at the corner, he thought he saw her loiter on the corner and talk to a couple of women he assumed were prostitutes; she then began to cross Chapeltown Road. The split in her skirt triggered his unnatural urges to kill, flicked the switch, her vulnerability encouraged HIS needs HIS desires. HIS selfless acceptance of HIS mission. HIS selfish disregard for HIS victims. Natural selection, the natural order, the wolf amongst the sheep, the fox in the chicken pen. Peter was no longer Peter, but he was a force for good, he had instinct and God to blame for his actions. Peter had an idea where Jayne was heading and pulled off Chapeltown Road to the left into Reginald Street and then turned first right and parked up in the car park of the Hayfield Hotel. Peter snatched the claw hammer and black ebonite handled thin bladed kitchen knife hurrying to exit the car and locate the woman. He fumbled with his tools speedily hiding them in the inside breast pocket of his jacket, by now fit for purpose with the pocket bottoms cut out to allow extra depth for full concealment. As Peter walked from the car park and arrived on Reginald Street, he surveyed the area. The once proud Edwardian terraced houses of Reginald Street and Reginald Terrace, victims of a reverse gentrification process, were a busy thoroughfare for the Chapeltown area, which developed a life of its own after dark. A sub, sub-culture of private parties, illegal drinking dens (Afro-Caribbean shebeens), prostitution, alcohol and substance abuse. The street lighting on Reginald Street was turned off at 23:30 hours this was not Leeds City Council's enlightened contribution to the reduction of light pollution, (photo pollution or luminous pollution), but a cost cutting exercise.

His earlier intuition as to the destination of his would-be victim was correct, he saw Jayne ambling up the narrow road oblivious to the threat the stranger possessed. Peter paused, had a cursory look up and down the street to assess any would be witnesses and let her pass then began to walk behind her. Jayne continued blissfully unaware, unconcerned, confidant in herself and her surroundings. No 'stranger danger' alerts, no internal bells ringing to prepare the body for fight or flight, just apathy, indifference and heavenly indifference, thoughts of a nice cosy bed less than half a mile away. The pair walked about thirty metres along Reginald Street. As Peter gripped the wooden handle on the claw hammer and pulled it out from the depths of his pocket, he raised the hammer in his left hand and swung it down onto the back of Jayne's head. Jayne fell to the ground in a heap, stunned! he then bent over her and dragged her face-down by placing his hands in her armpits, the brass studs on her shoes scraping on the road he began to panic him thinking it would alert others. He dragged her unconscious body down the sloping wasteland, across the patchwork tarmac path bordered by rough sun scorched ankle length grass and discarded detritus; the continuity of the tarmac broken by tufts of rough grass unkempt uncared for unrequited. He dragged her body twenty metres across the tarmac and out of sight onto the adventure playground situated on the left of Reginald Street. It was here that Jayne's brown fake leather handbag fell completely from her shoulder onto the rough grassland. Alone, unsecure and unnoticed. He dragged her behind the high wooden fence that surrounded the adventure playground to his right, so the couple were obscured from view by a fence which allowed him the privacy he needed to proceed. As he pulled her into the corner one of her high heeled shoes fell from her foot. They were now in a darkened dead end - some twenty metres from the hustle and bustle of the main road, the red brick gable end of a derelict factory forming the final section of the ad-hoc cul-de-sac. Peter hit her on the head with the hammer again once, twice more. He fumbled at her clothing tearing open the blue/grey gabardine jacket and lifting her bra to reveal her breasts and then he plucked the knife from his inside pocket. Grasping the ebonite handle he plunged the knife into her chest. He repeated the process almost pulling the blade out of the original entry point but then reinserting the blade thrusting at different angles to incur maximum damage. As he flipped her body over, her upper chest fell on a broken bottle top, the shards on the screw cap stabbing and embedding themselves into her flesh. Peter crouched over Jayne and continued his assault on Jayne's unconscious and defenceless body. He stabbed at her back again and again he continually thrust the blade into the same wound, almost fully retracting the tip of the blade from her body and then changing the angle and trajectory of the blade to maximise internal damage but minimise external damage. The process of repeated stabbing in one solitary entry wound distended the injury creating a large and gaping stab wound in the pale flesh of her back. In total Peter stabbed her twenty-seven times. When the fury had passed he pulled the slim bladed knife from her body and carefully wiped the blood covered blade clean on the skin of Jayne's back, he flipped the blade over and replicated the process. Peter had now regained his composure and began to concentrate on his getaway.

His work done and his mission complete Peter walked casually from the playground and its high fences that held a secret that would remain undetected for a further seven hours and forty-five minutes. He walked onto Reginald Street, then back to his car still parked in the Hayfield Hotel car park. On reaching the car park Peter heard voices and saw a crowd of people walking up Reginald Street, following the footsteps that Jayne and he had recently walked. Peter remained calm. He let the people pass then started the engine, this time he drove down the car park and exited it via the Reginald Terrace entrance/exit. He turned left on Reginald Terrace and then onto Chapeltown Road. Down into Sheepscar, down Clay Pit Lane into the city centre, south west onto Armley Road (A647), onto the outer ring road Farsley (A6110), then west and into Bradford, once again disappearing like a phantom into the safety of his natural surroundings of Bradford Metropolitan District Council. He drove across the city centre making his way up and out of the city's naturally formed geographical basin. He eventually reached Clayton Road and pulled up in a reasonably secluded area where he gave himself the once over under the dim interior light to ensure there was no tell-tale signs of his earlier excursions, the claw hammer was a slight deviation from his preferred type, it reminded him of Tina Atkinson and her blood stained sheets. That was a messy one he recalled.

Reginald Street adventure playground, if the primary use of the area was designed to be an adventure playground, the secondary land use was seemingly waste disposal, a DIY city centre land fill site. An old abandoned metal sprung mattress, the coils of metal poking through the holes in the fabric lay alongside Jayne's lifeless corpse which was situated within the proximity of a cheap carpet that had seen better days. The remaining area was littered with rubbish, debris and detritus. The remaining area was littered with rubbish the remnants of twentieth century, late 1970's CE working class northern England, a collage of junk that obscured the stark harsh concrete that formed the excuse of a child friendly zone, a twentieth century health and safety risk, a twentieth century killing ground. The Wild West stockade effect of the fencing raised echoes of the lawless frontiers in America and similarities although exaggerated could easily be found. Illegal activity attracted the money, the money drew the prostitutes, and the prostitutes drew the punters. Someday a real rain will come and wash all this scum off the streets. The high timber fence that surrounded the loosely named (mis) adventure playground was used to hide a dark secret. Graffiti adorned timber fence panels underlined the stockade style perimeter black painted letters dyslexic in their meaning 'T CGL DA', white painted letters of various sizes positioned on the timber style fortifications. Black painted almost illegible scrawls 'JACKIE W = CARL, CLAUDE HOPPER, GAZ, LEEDS ARE CHAMPS, BAY CITY ROLL'. One half of the hinged timber gate was missing, possibly a casualty to bonfire night 1976CE, inside the playground to the right when accessing the area via Reginald Street was a club house, its white painted exterior also splattered with graffiti and its structure acted as a man-made barrier obscuring visibility of this area from the higher storeys of the terraced houses on Reginald Terrace.

The adventure playground that filled part of the land that separated Reginald Terrace and Reginald Street. The playground kept its counsel and held the sinister secret. Sunday the 27th June 1977CE at 09:45 hours two young children discovered her forlorn and lifeless figure where it had been abandoned at the foot of the timber fence, two metres shy of the factory wall. Jayne lay face down her legs outstretched with her feet crossed, her left arm was bent with the palm of her hand cradling her face whilst her right arm lay down by her side; her body was surrounded by bric-a-brac and debris, broken bottles and abandoned beer cans. Jayne's blue and white checked skirt was wrinkled on her upper thigh. Whilst the pale blue of Jayne's underskirt was visible, it was crumpled and had been pulled up, whilst her tights remained untouched and unscathed. Her blue and white gingham skirt, blue and white halter-neck sun top were soiled from the marks that betrayed the remnants of her attack. The jacket she wore was pulled up over Jayne's head and it lingered on her body, a single intact undamaged and resolute button, maintaining its purpose and clasping the garment to her body. Underneath Jayne's white sun top had also been lifted towards her head and revealed the pale skin of her left breast and the light pink of her nipple. The naked skin of her lower back was also visible to the unfortunate onlookers. The two children quickly raised the alarm and the authorities were notified, about their macabre discovery.

News quickly broke of Jayne's murder, Jayne was quickly identified by the police from the contents of her handbag. Two uniformed officers were sent to dispatch the despicable news of Jayne's death to her nearest and dearest. The coarse northern rationale shallow in emotional intelligence at the best of times sank to new depths as the officers crassly fulfilled their remit. He knocked on the door of 77 Scott Hall Avenue and the door was answered by Wilfred. *"Hello officers can I help you?"*

"Are you the father of Jayne MacDonald?" asked one of the officers.
"Come in lads, yes, I am, what's up? She stopped out all night and didn't let us know. I'll kill her when I get my hands on her".

"You won't get chance, someone's already done that". came the tactless response. Dumbfounded Wilfred struggled to comprehend the news, his condition deteriorated catastrophically, he went into nervous shock unable to cope with the horrific news as it sank in. His inability to cope plummeted and he was unable to function. A doctor was called and had to administer a strong sedative

Monday the 28th June 1977 CE 'GIRL, 16, IN A JACK THE RIPPER MURDER HORROR' the red top headline acted as harbinger for the sadistic murderer who stalked the streets of Leeds, Bradford and possibly Preston, (but not Keighley, Silsden or Halifax). Chief Constable Ronald Gregory decided to appoint Assistant Chief Constable George Oldfield to take charge of the investigation of the murders and headed up the team that was to be ultimately known as 'The Ripper Squad'. An interview with George Oldfield appeared on BBC's 'Look North' circa 17:35 hours and YTV's 'Calendar', circa 18:00 hours, where he spoke of the latest murder.

"I think it was a mistake that he attacked Jayne MacDonald. I think probably in her case he mistook her for being a lady of the streets because she was out in that area at the time she was on a Saturday night".

Peter was horrified when he read and heard the news and found out that his latest victim was only sixteen years old and was not a prostitute. Was it the devil that was driving him on encouraging him to kill, had he been the victim of some higher order confidence trick, he was unsure and questioned what a beast he was. He believed at the time he did it, she was a prostitute. The lurid headlines unnerved Peter however he had made a pledge, he had a mission to continue. He wondered if he was out of his mind and he thought he could not be held accountable for his actions. Peter sought solace he reconciled himself that Jayne was definitely one of them. Peter read the lurid headlines and was shocked by his actions, an inhumane beast controlled by the devil, a monster but the inner urges to kill prostitutes was too strong to deny, it must be sated, the urges were driving Peter to distraction, the urges were driving Peter out of his mind.

The Yorkshire Ripper was a popular topic of conversation throughout the West Riding, he continually cropped up in conversations, in the pubs, clubs and corner shops of Bradford and Leeds. Peter could distance himself from his dark persona, his evil alter ego. He would actively contribute to such discussions un-phased, detached, calm and collected, plausibly aloof, he would repeatedly refer to the Ripper as a head banger.

Eleven/Six
Leeds, Sunday 26th June 1977. (02:15 hours) The beast inside had taken over, Peter realised what a monster he'd become. *"I thought she was a prostitute".* He felt inhuman and wondered if it was the Devil turning him.

The hypocritical nature of seventies society came to the fore. Jayne's youth and her apparent innocence inferred that the other victims were not innocent, guilty of prostitution, a society that was indifferent to draconian DIY punishment administered by a mad man to these seemingly sub-human women. The inhumane malady, a sad indictment of a world that doesn't care! The disenfranchised women risking life and limb for small change and financial survival were the wrong doers, the punters who used and abused these women and the situation were innocent bystanders ensnared by these females' filthy ways. Such media signals reinforced Peter's perceptions that his mission was right, concerned as he was by his mistake in the war against vice. As in any war there was always going to be collateral damage, unfortunately for Jayne, Peter viewed her as exactly that. The national media catapulted the case into the British consciousness. 'GIRL, 16, IN A JACK THE RIPPER MURDER HORROR'. And projected the Yorkshire Ripper to a national audience.

Chapter 14
Maureen

Maureen Long a 42-year-old mother of three 'grown up' children, who lived in Farsley, four miles to the east of Bradford and six miles to the west of Leeds, Farsley was in the district of Pudsey. Her Farsley address was 22 Donald Street, Farsley, Pudsey, LS28. Maureen was also known to reside at 1 Rendel Street, which was in Laisterdyke a neighbourhood on the outskirts of Bradford, where her estranged husband Ronnie lived.

Maureen was a regular social drinker and was no stranger to embarking on an evening drinking in and around Bradford, she was a friendly sort and well known in many of the Bradford hostelries. Maureen had earmarked Saturday the 9th of July 1977CE for one of her regular nights out in Bradford and a mini tour of some of her favoured Bradfordian public houses. Whilst out drinking on her latest sojourn to the City she bumped into her estranged husband, Ronnie. They had a good drink and mulled over old times, generally enjoying the ambience of a Bradford, (Leeds Road) night out. Ronnie and Maureen visited an enclave of public houses on Leeds Road, some four-hundred meters from his humble abode, a humble abode he still sometimes shared with his estranged wife Maureen. One of the pubs was The Lemon Tree 854 Leeds Road, Bradford, BD3, another The Waggon and Horses, 839 Leeds Road, Bradford, BD3 and the third was The Cemetery at the junction of where Myrtle Street and Leeds Road met. This enclave was by no means an oasis in total, Leeds Road boasted at least sixteen pubs along a mile long stretch of road, The Junction at the bottom of Leeds Road, could be classed as a city centre pub and was the first Bradford pub to 'come out' being a well-known gay pub, The Napier, The Victoria, The High Flyer, The Waggon and Horses, The Albion Inn, The White Bear Inn, The Lemon Tree, The Cemetery, The Funhouse Bar, The Oak Inn, The Waterloo, The Garnett, The New Exchange, The New Inn and The Adelphi (this did not include the various social clubs).

Smoke filled room, nicotine stained decorations, drunk addled loud voices with nothing to say, people treading time going nowhere, without a care. Vibrant pubs full of life but devoid of life experiences, horizons shackled to the mills and factories whose chimneys and hostile facades sapped the life from the inhabitants. The cosy snug of the pub, if you were known and accepted was an inevitable safe port in the storm that was everyday life.

22:30 hours the bell rang for last orders, and Maureen quaffed at the pint of lager, it was the fourth pint Ronnie had bought her that evening, and Maureen was just starting to warm up. She decided that the night was still young.

"I fancy a dance. Are yer gonna take us to Mecca?" she asked Ronnie. *"No, I've had enough. You go Mo. You can stop at mine toneet; it'll save on't taxi fare".* came his considered response.

"Yer a spoilsport Ronnie, a bloody spoilsport".

23:10 hours their drinks drunk the couple parted with a friendly kiss and loose arrangements were made for Maureen to sleep over after she'd visited the night club. Ronnie returned home Maureen hailed a taxi to take her into town to continue her night on the tiles.

Maureen decided to finish her evening at the Bradford Mecca Locarno Ballroom, (AKA Tiffany's) 110 Manningham Lane, Bradford. BD1. In 1960CE the Mecca Locarno Ballroom was erected on the site of a former Roller rink on Manningham Lane in Bradford. This huge ballroom evolved and changed much over the passing years. The out of place ugly flat roofed exterior of the building set back from the main road belied the beauty within, this was night clubbing on an industrial scale. Bradford's premiere nightspot was full of life, bustling with the pulsating, energetic, effervescent revellers crowded under its flat roof. The toilets here were well known for being the best in any nightclub. Fountains with fish in and a perfume counter for the ladies. Over twenty-ones only. Wide lapelled jackets, bomber jackets, duffle jackets, afghan coats, pattern fitted shirts, high waist trousers, Old Spice, Hai Karate, chest hair, medallions, Jason King lookalikes, mirror balls, fake palm trees, chicken and chips in a basket.

She attended the Bali Hai disco, where she danced the night away until 02:00 hours when she decided to call it a night. She went to the cloakroom to pick up her light green crimpolene jacket, that she'd borrowed from her daughter, then out of the nightclub into the night air. The fresh summer air was playing havoc with her drink dulled senses. All danced out and drunk to boot, a regular to the Bradford night scene, Maureen said her good nights, with kisses and waves, a walk, a stagger, a lurch down Manningham Lane, down town past the massed hordes of revellers queueing in a drunken fashion revelry, rivalry, fear, loathing, skimpy clothing, loving couples a swathe of humanity, that Maureen wanted to avoid, she was devoid of interest and had other things in mind. Past the hot dog salesman, past the hamburger stand, then further on down Manningham Lane, still busy but the crowds thinning down, with a bit of luck she'd grab a taxi and beat the crowds.

Peter was on his usual lads night out round Bradford with David and Ronnie Barker, the Tanton Crescent Crew had decided to call it a day, so Peter duly drove them and dropped them off at their Clayton abode. To Peter the night was still young and he had an unquenchable thirst for blood, a thirst that must be quenched. The murder of Jayne MacDonald was becoming a memory, one he wished to erase. He needed to set the record straight, expunge the blot on his copy book record. He needed to set the record straight. A warning needed to be despatched all prostitutes should walk the streets in fear, this was Ripper country. Peter knew that he had to kill a prostitute, his inner urge, inner desire had become too strong, it had taken control of his life, his senses, his very being. Peter wanted to tell someone, release the pressure, but he didn't want to hurt his wife and family. Peter didn't care what happened to him, he knew that only God could be his judge and he was working for him, he placed one hundred percent trust in the Lord, his mission was a curse, but it was a theological necessity to save the morality of the world.

Peter was driving down Manningham Lane when he first saw Maureen, she was walking down Manningham Lane into the city centre on the same side as Tiffany's/the Mecca and the crowds and queues were beginning to thin, her five foot one inch figure walked unsteadily through the decreasing crowds. Peter pulled up his white Ford Corsair, with a black soft top roof, some ten metres in front of Maureen who continued on down the pavement. Each step Maureen took making her more vulnerable, more alone, more enticing a victim for the Yorkshire Ripper. He leant over the passenger seat and wound the window down. As Maureen drew level with the opened window Peter said in his soft friendly voice, *"Are yer goin far?"*

"Why are yer gonna give me a lift?" came Maureen's response.

"If yer want one". Peter confirmed. Maureen climbed in and thanked Peter in advance, *"Thanks love, have just been to't Mecca. Am off to me boyfriends up Laisterdyke, he wor a boxer, he dun't like me gonna Mecca. He won't take me to't Mecca, he's a spoilsport".* This flow of drunken rhetoric continued throughout the journey interspersed by directions to the desired destination.

Peter remained politely quiet talking was kept to a minimum, he was biding his time, waiting for the right moment to strike. He drove down Manningham Lane and through Manor Row.

"Do yer fancy me then?" Maureen enquired.
Down and through Cheapside.
"Yeah". Peter responded.
Onto Petergate, then onto Leeds Road, he then drove up Leeds Road.
"It's off Leeds Road love, on yer right". Peter indicated and turned right down Birksland Street.

"Carry on across the junction". Peter obliged and drove straight across at the junction with Mount Street. Maureen then pointed to a cluster of terraced houses to their left. A journey of approximately one and a half miles. In the lonely night streets Peter made good time.

When he was driving down Birkland Street and approaching Rendel Street Maureen muttered further instructions.

"It's that un love, don't stop outside, drive past and park up. Whatever you don't park up outside". Peter complied. He turned left driving into Rendel Street which was a horseshoe shaped road that connected twice to Birklands Street, there was also a narrow path at the far east of Rendel Street that connected it to Mount Street, so Peter drove about twenty metres past the property and then pulled over.

"If there's no one in you can come in". she explained before withdrew from the vehicle, she walked slowly to the house she'd pointed out earlier. Maureen knocked on the door and tried to gain entry for the next couple of minutes, but to no avail, defeated she returned to Peter and the car, she had a treat in mind for Peter.

"I know a place we can go. Just down't road," Maureen suggested as she climbed back into the passenger seat of Peter's car. He turned right back onto Birksland Street and started driving back up towards Leeds Road, Maureen instructed Peter to turn right into Birkshall Lane, was a cobbled street, Peter initially drove up the short slope, then proceeded over the brow and down the slope, to the right were the remnants of soon to be former streets, half houses, some demolished, some derelict, some boarded up, others half pulled down, some still lived in. Peter pulled up, he made a quick inspection of the area, which were quite possibly and ironically the last remnants of Sutcliffe Street, through the darkness he saw the uneven wasteland and his mind raced at the possibilities. He had scant regard for his decaying surroundings, the area was soon to be a litany of lost street names, lost lives and lost histories. Sutcliffe Street, Marsden Street, Hare Street, Cabinet Street Carpenter Street, Haydn Street, Beck Street, Hall Street, Birk Street, Cope Street, Furnace Street, Lake Row, Lake Street, Jewel Street, Aeolus Place, Long Court, Violet Court, Violet Street, Iron Street, Muff Street, Binns Street; to name but a few. Unlike Maureen who would remain synonymous with the darker side of Bradford's history.

Gasometers, disused gasworks, engineering works, scrap yards, factories, railway lines, railway yard, the Bowling Junction line, J McIntyre Ltd. Dudley Hill, the remnants of Bradford Metropolitan District Councils unwanted housing stock and Travellers camps. An industrial wasteland that heralded the degradation that was to befall Bradford and the north of England in general over the coming years.

"I need a pee," proclaimed Maureen. Maureen then climbed out of the car into the darkness of the night, she lifted her black dress pulled her tights and knickers down to her knees and crouched down to urinate. Sunday the 10th of July, circa 3:00 hours, it was the moment Peter had been waiting for and he took his chance with open arms, well a swinging right arm. Peter had quickly followed Maureen out of the car, but before doing so had picked

up and concealed his trusty tools from underneath the driver's seat, he'd second guessed Maureen's actions with the aid of a drunken commentary and seeing his opportunity struck Maureen with all his might. Maureen collapsed to the pavement, unperturbed by the caravan lights in the near distance; Peter replaced the hammer back in his jacket pocket and pulled her by her hands onto the urban wilderness further away from prying eyes. He then prepared to get to work ripping Maureen's black dress up to the waist and her bra had been pulled down to reveal her breasts, whilst her pants and tights remained around her knees. He pulled out his thin bladed knife from his back pocket and holding the black ebonite handle began to slash and stab, in total he stabbed her five times, once on her left shoulder, then he stabbed her four times in the side and front of her torso, one slashing stab wound tracking down from her breast to below her naval. A large dog barked in the distance slightly disturbing his work, but Peter persevered and concentrated on his work. When he felt his job was done he left the scene, on leaving he stumbled, lost his balance and fell, he put out his right arm to cushion his fall, his blood stained hand stopped his fall when it met a discarded wash hand basin/sink. Peter left a blood-stained partial palm print in the porcelain of the basin. He regained his balance and his composure and returned to his car. The dog began to bark again it seemed to be getting closer, the noises emanating from the Alsatian guard dog at Tanks & Drums Ltd. Peter hurriedly clambered into his car and sped away reversing at speed from the scene, back up Birkshall Lane and onto Bowling Back Lane. He was facing towards the city centre and his route back to domestic camouflage until it was time to kill again, he turned on the cars headlights and headed back to the home of his in-laws, at Tanton Crescent. Peter again pulled over before he reached his home and checked his appearance, to see if there were any clues to his recent actions. He then drove to Clayton washed his hands in the kitchen sink and then went to bed, as if nothing untoward had happened.

Sunday the 10th of July, 08:45 hours two traveller women were roused from their caravan, they decided to investigate what they thought to be a baby crying, the Mary Street caravan park, BD4 where they lived was adjacent to the wasteland from which the sounds emanated. They followed the noise until their inquisitive actions revealed the source, a middle-aged woman, a middle-aged Maureen Long, lying, crying, dying, disorientated but still alive.

"Your all right love helps on its way," they comforted Maureen, but their expressions told a different tale. Maureen mumbled and moaned incoherent, unaware how close to death she was. Alarmed at their discovery the two women quickly raised the alarm and the emergency services were called. The general consensus was that Maureen Long was lucky to be alive, but would she survive? Some luck! Her constant companion throughout the cold clear night and a black velvet backdrop which set off the brightness of the stars that decorated it, these were her companions (other than the Grim Reaper) as she fell in and out of consciousness, her life-force seemed to ebb and flow with the light morning winds. Maureen kept trying to get up and in her disorientated state kept falling over, she couldn't

understand why. The cool clear night had contrived to take her life and collaborated with Peter to finish his handy-work, hypothermia along with the hammer imprints and stab wounds ensured Maureen was critically ill, death's door was open and she was part way through it. An ambulance arrived and rushed Maureen to Bradford Royal Infirmary, where they saved her life, she was then transferred to Leeds General Infirmary where she was rushed into theatre and a complex operation at the hands of neurosurgeons saved her life. In total Maureen was hospitalised for nine weeks.

Twelve/Six
Bradford, Sunday 10th July, 1977CE. (03:20 hours) The inner desire to kill prostitutes had taken over totally, Peter wanted to come clean, confide, tell somebody what he was doing, he was in a dilemma, if he did confide, who would it be to, how would it affect his family and wife? Peter didn't care about how it would affect him, *"I wasn't too much bothered for myself"*.

Peter scanned the press, watched the television and listened to the radio for a media report on his earlier exploits. He received a nasty shock when his weekends work was described as an attack and not a murder, he was distraught. Peter heard the chilling news that Maureen was still alive, he assumed his killing spree had come to its natural conclusion, God must want the mission to end. Another failure! This was an unwanted complication but he'd travelled this road before, although unwillingly. His actions were protected by God, so there was no need to worry, but worry he did. He believed that his mission again was undermined, Maureen would be able to tell the police everything and she would be able to identify him, Peter thought the final curtain was fast approaching. Tuesday 12th July 1977CE, a relieved Peter breathed a sigh of relief when he heard that Maureen's memory was not what it was. He scoffed at the description of the assailant released in the press a six-foot one-inch blonde hair man with thickset eyebrows and fat cheeks, thirty-six or thirty-seven years old. However he was concerned that she'd remembered the fact that her attacker was driving a white Ford car with a black roof. This coupled with Frank Whitaker the night-watchman from Tanks & Drums Ltd. ((Unit 11 Iron Works Park) Bradford, BD4) he reported that he'd seen what he incorrectly believed to be a white Mark Two Ford Cortina drive away at speed from wasteland off Mount Street at 03:27hours. It was in fact Peter's white Ford Corsair, when he digested this information he resolved to offload his trusty vehicle. This re-assured Peter that God was protecting him orchestrating events to prevent the police from capturing him. Inside urges surged, his desire to kill prostitutes was stronger than ever.

Peter pondered the implications of capture and incarceration, he weighed it up against his mission, his thoughts were not for himself, but for his wife and family, how would it impact on them. The Lord God his protector had put him in an irreconcilable position. Unable to remember, unable to forget, left to live a life of regret.

Maureen Long and Peter Sutcliffe's paths were destined to cross once again, before Peter was deserted by God and arrested and charged with the Ripper murders. Peter would come face to face with Maureen on Saturday the 19th of December 1980CE in the Kirkgate Centre, Bradford, BD1. He was out with Sonia shopping when he turned around and almost bumped into Maureen. Three years and five months after their initial first fateful meeting, Peter was sure she would recognise him but his fears were misplaced, Maureen carried on regardless unaware that she had come face to face once more with the Yorkshire Ripper. Peter knew it was God who was protecting him once again and disappeared into the throng of festive shoppers.

Chapter 15
Scottish Jean

October 1973CE, a teenage tearaway runs away from home. Jean Jordan is that teenage runaway, she arrived in Manchester to chase her dreams, unfortunately Jean did not meet her Prince Charming; although she did meet and fall in love with a member of the Royle family. Alan Royle was the chivalrous chef returning home via Manchester's Victoria Railway Station, he noticed the forlorn figure of Jean and offered to buy her a drink and a bite to eat. Taken aback by this random act of kindness, she agreed. He then offered to take her home so she could clean herself up and romance duly blossomed. Perhaps not the best foundations for a fledgling romance, but love is blind and love knows no bounds. They set up home in a small Newell Green flat in Wythenshawe, south of Manchester city centre. The salad days of their relationship soon turned sour and the pressure of extra mouths to feed and growing economic hardship saw the couple grow apart. They continued to live together however they led very separate lives. Jean met her friend Anna Holt and they spent more and more time together, desperate for money the pair turned to prostitution. Turning tricks for a fiver on the streets of Cheetham Hill and Moss Side.

1977 CE, the year of Queen Elizabeth the second's Silver Jubilee, a major national celebration, street parties, red, white and blue bunting abounds, as do replica miniature union flags a unifying force for good, set to the back drop of financial, economic, industrial crisis and racial tension. Hulme, Manchester, the late 1960's CE, the old communities deleted expunged, recreated, rehoused, deloused and decanted into purpose-built tower blocks. In 1971CE the new dawn had become a false dawn, people were moved into the new Crescents, and high-rise tower blocks populated by low income, no income residents. Inappropriately badly designed buildings, low quality materials exasperated by poor workmanship ensured an ever-increasing repairs/faults/maintenance demand that the Council could not, would not tackle. The sky rocketing oil prices due to Middle East instability and the ongoing 'oil crisis' compounded heating costs and ensured fuel poverty was compulsory. Notorious dens of iniquity, damp, cold, rat and cockroach infested, and a hot bed for crime. A police no go area, the decks of the flats were not classed as streets, so the police did not patrol them. The dark dangerous decks contributed to the crime, mini stages, private and intimate performances of all manner of crimes, burglary, muggings, drug dealing and assault. Away from the prying eye and interference of the police. Government statistics for 1977CE underlined the living hell hole Hulme had become, individuals in the Hulme district were seven times more likely to commit suicide and thirty-one times more likely to be a victim of crime, when compared to the national average. It was within this context that Jean Jordan scratched a living for herself and her family.

The infamous Hulme Crescents crassly named after architectural demigod's Charles Barry Crescent, John Nash Crescent, William Kent Crescent and Robert Adam Crescent but this was a Godless enclave of the country. A final insult to the individuals and families that had to suffer the indignity of everyday life in this failed sociological experiment. The design of the Crescents was based on the regency terraces of Bath. Sir Charles Barry (1752CE to 1860CE), boasted the Palace of Westminster on his curriculum vitae (CV), John Nash (1752CE to 1835CE), designed Buckingham Palace, William Kent (1685CE to 1748CE) a famous landscape architect and furniture designer. Robert Adam (1728CE to 1792CE), integrated various elements of historical design in his work, Roman, Byzantine, Baroque and Greek; architectural aristocracy flaunted on the lower working class and fast emerging underclass. An irony that would not be lost until their demolition in 1993CE.

In 1965CE John Lewis Wommersley, MBE (Member of the British Empire) and Leslie Hugh Wilson submitted a four-million-pound plan to transform Hulme into a futuristic utopia. Multiple low rise concrete blocks would intersperse the thirteen tower blocks, all would be interconnected via the aerial walkways (the decks), at the heart of this lay the four Crescents, south facing blocks, 'streets in the skies'. However the gap between theory and reality was a big one.

Local authorities, central government & the National Building Agency were also culpable, along with the cartel of construction system-built housing companies inept at quality control adept at profiteering. The Ronan Point disaster in1968CE impacted on the Crescents, gas was considered an inappropriate energy source for communal living. Gas-fueled central heating was discarded in favour of a system of electricity powered underfloor heating. The 1973CE oil crisis, OPEC (Organisation of the Petrolium Exporting Countries), the Yom Kippur War saw fuel prices rise massively causing the knock-on effect of fuel poverty amongst the estate's new residents. In 1974CE a five-year old child fell from a top-floor balcony and died, as a result six-hundred and forty-three residents put their names to a petition requesting an immediate move. In 1975CE, ninety-six percent of Crescent inhabitants wanted to leave the Hulme estate. The Council attempted to appease these demands and agreed that no family should be required to live above the ground floor in any of its deck-access homes. The new Hulme was not made up of former Hulme residents who were simply decanted, the former Hulme residents were rehoused in out-of-town estates, so this was a community with no roots, no bonds, just desperate people forced together. Due to the estates continuing problems and worsening reputation as hard-to-let, the council then exacerbated the situation by introducing 'problem families' and vulnerable tenants, who were desperate for a home and would accept anything.

High rise, factory-built housing, industrial building techniques, monotony, a habitation lobotomy. Vandalised, disenfranchised, theft, truancy a social nuance, prostitution, pilfering, pest control, piss stench communal corridors, alcoholism, drug abuse prescribed and street. Sleep deprivation, damp, mould, noise and cold. Bookmakers, risk takers, pubs, clubs and bingo halls. Money laundering, loan sharks and 'Prudential' loans (a company which leant people money). Out of order lifts, broken rubbish chutes. Anti-social, social security.

Cutting edge architecture, cheap materials, thousands of pounds squandered, millions of pounds made, renegade builders, corrugated concrete, corrupt councils. Haphazardly built, corners cut, and reinforcing ties and bolts omitted, little or no quality control. Condensation from inadequate ventilation, insulation and heating.

Pests and vermin soon infested the blocks ducting. Life is cheap on cutthroat estates in the sky. Flawed design, enhanced isolation, in effect Hulme was cut off from the city, the area enclosed by Mancunian Way and Princess Parkway. Muggings, break-ins, crime, graffiti went unchallenged, ignored, the sink estate was born. Unsanitary, unsavoury and unkempt.

The Junction, The Iron Duke, Hulme Hippodrome, The Eagle (Honey Boy Zimba, the ebony Hercules), The Spinners Arms, The Grey Parrott, The Cavendish, The Grants Arms, The PSV Club, Moss Side Brewery, fuel poverty, Perry Boys and corduroy's. A no go zone.

Champions of the underclass, The Hulme Tenants' Association and Hulme People's Rights Group saw through the sham and battled the injustice, a perpetual flea in the ointment for the powers that be. *"Life in some parts of Manchester is as unsafe and uncertain as it is amongst a race of savages".* Judge Willis 1887CE. This quote could also apply to Hulme in the 1970's CE, northern savages left to their own devices.

Monday 26th September 1977CE Sonia and Peter moved into their fifteen thousand pounds new home 6 Garden Lane, Heaton, Bradford, BD9. Only thirty miles as the crow flies to the north west of Manchester, but a million miles away in regard to the living environment when contrasted to that suffered by Jean and her family in Hulme. Not only had Peter bought a house he also bought a new used car, a red Ford Corsair, a busy time in the new Sutcliffe household, a busy time soon to be made busier by Peter's nocturnal hobby.

Saturday the 1st of October 1977CE, Peter passed the day tinkering with his new toy on the driveway of his new home, he later decided to put it through its paces. Peter thought things were hotting up in Bradford and Leeds, especially after the adverse publicity he'd received in the Jayne McDonald attack. He'd recently read an article in a church magazine, where a priest warned about the dangers of prostitution in the Manchester Moss Side area. It was time the regional Yorkshire Ripper expanded his horizons and took his homicidal tendencies on tour, it was time he went provincial. Therefore Peter drove the forty miles across the Pennine hills, the back bone of England, he set off from his new home with a walling hammer that had been left in his new double fronted garage, in his new used car registration number PHE355G armed with one of his many road atlases. Peter drove south along the M606, then onto the M62 West along the M63 link, west along the A635 to Ardwick onto the Mancunian Way into Manchester city centre then south down Oxford Road, past the University of Manchester West along the B5129 along to the junction with Princess Road onto Moss Lane East heading towards his objective, Moss Side. He arrived at his destination at approximately 21:00 hours. It was a visibly run-down area, in effect a Lancashire replica of Chapeltown or Manningham, a home from home for the prostitute hating killer. The girls of the night were out in their numbers trading their wares in the cool autumn night.

Jean Bernadette Jordan (AKA Royle, AKA Scotch/Scottish Jean), was a twenty-year-old mother of two boys. Alan aged three and James aged one, originally from Motherwell she lived at 204/18 Medlock Court a sixteen storey tower block on Lingbeck Crescent, Hulme with her boyfriend and common law husband Alan Royle, an unemployed bingo worker/qualified chef and their baby-sitter friend. In what was to be a strange twist of fate a previous resident of 204/18 Medlock Court had also met an untimely end, Amina Thorne a twenty-three-year-old woman had recently been killed after falling from the cabin of a travelling lorry. In a strange twist of fate Jean too would be killed at the hands of a lorry driver. Jean had been cautioned twice previously for soliciting. Jean went out on Saturday the 1st of October 1977CE and there was some argument as to whether or not she was actively prostituting her body. Although the couple lived together they sometimes led very separate lives, Alan would think nothing of disappearing off on a three or four day 'bender' with the lads, whilst Jean sometimes disappeared for days on end, often returning to her native Scotland, (Glasgow particularly to stay with friends and relatives), catching a bus to the motorway and then hitching a lift up north, all this without any communication or discussion between the two. It was an unwritten understanding an unwritten agreement that both needed this pressure relief valve to help them survive the situation in which they found themselves. A somewhat unconventional relationship to say the least. An unconventional unnatural relationship that was reflected in their unusual social environment, an environment that stifled any aspirations any dreams. A half-life of has-beens and never will be.

Alan and Jean were sitting in the kitchen of the flat they'd recently begun to rent from the council, *"I'm off out with the lads tonight love,"* Alan explained putting his coat on.

"Nae problem doll, I'll see ya in the morrow," Jean replied taking a sip of the lemonade she was drinking and went back to the living room and continued watching Saturday evening television. Unimpressed by what Saturday TV had to offer Jean saw an opportunity to make a little extra money. A possible final foray into the red-light scene into which she'd been dipping her toes for the past two years, after all it was money and she had mouths to

feed. Money can't buy love, but it can buy sex and money will put food on the table, unlike love, what was that worth in Hulme. The humour of the Hulmerist.

Standing five feet six inches tall, a slim build, weighing a mere seven and a half stone and with long shoulder length auburn hair and an attractive face and a sultry shy smile that suggested an air of helplessness, a selling point for the chivalrous punter who was doing his damnedest to help this street urchin of low morals to live a more meaningful life. The blame transferred his sordid sexual transactions transformed into a charitable act.

Jean decided to take advantage of this unforeseen opportunity and quickly arranged with her live-in babysitter and left her flat at around 21:00 hours, with the parting words

"Am just nipping oot far some fresh air". Jean walked through the Moss Side Precinct buying a packet of cigarettes and asking the female shopkeeper for two five pounds notes to buy an electric card from the machine located outside, unfortunately the shopkeeper had no change and the electricity meter credit outside the shop was empty. So Jean set off on to her journey along Moss Lane West, puffing on a cigarette as she passed the 'Little Alex', to the right on Alexandra Road, (M16 7BU) heading towards 'The Big Alex' (The Alexandra Hotel) which was on the corner of Moss Lane West and Princess Road or diagonally adjacent to The Reno Club or The Nile Club, two clubs within the same building, again on the corner of Princess Road but now at the junction with Moss Lane East. The two clubs stayed open until 05:00 or 06:00 hours, extremely unusual for 1977CE. The Reno catered for funk and soul connoisseurs, whilst if jazz was your thing, it was in the basement down some seriously steep steps. The Nile was on the first floor and was the bigger of the two venues and played reggae. Jean wasn't interested in the music though - not tonight, she had decided to supplement her income by tried and tested means, one last time wouldn't do any harm. The temptation of an easy 'buck' had grasped her and she had been forced out onto the streets by the ineptness of terrestrial television. On she walked still heading towards the Big Alex, The Reno and the Nile, exotic names for a not so exotic Manchester night.

Peter pulled up at the kerbside and approached a young woman he asked, *"Do you want business?"* The young woman in question was Jean Jordan.

"Park up down there & I'll meet you in a minute". Peter complied, driving some two hundred yards, taking a right into Hulme High Street, he then performed a three-point turn and waited dutifully for his newfound business colleague. About two minutes later and Jean was preparing to attend her 21:30 hours meeting. At the same time a fawn coloured Austin 1100 car pulled up, the driver caught her attention, however Jean did not get into the 1100 she held true to her verbal contract and walked to Peter's red Ford

Corsair, a moth to a bright red flame. Jean took the lead, opened the front passenger and plonked herself next to Peter.

"I was ganna go wi him til I saw youz. It'll be a fiver, I know a place we can go, it's dead quiet" Jean quipped and smiled at her in joke for they were headed for the Southern Cemetery and directed him, a left back onto Moss Lane West, a right onto Princess Road a journey of around two miles south past the Southern Cemetery, down and around the roundabout back north up Princess Road and a left turn off the dual carriageway through the entrance to the allotments, then a sharp right turn towards the old allotments, somewhat overgrown, careworn and abandoned. Jean had brought Peter to the Southern Allotments, Chorlton, adjacent to the Southern Cemetery that served the city. This area was bordered by high hawthorn hedges that obscured the busy traffic from Princess Road. A small area of countryside in the urban sprawl of Greater Manchester, an open secret garden used and utilised for the greater good, late night lovers and Moss Side prostitutes and their punters were habitual attendees on the roll call of the night. Peter brought the Corsair to a halt, he dimmed the lights and turned to Jean.

"Fancy bringing me ere, yer see that greenhouse". Peter pointed to a greenhouse further into the allotment, further from the main road and away from possible prying eyes. *"It belongs to me uncle, there's plenty a room in there and it's heated".*

"Ya nae fargettin tha monae ar ye?"

"Of course not". Replied Peter and handed over the crisp new five-pound note, fresh from his Thursday pay packet. Jean exited the car and placed the five-pound note in a small side pocket on the outside of the handbag and cautiously walked towards the greenhouse, trying to concentrate on her footing in the uneven ground. Peter followed behind delaying just enough to allow him time to take the walling hammer from its hiding place under his seat. Peter then followed, Jean stopped at the physical barrier of a small fence surrounding the greenhouse blocking their progress. Peter was cradling the hammer in his left hand using the night, his jacket and body to obscure it from Jean's view.

"Wi'll have to climb over," Peter explained. Jean began to manoeuvre herself over the low fence, concentrating on the job in hand. Peter invited by the opportunity struck with the walling hammer, Jean fell back groaning loudly, Peter struck her on the head once more, then once again; eleven times in total, until the groaning stopped. Peter was just to get down to his second phase work, when an area some fifty-five meters away was illuminated by the headlights from another business meeting. Unbeknown to Peter his, their (Jean and Pete) would be tryst had not been private, they had not been alone, others were in the wasteland cavorting and cohorting, distorting the moral fibre. Had they seen him? He could not decipher. Witness or unwanted interlude, the car's engine ignited, Peter

inwardly panicked but outwardly went into survival mode, he pulled Jean's lifeless, limp and listless body to the cover of the apron of the hawthorn bushes. There was a natural ditch at the base of the hedge, he then covered the corpse with an abandoned wooden door, to obscure the obvious from a searching eye.

The car began to move out of the darkness of the old allotment towards the hustle and bustle of the traffic on Princess Road only yards away. Peter turned his back on Jean and the hedge; he was holding Jean's green coloured imitation leather handbag, he threw it to his right, into the night. The car passed by out onto Princess Road, Peter prepared to revisit his victim, but was interrupted. From his vantage point he could see the lights of the cars on Princess Road through the bushes and he noticed another vehicle slowing down on the dual carriageway and indicating left, another punter and prostitute double act, two lovers entwined, but to Peter they could be unwanted witnesses. He crouched down behind his car, shielding him from prying eyes, Jean's dying cries were now forlorn memories lost in the night. Peter watched the new car drive into the allotments, up the road recently traversed by the other unwelcome vehicle, he watched it turn around and then park in exactly the same place as that previously vacated by the former unwelcome guest. Peter decided to cut his losses and not Jean, he quickly climbed into his car and started the engine, his journey begun he was soon heading north on the dual carriageway, his handy work hidden under the hedge of an old Mancunian allotment. His urge fulfilled, his thirst quenched Peter decided to call it a night and head home. Driving along the M62 somewhere between Rochdale and Huddersfield a thought crossed Peter's mind, Peter paid Jean with a crisp new fiver from his pay packet. Should he return and attempt to retrieve his money a possible clue that would link him to the crime scene, he was unsure. Jean's body might have already been discovered and if he returned he would in effect be offering himself to the authorities on a plate. Peter weighed up the options and decided to keep on with his present course, he would return home and see what tomorrow would bring.

Alan returned home to the Medlock Court flat from his evening of overindulgence of alcoholic beverages, he found the children fast asleep, but no Jean. In his drunken stupor he didn't really care and supposed that Jean had gone out with her friends. He went to bed unconcerned and unaware of Jean's fate and soon fell into a slumber.

Sunday the 2nd October 1977CE, Alan woke mid-morning hung over and indifferent as to the whereabouts of Jean, he thought she'd done one of her disappearing acts, making a spur of the moment decision and travelled to Scotland to see her family. It wouldn't be the first time she had inexplicably disappeared, however it would be the last.

Monday morning the 3rd of October 1977CE came and went and there was no news in the daily red tops, Peter continued to pay particular attention to all forms of news, TV,

(BBC 1, BBC 2, and YTV), radio and newspaper, for a Yorkshire Ripper type murder across the Pennines. The Lancashire Ripper didn't quite ring true, he thought to himself, he pondered this thought further and the seeds of an idea for a further development were sown, if the opportunity arose. There was no news that the Manchester police were searching for a missing person, there were no lurid tales to tell not quite yet. No news is good news, or so the phrase goes, his ego had taken a beating he looked forward to the lurid headlines that captured his escapades in black and white for all eternity. No newspaper reports, no TV coverage, no free anti-prostitute propaganda. Peter was concerned, what had become of the body, what had become of the five-pound note, what would become of him, a puzzle that Peter pondered for the next seven days. He figured that he had hidden the body too well in an area that was only really active after dark, and when it was in full use, the people using it were enthralled in themselves in the security of their cars, why would they search an abandoned allotment in the middle of the night. The lack of news led Peter to the conclusion that he would revisit the Southern Allotment and revisit the body of Jean Jordan in an attempt to retrieve his money, but he needed an appropriate excuse to make the return visit to Manchester.

On Sunday the 9th of October 1977CE, Mr. and Mrs Peter William Sutcliffe held an open house for Peter's relations and Sonia's in laws, this was a housewarming party a chance for Sonia and Peter to show off their recently purchased dream home, the property had been their home for some thirteen days. It also gave Peter the chance to revisit Jean, in her Southern Allotment cemetery, just north of the Southern Cemetery. When the party reached its conclusion Peter offered to take John and Kathleen (his mother and father) and Jane and Ian, (his sister and brother in-law) home to Bingley. Peter dropped his mum and dad off at Cornwall Road in Bingley, around 00:15 hours on Monday 10th October, this was his opportunity, he drove directly to Manchester.

He arrived at the deserted disused allotments around 01:15 hours and set to work. In a re-enactment of his previous visit Peter turned a sharp right and parked his vehicle, he exited his vehicle and located and uncovered Jean's body, lifting the wooden door that concealed and covered Jean's rotting corpse. He struggled to manhandle the dead weight and ungamely size of the door away from his objective. He propped the door against the wooden shed that was serviced by the pathway and was adjacent to the makeshift grave he'd created on his previous visit. He manhandled her body from under the hedge and began to undress her. To hurry the process Peter produced the knife from his jacket pocket and he cut into her clothes from the top of her left shoulder, diagonally all the way down to her right knee. The force with which he made this cut penetrated the skin and contributed towards the ghastly catalogue of injuries Jean's body had to endure. Peter began the search for his fiver he began to undress the body and search through the clothing, first the coat, then the cardigan, the skirt, the tights, the jumper, the bra, the knickers and lastly her boots. As he removed each article of clothing he frantically searched it methodically and once unsuccessful he discarded the item by throwing it away. A macabre game of strip poker, no cards, no rules, the clothes fell around the body in an untidy manner. The five pound note was nowhere to be found, Peter then remembered that on the night of their initial meeting Jean was carrying a handbag, the five pound note, that could possibly link him to this crime must be in the handbag. Peter began to search the disused allotments and the used allotments in an attempt to locate the handbag and hopefully the prize within. A fruitless folly that saw Peter descend into a furious mood, his frustrations needed a release. Peter had planned a little surprise, he'd used the past few days to ponder his options and had come up with a creative twist, which he intended to play in his sick game with the police force. Peter had come prepared, he returned to the red Ford Corsair's boot, he returned to the cadaver with a hacksaw, over the previous week he'd hatched a plan to behead the body and then hide the body again then place the head somewhere else in a prominent place to create 'a big mystery of it'. Simplistic in theory however the practicality of it was to defeat Peter.

Peter formulated a search plan in his mind, he started from the body then circled it each time increasing his orbit to Jean's body. The circular orbit was punctuated by a wooden shed a metre away from Jean's current resting place, Peter continued his search in vain. During his search of the area Peter had come across a broken pane of glass from a derelict and vandalised greenhouse, he looked at the naked body of Jean and felt she was taunting him, scorning him. One of her last actions to conceal the five pounds in a secret compartment in her handbag had resulted in his re-visit, Peter thought it was her fault, if she hadn't hidden the fiver. He wouldn't be here now. He picked up a broken pane of glass, about three quarters its original size with a broken corner that had a sharp cutting edge and used it to slit her stomach open, the cut released a sickening stench from the decomposing corpse the smell was palpable and caused a reflex action from Peter, who retched, gagged and spewed up the party food he had happily eaten only a few hours previously. He regained his composure and assaulted Jean's body with the knife cutting, goring, gouging with the blade, hacking, slicing, slitting, stabbing, lost in violence. In total his second visit to the disused southern allotments, but much used southern open-air brothel of Manchester saw him stab the body a further eighteen times, he targeted her chest, her breasts, her stomach and her vagina. The gashes caused by the glass gaped open and were up to eight inches in depth. The Yorkshire Ripper had plummeted new depths of depravity, Jean would pay for her dying secret, for Peter must have a semblance of revenge. Her entrails, her intestines, her internal organs gushed out of the open wounds in her body from the deep slashing wounds he'd caused, gravity caused them to spill onto the ground. Peter manhandled her body further causing her innards to wrap themselves around her waist in a grotesque taxidermy belt styled fashion accessory.

His plan - to deface, damage, disfigure, dismember and decapitate his victim to disassociate and distance this attack from his previous crimes, hoping the police would believe there was a deranged copycat killer up and running in Manchester. If he could remove the head he could remove his tell-tale signature strike of the hammer wound to the back of the skull.

Peter took the hacksaw and began to cut at Jean's neck, the blunt blade made little progress, Peter decided it was a pointless venture. He used the piece of broken glass again and brought it down on Jean's neck in a final act of desperation, he felt that the net was tightening and the fact that he had not found the fiver meant that he was on borrowed time, if his freedom was to be short lived, this bitch would take the brunt of his anger. He kicked Jean's body, once, twice, three times and then rolled the body over so she was on her back. Peter knew he had to find the fiver, Peter knew he'd failed in his objective to retrieve the fiver, but Peter also realised that he'd spent too long and he must extricate himself from the situation and let time take its course, however he also felt he could aid the ravages of time by having an early bonfire, a human pyre that would help hide her identity and keep them guessing. He set fire to wasteland underneath her body, the flames licked at her face and hair a final punishment for her secretion of his fiver.

Caught between a rock and a hard place Peter gave up his search for the fiver (and therefore he supposed his freedom) and fled the scene. He drove home slightly reserved contemplating his next move, he returned home to Bradford and was astonished to find hardly any blood on himself or his clothes, he wiped his dark brown soft slip on shoes with a sponge to remove the blood stains, he also washed the blood that was on the back of his hands. His old pair of grey casual slacks had some blood staining, he tried to wipe them clean, but to no avail and therefore stored them in a cupboard in the garage, until he had a garden fire where he would burn the offending item along with other garden rubbish, he made a mental note to do this sooner rather than later. He also threw the pathetic excuse for a hacksaw blade in the dustbin with the household rubbish, after all what possible use could it be. Peter decided to stick to the tools he knew best in future, if there was to be a future attack. If God was to continue to protect him.

Monday morning 10th October 1977CE, Mr. Jones and Mr. Morrisey, two allotment holders are working on their allotment, they had recently bought a second hand shed and were in the process of sorting out the platform on which to build it. Bruce Jones (later to become Coronation Street Les Battersby) rolled his wheel barrow along the overgrown path at the edge of the abandoned allotments, one way empty with the exception of a hammer and chisel, the other way heavily laden with red house bricks synonymous with Manchester, that he had recently liberated from the disused former allotment building. He repeated this process twice and was on the return journey of a third trip with a red house brick laden barrow that he saw what he initially believed to be the arm of a tailors dummy, he then realised it was not, he could see that her hair was burnt, her face was smashed in and she had been disembowelled, Bruce had, it seemed walked onto the movie set of a Hammer House of Horror, unfortunately for all concerned it was very real, the time was 10:30 hours. In his efforts, his exertions he had inadvertently uncovered, unearthed the grisly secret of Jean Jordan's body. Bruce shouted to his friend in horror, his mate came over followed by a fellow allotment holder and his Jack Russell dog. Bruce then ran over the road and rang the police 999, the area was soon swarming with police, flashing blue lights, blue and white tape, sirens wailing, and a whirlwind of the Manchester constabulary. Bruce Jones was put into the back of a police van and taken from the scene.

Circa 12:30 hours Detective Chief Inspector (DCI) Tony Fletcher, the head of the Fingerprint Bureau of Greater Manchester Police was called to attend the murder scene. An abandoned section of the allotment off Princess Road, in the Chorlton district of Manchester. He was greeted by a frenetic scene of police activity, the naked body of a woman lay face down, her arms wide apart. The maimed bodies grisly appearance was exaggerated by the rotting intestines that were wrapped around her waist. His first impression was that a grave robber had taken the body from the nearby Southern Cemetery and desecrated the body. When items of Jean's clothes were found strewn around he began to think along different lines, it then became obvious that this was the scene of an appalling attack. DCI Fletcher fingerprinted the mutilated corpse.

18:30 hours, Alan read an article in the Manchester Evening newspaper report that a mystery murder victim had been found, the short description of the female body set alarm bells ringing in his head. He rang the police and voiced his concerns that the victim may be Jean Jordan, his common-law wife, who he had last seen on Saturday the 1st of October. The police picked him up and brought him to the Longsight police station, Grindlow Street, Manchester M13 0LL, where he became the prime suspect for Jean's murder. He was held for the next forty-eight hours. During the proceeding Alan was able to provide the police with a photograph of Jean and reliably recall the clothes she was wearing on that fateful evening.

18:30 hours, Anna Holt, an old friend of Jean and a fellow prostitute, also saw the article and called in to her local police station, Anna had the misfortune of formally identifying Jayne's body, a cursory glance in a state of the art mortuary on Rachel Street in central Manchester. A traumatised Anna confirmed that the body was that of Jean Bernadette Jordan (AKA Royle, AKA Scotch/Scottish Jean). Anna would later confirm that Jean had a duet of police cautions for soliciting and was struggling to find alternative methods of earning money, other than selling herself on the squalid sleazy streets of Manchester's red-light district. Anna explained how Jean struggled with overriding, undermining feelings of remorse and seemed out of place in this dark underworld. Jean was a quiet, reserved and timid person, wracked with guilt, a troubled soul doing her best under very difficult circumstances. Jean was trying to settle down and lead a normal life, but what was normal in Hulme.

19:00 hours Tuesday 11th October 1977CE a team of officers visited 204/18 Medlock Court, Hulme, in an effort to find fingerprints that belonged to Jean, they were greeted by a disconsolate Alan Royle, the common-law husband of Jean. The team were unsuccessful in their efforts and at 24:00 hours they were instructed to collect various items and return them to their office and powder and brush test them for latent fingerprints.

08:35 hours, Wednesday 12th October 1977CE six officers commenced work on the household items procured from Medlock Court. They dusted and powdered the lemonade bottle that Jean had sipped the lemonade from eleven days previously, it was this bottle that provided the single thumb print, which provided the positive identification, along with Alan's description of the clothes she was wearing on the fateful night. The body that had been found a little more than forty-eight hours ago was the last worldly remains of Jean Royle as the sixth murder victim of the Yorkshire Ripper.

There was a distinct difference between the different layers of discarded clothing that surrounded the body. The external clothing, coat, cardigan and jumper, were all heavily bloodstained and on close examination were seen to be teeming with well-developed maggots. On examination of the murder scene it became apparent that Jean's body had laid in a makeshift grave at the foot of the edge that bordered the pathway and divided it from the allotment. The natural trough in the ground was also crawling with maggots.

Saturday 15th October 1977, 10:00 hours, Mr. Cox an allotment keeper at the 'new' Southern Allotment's, rang the police to explain he'd found a green coloured imitation leather handbag he'd found it hidden in long grass, underneath a fence that divided the working allotment from the abandoned allotment, one side for the horticulturalist, the other side for the whore culture. Mr. Cox handed over the handbag to the authorities, he had found it lying open, the contents soaking from the inclement Manchester climate, a quick search through it revealed some cigarettes, matches and make up in the main compartment. In a compartment on the exterior of the handbag in which he found two bank notes, one a pound note, the other, the all-important five-pound note handed over by Sutcliffe. Police later believe that the handbag had been previously searched due to the fact that it was lying open, a theory supported by her common law husband, Alan who'd calculated that there should have been fourteen, or fifteen pound in the handbag. Mr. Cox found the handbag fifty-seven metres away from where the body of Jean Jordan had been found nearly five days ago give or take half an hour. Unfortunately the area searched was not within the area searched by the police, it was literally just outside the search zone. Fortunately for Peter the delay in the discovery of the body and the delay in the discovery of the handbag had distanced Peter further from the crime. The passage of time allowing serial number sequenced bank note in his possession to be offloaded.

In Bradford, Peter kept a self-interested eye on the press, he saw the newspaper coverage of Jean Jordan's murder and became convinced it was just a matter of time until he was caught. However these feelings were nothing new and he had been wrong before. Peter sat tight and didn't try to bother to second guess the industrious efforts of the boys in blue.

His assumption that the crisp new fiver would lead them to his door seemed to have developed into a self-fulfilling prophecy, he'd read with interest about the five pound note enquiry AW51 121565 and how it had been traced to the Shipley branch of the Midland bank. Peter felt the net was tightening, he knew that T and WH Clark (Holdings) Limited wage money, his wage money was delivered from the Shipley branch of the Midland bank, so he decided to sit tight and expect the inevitable. After all everyone knows that the British police are the best in the world, a statement that even back in the heady heights of the Jubilee and all things British seemed to resonate no real substance and an echo of hollow bravado. Peter took the blood-stained pants from the garage cupboard and burnt them with garden waste he'd amassed, he did this on the field adjoining the garden wall of number six Garden Lane. Peter waited for the inevitable.

Thirteen/Seven

Manchester, Saturday 1st October 1977 CE. (21:30 hours) A priest writing for an article in the church magazine articulated an argument warning about prostitutes in Moss Side Manchester. Peter knew this was most certainly a message and alighted for Manchester tools in hand. Proof positive in print of his mission, the church magazine was the expeditionary voice to the voices that would confirm his raison d'être.

INTERVIEW WITH A SERIAL KILLER NUMBER ONE:
Wednesday 2nd November 1977CE

Mr Peter William Sutcliffe, F44 received a five pounds note, serial number AW51 121565 in his pay packet, a five pounds note that he gave to Jean Jordan on an autumn evening in Manchester. This was the very same five pounds note that was found in her discarded handbag on a Manchester allotment. But the police did not know that Peter William Sutcliffe was the one who had actually received it. What they did know was that he was one of an exclusive club of eight thousand men all of whom could have received the all-important five pounds note. Police believed that if they found the man who had received the five pounds, they had found the killer.

Detective-Constables Leslie Smith and Edwin Howard of the unofficial newly created Trans-Pennine Police Force paid a visit to 6 Garden Lane Heaton. Wednesday 2nd November 1977 CE, 19:45 hours, Mr Peter William Sutcliffe and Mrs Sonia Sutcliffe seemed unperturbed by their unexpected guests. Mr Peter William Sutcliffe was asked if he could provide any of the five pounds notes received in his pay packet from Thursday 29th September 1977 CE. Almost five long weeks had passed and Peter thankfully had relieved himself of the offending items.

When asked his whereabouts on the night of Saturday the 1st October and Sunday the 9th October. Mr Peter William Sutcliffe responded that of course he was at home on the night of Saturday 1st October 1977 CE and had retired to bed at 23:30 hours. Whilst on Sunday 9th October 1977 CE he had been at home, in fact the couple had had a housewarming party; this was later corroborated by Mrs Sonia Sutcliffe.

Second interview to substantiate this information.

INTERVIEW WITH A SERIAL KILLER NUMBER TWO:
Tuesday 8th November 1977

Tuesday 8th November 1977 CE and another two police officers visited the Sutcliffe house, number 6 Garden Lane, Heaton, Bradford, West Yorkshire BD9. Mr Peter William Sutcliffe was questioned again about his whereabouts on the night of Saturday the 1st October and Sunday the 9th October. Mr Peter William Sutcliffe responded that of course he was at home on the night of Saturday 1st October 1977 CE and had retired to bed at 23:30 hours. Whilst on Sunday 9th October 1977 CE he had been at home, in fact the couple had held a housewarming party; this was later corroborated by Mrs Sonia Sutcliffe.

They also asked him questions about his car, a red Ford Corsair and also the tools he owned and asked about his footwear and boots in particular.

A covert tracking operation was ongoing by the West Yorkshire police, vehicles were observed in red-light districts, multiple sightings and cross area multiple sightings were of particular interest to the constabulary. The West Yorkshire Police Force was joined by Greater Manchester, South Yorkshire and Humberside police, by the middle of 1978 CE, Bradford, Leeds, Manchester, Sheffield and Hull's red-light districts were all under covert police observation. The data was collated by the Police National Computer, in Hendon and the number of vehicles kept increasing, spiralling out of control. Therefore a trigger point criterion was adopted to make the follow up work more manageable; the trigger point criteria was a vehicle sighting in at least two separate red-light locations. A criterion that Mr Peter William Sutcliffe and his red Ford Corsair, PHE 355G met. Hence interview three, hence a hat trick of interviews. An officer was dispatched with a surreal To Do list. Whereabouts on key dates and verification of alibi's? Do not mention ball-pein hammers. Keep the covert Tracking investigation covert. Does he have a car, could the car have left the tyre prints in Leeds and Manchester? If affirmative record position and make of the tyres, front offside, front nearside, rear offside, rear nearside. India Autoway, Esso E. 100, Pneumant or Avon Super? Ascertain if he is a punter?

NO FURTHER ACTION REQUIRED.

Chapter 16
Marilyn

Marilyn had experienced an eventful twenty-five years and lived on the seedier side of life. Marilyn was a qualified veteran of a life of hard knocks, even at such a relatively young age. A teenage tearaway who ran away from home at the age of fifteen years old and who was married at the age of sixteen. A failed marriage and an income supplemented by prostitution at the age of nineteen. Marilyn was slightly overweight, with long red hair with a cheeky and attractive smile. So come 1977 CE when two sevens collide Marilyn Moore was a twenty-five-year-old divorcee, with a previous conviction for soliciting. In fact she had a career spanning six years on the game and had traded her body in London, Slough, Bradford, Halifax and Leeds. She had two children a son aged six and a daughter aged one neither of whom lived with her at the Bayswater Mount property in the Harehills district of Leeds, LS8 5LW, where she lodged in a rented upstairs room. Mr Peter Sucvic was the owner of the terraced house and therefore Marilyn's landlord, he knew nothing of her secret life.

Wednesday the 14th of December 1977 CE, home alone Peter had time on his hands and nobody to share it with and as we know the devil finds work for idle hands, the urge surged through his body, he didn't try to fight it, he'd given up trying to resist the all-encompassing force, resistance was futile. But Peter wasn't in league with the devil, he wasn't a puppet at his command, a servant at his beck and call. Peter was a servant of God his actions and his mission were ordained by God. God the Supreme Being, perfect in power and wisdom, the creator and ruler of all. Why beat yourself up over it, use those negative emotions in a positive way, Peter decided a trip to Chapeltown was in order. Peter decided a prostitute's life should be expunged.

He climbed into his car, reversed down the steep drive then set off with murder in mind, he drove through Manningham his usual hunting ground then along Queens Road onto Lister Lane onto Valley View Grove onto Northcote Road then onto Killinghall Lane, up to Thornbury and the outskirts of Bradford, then Leeds. The car heater reached an ambient temperature, Peter unbuttoned his old brown car coat and loosened the collar on his yellow shirt. Into Pudsey then Stanningley on through Armley into Leeds city centre then into his old hunting ground, Ripper country, Chapeltown. McCann, Jackson, Claxton, Richardson, MacDonald and soon to be Moore. This was to be the last Chapeltown attack, but not his last visit to Leeds.

Maureen had told Mr Sucvic that she was off to see a friend and would be back no later than 23:00 hours, she had originally arranged for her friend to call round, however when she did not turn up she decided to visit her. It was a cold but dry evening and Marilyn walked the two hundred and fifty metres where she spent the early evening at her friend's house who lived in Gathorne Terrace. She left the property at 20:05 hours, walked down Gathorne Terrace and turned right and sauntered up Gipton Avenue advertising her wares. She continued to walk up Gipton Avenue, crossing the junction with Gathorne Street. She then turned left and began to walk down Spencer Place as she approached the telephone boxes at the junction with Leopold Street a slow driving car stopped adjacent to her and began to talk business. Marilyn looked at the occupant and wasn't impressed, she made her feelings perfectly clear.

In the near distance approaching slowly was the red Ford Corsair being driven by Peter William Sutcliffe. The way the car manoeuvred it was obvious to Marilyn that it was driven by a punter who was on the prowl. The failed business transaction saw the recently parked vehicle depart with a barrage of expletives, both parties giving as good as they got. Marilyn, ever the professional was two steps ahead of the game, her experience on the game giving her an almost second sense. Peter passed slowly as the parties broke, he too was an experienced punter, but also an experienced murderer. He also had a second sense and was two steps ahead of the game, not to mention he was endorsed by God.

Marilyn saw an opportunity. The driver of the red car might be up for a bit of business, if she walked down Leopold Street and if he did another circuit of the streets their paths would cross and then they could talk business. Peter realised that Marilyn was a likely target, he also realised that he would have to ease her fears. His overactive year had instilled hysteria and panic on the night streets of the north of England, especially Bradford and Leeds. Peter had a plan - a trap to ensnare his next victim, like the spider to the fly, jump straight ahead into my web. Peter kept a close eye on the woman, using both of the rear-view mirrors attached to his windscreen to scrutinise his prey. Marilyn continued to stroll down Leopold Street. Would her slow sultry stroll have its desired affect? The window of opportunity was still open for both parties, however Peter needed to act quickly to ensure it didn't get slammed shut.

Peter put his plan into action, he turned left into Spencer Place and then left again onto Louis Street and then left again down Frankland Street pulling into the kerbside down at the bottom of the street close to the cross road with Leopold Street. Peter hurriedly scrambled from his red Ford Corsair and set about ensnaring Marilyn into his honey (for money) trap. Because he had witnessed Marilyn rebuff the previous punter he had to put her at her ease, after all there was a crazed prostitute killer around that had a penchant for Leeds tarts. Peter walked to the corner of the street, where Frankland Place met Louis Street, safe in the knowledge that Marilyn was approaching from the opposite direction to which he was walking. Peter then stopped and waited until Marilyn came into sight, he then turned on his heels and walked back to his still warm car as Marilyn rounded the corner and came into view once again. Peter waved in the general direction of 112 Louis Street and shouted pleasantly at nobody in particular.

"Bye now, see yer later. Teck care". Soft voiced unassuming disarming.

Peter unlocked then opened the driver's car door and started the engine, he then lent over and opened the passenger window, just prior to Marilyn drawing level.

"Are yer doing business?" Peter asked in his high-pitched voice. Marilyn looked at Peter turned to the house, where she witnessed Peter wave and thought why not.

"Yes," She said has she climbed into the passenger seat. Marilyn thought Peter looked like Peter Wyngarde who starred in the 'Jason King' ITC Entertainments action drama, TV show about a secret agent, like Jason, Peter was on a secret mission, however Peter's mission was ordained by a higher order than the fictional Jason who worked for the British Government. Peter worked at Gods behest and unfortunately for the population he was not fictional, he was real a true manifestation of evil in the human form, he was the Yorkshire Ripper.

His demeanour put Marilyn at ease, his friendly chatter disarmed her defences, left her ripe for the plucking, for the killing no need for fucking. Although she navigated it was apparent that he had a good local knowledge.

"I know a place we can go". Marilyn offered. The couple had to travel about a mile and a half to reach the destination and small talk patterned their journey.
"Is it a fiver?" Peter verified.
With his sultry come to bed eyes or more accurately come to the back of my car eyes.
"I'm David". as Peter introduced himself, lying through the noticeable gap in his front teeth. *"Who were doing in Frankland Place then Dave?"* Marilyn enquired.
"I prefer David". Peter corrected, then continued *"Waving to me girlfriend, she's ill".*
"I've not seen you before do you know any of the other girls?" Marilyn asked him.
"Yeah, a few, I know Gloria and Hilary, I know Hilary better, she's the one with the Jamaican boyfriend". David's local knowledge further reassured Marilyn.

Peter turned right onto Leopold Street and drove up to the crest of the hill where Leopold Street meets Cross Louis Street, then down the slope towards Savile Mount, across Chapeltown Road and down Savile Mount to the bottom of the hill, then follow the road to the right onto Buslingthorpe Lane, then up the short steep climb to the dual carriageway of Sheepscar Street North/Scott Hall Lane. Then a quick left turn onto Buslingthorpe Lane once again. Up the narrow winding lane, woodland to the right, high stone walls and industry or the remnants of industry, tanneries, mills, workshops and forges to the left. An urban desert after the slum clearances of the 1950's CE. Then drove to the brow of the hill then down into the valley, a right turn onto Scott Hall Street, just before the bridge that was built to cross Sheepscar Beck, the red brick factory to the right hand side and grassland leading to the woods on the right. The tarmac of the lane gave way to the cobbles of the Street and they then faded into a quagmire of mud, as Peter pulled over and parked his car on the now unnamed dirt track.

Decline and decay; watchwords of Sutcliffe's night-time alter ego proliferated, it may not be Ripper country, but it was a favourable location for an armed man to blitz attack an unarmed woman and have a very good chance of avoiding capture.

The red brick façade of Alfred Brown (Worsted Mill's Ltd) factory loomed to the left and the running water of Sheepscar Beck could be heard in the distance, the couple were on the waste ground behind the mill, there was a caravan parked in an adjacent scrapyard the lights were on making it more prominent in the near distance. This unsettled Peter but Marilyn was unconcerned. 20:20 hours, but unlike the time of day Marilyn and Mr Jimmy Pearson (the occupant of the white caravan) did not have the luxury of 20/20 vision, or even 20/20 hindsight vision. The car engine noise had awakened the curiosity of Jimmy and his partner who were preparing to go out for the night. He opened his caravan door and assessed the lay of the land, he surveyed his surroundings and his attention was drawn to the solitary parked car approximately two-hundred metres away. The car was static, its engine and lights were off, and he thought he could make out two figures but was not entirely sure.

Peter's attention was grabbed by the activity in and around the caravan, a female figure emerged from the caravan and followed the man down the makeshift steps. The man locked the door, checked it by pulling down the door handle and then he followed the woman to his parked car. Peter's inward panic was allayed somewhat by Marilyn's blasé indifference, *"Don't worry David, they're used to it,"* she threw into the conversation to try and counter the discomfort apparent on David's countenance.

The caravan couple's car sparked into life, its engine breaking the still silence of the evening, the headlights came on and the beams cut through the dark. Peter turned his face away from the approaching vehicle, even after it had passed and disappeared in the distant night. He was unsure, unnerved and was in two minds whether or not to proceed.

It seemed that Peter was externally driven to reoffend in the same geographical area, like a dysfunctional homing pigeon, like a moth drawn to a flame; the site of his latest attack was only two hundred metres (as the crow flies (a murder of crows)) from the scene of his first murder that of Wilomena 'Wilma' McCann and the Prince Philip Playing Fields that witnessed this atrocity. Sutcliffe's one-man killing wave, which the forces of law and order seemed incapable to halt, had stuttered once again but had it stopped, only time would tell.

"Don't forget the money". Marilyn reminded.

"OK, I'll pay you when wiv done," he replied, thinking of his mistake in Manchester, thinking you'll pay not me. YOU WILL PAY WITH YOUR LIFE, YOU WILL PAY WITH YOUR BLOOD. Hatred boiled up within, it was all he could do to contain himself. His mission, clean the scum off the streets working in partnership with God.

Marilyn began to unbuckle her shoes in the front passenger seat, preparing to honour their verbal contract and allow him to access her wares. Peter stopped her.

"We can do it in't back o't car," Peter suggested. Marilyn submissively agreed by her actions, opening the passenger side door and exiting the car, she tried to open the rear passenger seat door as requested but found it was locked.

"David, it's locked".

"Hold on I'll come rarnd an open it," he replied reaching down and taking the almost trademark ball peen hammer he had strategically placed under his seat prior to commencing his journey. Peter held it in his right hand, he climbed out of the car and walked around the front of it to get to the nearside rear door at which Marilyn was waiting politely. 20:45 hours, Peter positioned directly behind his prey raised his left arm and swiftly swung it down, however his brown Doctor Martin boots slipped on the mud and the impetus of the intended blow dissipated the impact of the hammer on the crown of Marilyn's skull, causing Marilyn to scream and raise her arms to cover her head a biological reflex action of self-defence. Normally the prey would have been completely incapacitated but the mud had impacted on two lives for eternity. The scream caused a dog to stir, its barking a backdrop to the noises made by the combating couple. The dog belonged to Mr Hayward who lived at Scott Hall (Farm) or latterly (Cottage) as sometimes referred to, LS7 2HR, this once proud building it's brown hand-made bricks in random and Flemish bonds, slightly obscured by the diminishing trees from Scott Hall Wood, set back some twenty metres from the crime scene. He thought it prudent to note the time and have a quick check outside to see what, if anything had spooked his dog, his brief reconnaissance along with his hounds interruption could have saved Marilyn's life.

Peter recoiled, re-sprung his hammer arm and brought it down on the same target again, Marilyn's hands deflected some of the force from the blow, but not enough as she fell her arms flailed and grasped at Peter's body to break her fall.

"Dirty prostitute bitch!" he grunted. Peter continued with his onslaught until an unconscious Marilyn offered no resistance. In total he brought the hammer down on her defenceless frame eight times. His attention was then caught by a couple some thirty-five

metres away. Peter did not want to test his luck further and beat a hasty retreat, he left Marilyn unconscious in the mud, he returned to his car hurriedly slammed the door, replaced his hammer under the driver's seat and fled the scene causing the back wheels to spin on the muddy surface as he reversed away from the crime scene. He turned right and drove onto Buslingthorpe Lane, then left onto Meanwood Road, down Meanwood Road and onto Clay Pit Lane, Armley Road, the ring road and then back to Bradford and home to Heaton. When he got back to Garden Lane, Peter had to clean up, not the blood from Marilyn body, but the mud from the scene of his latest escapade.

Marilyn's body went into survival mode and collapsed to the muddy floor, a crumpled heap of a body haemorrhaging its life-force. She spluttered back into the conscious world and clambered to her feet, her instinct to survive spurred her on as she scrambled towards the sodium yellow light of the street lights in search of a red phone box, in search of help. She emerged from the darkness and stumbled onto the tarmac of Buslingthorpe Lane.

A young couple saw the blood covered zombie like figure of Marilyn emerge from the gloom of the night.

"Jesus Christ!" said the shocked boyfriend and placed his arm around the distraught woman's shoulder; she looked in danger of collapsing. The girl aided and comforted Marilyn as best as she could whilst the young lad ran to find a phone box to request an ambulance post haste. He rang the emergency services from a telephone box located at the junction where Buslingthorpe Lane meets Meanwood Road, just outside the Primrose public house 280 Meanwood Road, Leeds LS7 2HZ. The commotion on the subdued and secluded street grabbed the attention of Gloria the prostitute that Marilyn and Peter had spoken about in the car journey as a mutual friend appeared.

"What's happened love". came the concerned reaction from Marilyn's work colleague. Marilyn was propped up, supported and comforted until the emergency services arrived, she was rushed to Leeds General Infirmary where surgeons performed an emergency life-saving operation. Fifty-six stiches were used to stitch her wounds, however the wounds went much deeper and the harm inflicted by the Yorkshire Rippers hand had shattered her life. If Marilyn was in a dark place before he struck, her life post attack spiralled into a desperate, dreadful existence of drudgery, fear and self-loathing. Marilyn discharged herself from hospital on Saturday the 24th of December 1977CE. In fear of a further attack, for the man who attempted to murder her, might return to finish the job. She fled to a friend's home firstly in High Wycombe and then she moved to Birmingham before eventually returning to Leeds.

Fourteen/Seven
Leeds, Wednesday 14th December 1977 CE. (20:30 hours) Man Interrupted. The

voice took control, dirty prostitute bitch. His body forced into action, his actions now a force of nature. The nature of the beast inside, the deed attempted but not executed to its conclusion. An outpouring of rage emphasised by the loathing words of the perpetrator, better out than in. *"Dirty prostitute bitch"*. Yorkshire's very own Jason King, not a Geordie man, he's a Yorkshire man. Or was that a Liverpudlian, a scouser, who could be sure?

Marilyn created a photo–fit and gave a description of her assailant, he was white, aged about 30, with a stocky build, about 5' 6" to 5' 8" tall, with brown eyes, thick eye brows, dark suntanned appearance, with dark wavy hair, and beard and a moustache like Jason King, the secret agent hero of a popular TV series and spoke 'softly' in what she mistakenly believed to be a Liverpool accent. The photo fit was very similar to the one described by a fourteen-year-old girl called Tracey Brown from Silsden nearly two and a half years previously.

She also described that her attacker drove a dark coloured saloon, with four doors and two rear view mirrors. This was supported by Mr Pearson from the caravan on Scott Hall Street. Marilyn after some deliberation and collusion with police from the stolen vehicle 'squad' and numerous test 'sittings' decided that the vehicle her attacker drove was a Morris Oxford. The interior of the assailant's car had pristine clean, almost sterile dark coloured upholstery. There was a box on the window ledge, central to the windscreen, with T. R. I. written on it.

The full locked tyre prints resurrected the tyre enquiry and linked the attack with the murder of Irene Richardson (Leeds) and Jean Jordan (Manchester), three tyre tracks in the Sheepscar mud were very similar to tracks found at these murders. India Auto way cross ply, Avon Super tyre and an ESSO 110.

Peter just dropped back into his normal routine. Oblivious to the possibility of capture, aware only that God was in charge of his destiny.

Chapter 17
Yvonne

Saturday the 21st of January1978CE a cold and crisp day disappeared into a cold and crisp evening, Yvonne Ann Pearson aged twenty-one years old, was five foot five inches tall and had a slim build. She was born in Leeds, she moved the short distance to Bradford in 1974CE aged eighteen, where she lived with Roy Saunders her Afro Caribbean boyfriend and common law husband in a back to back terraced house on Woodbury Road, Heaton, BD8. It was around this time that she turned to prostitution to supplement her income.

Soon to become a regular figure in the haunts, pubs, clubs and dens of iniquity that constituted the red-light district of Bradford and more specifically Manningham. On occasions Yvonne would branch out and take flight, chasing that all elusive big deal in the big city, she wanted to break into the big time, break the 'Arab Market'. Yvonne attempted to become a 'career prostitute,' well known on the national circuit. She travelled the country visiting prostitute hot spots and plied her trade, after one such visit south she returned from London bragging that she'd cracked the 'Arab Market'. The Shepherd Market neighborhood, the Hilton, Park Lane, Dorchester and Sheraton hotels of London. Mayfair, Marble Arch, Edgeware Road, Bayswater Road, Knightsbridge, Kensington and Soho. Not the sordid seedy street sex working environment, but the up market, high end, good money, good times, the same but not the same. Somehow acceptable on the moral compass of society. The woman selling herself to feed and shelter her kids a pariah, an outcast, undesirable, a reject, a social reject, a half person.

However the double standards of society applaud the entrepreneurial high-class hooker, the unequivocal good time girl, a figure seemingly to be aspired to. Yvonne was obsessed with breaking what she termed the Arab Market and boasted to her northern friends of her exploits. Her sex-exploits the super oil-rich, Saudi sheiks, middle east money without the religious excess, just triple X sex. Although Yvonne had the looks she didn't have the accent, the upper-class airs and graces. Unrefined, unlike the Saudi oil, her plain Yorkshire accent didn't fit into these circles, like a fish out of water. A working-class northern lass unable to compete against the high-class hookers who owned the West End and the elusive 'Arab Market'. This failing was not lost on Yvonne and was possibly the reason she kept returning to Bradford, that and her beloved children, who she idolised. Her northern roots, her Achilles heel, that would ultimately seal her fate.

Echoes of duality the mad, bad and dangerous to know aristocrat allowed to indulge his inadequacies deemed a mere eccentricity. The young unmarried mother who he abused, gets carted off to Bedlam, the dark secret of the Lord of the Manor, hidden away under lock and key, undermined and so it continues. She had two daughters, Lorraine who was two years old and Collette who was five months old. Yvonne was streetwise, stylish, fashionable and fully aware of the dangers that her work entailed. She had often been seen out drinking with Patricia 'Tina' Atkinson, the Yorkshire Rippers ninth victim and fourth murder.

During the build up to the fateful evening, Roy was away in Jamaica visiting family and friends, to console himself on his failed relationship. Whilst Yvonne was worried, concerned about her upcoming court appearance and what would happen to her children if she was incarcerated. She'd taken to drinking to excess as her relationship floundered. Roy and Yvonne had decided to pull the plug on their relationship just before Christmas 1977CE. Yvonne was about to accrue a hat trick of court appearances for soliciting, an acrimonious achievement she never managed to fulfil. She had been arrested in the Bradford red-light district approximately two months previously and was now on police bail. She had a date with justice booked into her diary for Thursday the 27th of January 1978CE, a date she would never keep. Conditions of her police bail, which she openly flaunted were a 19:00 hours to 7:00 hours daily curfew. No stranger to the penal system Yvonne had done time before, it was an occupational hazard, she had recently preparing a worst case scenario plan of action, just in case the day went against her, who would look after the kids. There was a very real possibility that Yvonne would receive the punishment of a three-month jail sentence. This was all time wasted on worry, for Yvonne had a date with fate.

16:00 hours Yvonne set off into Bradford on the premise, or with the intention of visiting her mother in Leeds. She told the babysitter her friend's sixteen-year-old daughter that she was off to Leeds to borrow some money from her mother. However this may have been a plausible excuse or alibi to hide her illicit dealings in street sex working. An elaborate falsehood possibly to protect her children, or even her reputation.

However Yvonne was quite open and blasé about her profession, she never did visit her mother, although she did go into Bradford where she did some shopping. First she walked around the clothes shops, a pastime she loved, assessing the fashions and trends, comparing the prices. Eventually her 'window shopping' done, she headed back up town, up to Westgate, where she visited Morrison's Supermarket, John Street Market, Westgate, Bradford, BD1. She did some grocery shopping, then decided to head home, a walk of just over a mile, up White Abbey Road, right onto Heaton Road, then right onto Woodbury Road. She arrived home circa 18:00 hours and asked the babysitter if she'd stay later, so she could go out. All the window shopping had got her into the weekend mood.

She prepared herself for an evening out, she dressed herself in a black polo-neck jumper, black trousers, a green and black striped woollen jacket, black shoes and a small black underarm handbag a type of urban camouflage blending in with the darkness of the evenings surroundings. Yvonne then walked the short distance from Woodbury Road, to Lumb Lane, she walked onto Bury Place into Lily Street, then onto Church Street and then onto the Lane, she traversed almost the full length of it, getting a feel for the evening, putting herself on display, seeing if there was any interest. She went to the Flying Dutchman, (31 Lumb Lane) to gain some Dutch courage, the reggae drum beat a backdrop to the smoke filled bar rooms: she played pool with an eye on any opportunity for business, sipping her pineapple juice - making it last and enjoying the ambience of a Saturday evening in Bradford. 20:45 hours Yvonne left the warmth of the pub and stepped out into the cold dark unwelcoming Bradford night in the hope of making some quick money. She strolled up Lumb Lane again always on the lookout for a punter, but again unsuccessful. The smell of ganja and curried goat, rice, black eyed peas and sweet Jamaican dumplings permeated from The YOUNG LION café and into the night air. She called into The Perseverance Public House (161 Lumb Lane) and ordered a drink. She sat at the bar considering the possibilities, it had been a slow night but surely there would be an upturn in her fortunes. Yvonne became a little maudlin at her current plight the upcoming court case, her growing debt. She spoke to the landlady Audrey.

"If yer numbers up, it's up. It'll be just my luck to get knocked on the head," She joked crying to put on a brave face.

"I reckon you've gotta better chance on the street. If a bloke gets you indoors, you're a goner look at Tina (Atkinson) and what about Jane (McIntosh)".

The ghosts of Jane and Tina haunted her working hours, there but for the grace of God go I. Everybody knew about Tina but Jane McIntosh's demise was not so well known on the harsh Bradford streets. Yvonne was ultra-aware of the circumstances of Jane's passing. Jane originated from the small North Yorkshire town, tagged 'The Gateway to the Dales' about twenty miles north west and like Yvonne had tried her luck in the small but lucrative prostitution industry located in the swanky hotels and streets of London. Jane unlike Yvonne was more adept at the social niceties required in servicing the clientele at this level, could adopt the social airs and graces required to flourish, unlike Yvonne who struggled in this important department. Jane lived well off the fruits of her immoral earnings, setting up a nicely furnished property in Southampton some sixty miles south west from the hustle and bustle of the Capital. However Jane's luck was soon to run out one evening in a hotel bedroom on Bayswater Road, she was murdered. These ghosts came to the fore when Yvonne went out to whore herself on the streets. For streets it was, Yvonne would no longer work out of a property, she felt that if you were attacked that at least out in the open there was a chance of survival or escape. A chance that was greatly diminished behind the closed doors of a flat, hotel room or house.

Yvonne finished her drink at approximately 21:30 hours.

"Do you fancy another," asked Audrey.

"No tar, am off to earn some money," she joked. She said her goodbyes picked up her big black strapless handbag by the handles. Inside the long-bladed scissors jostled with the

loose ganja and cosmetics, then disappeared into the cold night air. She sauntered up Lumb Lane towards Southfield Square and destiny.

Peter spent the afternoon and early evening with Mick, helping his mother Kathleen and Father John prepare to move to a new house from Cornwall Road to 8 Rutland House. Peter drove his brother Mick and father John to the far south east of Bradford in an unsuccessful attempt to hire a van, they arrived too late and the company had closed for the weekend; typical of Peter always late always last minute, he'd be late for his own funeral. The trio had to revise their plans, eventually they decided that Keighley was a viable option and in a last gasp effort arrived at Budget rent a van Station Garage on East Parade at 16:30 hours and procured a vehicle for the remainder of the weekend. A plan was hatched. Peter took the wheel of the hire van, due to his professional expertise, whilst Mick and John drove Peter's car back to Cornwall Road. The group returned to Bingley arriving circa 17:00 hours. The group then moved the furniture and belongings accrued in the family home over the previous eighteen years, lifted the carpets and rolled them up, placed them in the hire vehicle and transferred them to 8 Rutland House, Mornington Street, Bingley, BD16. A 1968CE built two bedroomed maisonette owned by the council, closer to Bingley town centre, easier access for Kathleen (Peter's mother) who had increasingly struggled with the hills that led to Cornwall Road due to her worsening angina. The trio then cut and laid the carpets in preparation for tomorrows move. 20:30 hours Mick and John found this thirsty work and invited Peter to join them for a well-earned pint or two at The Fisherman's pub, Wagon Lane, Bingley, BD16. A seemingly rural backwater on the margins of the small town of Bingley. Peter duly drove the hire van up to Cornwall Road, leaving the van there ready for the morning. The trio then decanted into Peter's car, along with the key for the hire van that was kept safely in Peter's pocket, much to Mick's disdain. He then drove the short distance and dropped off the duo but declined to join them, they assumed he had to be home to spend an evening with Sonia.

Peter didn't want a drink, but wasn't quite ready to go home, he decided to have a drive down Lumb Lane and around Manningham to see if there was anything happening. Left at the end of Wagon Lane onto Bradford Road, over the River Aire surrounded by middle class housing with their rolling gardens, past the junction with Cottingley New Road, another area with strong ties for Sutcliffe. He continued to drive past the gothic grandeur of the Bankfield Hotel to his left, on his right the playing field of Nab Wood Grammar School the road remains the same however the name changes for a brief duration to Bingley Road. Upper middle class Nab Wood, the tree lined roads and the woodland to the left that leads to Nab Wood Cemetery lower down in the valley. Up until he reached the notorious Saltaire roundabout, Peter drove straight on at the roundabout, The Rosse pub to his right, where Bingley Road, once again returned to Bradford Road, through the high street with various shops that formed Saltaire/Shipley high street. And on into the suburban semi-detached houses on the outskirts of Saltaire and Shipley, past the Ring 'O' Bells pub to his left. The semi-detached houses disappear replaced by rows of terraced houses, the Prince's Hall cinema or Studio 1234 cinema on the left that soon make way for the Branch pub. Row upon row of terraced houses to the right sloping sharply down the valley, on the right larger terraced houses bordering the road and disappearing up the hillside. Bradford Road becomes Keighley Road on into Frizinghall. However he didn't turn right up Emm Lane, which would have taken him home, he drove on past the castellated gatehouse, the ornate arch with its black iron framed gate supported by octagonal turrets then the smaller arches for pedestrian access. This Yorkshire stone gateway was known as the Norman Arch. The raised lush green landscape of Lister Park bordered by trees to his right, hidden in the shadows of the evening. To the left the grounds of Bradford Grammar School, further along the way, the lights of the Cartwright Hotel to his left heading towards the city centre to deprivation, a multicultural oasis in the heart of Yorkshire. To his right the junction with Oak Lane, its wide expanses empty in the cold night air. Onto Manningham Lane his eyes half on the road half on the pavements, checking the shadows, old habits die hard, but prostitutes die harder in this part of town. The Bell Vue Hotel to his right, houses are interspersed with shops, exotic, erotic names adorn their fascia's and shop fronts. Ripper country! But Peter wasn't the Yorkshire Ripper, he was Peter the mild-mannered truck driver. The YMCA building and The Royal Standard on his right, Tiffany's nightclub on the left, the icy winter weather meant the revellers, prostitutes, perverts and pimps were at a premium. Austerity, decline and degradation, watchwords for a city stuck in the doldrums, a moribund mass of misery, despair, dejection and growing despondency. Peter turned right into Drewton Street, he decided he'd check out Lumb Lane before he went home, a sharp right onto Infirmary Street then onto Lumb Lane. Manna from heaven, Peter was driving up Lumb Lane, the epicentre of Bradford's red-light district. Lumb Lane and prostitution were synonymous with one another, they went hand in hand. Into the abyss of the lost world of lost souls that was Bradfords sin city.

Peter in his red Ford Corsair was driving along when a fawn Mark II Cortina car reversed from Southfield Square, a side street into the path of Peter's car. Peter took evasive action to avoid an accident. At the exact same time Yvonne appeared around the corner as if from nowhere. The screech of his brakes emphasised the evasive action taken by the professional driver, Peter remained confident in his driving ability and his ability in fulfilling his mission aided and abetted by God. Yvonne tapped on the front passenger side door window and opened the front door of the car uninvited.
"Are you looking for business?" Yvonne asked abruptly.
"Where did you spring from?" A startled Peter questioned.
"It's just good timing, or you could put it down to fate". Peter took this as the green light for go from God. A direct signal from God.
"How much?"
"It's a fiver".
"Alreight, but where?"
"I know a place".

No instructions from God, no message. Just a directness, her words, how everything fell into place. It was arranged by God. He turned the car around using Southfield Square to reverse into and turn around, they then drove down Lumb Lane, past the iconic Drummonds Mill on their left hand side, then a right hand turn onto Greenchurch Street down onto White Abbey Road, a right hand turn up White Abbey Road and then a left turn onto Arthington Street just before White Abbey Road becomes Whetley Hill. Onto Arthington Street just behind Silvio's Bakery and then onto the end of the street, where the road peters out into non-existence, soon Peter would make Yvonne non-existent. Peter slowed up his car at the end of the road, close to the waste ground, he performed a pinpoint three-point turn, then reversed back to the edge of the road.
"How much did we say?"
"*It depends on how much you can afford?*" She laughed, employing her best sales tactics. "*A good time a fiver, more than a good time, a tenner*".
"Not ten pound".
"Shall we get in the back?"

Put there by God and therefore must be killed from alfresco to ad-lib, this was another scenario to add to his growing arsenal. There was no direct message that instigated this attack, Yvonne just stumbled across his path. Peter was now primed to kill at any given opportunity

Yvonne and Peter then got out of the car, almost simultaneously, Peter carefully and inconspicuously picked up the lump hammer - he'd hidden there many days earlier, from underneath his driving seat. Yvonne walked to the passenger side back door, unfastening her black flared trousers and tried the door handle, but the door was locked. Peter had walked around the front of the car and witnessed Yvonne's failed attempt to open the Corsair passenger side back door, he held the lump hammer in his left hand, tightly into his body, using his leg to obscure it from view. In reaction to Yvonne's movement he opened the nearside/passenger front door and leant into the interior reaching with his outstretched right arm and he flicked the rear door catch open.

Yvonne reacted to the click and went to open the passenger side back door again. As Yvonne did this, Peter hit her twice on the back of the head, her skull imploded and she fell onto the car door then dropped backwards to the floor groaning raucously. Weighing eight stone and standing at a height of five foot five inches Yvonne was no physical match for her attacker. Just the way he liked it. Peter hit Yvonne with the lump hammer, (a veritable heavy weight in the hammer, hand tool range). It incapacitated her immediately, he then grabbed the collar of her black turtle/polo neck sweater and dragged her further into the darkness of the wasteland, into the night away from possible praying eyes, her back hauled over the uneven hinterland into the abyss, the ground tugged at her pants and slowly pulled them down further, adding to the degradation of her final moments. Some twenty metres away from the road towards a discarded and upturned settee that was the focal point of this dystopian backdrop amid Yvonne's voluble groans. He then attempted to use her ribcage as a trampoline, to silence her noise, to extinguish her life.

At this instant the calm darkness of the night was broken, as another car travelled down Arthington Street, it stopped adjacent to Peter's Corsair. Peter ducked behind the cover of the settee, almost laying on Yvonne's supine form, a gurgling mass of indifference. The silhouettes of a punter and prostitute could be clearly seen inside the car, the blonde woman in the passenger seat and the dark-haired man in the driving seat. For a fleeting second it reminded him of Yvonne and him and their actions only minutes earlier. Concerned at the continuing commotion emanating from Yvonne's throat, Peter took evasive action, he clutched at the settee and the horsehair stuffing presented itself to him, as if by magic. He grabbed Yvonne's nose, nipped together the nostrils forcing her body mechanics to kick in and her mouth to open. He took his opportunity to stuff her mouth with horsehair to quell her noise, pushing it down her throat to shut the bitch up. Peter kneeled above Yvonne, her mouth and throat were jam-packed, stuffed with the horsehair stuffing, he continued to hold Yvonne's nose to stifle the noise, not wanting to attract the attention of the couple in the car. Fatigue told in his fingers and he released his grip on her nostrils, but the noise returned immediately. Peter cursed his luck, the couple were taking forever. He tightened his grip on her nose again and enjoyed the silence. Filled with fear at his vulnerability Peter could only hope and trust in God, he was by now a willing servant and he knew that his fate was in the hands of a higher force. Time seemed to stand still, when would this torture end? It was as if events were unfolding in slow motion, he felt frustration building but was helpless to vent it. He thought back to Manchester, Jean Jordan and the disused allotment that seemed to double as a car park for every prostitute and punter in the Manchester district. Eventually the car and the unsuspecting onlookers, short sighted with grubby deals and pleasure-seeking antics, (they will never realise they attended the drive-in version (Act I of) The Murder of Yvonne Pearson) left the scene. The punter reversed away, turned his vehicle around and returned to the underbelly of the city.

Anger erupted from within Peter's very being, he stood above her body, Yvonne's black trousers were almost around her ankles, and Peter tugged them violently from her form and flung them into the night. Peter could hold in his anger no longer and began to kick the helpless Yvonne to death. Frenzied thrashing, kicking, hacking, attacking her head, body, arms, legs and head until the fury dissipated into calm. Peter undertook his signature tasks; his grotesque fashion show with added Ripperesque chic, lifting Yvonne's bra above her breasts, also pulling her black turtle/polo neck jumper up to reveal her breasts. Peter, a spent force, his body used as a vessel by a higher being felt deflated, peculiar as if distant from the proceedings.

21:00 hours his deed done. Peter slumped to a standstill.
"Sorry love get up you'll be reight". He consoled. *"A don't know what come over me".* He explained. Silence was her only response. He knew that if he'd have acted inappropriately or incorrectly Yvonne would have been perfectly fine, when she didn't move Peter realised it was meant to be. Like a witch hunt in the 'Elizabethan Age', an alternative version to 'Ordeal by Water'. Yvonne was the accused woman, the witch, to be bound and dunked into a river, pond or lake. If the accused was to sink and drown they were proven innocent and their soul would be saved. If they floated they were believed to have been guilty and would therefore face execution. Double jeopardy! Peter questioned his actions, but realised that only God could judge him, when he realised that Yvonne was dead it was obviously meant to be. Yvonne had passed the 'Ordeal by Hammer', she had died at the hand of a missionary and her earthly death had ensured her eternal life and ultimately her saviour.

Peter became emotional, remorseful and began to cry, however he held his composure, he knew that he needed to hide his handy work, buy some time, and ensure the police had only a cold trail to work with. He found a naturally pitted area of the wasteland and manhandled the mortal remains of Yvonne towards it. He thought back to his early grave digging days as he threw stones, rock, rubbish, rubble, soil, sods of grass over her body, completing the improvised mound; an alfresco mausoleum with his 'piece de resistance' of a discarded settee acting as a casket for the cadaver. Once again his do-it-yourself grave surpassed all expectations and unbeknown to Peter at the time his handy work would not come to light for another two months.

Business expenses for appearances is critical, bleach blonde, platinum blonde, peroxide blonde, blonde. Page boy hair cut Altar boy head cut, Purdey, The New Avengers meets Jason King, lumps on the head caused by a lump hammer. New Avengers meets the avenging angel, the Angel of the North.

Oblivious, uncaring, his urges sated but not for long, the depraved creature he had become, the depraved creature he was. He had no qualms or concerns for no one other than himself. His graveyard and mortuary days had proved a good apprenticeship for his macabre murders and the repeat attendances to the scene of his kills and the corpses of his victims to inflict further indignation on the unfortunate fatality.

Peter then drove away from the scene, turning left and driving up Whetley Hill onto Toller Lane, he pulled over to check himself for the tell-tale signs of his activities and to compose himself after the excitement of his attack, however self-doubt and an inability to comprehend his actions left Peter confused. Unplanned, unpremeditated a freestyle killing what had he done? Why had he done it? Chaos controlled his action, confusion, turmoil, turbulence and tumult made him question his action. He composed himself and thought he'd sleep on it, God would come to his aid, and God would assist him. Peter started the engine of his car, then drove down Leylands Lane and took a right turn onto Garden Lane. He pulled into the driveway and returned to domestic bliss as if nothing had happened.

Sunday the 22nd of January 1978CE, Peter reconvened his removal services, calling at his parents' home at Cornwall Road to continue with the move. But first came the most important moment of the day, he presented his mother Kathleen with a birthday present. Kathleen Frances Sutcliffe (nee Coonan) born 22nd January 1919CE; it was her fifty-ninth birthday and also her last. Kathleen's birthday was somewhat overshadowed by the move, which started in earnest circa 09:15 hours. They loaded the hire van and travelled the half mile down Cornwall Road, across the junction with Ferncliffe Road and then into Mornington Road past the Methodist Church on the left then past the flat roofed rectangular three storey block of 9-18 Rutland House, on the left and Mornington Road School on the right, a left turn into Norfolk Street, the Yorkshire stone terraced houses to the right and 1-8 Rutland House on the right. He then pulled up on the left side of Norfolk Street, close to the flagged steps that advanced to the preformed concrete stairs, the fourteen steps leading to the first storey maisonette flat. The party exited the vehicle where they were greeted by various members of the Sutcliffe clan to help set up their new family home. The first load unloaded, the trio decided it was time for a liquid lunch, they had worked up a thirst and decided to visit the pub, they drove back up to Cornwall Road, past the soon to be ex-Sutcliffe family home, took a right turn down Primrose Bank and a right turn onto Primrose Lane over the narrow humped back canal bridge to The Fisherman's Friend. A couple of pints later the trio returned to their work suitably refreshed calling back to Cornwall Road, where the hire van was reloaded with the last of the Sutcliffe's belongings and then transported to their new abode. Peter showed no signs of his antics of yesterday, the Yorkshire Ripper had been vanquished, but for how long?

Monday the 23rd of January 1978CE, Yvonne Pearson of Heaton was reported missing to the Bradford police force, the verdict was out as to whether Yvonne had been the victim of a foul deed, of course the West Yorkshire police force were in the middle of tracking down an homicidal murderer with a penchant for prostitutes, and realised that Yvonne would be a prime candidate for a victim. However there was also a school of thought that Yvonne could have made herself scarce, decided to lie low, to avoid her oncoming court case and a possible trip to prison. The police pursued both schools of thought conducting cursory searches of dilapidated buildings, run-down industrial areas and abandoned wastelands. They also made tentative explorations into her possible location, but all investigations proved fruitless. There were alleged sightings of Yvonne in London and also Wolverhampton and this made the police more inclined to believe she had 'done a runner'. Although friends and neighbours discounted these claims and were concerned that Yvonne had not taken anything with her, no clothes, no bank book, no cheque book and no family allowance book. But more importantly they rightly felt that she would not abandon her children.

Saturday the 28th of January 1978CE, saw Detective Inspector John O'Sullivan of the Bradford police Criminal Investigations Department (CID) address the press and release a statement to the media in relation to Yvonne's disappearance.
"We are concerned for the whereabouts of this girl. We have to have an open mind about the Ripper".

Peter regularly visited Monica Flaherty, a thirty eight year old street worker on Lumb Lane who Peter had got into the habit of patronising, she was a little more expensive than the other girls, but he thought she was well worth the investment. Tuesday the 21st February 1978CE was one particular occasion when Peter procured the services of Monica, this was a dangerous liaison for all parties concerned, a little more dangerous than Monica realised at the time. The pair sat in Peter's car on the northern extremity of Lumb Lane, close by The Queens Hotel (195 Lumb Lane) both parties were relaxed. Monica was happy to be inside, out of the cold and the dark, in the relative comfort it offered from the elements. Peter spoke to Monica.
"Be careful love, with him about," he warned. *"Is that friend of yours the Yvonne who got killed,"* he enquired. Monica looked puzzled, she felt unnerved and sensed something very strange about her punter.
"Nobody knows if she's been killed, she's just missing. How do you know she's dead?"
"Well naturally she will have been". He stuttered and became agitated. *"She's been missing for ages and papers are asking if she's a victim".* His ire raised, his veneer of 'respectability' broken.
"Now get out!" He shouted at Monica and manhandled her out of his car. And he drove off at speed southwards down 'The Lane', he took the sweeping corner at speed attracting the attention of two plain clothed police officers parked in Green Lane.

He continued driving his mind troubled, he retraced his steps reminiscing about his debased antics a month ago, and he drove to Arthington Street and parked up. Through the darkness he could see the settee, where he knew she lay. He picked up the Daily Mirror and began to read it. It carried an article about the Yorkshire Ripper and the murder of Helen Rytka in Huddersfield. His warped brain began to wander, voices filled his head. He thought of Jean Jordan in the Manchester allotments, he thought of his time as a gravedigger, working in the mortuary for extra money and, the enjoyment. He felt compelled to revisit his victim. Checking the coast was clear, he pulled the settee back and carefully placed the paper under her arm. That would give them something to talk about he thought, as he replaced the sofa to obscure his handy work. The public-spirited Peter had an eye for publicity and knew that any press was good press, his actions ensured media coverage and raised the profile of his moral crusade, his mission against prostitution. This also fed into the fear factor and fueled the fear of attack and exaggerated his actions far beyond the districts he inhabited.

12:00 hours, Easter Sunday the 26th of March 1978CE a pale naked arm hangs loosely, lies motionless, sticking out from the discarded and overturned settee. The lifeless limb jutting awkwardly ill at ease, the onlooker took a closer more involved inspection, his first cursory glance suggested the usual and understandable tailors dummy, but this was Bradford, Ripper central, things weren't normal they were mental. The unfortunate gentleman walked towards the horror intrigued at its existence, as he approached he was beaten back by the stench of rotting flesh, by the acrid stench of death, he retched at the wretched scene that enveloped his gaze. Then panicking, he hurriedly retreated to the reality of an uncultured uncivilised Bradford, there was to be no Resurrection Sunday, no Passion of Christ, no Easter Bunny, no egg hunts, just murder hunts. He found a phone in the nearby Lindfield Auto (Bradford) Limited garage, that bordered the wasteland and rang the police.

A copy of the Daily Mirror dated Tuesday the 21st of February 1978CE was found with Yvonne's body, it was tucked under her arm within the damp and soiled off white newsprint paper was a lurid headline relating to the Huddersfield murder of Helen Rytka at the hands of the Yorkshire Ripper. The headline grabbing twin (Helen) the successor who was also the precursor, curse the Yorkshire Ripper, wish him dead, wish him caught how many more must endure this evil onslaught. Murder, mystery and suspense!

Her body had been missing for sixty-four days, from 21:30 hours on Saturday the 21st of January 1978CE through until 12:00 hours on Sunday the 26th of March 1978CE. Close to the morning and evening commuter run into Bradford city Centre, close to the children who played daily on the wasteland, close to the comings and goings of a city at work and play, hidden clearly and cruelly within plain sight.

The police were concerned that they had a copycat killer on their hands, the modus operandi linked it to the murder of Carol Wilkinson, a Ravenscliffe teenager who was bludgeoned to death by a fifty-six pound coping stone hammer on Monday the 10th of October 1977CE. However there was also the tell-tale staging/posing of the body, a Ripper trademark, her breasts were exposed, although there was no knife work.

The police used what they could find of Yvonne's finger prints and the remnants of her teeth, through the skills of the Bradford Finger Print Bureau and Yvonne's dental records, along with a ring on her finger they positively identified the corpse as that of the late Yvonne Anne Pearson. Yvonne's cream and gold diary that also acted as an address book, boasted the names of many a client and also underlined the contacts and networks in relation to the areas where she plied her trade. However offered no clues to her assailant.

Donna Dent was another lost soul that he saved, Donna was a twenty-three-year-old prostitute and friend of Yvonne, on occasion's she had baby sat for Yvonne. Donna appeared before Bradford Magistrates Court (circa April 1978CE) shortly after Yvonne's body had eventually been found, charged with two counts of soliciting. Donna's solicitor told the three magistrates that Donna had decided to turn her back on the vice world since her friend Yvonne Pearson had been murdered, the magistrates responded leniently to her plight and handed down a three month suspended sentence.

Peter William Sutcliffe, AKA The Yorkshire Ripper, saved the soul of Donna Dent from eternal damnation. There were similar stories of salvation throughout the north of England, therefore Peter was the saviour of a thousand souls. But at what impact, how many families would decline into the poverty trap that was to become a way of life to a new underclass of individuals, born at the wrong time, in the wrong place. The 1970CE where the First World, becomes the Third World in the change of a postcode. But worse was to come.

Fifteen/Eight
Bradford, Saturday 21st January 1978 CE. (21:30 hours) *When opportunity knocks Peter could not look a gift horse in the mouth, "It was a complete surprise to me because I wasn't looking for a prostitute at all". Fatal fate, "Unfortunately for her, I thought this was a direct signal". Peter was sorry for hitting her, he apologised telling her to get up and everything would be alright. Unlucky, untoward, unfortunate, ill-fated, ill-timed and inopportune, however it was meant to be.* Yvonne Pearson born Thursday the 2nd of February 1956CE died Saturday 21st January 1978CE, twenty-one years old.

Chapter 18
Elena (Helen)

Bernardina De Mattia married Zygmunt Rytka in Leeds in 1951CE, the couple had a baby girl called Helena in 1953, but unfortunately she died in infancy. In 1957 CE the couple had the first of three sets of twins Alexander and Helen again both passed away. Elena and Rita Rytka were twin sisters, both were born on the 3rd of March 1959CE. It came to pass that Elena didn't like her birth name and preferred to be called Helen. Bernadine gave birth to her third and final twins in 1960CE, Antonio and Angela. The twins attended St. Charles Roman Catholic School in St. Mary's Street in Burmantofts, Leeds. Unfortunately Zygmunt and Bernardina's marriage floundered and the children were taken into care in the late1960's CE as Bernardina was unable to cope with her offspring. The Rytka children were taken into the care of Leeds Diocesan Rescue Society. Throughout this period Helen and Rita had stayed together, an amazing feat in social care for the time. The Rytka twins had spent time in both local council care and also Catholic care homes.

May 1974CE a poem by the Rytka twins appears in the letter page of the Yorkshire Post, the twins post pubescent teenage angst adolescent poetry published in the Yorkshire Post. If we were to be fostered out together it would be like winning £1.000.00 on the football pools, but money is not involved LOVE is. The poem was entitled *'Lonely and Unloved'*. *Loneliness, care, there, despair, prayer, spare, day, pray, way. Yet I know I shall die, as my years drag by, Oh why was it me Lord? Why?"* Were all key words in the poem.

The poem resulted in Rita and Helen being adopted by a couple in Dewsbury. The girls left Saint Theresa's Roman Catholic children's' home for girls, which was situated south of Knaresborough in a building called Queensmead although it was also called Kingsmead. It is sited on Thistle Hill, near Calcutt for their new home and remained living with their new foster parents in their Dewsbury home.

The twins new foster parents were reasonably affluent civil servants and also good Catholics, in fact they had been cherry picked and earmarked by the local diocese to fulfil the foster role. Helen and Rita lived in their Dewsbury home for a further two years until the autumn of 1976CE when they moved out of their foster home to reconvene a Rytka family environment with their younger brother and sister, Antonio and Angela, who were also twins, in their Laisterdyke flat after a twelve year hiatus. Rita had won a scholarship to Batley Art School, whilst Helen took a job as a sweet packer at Bysel Limited, Batley Road, Heckmondwike, WF16.

Eventually Rita became depressed and abandoned her studies. Rita the former art school student moved to Huddersfield in November 1977CE disappearing from her family in Laisterdyke and not leaving a forwarding address. Helen visited her mother Bernardina in her Victoria Terrace home, Hyde Park and Woodhouse, Leeds, (LS3 1BX); over the Christmas holiday period and although her mother had not seen Rita, the pair eventually tracked her down to Hillhouse, Huddersfield.

In early January 1978CE Helen moved to Huddersfield to resume the terrible twosome. Friday the 13th of January 1978CE Helen left Bysel Limited for the last time. She collected her twenty-pound weekly wage and other monies that were due to her and said her fond farewells, never to return to Heckmondwike again. These out of the blue actions were a shock to her work colleagues who wished her well in her new life.

The twins priorities were not in line with the moral consensus, Helen had attempted to assign herself to the protestant work ethic, (or should that be Catholic) and worked for forty-hours a week for twenty pound and had decided that this was not the life for her. Fashion is a fickle mistress. Fashion, fun and frivolity were to be the order of the day. Pop stardom the aspiration, however it didn't take a genius mathematician to conclude that selling sex was easier money and a better hourly rate than the factory, or was it? If business was brisk she could earn the weekly amount she'd earned in the factory in an hour and a half. This did not include travelling time and expenses. Therefore prostitution was a no brainer. Although what about the psychological, physiological effects, but when your young you know best. Chasing the great American dream in Huddersfield. Her passion curtailed, priorities wrong, misaligned, her ambition destroyed or misdirected to Endersley in the Hillhouse district of Huddersfield, next stop Hollywood? Next stop Scholemoor Cemetery!

Friday afternoon the 27th of January 1978CE Peter had a delivery to make in an area close to Huddersfield town centre, he saw some women quite openly soliciting on a road close to the Market on Lord Street and Union Street, it was then that he chanced upon Great Northern Street and ultimately the fulcrum of Huddersfield's red-light area. He paid particular attention to two half caste/mixed race girls he saw, ultimately these girls were Rita and Helen Rytka. This chance find was to lead to the untimely passing of an unfortunate prostitute as Peter continued his theological mission, but not today, he had a delivery to make.

The inner compulsion to kill prostitutes, women, and girls had become an uncontrollable craving. Peter made a note in the inbuilt satellite navigation system that was his brain, he would return later at a more appropriate time equipped with the correct tools to enable him to ply his trade and stop them from plying theirs for this was his raison d'etre. Peter was going to despatch the next girl at the first possible opportunity, the (self) righteous lean, mean killing machine with fourteen attacks and seven killings the urges were growing stronger, the messages clearer, it was barely over a week since he'd last killed/saved but the voice needed more and who was he to deny the voice. The visit to Huddersfield was undertaken with a purpose, to kill.

Tuesday the 31st of January 1978CE it was a cold day with bouts of snow contributing to slush puppy conditions underfoot. The twins lived 31, Flat 3 'Enderley' in a once proud stone built Edwardian house, Elmwood Avenue, Huddersfield on Highfield Hill, in a downstairs living room, which was accessed by the shared stone flagged hallway, the twins also shared toilet facilities with the rest of the household. The house overlooked the flyer of the M62 Motorway. The damp squalor was eased slightly by some sparse furnishings, a double bed with a bright blue bedspread, a table, some chairs and a wardrobe. The small gas fire did little to take away the chill from the room.

These free spirits these bohemians from the Bradford borderlands awoke from their slumber in the early afternoon, 13:30 hours approximately. At 14:00 hours they enjoyed an intercontinental breakfast of meat stew, sweet potatoes, sweet dumplings, yam and some black-eyed beans and then struggled to maintain their internal warmth. Later they would enjoy tea and biscuits circa 17:30 hours.

Helen and Rita decided to leave their cold flat, exchanging it for the cold winter night air, at least this way they were moving about and generating heat not just sitting huddling around the lonely gas fire with the off white walls interspersed with black mould supressing their very life force. Better to be out making money than in, spending it. Helen and Rita prepared for their evenings work, dressing against the elements.

The pair left 'Enderley' at 20:30 hours and began to descend the well-worn single dirt track carved into the hillside by the daily steps of the Huddersfield town folk. Snow was settling on the grassland and the well-worn narrow dirt track etched into the steep hillside became more prominent. Like sheep tracks on the moorlands above the town, an evolutionary parallel where sentient creatures through instinct find or create the path of least resistance. A shortcut to survival, from the wilds of the hills, to the relative safety of lowland civilisation. However in Huddersfield on this day there was a lot of parallels, mirror images, carbon-copies, twins. Unfortunately the actions of the Yorkshire Ripper would smash and fracture the lives of his victims, smash and crack the mirror, but when broken this did not result in seven years bad look, it created a lifetime of desperation. The Yorkshire Rippers actions would result in a great deal of reflection, consternation and unrest. For his foray into immortality was a part of his fight against immorality and also to create his own immortality, for after all he was one evil and sick bastard, but sometimes you have to be cruel to be kind. Helen followed Rita down the human sheep track, a veritable lamb to the slaughter.

Fledgling floozies the Rytka twins were new to the sex game having only been working the streets for a few weeks. Rita was the most experienced of the pair but both were young and gullible. They may have thought that they were street wise but they were far from it, even in the relative 'rural' backwater of the town. Huddersfield's red-light area of Hillhouse had taken over from the town centre Venn Street as the venue for women to sell their bodies in the late 1960's CE. The red-light commerce was subsequently to be found in the triangular area formed within the boundaries of Great Northern Street, Hillhouse Lane and Lower Fitzwilliam Street and bordered by the natural boundary of the railway lines, the streets in this area formed the regular pick-up points for punters seeking sex. The area is bordered by rows of terraced houses, the homes of families who had to put up with the unwelcome visitors, their unwelcome attentions and multitude of subsidiary issues.

Occupied houses were few and far between on Great Northern Street itself. Mrs. Ethel Cowan a resident of the street was often disturbed by the noise pollution that came from the illicit sex trade that thrived in her back yard. Mr. and Mrs. Fred and Gwen Smith also lived on the street with their son Paul, they often saw the girls flaunting their wares. Fred was the supervisor at Huddersfield open market on Brook Street just over half a mile to the south of Great Northern Street, he was well aware of the red-light district and the problems it incurred. Gwen and Paul saw Helen & Rita at 21:00 hours, they had assumed their usual positions on the street close by to the public toilets, none of the four people knew that one of them had less than an hour to live. The twins worked Great Northern Street and their patch was either side of the road next to the public conveniences at the junction where Great Northern Street meets Hillhouse Road.

The girls devised and employed a system for their own safety and security, but unfortunately the system was flawed, ultimately it was far from fault free, but it was a system, a safety net, a reassurance that all is well. It enabled the girls to put the Rippers reign of terror to the back of their minds. This false sense of security was supported by the fact that Peter had not yet visited Huddersfield under the guise of The Yorkshire Ripper, his farthest foray south had been to the Boothtown district of Halifax circa six or seven miles away.

The girls would commence work outside the public toilets on Great Northern Street they would then accept customers and simultaneously set off for a sex session and return to the rendezvous point of the public toilets, to repeat the process again and again. The girls allocated each punter a twenty-minute time slot, the command and control management model. A similar tactic was employed across the north of England by the good time girls on the streets, slightly more water tight than the Rytka system, the girl s would work in pairs and at the moment of inception that 'business' was to occur the non-bartering prostitute would turn note taker, writing down the vehicle details and registration number of the punters car. The selected prostitute would then enter the punters car and stall proceedings until the second prostitute had agreed terms and the second girl would act as administrator in return. The sisters system would in theory see the two punters and two sisters simultaneously disappear to perform various sexual favours for various amounts of money, for a twenty minute duration and then return back to the public lavatories at the junction with Great Northern Street and Hillhouse Lane; however this was not the reality of the situation. In theory once proceedings had been completed, the failsafe was no longer required and the car details and registration number were destroyed in-front of the happy/hapless punter, but reality is a pale imitation of theory.

21:10 hours Rita saw Helen climb into the passenger seat of a dark coloured Ford Consul or Granada, this was to be the last time she saw her sister, her twin, her flesh and her blood alive. The punter in question was Joey, he was known in the area, amongst the prostitutes, but not known to Helen.

21:15 hours Rita climbed into the passenger seat of a Datsun and set off into the night to turn a twenty-minute trick and earn a blue five-pound note. (System flawed, abort, abort! But this was a laissez faire business system, free love at a price).

21:20 hours Helen is dropped off on Great Northern Street by a satisfied customer who had been a little quicker than his allotted twenty minutes. Helen ever the free market economist employed her entrepreneurial zeal to obtain a new fare, she wandered south down Great Northern Street to keep warm, she also had half an idea to buy some cigarettes, after all she had time to kill until Rita returned, what harm could it do?

M606, M62, A641, Willow Lane East, Hillhouse Lane, Great Northern Street. However Peter William Sutcliffe had a good idea that somebody was to die, although he was unsure who it would be, he would see what mission God would entrust to him. Peter arrived in Huddersfield and was driving down Great Northern Street when he saw Rita, he pulled his red Ford Corsair over and approached her with a view to 'doing business?'

"Are you doing business?" Peter enquired in his gentle voice.

"Yeah, but you'll have to wait until I've seen a regular, he'll be here any minute now then I'll be able to fit you in," Rita responded aware of the system aware of the risk.

"Alreight maybe later then," Peter said and turned his attention to the road. He continued to drive down the road, trying to supress the urge, trying to locate a suitable candidate, a soul to save, a message to send to the seedy underworld of this gritty northern town. He didn't have far to go and long to wait as he drove around the corner he saw a second girl, a carbon copy of the one he'd just met, young, mixed race, and slim build with a bushy Afro hairstyle. He slowed his car down and propositioned Helen.

"Are you doing business?" Peter once again enquired in his gentle voice. Helen looked hesitant; new to the game, naïve and eager to please she forgot the system. Peter persuaded Helen what harm could a quick trick do, it was money in the bank; she was comforted by his soft voice and mild manner and enticed by the in-car heater.

"Yeah," came Helen's hurried reply has she climbed into the warm sanctuary of his vehicle.

"It'll cost a fiver," Helen negotiated.

"Alreight," Peter confirmed.

"We can go to timber yard and do it there," Helen explained. *"It's just down the hill on your left".* As they rounded the corner Rita came into sight walking down the pavement on the right-hand side towards the public lavatories.

"That's me sister," Helen explained, *"We share a flat".* Peter nodded in acknowledgement, then turned left onto Lower Viaduct Street, he took a sharp right into Garrard's Timber Yard, Great Northern Street, Huddersfield, HD1. Peter parked up in the timber yard the railway embankment forming a dead end, the sides of the street were formed and pronounced by the patch work sheds and garages that formed the timber yard. Rita continued to walk oblivious to Helen's impending danger. Peter then briefly assessed the area taking into account his possible need for a quick exit, he then turned the car engine off and turned to Helen.

21:30 hours and ever one for punctuality Rita returned to the public lavatories. Satisfied punter, guaranteed twenty minutes for five pounds, the deal was exactly what it said on the tin. Rita remained at the public lavatories. Where was Helen? Eventually Rita made the decision that Helen was not going to meet this rendezvous. Kicking her heels and stamping her feet against the bitter chill Rita was angry with Helen. Rita felt unnerved, where was Helen, the punter with the dark hair, dark eyes, beard and moustache had unnerved her slightly. However she was starting to get used to the low life and perverts that came with the job. But still she could sense something was wrong, she became unsettled, uncomfortable. The discomfort made worse by the appalling weather conditions. A punter pulled over in his white sports car, Rita and the man agreed terms, then went off to consummate the agreement, unbeknown to the pair a brown van followed the couple, to the secluded car park adjacent to Huddersfield Town Football Club's Leeds Road stadium. The kinky covert van driver enjoyed watching prostitutes and punters in the throes of action. It takes all sorts!

Peter had hatched a plan, a formula to which he hoped to adhere. Stage one - recommend they use the back seat of the car for sex, because there is more space. Stage two - when the woman turns her back on him in the process of opening the rear car door he strikes her repeatedly to the back of the head with a hammer, incapacitating his victim. Stage three - drag the body further into wasteland and stab, cut, slash and kill them. Stage four - arrange clothing and body as required, (possibly conceal depending on the location) to create appropriate reaction. Stage five - exit the scene of the crime and drive directly to a safe place to clean up if needed. What could possibly go wrong? Peter hid the truth from himself - stage three and a bit - reveal your genitalia and crouch over the body and masturbate, whilst stabbing, cutting and slashing his unfortunate victim.

Helen took the turning off of the engine as her cue to undo her jeans, raising her pelvis off the car seat and peeling the jeans down to free them from the grip of her buttocks and prepare for sex. Peter's body responded to her actions and he became aroused, this was not in his plan of dispatching the sinner at the earliest possible opportunity.
"Hold up love, I need to take pee," he mumbled contritely. The impetuousness of youth had cramped his style, but only for a while, he regained control and was now manipulating the situation to end her youthful life but also eternalise her youthful looks, for Helen's luck was about to run out and the self-proclaimed divinely ordained theological missionary was to save yet another pitiful soul.

Peter got out of the car and was now in the open yard of the timber yard, surrounded by various piles of timber of all shapes and sizes, haphazard out buildings of corrugated sheeting and dilapidated roof tiles and mismatched felt loomed large in the shadows. He used the time wisely to regain his composure, deep breaths, regroup and re-think, 'no plan survives engagement with the enemy'. He returned to the car his mini reconnaissance mission complete he climbed into the car and prepared for stage two and his ultimate mission, to clean the streets of prostitute scum and intimated that the best place for them to get intimate would be the back seat of his car, Helen with half an eye on the clock wanted to close this encounter and return to the sanctuary of her sister and the public toilets a little less than one hundred metres away.

She clambered out of the cars passenger seat and headed towards the rear nearside door. Simultaneously Peter's left hand felt for the handle of the hammer, his fingers tightened around the handle. He too clambered out of the Corsair and strode with purpose around the front of the car. Helen was struggling with the rear door handle, with her back to Peter and unwittingly vulnerable to his trademark tool of incapacitation and unprepared for the oncoming onslaught. Helen finally opened the door and went to climb into the back of the car, so in essence she was partially shielded from Peter. Peter lifted his left arm from the side of his body bringing the hammer away from its half hidden state and creating the shadow of a monster in the half-light emanating from the half hidden street lights, his opportunity engineered, Sutcliffe swung the ball-peen hammer in the general direction of the back of Rytka's head. His eyes must have still been adjusting to the darkness and his aim faltered, the hard face of the hammer - heat treated and forged from high carbon-steel, was more than a match for the skin, flesh and bone it would soon be striking, the blow caught the edge of the top door sill bouncing off the metal with a dull thud and providing Helen with a glancing blow. The force of the initial blow nullified Helen believed that Peter had struck her with the back of his hand; Helen's hand automatically covered her head, she turned to face her assailant and put some distance between her and the confines of the back seat of the car.

"*There's no need for that, you don't even have to pay*". Startled at this turn of events and expecting Helen to scream out aloud at any moment, Peter once again tried to regain his composure, deep breaths, regroup and re-think, 'no plan survives engagement with the enemy'. "*What was it?*" Helen demanded. Peter already raising his left hand for a second bite of the cherry retorted.
"*Just a small sample of one of these!*" Almost grunting the words with the exertion and effort he put into this strike. He repeated his efforts just to make fully certain there were to be no further unpleasant surprises. Unable to respond quickly enough Helen took the full force of the hammer in the crown of her skull and crumpled to the floor, a loud groaning sound emanating from her throat, Peter briefly pondered it was reminiscent of Yvonne and Arthington Street some ten days previous. The continual noise broke him from his thoughts and made him aware that he needed to check if his actions had been witnessed and if he was safe to continue without being rudely interrupted. The premeditated plan well under way saw instinct take control, like a Meerkat sentry in the Kalahari Desert, Peter surveyed his surroundings, and like a guilty schoolboy he quickly assessed any possible danger to calculate his next action. He was horrified at what he saw! Two taxi drivers had front row tickets to the action in the wood yard. Fortunately for Peter they were standing outside their vehicles deep in conversation and oblivious of his attempts to dispatch Helen into oblivion. Their cars were parked up one behind the other about thirty metres away, both facing the wood yard. Their taxi roof signs illuminated, saying they were available for hire with their drivers stood in the cold night air deep in conversation, oblivious to Peter's murderous exploits.

21:40 hours, a man driving home down Great Northern Street caught a glimpse of a shadowy figure skulking in the wood yard; he described him to the police as being about thirty years old, five foot eight inches and wearing dark clothing, although he thought little of this at the time.

Helen had fallen forward away from the rear door and taking his prompt Peter dropped the hammer and duly dropped on top of Helen and placed his hand over her mouth to muffle the noise. At this lower level the pair were obscured from the unwanted view of the taxi drivers. Helen scared half witless and beaten almost senseless tried to struggle and evade her attacker, but he was resilient and too strong. Helen's eyes fluttered in a blind panic she raised her arms trying to protect herself further. Peter pulled off her boots and then her jeans from her legs, he then pulled down her black lace knickers.
"*Keep quiet and you'll be reight,*" Peter lied. Then finding himself in the close proximity of Helen once more and still partially aroused he decided to have intercourse with Helen. His

mission, the divine mission needed him to submerge himself in the role to prevent detection, Peter needed to go native; a covert sleeper cell in the sordid sex sale supermarket that was street prostitution. He was a foot soldier obeying Holy orders as the old adage goes, it's a dirty job but somebody has to do it. Street cleaning means that you sometimes have to get dirty to ensure a thorough clean, this was a situation of that ilk. Unfortunately for both parties they found themselves at the whim of higher powers, they were the lead players in a tragedy that would have to run its course. The thought process employed by Peter was that this was what Helen expected of him and would therefore put her at ease if he obliged, the sex mechanics were a necessary function in the attainment of his mission.

Peter undid the fly on his Levis, he spread Helen's legs and penetrated her. This seemed to focus Helen's attention and stopped her from moaning. Helen's body lay limp below the unwanted attention of her admirer/attacker. Peter continued until he ejaculated and then rising from his work he checked to see if the taxi drivers were still in place, they had gone. Sutcliffe went to retrieve his hammer.

His job was only partly done, he didn't want another failure; another survivor on his curriculum vitae, he fumbled for the hammer and finally found it, meanwhile Helen had mustered up enough strength to struggle to her feet and she made a rush towards the street lights and the open public space of Great Northern Street, the car and timber racks acted as a funnel if she was to be successful in her bid for life, she would have to circumnavigate one Mr Peter William Sutcliffe. This extreme game of 'British Bulldog' had high stakes, stakes of life and death and both parties knew this. He turned to face her at the exact moment she flung herself forward, unsteady and blood soaked she half stumbled half ran towards the entrance but was stopped almost immediately by a hefty hammer jolt to her head. Helen reeled with the blow but Peter gave her one more blow for good measure. She fell to the floor! Peter crouched over her crumpled form, he hauled her, pulling her by the hands in front of the car and further into the wood yard, into the blackness and the obscurity out-of-the-way of the prying eyes of humankind.

As he dragged her into the isolation he stripped off Helen's clothes flinging them over a nearby wall bordering the viaduct which housed the railway line from Liverpool to Hull. Peter saw that Helen was still alive and wanted to draw a curtain down on this evening's performance, he returned to the car and his little hiding place beneath his driver's seat, collecting the concealed weapon a rosewood handled kitchen knife. Helen was dying but Peter decided to help her on her way. He revisited his earlier task and stabbed Helen three times, however he repeatedly used the same entrance wounds therefore he stabbed Helen thirteen times in total, the trajectory of these additional hidden wounds striking the heart, liver and lungs.

He knew he had successfully completed his mission, although he was not yet fulfilled, there was the second twin, this would be a fait accompli, this would be him showing the public and police who was in charge. It would also please God. He briefly checked his appearance, it seemed in order, unruffled, unsoiled, and untouchable. He observed the surrounding area, there were no longer any taxi drivers, no witnesses. A clean conscience, a clean slate on which to write history, HIS story!

21:50 hours Rita returned once more to the Great Northern Street rendezvous point, still no Helen, her concern was almost tangible as she paraded the street close to the toilets. Rita had more street knowledge than Helen, she'd been on the game longer and had working knowledge of the locality and the men who frequented the area. Rita decided enough was enough and headed home, hopefully to find Helen.

22:05 hours, Peter put his car into reverse and drove out of the wood yard, he turned onto Lower Viaduct Street, then left and back up Great Northern Street, past Garrard's timber yard, now his makeshift cemetery and up towards Hillhouse Lane looking for the mixed race prostitute. Slowing down almost to a crawl near the public toilets, the flat roofed unspectacular stone built rectangular building, home and office to prostitutes, pimps, perverts, rent boys, homosexual's; Huddersfield's cottage industry. No sign, a deep sigh emitted from Peter's mouth, not tonight, his spectacle of a double-header murder mystery suspense, an additional angle, the murder of twins. Nothing was immune from his power, his righteous crusade. But fortune favoured Rita, a sixth sense, possibly the psyche of Helen alerting Rita to the danger.

He turned left onto Hillhouse Lane, under the arch of the viaduct, a left turn onto Alder Street, rows of terraced houses disappearing to his right, the wilderness bordered railway embankment and the viaduct domineering the view to the left. He hatched an alternative plan, his circling like a great white shark brought back memories of May 1976CE and Marcella Claxton, however he'd learnt a lot since then. To his left he now saw unhindered easy access to the east side of the railway line, to Helen's body. But he'd have to chance his arm once more, look for Rita, the unconventional meter maid, kerb crawling wasn't an offence in her book, it was a necessary evil. Parking tickets weren't doled out but sexual favours for an exchange of cash. Left onto Northgate, his nerve still holding, as it always had done, left again onto Ray Street, then left and back onto Great Northern Street.

The weather was worsening, girls were getting sparse, and each additional moment he spent in the area risked later identification and desertion of his missionary duties. Unsuccessful on his trawl for Rita, he drove onto Alder Street which ran parallel to the railway line west of Great Northern Street, he exited his car and dissolved into the wasteland of the embankment, viaduct and down the mound through to Garrard's timber yard. The scene of his earlier atrocity. He re-cooped, re-gathered and re-convened his work.

He returned to the lifeless body of Helen. In a frenzy the West Yorkshire whirling dervish began to tug and tear at Helen's clothes, once discarded he threw them into the darkness of the night, towards the steep sidings of the railway line. Always wasteland, always desperation, always God, always Peter. He saw her bare breasts, her naked flesh. He took out the remnants of his anger on Helen, blaming her for his inability to find, attack and kill Rita.

Peter worked to conceal his horror, dragging Helen by the arms to a more secluded resting place. His initial onslaught was to the rear of Garrard's timber yard's foreman Melvin Clelland's office, the corrugated panelled sheets of the hut were stained with an arc of blood that had haemorrhaged from Helen's head. A Huddersfield Jackson Pollock, drip painting. Extreme abstract expressionism. Now where to hide his work, where best to buy him some time. Peter pulled Helen's corpse behind some bushes that bordered the rough shrub land slope that supported the railway tracks. The eighteen-inch access/egress point for Helen's makeshift mausoleum forced him to lift, push and pull Helen into her final hiding place. Difficult to manoeuvre, he used his lorry driving dexterity/expertise and his 'Bullworker' strength to complete his task. Once she was wedged he covered her with a sheet of corrugated asbestos. Out of sight out of mind.

22:20 hours, Peter scrambled back through the viaduct, under the railway and back to Alder Street, although his earlier actions were irreversible, that was the past, that was done compartMENTALised into the missionary work section of his life. Rita may have escaped but Helen certainly had not, there may be time for the twin later, only God knew the answer to that one. Prying eyes, dying eyes, blood and lies, Peter thought he had outstayed his welcome. In theory his audacious plan seemed an excellent and attainable idea, in reality it was not. Peter drove straight home, Sonia was working at the Sherrington House Nursing Home so he drove home and pulled up onto the drive at Garden Lane and went into the kitchen. He found that he had some blood on one of his fawn court shoes. He rinsed it off with a sponge and water in the kitchen sink, he washed the kitchen knife he'd used on Helen and replaced it in the knife block. He checked his Levi jeans and dark blue pullover for blood, there was none. He then made himself a pot of tea and went to bed.

Wednesday the 1st of February 1978 CE and a delivery driver to Gerrard's timber yard found Helen's discarded bloodstained black lace knickers, these were duly hung on a rusty nail in a prominent place on a shed door within the yard, much to the amusement of the general workforce. The mud and blood soiled black lace knickers were the talk of the timber yard but regrettably all too common place, was that a blood-stained patch of mud or was it just their imagination running wild and free in the Kirklees air. For when dark descended and work ended, the low life came out of the woodwork and often into the wood-yard. Homosexuals, heterosexuals, bi-sexual, try-sexual (so named because they will try anything sexual), alcoholics, drug addicts, down and outs would come down to the wood (yard) and practice immorality of the highest order. Tales of the after dark antics were legendary amongst the Garrard's staff.

Rita eventually plucked up the courage to report Helen's disappearance to the police, it was not until 20:00 hours, Thursday the 2nd February 1978CE that she walked down to Huddersfield's Castlegate police station HD1. Rita sheepishly explained that she was concerned as to the whereabouts of her twin sister Helena Maria Rytka. Rita told the desk sergeant that she last saw Helen at 21:10 hours on Tuesday the 31st of January 1978CE on the notorious Great Northern Street. Once he'd heard the location it didn't take the desk sergeant long to establish the real reason the twins were in the red-light area of Huddersfield and Rita quickly cracked and told them the whole sorry story. Normal avenues were pursued, family members contacted Antonio (or Anthony as he preferred) and Angela in their flat at Laisterdyke. Rita and Helen's foster parents in Dewsbury. Bernardina the girl's mother in her Leeds home. All avenues pursued led to dead ends. The desk sergeant notified Detective Chief Inspector John Stainhope. Alarm bells rang, two 'good time girls' missing in action in West Yorkshire, with Yvonne Pearson missing since Monday the 23rd of January 1978CE, was this the work of the Yorkshire Ripper? The Huddersfield police sprang into action, hoping to find the monster, hoping to find spring heeled Jack.

Friday the 3rd of February 1978CE, Melvin Clelland received a telephone call in his Garrard's office, the call was from the Huddersfield police station, asking him for permission to conduct a search of the timber yard. 15:00 hours, two uniformed officers, dog handlers, attended the wood yard, they were from the Dog Support Unit, they brought a police dog with them. The dog was an Alsatian or German shepherd, the handlers had items of Helen's clothing from which they let the dog smell the scent and they then released it to do its job, almost immediately the dog went to the area of the yard in which Helen's corpse was hidden.

"I think this is it," said the police dog handler. Helen's lifeless body was found at 15:10 hours and a new Ripper murder was suspected. The dog handler asked Melvin to guard the grisly find and also secure the integrity of what was left of the crime scene, whilst he went to put the dog back in the van, alert the other officers and radio in his findings. He returned to the crime scene and relieved Melvin, cordoning off the area with police tape and then waited for the assembled hordes of West Yorkshire's finest.

White snow, red blood, brown sludge. Puddles formed on the tarmac, concrete and dirt of the floor. Stacks of timber, planed, rough sawn, crown cut, quarter sawn, board, bead, block board, chamfered, dado, fascia, fibre board, floorboard, tongue and groove, laminate, moulded wood, newel posts, sanded, sap, short grain, skirting boards, shingle, scant, sill, soffit, sash, softwood, hardwood, spandrel, stave, stile, stopper, warped, tanalised, plank, lathes, and strip. A funeral pyre, lack lustre innate devoid of desire. Backyard, back water, discarded off cuts of timber, trolleys up-ended, plastic straps littering the local debris and detritus. A shanty town of spit and sawdust, under the backdrop of the Victorian monolith supported in places and elevated by a mound of wasteland, interspersed by the odd shrub of a tree. A four-foot-high dog ear cut fence separated Garrard's yard from the railway embankment, missing pickets were strewn on the floor, unrepaired, undermining the function of the fence as a barrier, ill designed, ill-treated, irrelevant. Helen's body was found in an almost inaccessible enclave of the wood yard, by a semi-derelict garage. Access/egress made more difficult by rubbish, rubble, rubber tyres, an iron metal framework for reinforced concrete and covered graffiti.

Helen's body was taken to Huddersfield Royal Infirmary, where hospital staff worked tirelessly to superficially undo the despicable work of the Yorkshire Ripper and lessen the hammer blow of the initial realisation for Rita that her sister, her twin, her Helen was a victim of this sadistic mad man. Cleaning, caring, calming and hopefully easing the inevitable pain. Helen lay in state, her body covered by a NHS (National Health Service) blanket up to her neck. The only discernible imperfection was a wound on her forehead, Rita duly did her duty and the nightmare of Huddersfield continued apace.

A spike in Peter's activity, the 'Devil's Staircase', a mathematical formula that argues that serial killers work to a 'rhythm' of brain cells firing, causing an overwhelmingly urge to kill. Simkin and Roychowdhury theorise that the probability of reoffending is significantly higher instantly after a murder and reduces significantly when time has elapsed since the last murder. They suggest that the neural impulse to kill engulfs the killer even after the calming effect of killing. This results in an eruption of homicidal activity. For Peter, not the 'Devil's Staircase', but 'God's Staircase'. Peter murdered Helen barely ten days after he bludgeoned the life out of Yvonne Pearson.

The Hull to Liverpool railway line was housed upon Huddersfield railway viaduct (1845CE - 1847CE) a grade II listed building comprising of eighteen rock faced stone arches, from the north and down to Bradford Road and then twenty-six segmental arches from Bradford Road to John William Street, these arches overshadowed Lower Viaduct Street, Great Northern Street and Garrard's timber yard that stretched along Great Northern Street and the railway viaduct. It was a prominent piece of architecture that marked another act of inhumanity committed by the Yorkshire Ripper.

Saturday the 4th of February 1978CE, Huddersfield, Assistant Chief Constable George Oldfield's home town, George Oldfield, of Grange Moor, Huddersfield went into press mode, he addressed the open hordes of the national press, photographers, reporters, red top and broad sheet, note books, lenses, lens caps and television cameras from the social club bar at Huddersfield's police headquarters. The media circus that was the Yorkshire Ripper had arrived in Huddersfield onto George Oldfield's doorstep.

"As the indications are at present I cannot discount the possibility that the man responsible for similar attacks on women in West Yorkshire over the past two and a half years. (The so-called Yorkshire Ripper). No woman is safe while this man is on the streets".

Tuesday the 7th of February 1978CE 15:00 hours the free-phone number 5050 calls in relation to this attack was promoted and all calls were directed to Millgarth Police Headquarters.

Thursday the 9th of February 1978CE, Assistant Chief Constable Oldfield appeared on The Jimmy Young Show, BBC Radio Two 10:00 hours to 12:00 hours. Mr. Oldfield became George for Jimmy Young disc jockey extraordinaire, the former singer and current housewives' favourite of the airwaves. A radio rating topper and an ideal attempt to appeal for information.

"The public has the power to decide what sort of society they want. If they want murder and violence they will keep quiet. If they want a law-abiding society, in which their womenfolk can walk freely without fear of attack from the individual we are seeking, then they must give us their help. The Ripper is someone's neighbour, someone's husband or son. Life's become very cheap in this civilised country of ours. There's a general state of apathy, an unconcern for violence". Jimmy Young the voice of Woman's Own and Woman's Weekly remained silent and nodded his head in agreement and hoped that this venture would contribute towards the capture of the so-called Yorkshire Ripper.

Sixteen/Nine
Huddersfield, Tuesday 31st January, 1978CE. (21:25 hours) *Ball peen hammer swung, slewing down a Pete Townshend windmill, but the blow was misdirected. It glanced against the top of the door frame diminishing the force with which it hit her. "There's no need for that, you don't even have to pay". Peter repeated the process on this occasion the hammer hit home, a fairground high striker, roll up, roll up, step right this way; welcome to the fairground freak show. Her eyes gazing, staring, uncaring, despairing whilst Peter indulged himself in obscenely abnormal sexual intercourse. He then dragged the body to its makeshift tomb and closed the lid by throwing an asbestos cement corrugated roofing sheet, over her prone and lifeless body. No health and safety at work, no asbestos awareness, just an empty vessel, just two empty vessels.*

Re-enact the act, a police re-construction of the Yorkshire Ripper's destruction. A living ghost, a replica reminder of her dear departed sister. A wanted 'type' poster - Rita the acting clothes horse, dressed in a fun fur coat and black trousers, Helen's head superimposed onto it.

The Mirror on Sunday, 12th February 1978CE and a Rita Rytka exclusive and more poetry. *"In innocence she lived, In innocence she tried, In innocence she tried, In innocence she walked the streets, Simply to survive, In innocence she died".* This preceded: - Sunday the 12th of February 1978CE, Rita was due to address the massed ranks of the media, but the Roman Catholic Church had become involved, they had a vested interest in Rita and also a reputation to rescue and protect.

After a delay of forty minutes Rita addressed the media, an echo from the grave Rita wore a figure hugging round necked multi coloured striped jumper, black, yellow and green. The black collar underlining and emphasising her tight-fitting silver torque necklace on her elegantly thin coffee coloured neck. Her striking bushy black Afro hair adding inches to her height. Her midriff was open to the elements with the crop top jumper bottom bordered by a dark black band as were the jumper's cuffs. Again her ebony skin on show. A thick large black belt with a rectangular Winchester rifle buckle held up her skintight blue denim jeans.

We be echo Peter recalled his brush with God back in Bingley Cemetery, back in 1966CE, his epiphany. An echo to Great Northern Street a fortnight earlier, to Garrard's timber yard. Rita was accompanied by her solicitor and read a pre-written statement, which she held in her right hand, in her left hand she held a handkerchief tightly scrunched into a ball. Rita spoke eloquently, emotionally, she was once again in the bosom of protection of the Catholic Church, the sisterhood, a lost soul saved. In the weeks since Helen/Helena's death, she had been under the protection of two agents of the establishment the Roman Catholic Church and the West Yorkshire police force. She had been hidden away in a secret address in Bradford, guarded day and night by the police twenty-four-seven.

Bernardina, the twin's mother (not to be left out), her house in Leeds had also been placed under police protection. Rita addressed the room.
"I could have lost nothing dearer than Helen. Nothing closer to my life could have gone than Helen. For his own sake and the publics sake he should hand himself over. I knew the Ripper was in West Yorkshire, but you don't expect it to happen to you. It just happened to Helen. We had a psyche between our minds. If she had a problem I knew I could feel it".
Rita closed on a positive if a little desultory, for these were surreal circumstances.
"I am young. I have my whole life ahead of me. I have to survive". The solicitor and Rita left the emotionally charged room, Rita to disappear into anonymity. Fabled legend and gossip suggest Australia and an antipodean nunnery. Away from the horrors of her homeland away from the clutches of evil and safe in the heart of the Roman Catholic Church, Sister Rita?

As ever Peter furtively scanned the newspapers for details of his crimes, the newspaper articles stirred his memories and he realised that he recognised both Helen and Rita from his time at Clayton, where they used to visit their friend, a relative of the Baker boys and regular visitors to Tanton Crescent. Too close to home, too close a call he thought, but what was done was done. It was God's will, under his guidance Peter knew he would prevail. Still no news on Yvonne Pearson, only speculation.

Friday the 3rd of March 1978CE, Rita's nineteenth birthday and what would have been Helen's but for Peter's intervention. It was also the date of the inquest to be held in relation to Helen's death.

Thursday the 9th March 1978CE, was the day of Helen Rytka's funeral. Canon John Murphy led a short service at Saint Anthony's of Padua Church, 20 Bradford Road, Clayton, Bradford, BD14. Canon Murphy was heavily involved in the Leeds Catholic Rescue Society, he was assisted in his duties at the funeral by Father Michael Killen, who had also worked with the twins and the Rytka family. The funeral cortege headed towards Scholemoor Cemetery in a sombre mood, approximately a mile and a half distance from the church, where Helen was laid to rest. Where Helen was reclaimed by the Catholic Church.

The police continued to provide round the clock protection for Rita and had her back out patrolling the red-light area, as live bait in the hope that the Yorkshire Ripper would have a second bite at the Rytka cherry.

Yet I know I shall die, as my years drag by, Oh why was it me Lord? Why? Born 3rd March 1959 CE Died 27th January 1978CE. The makeshift wooden cross and attached piece of UPVC with 'Helen Ritka. (incorrectly marked) Aged seventeen years, IN PRIME OF LIFE' written on the white UPVC background in black marker pen ink. Helen was in fact eighteen at the time of her death.

In an envelope addressed to: - Chief Superintendent George Oldfield, Central Police Station, Leeds, West Yorkshire.

Pen-pal One Wednesday 8th March 1978
Dear Sir, I am sorry I cannot give my name for obvious reasons. I am the Ripper. I've been dubbed a maniac by the Press but not by you, you call me clever and I am. You and your mates haven't a clue that photo in the paper gave me fits and that bit about killing myself, no chance. I've got things to do. My purpose to rid the streets of them sluts. My one regret is that young lassie McDonald, did not know cause changed routine that nite. Up to number 8

now you say 7 but remember Preston '75, get about you know. You were right I travel a bit. You probably look for me in Sunderland, don't bother, I am not daft, just posted letter there on one of my trips. Not a bad place compared with Chapeltown and Manningham and other places. Warn whores to keep off streets cause I feel it coming on again. Sorry about young lassie. Yours respectfully Jack the Ripper Might write again later I not sure last one really deserved it. Whores getting younger each time. Old slut next time I hope. Huddersfield never again, too small close call last one.

In an envelope addressed to: - Chief Editor, Daily Mirror Publishing Office (STD code 061), Manchester, Lancs.

Pen-pal (Daily Mirror) Two Monday 13th March 1978

Dear Sir, I have already written to Chief Constable George Oldfield "a man I respect" concerning the recent ripper murders. I told him and I am telling you to warn them whores I'll strike again and soon when heat cools off. About the MacDonald lassie, I didn't know that she was decent and I am sorry I changed my routine that night. Up to murder 8 now you say seven but remember Preston '75. Easy picking them up don't even have to try you think they're learn but they don't. Most are young lassies, next time try older one I hope. Police haven't a clue yet and I don't leave any I am very clever and don't look for me up there in Sunderland cause I not stupid just passed through the place not a bad place compared with Chapeltown and Manningham. Can't walk the streets for them whores. Don't forget warn them I feel it coming on again. If I get chance sorry about lassie I didn't know. Yours respectfully Jack the Ripper Might write again after another week gone maybe Liverpool or even Manchester again. To hot here in Yorkshire. Bye. I have given advance warning so its yours and their fault.

Scrutinised, assessed, evaluated and cross checked and ultimately dismissed along with many others as a crank, a hoax, a time waster and an oddball. The writer was written off as a sensation seeking misfit with an unhealthy occupation in the celebrity of infamy, a box bedroom felon an armchair killer. With fifty other similar anonymous letters purporting to know of or from the killer in the wake of the latest murder.

The letters put one new slant on the murders, by re-introducing, re-insinuating, suggesting that the killing of Joan Harrison should be brought into the Yorkshire (Ripper) mix but was unmemorable in all other aspects. Although there were comparisons to the 'Yorkshire Ripper' attacks, the staging/arrangement of her body and clothes; however there was many dissimilarities, Joan had been robbed, she had not been stabbed and her killer had sex with her. The police had discounted this murder as a possible 'Ripper' killing in the early part of 1977CE. The Daily Mirror ran a story in April 1977CE that stated police were investigating possible connections with Harrison's death and the so called 'Yorkshire Ripper' case.

A factor that contributed towards its lack of authenticity was the fact that Yvonne Pearson, who had been killed some forty-six or fifty-one days before the letters were posted and her body wasn't found until thirteen or eighteen days after the letters were posted. If as was believed at the time that the Ripper killed Pearson, why had he not revealed this in his writing, after all on face value the author was no shrinking violet, possibly just violently deranged? Also at the time the modus operandi of Yvonne resembled more the attack on Joan, so why not the mention. This created more questions than answers and told them nothing new and nothing that they didn't already know.

Were the two letters from Sunderland a red herring that hooked the West Yorkshire Police Force? Unbeknown to Peter William Sutcliffe someone (other than God) was on his side, another missionary working in tandem on the Holy mission, another prophet, a disciple of the Lord. Working tirelessly, relentlessly to eradicate the filth and scum stagnating, impregnating and undermining society.

Chapter 19
Eva (Vera/Mary)

The first ever May Day Spring Bank Holiday was created, it was held on Monday the 1st of May 1978CE. Vera, Cy and the children enjoyed this newfound family day, even if the weather did its best to dampen this new government endorsed holiday. For this was to be her first and last Spring Bank Holiday. Just over two weeks later she would be another crime statistic and another notch on the growing portfolio of Peter Sutcliffe

Vera Evelyn Millward AKA Vera AKA Anne Brown, AKA Mary Barton was a forty-year-old mother of seven, she lived with her common law husband Cy Burkett. Born in Madrid the capital of Spain in 1937CE during the upheaval of the Spanish Civil War she fled the persecution of General Franco's Spain in the 1950's CE to take up work in domestic service. She lived with Mr. Yusef Mohammed Sultan and the couple had five children together. Their relationship floundered and they separated in the late 1960's CE when Vera started to work as a prostitute in the Moss Side area of Manchester to supplement her family budget. It was around this time that she met Cy Birkett a forty-nine-year-old Jamaican, who fathered two further children with Vera. Cy did not know that Vera was the mother of five other children. Vera amazingly managed to hide this important information from him. They lived in their Grenham Avenue flat, on the Hulme estate in Manchester, M15.

Tuesday the 16th of May 1978CE, Vera had been suffering all day, the chronic stomach pains would not go away, it was nothing new for she was a poorly lady. She was unwell only having one lung and having to undergo surgical operations on three separate occasions between 1976CE and 1977CE.

"I'm off to get some cigs from the pub," Vera notified Cy as she put on her reversible coat, which was blue/brown chequered on one side and blue on the other, this evening she wore the chequered pattern on the outside. The inferred cigarette purchase was a front that was mutually beneficial to Vera, (or Eva as Cy liked to call her) and Cy. An unwritten understanding between consenting adults, the extra cash, came in handy and allowed Cy to turn a blind eye to Eva's Tuesday's and Thursday's extra marital liaisons. Cy knew the true meaning of Eva's excursion and did not expect her to return for the usual couple of hours.

It was 22:00 hours Vera left her Grenham Avenue flat and walked slowly, dragging her right foot slightly, the short distance to the Mancunian public house which was situated on the City Road, Royce Road convergence in what was deemed one of the better areas of Hulme. She left the high-density deck housing a designed flawed façade of Bath, Georgian crescent housing, but on a cheaper and more industrial scale. Run down, in rack and going to ruin their tenants forgotten, out of sight out of mind. Vera had last been convicted of soliciting in the November of 1973C. She tried to forget this, just as she tried to forget the hell hole in which she lived.

She entered the Mancunian pub and used the cigarette machine to purchase two packets of twenty Benson and Hedges cigarettes, the vending machine took payment for the cigarette packets and dispensed packs containing seventeen cigarettes, although the packaging and dimensions were the same as counter purchased equivalent that contained the regulation twenty. Discreet, meek and mild, Vera edged into the night immediately tearing the transparent cellophane wrapping from the packet and absentmindedly dropped it to the floor. Concentrating on opening the packet and getting to the cigarettes they housed.

She looked up the road in expectation, she was awaiting the flashing headlights of a 'regular' friend, confidante and punter, she sucked on the cigarette as deep as her one lung would allow, leaning on the timber post that supported the pub sign an elegant free standing pub sign recreating the Manchester ship, as featured on the city's Coat of Arms symbolising trade and enterprise. A fitting signpost that echoed Vera's own flirtation with the free market economy although there was to be no enterprise allowance or commendation for Vera. Behind her stood the flat roofed one storey Marston's tied house estate pub, The Mancunian that she had just vacated. Vera's eyes were peeled, she was on the look-out for a white 1968 CE Mercedes; and the money she would get from her concerned benefactor, her wait was in vain, however another opportunity soon came her way.

The external influence of the Lord forced Peter to do things that he was uncomfortable with. However he was reconciled to the fact that it was his calling and in some ways he felt special to have been singled out to pursue the mission. Although on occasions it sat somewhat awkwardly with his value consensus, when the urge came it had to be satiated and he knew ultimately that he was not responsible for his actions, a higher power dictated his actions his responsibility was diminished, he was a herald, a harbinger that immoral behaviour was unacceptable and those indulging in such behaviour may be judged at any time, they didn't have to wait to see their maker for their day of judgement for he had a servant, a messenger bidding his wont.

Peter crossed the Pennines again in his red Ford Corsair to the Manchester Moss Side red-light area he had visited twice during October of 1977 CE. Peter drove past The Factory Club AKA The Russell Club AKA The Caribbean Club, the nightclub was on Royce Road at the junction with Bonsall Street, and there was no trace of any girls. Peter was feeling his age, it was his thirty second birthday in just over two weeks and as he surveyed his surroundings, *'Use Hearing Protection' the poster read and boasted the talents of The Durutti Column/Jilted John on Friday the 19th of May, the week after Friday the 26th Big In*

Japan/Mancured Noise. THE FACTORY. Friday the 2nd June 1978CE, Peter's thirty second birthday would see The Durutti Column/Cabaret Voltaire perform at the club, finally he read that on the 9th June The Tiller Boys/Joy Division. What was the world coming too?

What was all that about he wondered? His inability to understand and relate to the poster reassured him, he was cultured, respectable his crusade would continue until God decided it had to end. In God we trust he said to nobody in particularly, shaking his head at the unfathomable content of the poster, it was like being in a different country, he smiled and said to himself, well we are in Lancashire. 'The past is a foreign country, they do things different there'. He longed for traditional values and a less secular society, he longed for the divine judgement of God to be passed upon Sodom and Gomorrah and the other 'cities of the plain' his five 'cities of the plain' were in northern England, not Israel, his 'cities of the plain' were Leeds, Bradford, Manchester, Huddersfield and Halifax. Peter was the fire and brimstone that would end impenitent sin, Peter was the tool of divine retribution that God was to unleash on the vice and sleaze in these towns and cities. Peter was an avenging angel.

Peter took his third left and followed Royce Road, a long street that ran the distance of the area, he was on the prowl, his thirst for blood needed to be quenched at the bottom of the road he saw the slight figure of a middle aged woman waiting propped against the pub sign post. Vera was just about to call it a day and return home, her Mercedes driving benefactor was a no show and there wasn't much else doing. It was then that she saw the red Ford Corsair cruising towards her.

Fate, fate, fatal fate. Peter pulled to a halt adjacent to the pub sign that towered over the fragile figure of Vera, he had already wound down his passenger window when driving through Moss Side. *"Are yer doing business?"* he asked.
"Yeah it'll cost you a fiver but we'll have to do it in the car," Vera bartered.
Peter nodded his agreement and Vera climbed into the passenger seat.
Peter quizzed *"Where can we go?"* There were two standard places where the Moss Side prostitutes would take their clients, one was the Manchester Royal Infirmary and its dark secluded car parking facilities, the other was the Southern Cemetery allotments that Peter knew all too well.
"Do you know where the MRI is?"
"What?"
"Manchester Royal Infirmary, the hospital. Never mind I'll give you directions".
He swung the car around using the width of the junction for this manoeuvre travelled to the end of Royce Road, briefly retracing himself, then right onto Chorlton Road, A57 (Ring Road Birmingham), left onto the A37 then onto Upper Brooke Street, right onto Hathersage Road, turning right onto the Boulevard, entering the hospital from the south, turning right before the overhead pedestrian walkway that bridged the expanse between

the two large buildings facing them. Peter thought by his surroundings that the couple had reached their destination he looked to Vera for confirmation.
"Anywhere here love, the quieter the better," she confirmed.

Peter could not have put it better and agreed internally whole heartedly, he proceeded and drove through the gap in the chain link fence and then using the vastness of the empty car park, he swerved harshly to the right until he neared the seclusion of the perimeter fence. Peter then reversed his car ensuring that the front bonnet was facing directly towards the exit, to enable a direct and swift exit once he had completed his mission. Peter parked the car in an area near a narrow road, they were at the far end of the car park away from the hospital lights and other the brighter floodlit areas of the car park, Manchester Royal Infirmary, Oxford Road, M13 9WL.

"It'll be better in't back," Peter suggested. He'd been in this position so many times before and was beginning to feel the adrenalin rush build, no mundane repetition, no going through the motions, this was going to be his moment and Vera's final moment. The expeditionary work he'd undertaken was about to take fruition and his mission was well on course he just had to bludgeon her unconscious and then stab her until the lifeblood ran out of her eight stone five-pound frame. Internally he whispered his mantra, his watch word: - method, concentration, thought & care. The blank canvas was prepared.

Happy to oblige and see through the transaction, receive her payment and return home to the security of her husband and children, Vera climbed out of the car. Happy to oblige as ever Peter reached for the ball peen hammer and picked it up from under the seat in which he was sitting, as he exited the vehicle he felt his breast jacket pocket for the hard rosewood handle of the kitchen knife, reassured it was there he walked around the back of the car. By now Vera was attempting to open the rear door and Peter grabbed his opportunity. 23:15 hours, Vera began to open the back door as Peter began to swing the hammer at Vera's head.

"HELP!" Vera plummeted backwards attempting to get past Peter, she was on her hands and knees scrambling to escape. Peter recollected a similar failed attempt to escape in late January when Helen Rytka tried to escape with her life. But that was a different time, a different place; the past is a foreign country.
"HELP!"
He concentrated on the task in hand, hitting her a full-blooded blow with the face of the hammer to her head.
"HEL!" Vera fell face first to the gravel surface of the car park and lay in silence. Peter quickly got to work her feisty final fight and attempt at flight had startled him, Vera was frail and fragile in appearance, however appearances can be deceiving. He was living proof of that he smiled wryly to himself. Peter pulled Vera's limp body by her wrists dragging

her about four metres from the back of the vehicle to the front, he used the vehicle to shield and obscure himself from unwanted onlookers. They were close to a perimeter chain link fence that had recently been erected to temporarily secure the area after a wall had collapsed. Peter reached inside the breast pocket of his brown car coat and pulled out the kitchen knife, he pulled up her short length floral dress and the white under slip and slashed her stomach, he watched as it opened up her guts, the eight inches long cut had jagged edges emphasising Peter's persistence and the north European work ethic he'd employed, the jagged edges were testament to the effort he'd employed, the stop start nature of the cuts underlining his commitment. He then switched to his trusty trademark sharpened Phillips screwdriver pulling it out from his breast pocket as he rolled her over onto her stomach. Using the screwdriver he stabbed through her back towards her liver, he partially pulled out the weapon and changed the angle, direction, trajectory to create further havoc, this time he pushed it towards her lung, and finally he repeated the process and aimed the blow down towards her stomach. His rage diminishing, his deed almost done, his epitaph was to puncture Vera's right eyelid with his makeshift weapon. Her intestines were beginning to spill onto the gravel floor of the car park displaying the depth and penetration of the wound as he hurriedly tried to wrap up his evenings work. Finally he flung her blue/green chequered reversible coat over her body and placed her blue canvas shoes carefully at the side of Vera's body.

23:30 hours Cy was concerned that Eva hadn't returned, she was never this long. He went out to check and see if he could find his absent wife in the near vicinity, however his search was to prove fruitless, he knew his place was with his children and he also knew in his heart of hearts that she would return. But unbeknown to Cy, Eva had become the ninth murder victim of the Yorkshire Ripper. Quiet, frail, unassuming and in constant pain from her stomach cramps Eva/Vera had previously visited Manchester Royal Infirmary for pain killing tablets and Cy assumed that's what she'd done this evening. Unfortunately Peter had ended her pain and suffering once and for all.

Peter rushed to his car and hurriedly reversed from the scene leaving the lonely, last earthly remains of Vera Evelyn 'Eva' Millward in the corner of a rubbish strewn car park. Peter used the hour long journey home to examine his clothing and remarkably he was largely blood free, he took this as a sign that his Lord protector had been watching over him, protecting his evangelistic apostolic missionary at all times. The open expanse of the M62 motorway calmed him. He reflected on his handy work, he thought of the small card of prose he had placed in his windscreen of his wagon some weeks earlier, it read, *"In this truck is a man whose latent genius, if unleashed, would rock the nation, whose dynamic energy would overpower those around him. Better let him sleep?"* His senses over indulged, overwhelmed by the divinity and the onset of Holy Madness, self-interpretation or misinterpretation of the Holy word; illuminated by the word of God, blessed by the voice within, the divine mission. Clean the streets of prostitutes and their unsavoury ways, kill prostitutes! Peter like his predecessors, Moses, Isaiah, Abraham et al had a job to do and he would do it to his utmost ability. This attack on Vera seemed to stifle the compulsion that forced Peter to kill, it doused the flames, but the inclination was not extinguished, it remained latent, a constant reminder that no woman was safe in the Yorkshire/Manchester area. He returned home arriving there around 00:30 hours, he washed himself, prepared himself for the morning and went to bed.

Wednesday the 17th May 1978CE, 08:00 hours, two yellow vans belonging to a Rochdale landscaping firm who had won the contract to work on Manchester Royal Infirmary pulled up into the secluded car park vacated by Peter approximately eight hours previously. The team of six workers were unloading their tools and preparing for the day's work ahead, when their charge-hand, Jim McGuigan's attention was captured by what he initially thought was a tailors dummy that was lying discarded against the boundary fence. Jim naturally inquisitive approached what he believed was a pile of rubbish, it was then that the realisation dawned upon him that he had found a body, the body of a dead woman. Discarded like a piece of rubbish in the corner of a central Manchester hospital car park; Vera was lying on her right side her face was resting in the gravel of the ground, a piece of paper covered her head like a makeshift shroud. Her arms were folded beneath her body and her legs were stretched out straight, her blue canvas shoes were placed on top of Vera's body. Her reversible coat, which was blue/brown chequered on one side and blue on the other, covered Vera's body from her neck down to her knee, the chequered pattern was on the outside. Vera was fully clothed she was wearing white knickers and a blue and white bra. Her short length floral dress and white under slip were still pulled up and Vera's intestines were clearly visible.

In her pockets the two vending machine packets of Benson and Hedges, seven cigarettes remaining in one packet, the other still wrapped containing the seventeen cigarettes vended only ten hours earlier. The cigarettes also paid testament to Vera's near chain smoking exploits, ten being consumed in the final hour of her life. In hindsight they were possibly a contributing factor to her chronic ill health.

Police arrived at the scene and tried to extract as much information from the murder scene as possible, the police were able to gain plaster cast impressions of Peter's car tyres. The police then used the measurements attained to calculate the probable make and model of the murderer's vehicle. The North-West Forensic Science Laboratory returned with a short list of eleven vehicles that could have left the tyre tracks, and on it was the Ford Corsair. Other constants were the India Autoway cross ply tyre tracks and the four foot two inch track width of the tyres; they were common factors in relation to this and two previous attacks (Irene Richardson and Marilyn Moore) that were attributed to the Yorkshire Ripper.

Peter had to move with the times, after the murder of Vera his killing compulsion laid dormant for the best part of the year. His desired audience for his practical theology, or his preferred victim group prostitutes, sex workers and good time girls were becoming more and more inaccessible. Police 'undercover' operations monitoring vehicles that frequented the red-light districts in effect flushed him out into the open. However Peter became more desperate, taking to the open streets of Halifax, Bradford, Leeds and Huddersfield. A true watershed in his work when the compulsion to kill came calling no woman was safe in the West Riding of Yorkshire, from the Yorkshire Ripper. His modus operandi changed, he ceased to pick his victims up in his car, rarely did he engage in dialogue with his victims. Random, reckless, haphazard, and Peter's urge to kill any woman was guaranteed to end in his capture but this was all out of his hands, he was a messenger an instrument of God, who had intervened on numerous occasions to ensure his freedom to continue with the divine mission. A part of Peter wanted it to end although who was he to argue with God, he needed to keep his head down and do the Lords will.

Seventeen/Ten,
Manchester, Tuesday 16th May 1978. (23:00 hours) *An all-consuming urge to kill any woman, Peter knew such an agenda would lead to his capture, but then again Peter was only acting under orders. This was a catalyst in reverse although the inner struggle raged on, Peter's compulsion within seemed to lie dormant but inevitably the feelings, urges returned, welling up from within, out of control. Peter was tiring of his mission becoming sloppy, his discipline had slipped, sharp edges blurred, when would his torment cease? His non-discriminatory attack on womankind he hoped would end his mission, but when? Commuter killing on the M62 corridor.*

INTERVIEW WITH A SERIAL KILLER NUMBER THREE:
Sunday 13th August 1978 CE

Sunday 13th August 1978 CE, Detective Constable Peter Smith visited number 6 Garden Lane, Heaton, to find Mr and Mrs Sutcliffe in the throes of decorating the kitchen, Mr Peter William Sutcliffe was dressed appropriately for the task in hand, in a pair of overalls. The trio retired to the living room to discuss the reason for the police visit. When asked if they could remember their whereabouts on the weekend of 16th and 17th May, 1978 CE, neither could remember, however Mrs Sonia Sutcliffe said.
"Peter would come home from work and stayed home all evening". Mrs Sonia Sutcliffe left the room and the two gentlemen were alone, the police officer took his opportunity. Detective Constable Peter Smith asked Mr Peter William Sutcliffe if he used prostitutes, Mr Peter William Sutcliffe replied
"No, certainly not".
When questioned about his car movements and if he'd recently driven through the red-light districts in the Bradford and Leeds. Mr Peter William Sutcliffe replied
"I don't know exactly but I drive home from work via the city centre".
"No, I haven't been to Leeds for ages".
When Sonia returned, she endorsed Peter's reasoning and whereabouts on specific dates recalling a visit to Rockafella's discothèque, Leeds, way back on Saturday 21st January 1978 CE. Detective Constable Peter Smith seemed satisfied with the initial interview, so satisfied that he did not deem it fit to check the tyres on the red Ford Corsair parked in the driveway. If he had taken more time to check out the car, he would have found out that Peter William Sutcliffe had recently purchased a black Sunbeam Rapier, this vehicle had by now already been spotted nine times in the Bradford red-light district. The officer put it on his to do list.

***

INTERVIEW WITH A SERIAL KILLER NUMBER FOUR:
Thursday 23rd November 1978 CE

Detective Constable Smith returns to number 6 Garden Lane, Heaton, and Bradford on the evening of Thursday the 23rd of November 1978 CE. He asks Mr Peter William Sutcliffe for his banking details, he also enquires about the red Ford Corsair and the black Sunbeam Rapier. Mr Peter William Sutcliffe explained he'd bought the Rapier to replace the Corsair, he'd subsequently sold the Ford Corsair. Detective Constable Peter Smith needed to visit the new owner. Detective Constable Peter Smith needed to check the tyres on the red Ford Corsair. Detective Constable Peter Smith put it on his to do list.

Riding high in the Punters index, Bradford, Leeds and Manchester a triple area sighting, another hat trick to add to his growing arsenal of achievements. The black Sunbeam Rapier was now his new vehicle of choice.

Chapter 20
Ann

Thursday the 22nd of February 1979CE, a black Sunbeam Rapier NKU 888 H driven by a solo man was flagged in the Manchester red-light district of Moss Side as part of the covert tracking investigation, thus becoming a triple area sighting. His car had already been logged as travelling through the red-light areas of Leeds and Bradford on multiple occasions again driven by a solo man. The accolade of a triple area sighting was that the Police National Computer (PNC) produced a printout report and an interview was automatically actioned so the police could check out the background of the would-be suspect and ascertain the reasons behind his frequent visits to these less than salubrious areas. Peter was flying high in the 'Punter's Index' for a second time, with a second vehicle.

Friday the 2nd of March 1979CE, killing prostitutes had become an obsession with Peter, this evening he travelled the seven or so miles from Bradford through Undercliffe, past Ravenscliffe, through Apperley Bridge up to Rawdon then east to Horsforth, normally he'd continue easterly onto Chapeltown, but not this evening. Tonight was to see a sea change in his working style, one that would not be acknowledged until 1992 CE.

Peter sat in his black Sunbeam Rapier looking for a suitable candidate for the urge was upon him, he'd struggled with the voices for so long now and was now an obedient servant to their suggestions. 19:55 hours Peter sat in his black Sunbeam Rapier NKU 888 H, he looked directly at Ann as she passed his car which was parked discretely on Brownberrie Lane, facing down the gradient of the hillside; Ann had enough time to note the general appearance the car and a more detailed account of the dark curly haired man, with the wilting moustache. She described him as in his twenties, he was at this particular juncture in time just three months shy of his thirty third birthday. She also said her attacker was approximately five foot ten inches tall and broadly built. She thought little more of this man assuming he was waiting to pick up a fellow student and Ann continued about her business.

At 20:00 hours Ann Rooney a twenty-two-year-old student from Ireland was walking in the grounds of Trinity and All Saints College in Horsforth off Brownberrie Lane, Leeds, West Yorkshire LS18. Peter slipped out of his car and hurriedly fell into step behind Ann. Peter waited until it was only the two of them, he followed her for a few more steps then felt for his trusty hammer, the handle bulged in his breast pocket, he pulled it out with his left hand it felt slightly lighter than the ones he preferred but he paid it no further mind and sensing an opportunity he hurtled towards Ann, he swung the hammer down upon the back of her skull, once, twice and three times for good measure.

Ann fell to the ground screaming Peter was sure that her cries would alert other people in the area and he felt threatened. No time to finish his work too much risk of capture. He left the prone figure of Ann to be found by a fellow student and fled back to his car, no knife work or other homemade hybrid tools on this occasion. Just time to escape evasion and abscond from the vista of his latest abomination. However in his haste to extricate himself from this horror, Peter panicked, he took a right turn onto North Road, a private road that was a dead-end street. Was this going to be the end of his killing spree? He took a few deep breaths, composed himself manoeuvred his Sunbeam Rapier through a three-point turn and retraced his route. He used the rest of the short journey home to reflect on his unprofessionalism, his desperation, his actions were shambolic and amateur. It was a botched attempt, opportunistic, a switch from his usual hunting ground, he would have to step up his game or his freedom would soon be lost. Peter was protected by an outside influence and knew that he could not be caught until the power that controlled him decided that was his fate. A force immeasurably more powerful than the authorities and the keystone cops they employed to track him down.

The aftermath of Peter's onslaught saw Ann being rushed to Leeds General Infirmary for emergency treatment. Professor David Gee - who was Head of the Department of Forensic Medicine at Leeds University and was the pathologist employed by the West Yorkshire police force to undertake the post-mortem examinations of all the Yorkshire Ripper victims killed in West Yorkshire, also examined his survivors and was an expert in all things Ripper, - soon arrived to appraise her injuries and see if this could be linked into the Yorkshire Ripper series of attacks, the semi-circular compression injuries to the skull were all too familiar. However pressure was growing on the police and hysteria about the murders had resulted in irrational reaction to possible Ripper crimes. Unwilling to further fuel this hysteria and aware that the Yorkshire Ripper had not attacked for over three hundred days, nobody wanted to confirm that their worst nightmare had returned, especially if there was a chance that this was wrong. In essence the 'political' climate dictated that this could not be a Yorkshire Ripper attack, a fact that was reinforced by the victim type and the attack location. But they didn't know what he knew, spring heeled Jack and out of control.

Referring back to the opening paragraph of this chapter, Peter was flying high in the 'Punter's Index' but the fact that Ann had pinpointed a black Sunbeam Rapier had not fallen on deaf ears. The police checked the 'Punter's Index' to create a Sunbeam Rapier or similar model short list in the hope of fast tracking their efforts to apprehend the attacker. The 'Punter's Index' produced a list of eight hundred and fifty cars. However if the officers investigating had understood the data and codes on offer they would have been able to decipher that twenty-one of the possible suspects had been double area sightings and short list the short list. Taken to its natural conclusion the information proffered highlighted that there were only three suspects that were triple area sightings enabling them to further short list the short list. Of course Peter William Sutcliffe was one of the three triple area sightings, but of course the police officers investigating the attack on Ann Rooney had not been trained in analysing the PNC printout and this again was a lost opportunity. Peter was truly blessed and under the protection of God and would continue with his divine mission until God saw fit for it to cease. On occasions he felt the blessing was a damnation; he was not in control of his actions and a mere tool that was at the whim of God. The officers had the information to place Peter as a possible prime suspect but it was not to be.

Fate intervened yet again in Peter's favour, the net was closing and he was oblivious to this blasé even, safe in the knowledge of his divine protection. The police did not link this incident to his previous work. Unbeknown to Peter the net was closing, however luck remained his firm friend the PNC was too new for the traditional ways employed by the Horsforth police officers. The past is a foreign country indeed, a fact that favoured Mr Peter William Sutcliffe.

Eighteen/Ten
Leeds, Friday 2nd March, 1979CE. (20:30 hours) *Now a triple-area sighting on the 'punters index', an interview was actioned police would be interested in Peter's fascination with the red-light area and the frequency of his visits, or would they? Indiscriminate, random and ring rusty. Discounted and overlooked, the sleeper cell was reactivated, but was operating under the radar. The luck of the Irish held but so too did that of Peter William Sutcliffe.*

In an envelope addressed to: - Assistant Chief Constable Oldfield, West Yorkshire CID, Leeds, West Yorkshire

Pen-pal Three Monday 23rd March 1979

Dear Officer, Sorry I havn't written, about a year to be exact, but I hav'nt been up north for quite a while. I was'nt kidding last time I wrote saying the whore would be older this time and maybe I'd strike in Manchester for a change, you should have took heed. That bit about her being in hospital, funny the lady mentioned something about being in hospital before I stopped her whoring ways. The lady won't worry about hospitals now will she. I bet you be wondering how come I hav'nt been to work for ages, well I would have been if it hadnt been for your cursered coppers I had the lady just where I wanted her and was about to strike when one of you cursing police cars stopped right outside the lane, he must have been a dumb copper cause he didnt say anything, he didnt know how close he was to catching me. Tell you the truth I thought I was collared, the lady said don't worry about the coppers, little did she know that bloody copper saved her neck. That was last month, so I don't know when I will get back on the job but I know it wont be Chapeltown too bloody hot there maybe Bradfords Manningham. Might write again if up north. Jack the Ripper PS Did you get letter I sent to Daily Mirror in Manchester.

The third and final letter of the trilogy arrived just over a week prior to the murder of Halifax's Josephine Whitaker. The contents of this letter provided more detail and eroded previous doubts and gave added credence to the authenticity of the author. The forensic evidence again reinforced the distinct possibility that this was their man.

It just so happened that the killer of Joan Harrison was very likely blood group B, this was deduced from a sample of semen which was taken from Joan's body and tested. This correlated to forensic findings on the saliva used to seal the envelope in March 1979CE and showed a possible link between the writer and the murderer.

This made the police revisit the previous correspondence. In the first of the series of letters the author had made a number of predictions about forthcoming crime he intended, an 'old slut', it said. In the second letter which he sent to the Daily Mirror, he reinforced his slightly earlier claim 'an older one I hope'; this was further supported by a possible location, 'Liverpool or...Manchester'. On revisiting these letters it seemed that the culprit had either inside information and was therefore either the killer or known to the killer or the predictions and actions of the killer were just coincidental. Vera Millward was the next in the sequence of victims, aged forty, she was in the higher/senior age spectrum of his victims. The location of her demise was Manchester.

In the third letter, there was mention of Vera Millward having attended the hospital, the grounds in which she'd been murdered; he wrote 'the lady mentioned something about being in hospital', this further enthralled the detectives who believed this was private and unpublished information that only they were privy too. The fact that the author knew, fortified the integrity of the literature and emphasised the nerve and depravity of the author/murderer. There was a further prediction about his next murder that did not transpire, the location of his next attack. However a clue left at the scene of Josephine Whitaker's murder, traces of engineers milling oil, traces of similar oil were found on one of the envelopes they had received.

The gapped toothed bite mark found on Joan Harrison's body was similar to the bite mark found on Josephine Whitaker, conjecture, coincidence or concrete evidence. A further factor to support the gap in the upper front teeth of the attacker was Marylyn Moore's description of a gap-toothed assailant, however at the time the police placed little weight on the photo-fit Marylyn produced. There were also other theories about the cause of the marks on Josephine's breast.

The third letter from Sunderland caught the attention of the Ripper Squad high brass. Unbeknown to Peter William Sutcliffe someone (other than God) was on his side, another missionary working in tandem on the Holy mission, another prophet, a disciple of the Lord. Working tirelessly relentlessly to eradicate the filth and scum stagnating, impregnating and undermining society.

Chapter 21
Jo

The winter that spanned between Thursday 21st of December 1978CE and Monday the 19th March 1979CE became known as the 'Winter of Discontent', it saw the country paralysed by a plethora of strikes and industrial action, the public sector faced with capped pay rises soaring inflation, saw strike action become an intrinsic part of the Great British way of life.

Monday the 18th of December 1978CE saw BP (British Petroleum) and ESSO Petroleum Ltd 'employed' lorry drivers commence an overtime ban in their efforts to secure a 40% pay hike, the disruption of the supply of oil resulted in a pay rise of 15% being agreed.

Wednesday the 3rd of January 1979CE saw all Transport and General Workers Union (TGWU) drivers join in the industrial action, their wildcat strike caused the closure of thousands of petrol service stations due to the decimation of fuel distribution. Striking lorry drivers sent flying pickets (a worker who travels to support workers who are on strike at another place of work or attempts to gain support for their strike from the place/workforce they visit) to the main ports to prevent the Government importing fresh supplies and also to the oil refineries to disable the internal supplies. The strike gained momentum and was made official on Thursday the 11th January by the TGWU and Friday the 12th January by the Road Transport Union (RTU). The lorry drivers strike brought transportation of goods and supplies throughout Britain by road to a standstill. The resulting standoff between the Government and the lorry drivers saw over one million temporarily laid off as a result of the dispute. On Tuesday 29th of January the Government capitulated to the lorry driver's demands and a pay rise of around 20% was agreed.
"What do we want 20%. When do we want it, now!" seemed to become the soundtrack to the winter of discontent.

Peter was a bit part player in a theatrical production that had threatened to force the Government into declaring a state of emergency during the lorry drivers strike, he was soon to become lead role in a sinister plot that would force police forces in the north of England to declare an unofficial state of emergency on the streets due to his alter ego the Yorkshire Ripper. Long gone was the puerile altar boy, lost beyond recognition. No longer did Peter scurry for the scraps thrown from the top table of the last supper, he now sat shoulder to shoulder with Jesus and his twelve Disciples. *'Now is the winter of our discontent, Made glorious summer by this son of York'* wrote Shakespeare and Peter misinterpreted, *'Now is the winter of our discontent, Made glorious by THIS SON of York'*; this had to mean the YORKSHIRE RIPPER, the theological mission must continue.

A familiar face returned to the perennial party that was Peter's life, Trevor Birdsall a man that would abut and encapsulate the Yorkshire Ripper's years of freedom. Re-united, thick as thieves (for both were, tried and convicted) Peter and Trevor made the most of the extended Christmas holiday period due to the bad weather and the lorry drivers strike to also reacquaint themselves with some of their favourite hostelries, Michael (Peter's younger brother) also tagged along to these daytime drinking sessions. The worst winter for thirty years, with the heaviest and most sustained snow fall. The TGWU played their part in the winter of discontent and Peter William Sutcliffe et al, although Peter's strike action consisted of afternoon drinking sessions in Bradford, with Mick, his brother in-law Robin Holland (married to Maureen Sutcliffe) also a lorry driver and Trevor Birdsall.

The Old Crown, 23-25 Ivegate, BD1, Yates Wine Lodge 9-19 Queensgate BD1. The Harp of Erin Chain Street, BD1. The groups favoured watering hole was the Belle Vue Hotel, which was located at 187 Manningham Lane, Bradford, BD8. The Belle Vue had two bars, one of which was a common or garden public bar, whilst the second bar catered for a different clientele. For the princely sum of ten pence the drinking connoisseur could gain admittance to the second bar - the strippers bar and savour the delights of a topless DJ whose performance was punctuated by an hourly performance of exotic, erotic striptease. Booze, birds and blokes always the constant, reaffirming, a hot bed of misogyny. A breeding ground for murder.

And so it begins, the beginning of the end, or the end of the beginning. Wednesday the 28th March 1979CE, Margaret Thatcher leader of the opposition tabled a motion of no confidence in the Labour government, this motion was successful forcing a general election for the 3rd of May 1979CE and a caretaker budget.

Lorry drivers - creators of destiny, one such lorry driver, Peter William Sutcliffe was starting to believe his own press. *'In this truck is a man whose latent genius if unleashed would rock the nation, whose dynamic energy would overpower those around him: Better let him sleep?'*

The Government planned a state of emergency, Army aid to undermine the TGWU and safeguard essential supplies. Band wagon jumping public sector workers striving to ensure their pay packets kept pace with soaring inflation. *"What do we want 20%. When do we want it, now!"* Iconic images that would undermine the Government and bring the death knell of consensus politics in Britain. Consensus was to become conviction, discontent was to be malcontent. *"What do we want 20%. When do we want it, now!"* Rubbish, uncollected piled high in the snow-covered streets, the dead were left unburied in makeshift morgues, mass rallies and demonstrations. WANTED! A living wage. WANTED! The Yorkshire Ripper. *"What do we want 20%. When do we want it, now!"*

The Winter of Discontent 1978CE, 1979CE. 'Now is the winter of our discontent' a phrase from the playwright William Shakespeare about the English civil war, King Richard the Third. The art of a genius encapsulates the actions of a heathen, Peter created a civil war, between the sexes his unchecked antics were out of control. Fom the industrial/political division of the Winter of Discontent and the lorry drivers strike, to 'Now is the winter of our discontent,' a civil war on the streets of northern England, protest marches, a reign of terror creating headaches and heartaches from Wakefield to Westminster. The Winter of Discontent had passed, but people, society was still recoilling from the fall out. Sociologically, economically and politically. *"What do we want 20%. When do we want it, now!"*

Peter was often assigned the Nelson run, as part of his work duties at T.H. Clarks Limited, this was a particular favourite with brother Michael who often accompanied him in his lorry cab. Mick would ride shotgun and enjoyed this particular delivery, because it meant the pair could drop off their load and be homeward bound for 14:00 hours. However they did not go straight home as the pair had discovered a pub in Burnley that was open all afternoon. The pair would enjoy the ambience of the East Lancs hospitality, drink and dominoes until 16:30 hours then back on the road Todmorden, Hebden Bridge, Mytholmroyd, Sowerby Bridge, Halifax, Northowram, Bradford to arrive at T.H. Clarks Ltd, Hillam Road depot for finishing time.

It was probably on one of these trips that Peter was introduced to the tale of the Pendle witches. The Pendle Witch Trial saw nine women and one man executed after a trial at Lancaster assizes on the 20th of August 1612CE, their crime to have bewitched to death 'by devilish practices and hellish means' no fewer than sixteen inhabitants of the Forest of Pendle. Peter was after some rough justice to end the plague of prostitution to break the contamination of their charm, the bewitching bitches, were taken onto the moors on the outskirts of the town and hanged. The 1604CE Witchcraft Act dictated that if found guilty it was a crime punishable by death, Peter's theological mission echoed similar sentiments, his epiphany in 1966CE saw him set out on a stuttering mission to eradicate the modern day witches of the north.

Like the Pendle witches, Shakespeare's Macbeth and the Thane of Cawdor, compromised by women of ill repute, supernatural, witchcraft, unnatural, ungodly, uncouth, unclean, unneeded; using their bodies to tease and torment unsuspecting men ensnared by these unscrupulous sirens. Peter knew he had to rid the streets of this scum, his main job was that of a lorry driver, however his second job was that of street cleaner.

The Mexican standoff, each party prepared, each party waiting for the other to make their move, the police and Oldfield's continued surveillance of the red-light districts of Bradford, Leeds and Manchester, realising that there was no real hope of catching their quarry until he attacked. The Ripper letters by now three in number remained hidden from the public eye and a media blackout was encouraged by the West Yorkshire police. Unable to operate in the shadows of the red-light districts of West Yorkshire and Manchester, Peter had to find a new hunting ground. Everybody was aware of the police covert operation to uncover the Ripper, the plain clothed officers stood out like a sore thumb in and amongst the usual characters that inhabited this underworld. This turn of events was not lost on Peter, he still continued to frequent these environs however chances were few, if not non-existent. He would have to find new killing grounds, in doing so he reverted to his initial haunts, the student hinterland offered a viable option, easy picking, easy meat but any opportunity would do when the mood was upon him. He'd dipped his foot in that pool in a failed outing in Horsforth, he would have to try again, elsewhere. Peter Sutcliffe duly complied, murdering Josephine Whitaker on a cold spring night in Halifax; after a killing drought of three hundred and twenty-two days he struck, killing outside the police/prostitute baited areas. The police in smoking out the Yorkshire Ripper had ensured that no woman was safe.

His enforced hibernation, police surveillance, inclement weather, a lack of libido, no direction, no sign from God, his mission stalled. During this killing drought Peter put his spare time to good use. He went to work on a proto type pair of 'gimp' leggings. Silky leggings, one lovingly handmade calf-length garment made from one of Peter's old green shirts, another from a V-necked sweater, aided his newfound professionalism. He'd taken time and care, creating knee pads to cushion the knee area, therefore allowing him to expose his genitalia whilst he bore down on his defenceless victim. He may be on a mission from God, but he could see no reason why he couldn't indulge himself whilst doing the lords bidding - the creature comforts this garment afforded him. He hadn't had time to check them out them practically in Horsforth on the Irish bird, but there would be no mistakes tonight. His incapacity exaggerated by their ineptness, it was just over a month since his unrecorded last attack, but closer to eleven months from his excursion to Manchester and fourteen months since his Huddersfield attack.

Wednesday the 4th April 1979CE, a cold wet winter continued into early, mid spring. Snow showers manifesting the extreme spectrum of the weather in the north of England. Wind, precipitation, undulating temperature, sunshine, visibility, cloud, pressure and humidity. Peter William Sutcliffe was becoming a pressure cooker, his guise of humility about to be lost in the clouds of a troubled mind, the voices had returned, his mission re-ignited. Hate seethed within his blood boiled, meek, modest, shy and unassuming body. Sutcliffe was soon to share the centre stage with his alter ego the Yorkshire Ripper, the ticking time bomb lying innate within had now begun to stir. The likelihood for blood was high, Sonia's acceptance of the night shift almost made it inevitable, but only time would tell.

Although Sonia was working as a supply teacher she continued to 'moonlight' doing relief work at the Sherrington Nursing Home, she worked her usual Saturday night shift, but often helped out at short notice, working Tuesday and Wednesday nights, this often left Peter to fend for himself. Peter referred to 'plan B' and arranged to check over his in-law's car. But beforehand he retired to the bathroom to exchange his underpants for his gimp leggings, the freedom he felt excited him and contributed further to his desire to kill, was this a message from God, or was this a massage from God.

Peter borrowed Mrs Szurma's, his mother in-law's Ford Escort car on the pretext that he was going to check it over, instead he drove the three miles or so over to Halifax, he drove around the town centre. At 21:00 hours he saw a lone woman and pulled over, offered the woman a lift and asked her if she wanted to have sex with him. The rebuff was direct and forthright, the woman hurried towards her destination of Halifax bus station and Peter quickly drove away down the A629 to the south of the town centre. Peter pulled up outside Halifax General Hospital, a police patrol car pulled up behind him, the first officer exited the Hillman Avenger and approached Peter in the driver seat. Ever vigilant the police officer spoke with Peter.

"Why are you here...what are you up to...do you mind if I take a look inside your vehicle...why have you got a toolbox in the passenger footwell?" Peter remained calm and quiet, obedient, respectful, reserved and struck the officer as a shy man. But the officer was far from satisfied, he spoke to his colleague and asked him to get on the radio and speak to the control room in Halifax, 'A' Division and request a Police National Computer (PNC) check on Peter and the vehicle. Unfortunately fortune favoured Peter, the operator in the control room, notified the patrol officers that the PNC was 'down'. The officer returned to Peter's vehicle and explained he was free to go. Peter thanked the officer for his time and drove back to Clayton, where he collected his own vehicle. The near miss had whetted his appetite, he thrived on the danger, the excitement, he'd decided on Halifax and Halifax it had to be. Peter set off from Clayton through Queensbury and onto Halifax, because the impulse was upon him. Peter cruised around Halifax town centre once again, this time in his black fastback Sunbeam Rapier on the hunt, searching for a victim.

Josephine Anne Whitaker worked for the Halifax Building Society as a clerk at the head office in the town centre, she was nineteen years old. She lived with her mother, Thelma (Hiley) a school teacher, her step father Haydn, a builder and her brothers, Michael (Mick) aged 15years and David, aged thirteen, in a stone built terraced house at 10 Ivy Street, Bell Hall, Halifax HX1. Josephine was the offspring of Thelma Priestley and Trevor Whitaker who were married in Halifax in 1955CE, Josephine was born in 1959CE in Bradford.

Trevor and Thelma's marriage failed and their marriage vows were annulled in 1961CE. Thelma returned to her parent's home after she was divorced. Therefore Josephine spent the formative years of her life, along with her mother living with her grandparents in their Halifax home. This went some way to explaining the special relationship Jo had with her Grandparents. Thelma subsequently met another man with whom she had two sons Mick and David, unfortunately this relationship was not to be and once again Thelma returned to her parent's home in Halifax. Eventually Thelma met Haydn Hiley and the couple married in Halifax in 1972CE.

Jo left school in 1977CE and got a job at the Halifax Building Society headquarters in the town. She had worked at the Halifax for about 20 months and she'd recently secured a promotion. She also had a part time job as a barmaid at The Tower House Hotel, Water Lane in Halifax and visited her Grandparent's religiously every Sunday. Jo had been engaged to Craig Midgley whose family lived in Gibbett Street, central Halifax, but had split up in the May of 1978CE, Craig believing the relationship was getting too serious. So life continued, Josephine concentrated on her career and her horse riding, often visiting Norland Moor. Josephine had recently decided to treat herself and had purchased a silver wristwatch from a work colleague's catalogue, the work colleague brought it into their Halifax office on Wednesday the 4th April 1979CE. Josephine had spent the extravagant sum of sixty-five pounds (the equivalent to three hundred and thirty-three pounds in 2015CE prices). Jo was ebullient at the expensive present to herself and returned home to share her delight with her mother. However her mother didn't feel quite as pleased with her daughter and thought that this would be an ideal time to try and instil in her daughter the real value of money. The gift inadvertently contributed to a little disagreement between Jo and her mother Thelma.

Circa 18:00 hours, Jo had a fish tank and the electricity for the filter was paid for by her parents, Thelma felt this would be an opportune time to teach her daughter the importance of thrift. This well intended life lesson was lost in translation. Thelma tried to highlight the cost of living, but Jo took umbrage at her mum's well-meaning words, Jo became frustrated as teenagers do, unable to see the wood for the trees. Frustrated at the fact that she was the focus of the conversation and she did not like what she was hearing. Typical teenager, Jo decided to end the awkward situation by retreating to the solace of her bedroom to avoid further unease. She pondered her predicament for a good hour then decided she'd pay a visit to her Grandparent's house and extricate herself from the house for the rest of the evening. Perhaps they may be more impressed with the prized possession of her new silver wristwatch? And it was always nice to see them.

The journey to her Grandparent's Tom and Mary Priestley, was one that Josephine was familiar with, just over a mile and predominantly downhill the leisurely walk took Josephine about twenty minutes and she arrived unexpectedly at her Grandparent's Huddersfield Road home circa 19:40 hours, Josephine was impatient to show her

Grandparent's her new silver watch, but when she arrived Mary her Grandma was out attending a church party across the road at Saint Andrew's Methodist Church, Huddersfield Road, Halifax, HX3. Tom was pleasantly surprised as he explained his wife's whereabouts.

"Your Grandma's out love, she'll be late back".

"Never mind, I can wait". Jo then disappeared into the kitchen to make a drink of tea for the duo. She then returned to the living room and the warmth of the fire. Jo then took on the role of a hand model and displayed her newly purchased silver wristwatch.

"It's looks lovely I bet that cost a pretty penny". The pair then settled down to a cosy night of informal chit chat and television entertainment.

The pair sat down and at 19:30 hours watched Coronation Street on YTV (Yorkshire Television), they talked and chatted and at 21:00 hours, there attention was drawn to the headline story of BBC1's (British Broadcasting Company) Nine O'clock news which was about the execution of the former Prime Minister of Pakistan Zulfikar Ali Bhutto, who had been executed by hanging at Rawalpindi district jail. 21:25 hours, they continued to chatter to the backdrop of the television, the Right Honourable Sir Geoffrey Howe, MP for the Conservative party in opposition to the government, gave his views on The Budget.

21:35 hours, Sportsnight, with highlights from the FA (Football Association) cup Semi-Final replay between Liverpool and Manchester United played at Goodison Park, which Manchester United won 1.0 to set up a cup Final with Arsenal. Harry Carpenter's feature on the Terry Lawless boxing stable played particular attention to a young Scotsman Jim Watt, who had an impending title fight in Glasgow.

22:55 hours, 'Tonight' hosted by Valerie Singleton and Donald Maccormick, however the television faded further into the background as Mary (Jo's Grandma) returned to the family fold.

"What are you doing here love? It's not Sunday" Mary quizzed pleasantly. This was a reference to the fact that Jo visited her Grandparents every Sunday, without fail.

"Look at her watch Mary," Tom interrupted.

Jo held out her wrist to show off the silver wristwatch that adorned her arm.

"It's lovely love".

"I decided to treat myself".

Mary was pleasantly surprised by her granddaughter's impromptu visit, she admired Jo's wristwatch and they had a good natter. They continued to talk and the time passed quickly.

23:35 hours, The Sky at Night, 'The Space Between the Stars' hosted by Patrick Moore with a guest appearance from Dr John Beckham, faded into the background as the trio discussed their farewells, both Tom and Mary tried their damnedest to get Jo to sleep over.

"Stay the night Jo, the bed's made up in the spare room".

"I'll be alright, I'm not bothered about walking home in the dark". Tom ever the gentlemen and chivalrous offered to escort his granddaughter home, however his failing health, his chronic emphysema and his ageing body belied his well-intended gesture, and all parties knew this was not a real possibility.
"I've got to get home, I need to take my contact lenses out and I've left the storage case at home". Jo said her goodbyes and left their company at 23:40 hours saying, *"I'll see you on Sunday"*. Josephine left her Grandparents home for the last time, she turned right off Huddersfield Road (A629) onto Dry Clough Lane (A646) following the road upwards onto Skircoat Moor Road (still the A646).

Like a rudderless ship and without direction Peter drove through the streets of Halifax, past the Bulls Head 5 Bull Green, Halifax HX1 first left on the Bull Green Roundabout down the A629 past the Victoria Theatre on the left then followed the road down and round past the Halifax Building Society Head Office, the Shay Football Stadium to the left in a natural bowl, past the bus depot - directed by a Holy force an ecclesiastic satellite navigation from the heavens, no woman was safe. He veered right off the road he was on and eventually found himself in the middle class Bell Hall district of Halifax and circling the green oasis of Savile Park, dog walkers broke the desolation of the streets, Peter circled the playing fields repeatedly on the prowl for his next victim. Peter felt the compulsion within, he was in the mood for murder, his state of mind meant that no woman was safe until the urge had been satisfied.

Skircoat Moor, Halifax, 'The Moor' not the wild windswept moors of Heathcliffe and Cathy, but a grassed haven amidst the once satanic mills of Halifax, known on the ordnance survey maps of Calderdale as Savile Park, a gift to the people of the town by Captain Henry Savile in 1866CE. 'The Moor' using the colloquial Haligonian title was going to witness the passing of Miss Josephine Anne Whitaker, she was to be the Yorkshire Ripper's tenth (official) murder victim.

Peter saw Josephine's five-foot eight inches frame walking up Skircoat Moor Road she was wearing a heather-mixture three-quarter length hacking jacket and skirt to protect herself against the elements. Peter immediately parked up outside the terraced houses of Manor Heath Road and swiftly grasped the large Phillips screwdriver and his favoured ball peen hammer, he'd spent some time sharpening the pointed end of the large screwdriver to ensure that it was fit for its sinister purpose. Like an old-time whaler, the seafarers that originated the art of scrimshaw in the 1750's CE. Scrimshaw, carvings and engravings in ivory and bone, whales, walruses, tusks and teeth. It passed the hours at sea, a hobby that became a trade, but Peter's sinister twist on scrimshaw was sinister twist, provocative an affront to humanity. His sadistic version of an ancient art corrupted, debased, with murder in mind and engineer oil in evidence.

Peter climbed out of the car and he placed his tools of choice in his breast pocket and scurried discreetly in an attempt to catch up with Josephine. He eventually caught up, falling into step with her after a couple of minutes.

"Do yer have far ter go?" A hushed question came from Peter's lips.

"Yes," replied Josephine, *"It's quite a walk".* Their initial conversation was interrupted as their attention was drawn to a man who passed them by on the pavement, he was out walking his dog. By now Peter had concluded that Josephine was not a prostitute, but was not concerned, he had decided that he just wanted to kill a woman. The couple walked together into the darkness of the grassland playing fields of Savile Park.

"It's late to be out alone, what have yer been up to?" Peter probed pleasantly.

"I've been to my Grandma's house, I nearly slept over, but decided to sleep in the comfort of my own bed".

"Why don't yer learn to drive?"

"No thanks, horses are my preferred and most satisfactory form of transport". There was a pregnant pause and a brief silence, Jo then explained *"I normally take a short cut across the field".*

"You don't know who you can trust nowadays," Peter straight forwardly warned. Peter thought she wasn't a prostitute, their chat and stroll planted the seed of doubt. Peter pondered the pros and cons, she sounded innocent, unknowing, visiting Grandma's, and liked horse riding. This was not a scarlet woman, although she soon would be, after he had hit her, her cries and pleas for mercy would be of no use then. But he believed she was innocent, he believed he was wrong, he looked upwards instinctively towards the clock tower, then up again to the dark sky, up to God and he questioned his judgement, 'You must be wrong. This is wrong. I shouldn't be doing this'.

'This is a likely story. She's playing you for a fool. She is very clever this one. You are not going to fall for all this. YOU QUESTION ME, THIS IS THE DEVILS WORK, SHE LOOKS INNOCENT AND IS THE DEVILS WORK'. Peter chastised set back on the righteous path continuing his work with a newfound verve.

The couple then walked together into the darkness of the grassland playing fields of Savile Park, walking diagonally across the grass.

As they walked the silhouette of Saint Jude's Parish Church, Savile Park, Halifax, (HX1 2XE) which overlooks Savile Park, domineered the skyline. Its clock tower rose to their right-hand side, it was in this very church that Josephine had been baptised and on a Sunday her family and friends were a part of the congregation. Peter felt at the wristwatch on his left wrist and smiled to himself in the darkness, he knew he was protected, he knew Jo would fall for his deception. When the pair were about thirty metres into the playing fields and thirty metres away from the tarmac of Savile Park Road.

"What time does it say on the church clock?" Jo turned her head towards the clock on the tower.

"Seven minutes to twelve. I forgot the time," Josephine continued.

"Well there's nowt wrong wiv yer eyesight," Peter replied, pantomime acting, arcing his head to the right craning to look at the clock face on the tower, he lagged behind Josephine, intent on putting his dastardly plan into action. Their dastardly plan into action for Peter was working with an accomplice, it was the voice that instigated the question about the time on the church tower, he - they knew it would get her to turn her head away from him and allow him to attack her at her most vulnerable. Desensitised, murder is natural, rid the world of prostitutes, desensitised, murder is natural rid the world of women!

Reaching into the depth of his jacket pocket, complete with cut pocket linings to allow extra space, extra depth to safely house his tools, with his left hand Peter pulled out his ball peen hammer, instinctively quickening his pace and actions, he swung the hammer down towards the crown of Josephine's head, once, twice until she fell face first into the soft ground of the playing fields her skull fractured from ear to ear. A loud groan emanated from Josephine's mouth, Peter began to panic, the euphoria of his deed coupled with the public arena, he instinctively surveyed the area, to his dismay he saw a lone figure walking down Savile Park Road to his right. He was already committed so decided to continue with his mission, grabbing Josephine by the ankles and dragging her ten metres further from the main road and further into the dark wilderness of the field. Josephine her face slightly buried in the dirt continued to moan, although the ground somewhat muffled her protestations.

Peter confident that he had manoeuvred to a position where he could safely continue his work undisturbed, was once again startled; he heard voices behind him and to his left, he turned to meet their origin and saw two people walking along the footpath that crossed Savile Park from west to east, Josephine was still moaning louder than he was happy with, possibly drawing attention to him, he needed to act fast, he flipped Josephine over manhandling her body and pulling at her clothing, he pulled up her pink jumper and her bra to allow easier access. He pulled out the sharpened Phillips screwdriver and stabbed her repeatedly in the chest and stomach. He continued to stab at Josephine a defenceless target, on twenty-one occasions he plunged the screwdriver into her stomach and chest. He pulled up her multi-coloured skirt, its white lace trimming discoloured and soiled by the mud, he stabbed at her vagina thrusting the screwdriver between her legs and then he continued lower down her body to her right leg, stabbing her six times.

Amateur gynaecology and a hybrid of sexual butchery, Peter continued to justify his debased actions as a theological mission to cleanse the world of depravity, although his actions only contributed to it further. A lightning fast blur of violence, a frenzy of abomination and his actions had the desired effect and her moaning stopped. In the frenzy of the attack the beast took over and he bit down onto her right breast, puncture marks outlining the quarter inch gap between his teeth on the site of the wound. Re-insertion, total submersion in the deed, patterned, callous, calculating, method, madness, concentration and care. In a world of his own oblivious to the surroundings, he dropped to the padded knees of his gimp leggings, opened up his trousers and due to his strange handmade under garments had easy access to his penis, he masturbated over the prone figure of Josephine

Peter relaxed a little, he repositioned Josephine's clothes to reveal the front of her body, he found one of her brown leather shoes and placed it gently between her thighs, he spent a moment or two searching for its partner but soon gave up the search. On a snowy and wet evening, she lost her life five minutes shy of midnight, 23:55 hours, her last journey finished some three hundred metres short of the desired destination. He then covered his handy work with Josephine's three-quarter length jacket. The muddy pitch had worn patches of grass and the muddy areas were ideal for capturing the clue of his shoe/boot size.

For whom the bell toll's, Ernest Hemingway's Spanish Civil War classic, for Josephine Whittaker read Robert Jordan, for Peter William Sutcliffe, read the Falangist fascist protagonists that rape and execute Jordan's girlfriend's parents. Fact like fiction is rarely fair, 00:00 hours the church bells tolled to mark the passing of one of Halifax's daughters, one of their flock, one of their congregation. A death knell to Josephine and the other hapless victims.

Peter started to walk away from her body directly towards Savile Park Road, he then broke into a run, he then slowed down because he saw a figure approaching walking up the road, so he retraced his steps and walked in the safety of the darkness a reverse of the journey he and Josephine had just taken. Peter returned to his car unhindered and unmolested, he drove home. He reached the sanctuary of 6 Garden Lane and took off his brown coat he painstakingly checked himself for signs of his evening's escapades, but other than the bottom of his jeans and his black boots being covered in Halifax mud, there was no evidence of his evenings work.

Thursday the 5th of April 1979CE, 5:30 hours Calderdale Metro bus driver Ronald Marwood passes Savile Park whilst driving the green and white number 6 bus, this routes first bus of the day, he noticed a pile of discarded clothes on the playing fields. On his return to the bus station he reported his observation to the office staff, however the fly tipping of some rags seemed low down on the priorities of the day and no action was taken in resolving/reporting the rubbish to the authorities. Unbeknown to Ronald and his colleagues he was the first witness to the discovery of Josephine Whittaker's body and a Yorkshire Ripper murder scene.

6:30 hours Jean Markham a factory machinist stood at the bus stop on Free School Lane at the junction with Elmfield Terrace, her early morning gaze drawn towards a single brown ladies' leather shoe on the grassed area known as Savile Park. Her attention gained and her line of vision then honed in on what seemed to be a discarded bundle of clothes, her inquisitive awakening senses were invigorated and she decided to take a closer look at the unusual package. To her horror and realisation it was the last earthly remains of a young woman. Jean quickly recoiled and ran to the nearest public telephone to contact the authorities.

A sad personal twist to the events occurred when David, Josephine's younger brother was going home after collecting the newspapers from the newsagents to begin his paper round and was crossing the grassland and was intrigued by the police activity, a plethora of uniformed officers mulling around, strategically placed traffic cones, police tape and duct boards; it was then that he saw and recognised what he believed to be Josephine's discarded shoe, brown with a stacked heel accompanied/guarded by the orange and white of a lone traffic cone. His eyes were drawn to a bundle, a body lying face down on the football pitch. Too far away to identify as an individual, close enough to know that it was a corpse. Talk was rife of a dead woman, whispers amongst the morning commuters. A hit and run, road traffic accident, a grisly murder nobody was sure. As the realisation of what he thought he'd seen sunk in, David hurried back to the Ivy Street family home to inform his mother Thelma, and stepfather Haydn of his fears.

They checked Jo's bedroom and found it empty and her bed unslept in, their worst fears partially confirmed they immediately rang Halifax police station, desperate for some answers.

7:20 hours, the police contacted Halifax bus station instructing them to move the bus stop on Free School Lane at the junction with Elmfield Terrace, away from the murder scene of Josephine Whittaker. This brought about the realisation that bus driver Ronald Marwood was in fact the first person to find Josephine's last earthly remains.

Friday the 6th of April 1979CE, 18:30 hours Assistant Chief Constable George Oldfield made a statement *"We have a homicidal maniac at large and I believe he lives in West Yorkshire. This man will continue to kill until he is caught...All women are at risk, even in areas not regarded as Ripper territory"*

NO WOMAN WAS SAFE! Women's lib, men's lib, adlib, spare rib, broken rib. Free fall, free for all. The time bomb ticking no resistance from Peter, now just compliance, acceptance and a religious zeal to repeal the ills of the moral decline of society. Undercover, overt covert plain clothed policemen were the order of the day in Chapeltown and Lumb Lane oblivious to their obvious advertisement for law and order. Their man smoked out unerringly unaware that their efforts had indirect implications for the safety of the women of West Yorkshire Ripperville. NO WOMAN WAS SAFE!

Wednesday the 5th of April 1979CE, 18:30 hours, George Oldfield faced the press.
"The dead girl is perfectly respectable, similar to Jayne MacDonald. It is more than a year since the Ripper last struck in Yorkshire." (The attack on Ann Rooney had not been recognised as Ripper at the time). *Josephine was badly beaten about the head and suffered injuries to her body".*

Friday the 7th of April 1979CE, George Oldfield once again addressed the massed ranks of the media, for murder sells papers, it also brings celebrity.
"We are looking for a clever person, if he is not living with us, he is not far out of West Yorkshire. The man is obviously mentally deranged, but now he has changed his pattern. We cannot stress how careful every woman must be. Unless we catch him, and the public must help us, he will go on and on. I warn all women to use lighted streets and to walk home with someone they know. In no circumstances accept lifts from strangers".

Peter continued his daily life indifferent to the anguish he had caused and was continuing to cause. Oblivious to the deranged monster that he had become. He scoffed at Oldfield's comments, no woman was safe, he thought of Sonia, Maureen and Anne. The only women who should fear him, were the ones who had upset God, or so he told himself. Although on occasions Peter felt deflated, dull disappointed, guilt ridden it was a penance he would have to suffer, it was all a part of his mission, a test that he would have to endure.

Palm Sunday the 8th of April 1979CE, the Reverend Michael Walker delivers his sermon at Saint Jude's Church, Savile Park, Halifax, West Yorkshire HX1 2XE, where Josephine et al were part of the congregation, in fact Josephine had been christened there in 1962CE. The Reverend Walker asked the fellowship to pray for Josephine and her family, but also for the perpetrator of this abominable deed.
"He needs help. He is someone's child, husband or father".

Holy Monday the 9th of April 1979CE, Peter reads with interest the newspaper reports, his inactivity had seen his alter ego the Yorkshire Ripper fall from the public spotlight. However he was now catapulted back into the headlines for all the wrong reasons, his interest was captured by the reporting of the recent comments made by the Reverend Michael Walker. He scoffed, for Peter had all the help he needed. Only God could judge him and seeing as he was acting as an instrument of the Lord, doing his bidding, he knew he need not worry.

The police found important clues at the murder scene, the footprints were that of a composition or moulded rubber soled boot, commonly found in the armed forces or for industrial protection and were reliably linked to the ones found at the scene of Emily Jackson's murder and also the bed clothes at Tina Atkinson's flat. The size of the footprints, size seven (although possibly up to eight and a half) also correlated to the previous murders. The police also concluded that the right sole showed wear consistent with repeated actions, there was a suggestion that the murderer might be a lorry driver. The fact that within the wounds on Josephine's body were tinges of milling oil used in the engineering industry drew unfortunate overtones. West Yorkshire Police had received a letter (the third in total) on Monday the 23rd of March 1979CE, on one of the envelopes which had contained a letter from a man claiming to be the murderer the press had dubbed the Yorkshire Ripper, there was traces of milling oil akin to that found within Jo. This was to prove a coincidence which would lead to the police investigation taking another unfortunate turn. Or was God ensuring his loyal servant Peter was given further scope to pursue his bidding and continue the divine mission. The police speculated that the murderer could be a semi-skilled worker with mechanical/engineering links, or perhaps 'he' was an electrical engineer or skilled machine tool-fitter.

Monday the 16th of April 1979CE, Assistant Chief Superintendent Mr George Oldfield called a special police press conference, he asked Yorkshire machine tool manufacturing companies, or Yorkshire based companies with interests in plant maintenance or engineering that have links with the North East to verify if they had any employees who worked or were working in Tyneside/Wearside on the dates the trilogy of letters were posted. Likewise he appealed to companies in the North East to check and see if Yorkshire based workers were in the North East on the dates in question. He also said he would be extremely interested to hear from employers who had employees that were absent from work on these dates.

Nineteen/Eleven
Halifax, Wednesday 4th April 1979 CE. (23:55 hours) *A real life Little Red West Riding Hood, the young girl and the big bad wolf and a visit to her grandmother, but no lumberjack. The voice in Peter's head said, "This is a likely tale. She is really trying to play tricks on me. She is very clever, this one. You are not going to fall for all this". God could not be wrong; Peter did the deed and disappeared into the dark.*

The goalposts had shifted, the NIMBY (not in my back yard) culture of middle-class northern England were now all possible victims. The roll call of recruitment to the moribund macabre misdemeanours of murder most foul. Mutilation became salvation, the reality of the situation, the gravity of the environment, down beat, down trodden synonymous with the 1957CE Harold McMillan speech *'You've never had it so good'* baby boomers juxtaposed with the nihilistic blank generation of post punk. The innocent woman analogy, the haves and the have never wills, they take it off. The dark cloak of the Yorkshire Ripper had descended on middle England.

In an envelope addressed to: - ASST. CHIEF CONSTABLE OLDFIELD, LEEDS CID, LEEDS CENTRAL POLICE HQ, LEEDS, WEST YORKSHIRE, came an audio cassette tape, the manufacturers label had been removed. The message on the C-30 cassette (a 30-minute audio cassette) faltered with the STOP and RECORD buttons used to produce the finished article.

Audio Red Herring Sunday 17th June 1979 (Chapter 22)

I'm Jack. I see you are still having no luck catching me. I have the greatest respect for you, George, but Lord, you are no nearer catching me now than four years ago when I started. I reckon your boys are lettin' you down, George. They can't be much good, can they? The only time they came near catching me was a few months back in Chapeltown, when I was disturbed. Even then it was a uniformed copper, not a detective.

I warned you in March that I'd strike again. Sorry it wasn't Bradford. I did promise you that, but I couldn't get there. I'm not quite sure when I'll strike again, but it will definitely be sometime this year, maybe September, October or even sooner if I get the chance. I'm not sure where, maybe Manchester; I like it there, there's plenty of them knocking about. They never learn, do they, George? I bet you've warned them. But they never listen. At the rate I'm goin', I should be in the book of records. I think it's eleven up to now, isn't it? Well, I'll keep on going for quite a while yet. I can't see myself being nicked just yet. Even if you do get near, I'll probably top myself first. Well, it's been nice chatting to you, George. Yours, Jack the Ripper. No good looking for fingerprints, you should know by now it's as clean as a whistle. See you soon. 'Bye. Hope you like the catchy tune at the end. Ha-ha. "Thank You For Being A Friend" by Andrew Gold was the closing tune.

The envelope in which the cassette was delivered was taken to Wetherby Forensic Science Service laboratories Audbey Lane, Wetherby, LS22 7DN. The adhesive gum on the envelope contained traces of saliva, from this they deduced that the person who licked the envelope and therefore very possibly the writer and therefore very possibly the 'Yorkshire Ripper' was blood type 'B' secretor. Handwriting experts concluded that the person who had sent the tape was also responsible for the three previous letters.

Thursday the 20th of June 1979CE, saw a high-brow, high-flyers, high level conference in Halifax. Representatives from Manchester, Lancashire and Sunderland were in attendance, guests of the West Yorkshire Metropolitan Police. The raison d'etre, what to do with this newfound information? The common consensus of the constabulary was to go public with the tape in the expectation of a quick arrest. An extended game of 'Call My Bluff' via the General Post Office/Royal Mail. This was truth or dare, a game of 'Call My Bluff' with high-stakes, lives, careers and reputations were all in the mix.

Monday 25th of June 1979CE an angered Assistant Chief Superintendent Mr George Oldfield feels his hand forced, the fact that the police are in receipt of, in possession of the 'Ripper Tape' is leaked to the press. A hasty re-hash of the original intended press conference, undermined by police in fighting, was this really for the best? Good intentions, bad vibes into the depths of a horde of scribes. Sinister forces at work or God protecting the mission?

Tuesday the 26th of June 1979CE 14:00 hours, an extraordinary press conference was held, Assistant Chief Constable George Oldfield, cut a forlorn figure sitting in front of an assembled audience of the massed media. The location was a lecture theatre at the police academy in Bishopgarth, 1 Bede Ct, Wakefield WF1 3RW. He was the focal point of the attention, on a table in front of him an industrial sized rectangular shaped audio tape cassette player, two tone grey, too big, with dimensions of approximately two foot, by one foot, by six inches, the plain C-30 cassette, the circles of the reels REC, PLAY, REVIEW, CUE, STOP/EJECT, PAUSE, MIN...VOLUME...MAX, MICROPHONE, AUTO STOP SYSTEM. The tape recorder was rigged up to a loudspeaker to ensure nobody missed a single word of the narrative. The black control buttons to the front of the unit.

Assistant Chief Constable George Oldfield moved forward to the tape recorder in an attempt to start the tape, the hushed audience watched in silence as he fumbled with the machine struggling to find the start/play button. Detective Superintendent Dick Holland surged forward from Oldfield's side and pressed the play button and the VOICE OF THE RIPPER was heard. The horseshoe audience of fifty plus reporters edged forward, closer to the source of the noise, closer to the sound of evil.

"I'm Jack. I see you are still having no luck catching me... 'Bye. Hope you like the catchy tune at the end. Ha-ha".
Six lines from the Andrew Gold song, 'Thank You for Being a Friend' a minor UK hit in 1978CE, peaking at an unremarkable number forty-two.
'Thank you for being a friend
Travelled down the road and back again
Your heart is true, you're a pal and a confidant
I'm not ashamed to say
I hope it always will stay this way
My hat is off, won't you stand up and take a bow'

Assistant Chief Constable George Oldfield, hard drinking, hard-working, hard; leant forward and pressed the black STOP/EJECT button, there was a pregnant pause, his audience waited with bated breath, all ears, the suspense tangible. Assistant Chief Constable George Oldfield broke the silence.
"*I believe we have now got the break we have been waiting for in our hunt for the so-called Yorkshire Ripper. I have already disclosed that I have received three letters from a person I believe to be the man speaking. I am satisfied that the tape and the three letters are all from one man - the man I believe to be the person we are seeking. This man was no doubt born in Sunderland or the Sunderland area".*
A member of the press asked Mr. Oldfield.
"*Why don't you call in Scotland Yard?*" Mr. Oldfield looked nonplussed, but Dick Holland. The larger than life character, a genial giant, a coppers copper, blunt and abrupt at times, he could be a veritable Rottweiler at times, when required and at nineteen stone, this police Rugby Union prop forward looked the part stepped forward, taking the stage. "*Why should we? They haven't caught theirs yet*".

Photographs of the envelopes were also released, white adhesive dots stuck to the top left-hand corner of the four envelopes, 1, 2, 3 and 4 written on them. Hold the front page. Local, regional, national and international news, fiction, fact and legend. Hot news cold hearted killer, cold case investigation, the nation's most wanted. Morality affronted, but Peter questioned by whom. Double standards, double murders. Copycat killers.

With the distinctive voice on the tape cassette police suggested that the author's days of freedom were numbered. This was the breakthrough that the police had hoped for, the pressmen were issued with a C-30 plain black cassette with a copy of the message. The tape received blanket coverage and filled the airwaves and was broadcast on ITV, BBC1 and BBC2.

The jury was out on the letters & tape. It raised more questions than it answered. Hoax, clue, Sunderland, I'm Jack, Yorkshire Ripper, Black Panther, Morley, West Midlands, David, Liverpool, Bradford, letters, mad as a March Hare, snare trap, CID, Lancashire, Northumbria, Manchester, West Yorkshire, George (Oldfield), Wilf (Brookes), Brian (Johnson), Peter (Docherty), Jack (Ridgeway), David (Zackrinson) and Dick (Holland). The Magnificent Seven. One lad that shook the north, yeah, yeah, yeah. Free-phone, Geordie boy, dial a Ripper. Whitechapel, Jack the Ripper, 1888CE plagiarism amongst the criminal fraternity. Hoax, clue, persona non grata, handwriting, forensics, hope, hate, repudiations and reputations. Landslide of information, overload, inundated, innuendo, propaganda, fear, revenge, reprisal, good intentions. Over time, additional resources. Handwriting samples, doctored extracts, commuter killer thrill seeker.

The summer of 1979CE saw the spotlight of police attention moved north easterly to Tyneside/Wearside, Northumbria. The net widening, the net tightening? Almost immediately the Northumbria Police adopted blanket exposure, in the hope that the voice on the tape is recognised. With an almost evangelical zeal they took the message of 'The Ripper' out and about to a bewildered public.

7th of August 1979CE, Stanley Ellis and Jack Windsor voice and linguistic experts from The University of Leeds used their skills to pinpoint the geographical source of the dialect recorded for posterity by a gentleman claiming to be the 'Yorkshire Ripper'. The finger of suspicion pointed to Castletown, a small village near Sunderland on the British Ordnance Survey map. Both men felt certain that the culprit originated from Castletown, however they had doubts as to whether or not the tape and letters were genuinely from the killer. They believed that his untainted, undiluted accent meant that he still lived and worked in the area and if the police did their job appropriately he would soon be arrested.

Castletown was a small mining village serving Hylton Colliery to the North West periphery of Sunderland city centre, with a population of around three thousand souls housed in one thousand six-hundred properties. Detectives visited all of these properties and conducted a detailed questionnaire, it was completed in ten days and produced no suspect.

(Thursday the 20th of October 2005CE, John Humble was arrested for the hoax correspondence, charged with four counts of perverting the course of justice and dubbed Wearside Jack; over twenty-five years later. George Oldfield scapegoated had to eat humble pie, a dish that he very nearly choked upon).

INTERVIEW WITH A SERIAL KILLER NUMBER FIVE:
Sunday 29th July 1979 CE

Detective-Constable Andrew Laptew and Detective-Constable Graham Greenwood visit number 6 Garden Lane, Heaton; mid-afternoon on Sunday 29th July 1979 CE. Pre-informed with the following information.
'P.W.Sutcliffe, lorry driver, triple-area sighting'.

It was the usual run of the mill Ripper case interview. The officers knocked on the front door and were shortly greeted by Mr Peter William Sutcliffe, who answered the door. Peter adjusted his clothing as he descended the stairs. Who could this be on a Sunday afternoon? Peter opened the door, the visitors introduced themselves and Peter ushered them into the living room.
"What is your full name?" Detective-Constable Andrew Laptew asked.
"Peter William Sutcliffe". Mr Peter William Sutcliffe replied.

"What is your date of birth?" Detective-Constable Graham Greenwood asked.
"2nd of June 1946 CE". Mr Peter William Sutcliffe replied.
"What is your occupation". Detective-Constable Andrew Laptew asked.
"Lorry driver," Mr Peter William Sutcliffe replied.
"Who do you work for?" Detective-Constable Graham Greenwood asked.
"T & W.H. Clark Limited," Mr Peter William Sutcliffe replied.

This began to set Detective-Constable Andrew Laptew's mind racing. But why? He tried to remember; the five pounds note enquiry? Detective-Constable Andrew Laptew decided that after the interview he would dig deeper into the background of what was at present a low level, run of the mill interview.

"Now's the time to get rid of your husband if you want to". Detective-Constable Andrew Laptew delivered the tried and tested line, the ice breaker, the hook line failed to do its job. It went over the couple's head, no funny bones were activated, no teeth were pulled, but the detectives possibly felt there were.

"Is there any chance of a glass of water please Mrs Sutcliffe?" Detective-Constable Graham Greenwood asked and Sonia the dutiful host complied, asking the officer's if they preferred *"Tea or coffee".*

With Sonia gone Detective-Constable Andrew Laptew asked the more personal, more prudent question.

"Have you ever used the services of prostitutes? If you want I could arrange a private interview where Mrs Sutcliffe is not within earshot".

"No, I don't have anything to do with them and I don't want a private interview, I'll answer your questions now" Mr Peter William Sutcliffe replied.

"You seem to travel through the Manningham area quite a bit, can you tell us why?" Detective-Constable Graham Greenwood asked.

"I don't know exactly but I drive home from work via the city centre or just visiting the city centre with the wife," Mr Peter William Sutcliffe replied.

"What about Chapeltown Leeds, have you been there recently?"

"Yes, I took the wife to a nightclub a while back".

"What about Manchester, have you been there recently?"

"No, I haven't been to Manchester for ages," Mr Peter William Sutcliffe replied.

When asked if they could remember his/ their whereabouts on Wednesday 4TH April 1979 CE, the weekend of 16th and 17th May 1978 CE and Tuesday 31st January 1978 CE.

Peter William Sutcliffe, replied calmly, quietly *"I dunno where I was, but if ever I go out, it's only with our lass".*

Sonia returned to the living room with a pot of tea, Detective-Constable Andrew Laptew asked, *"So Mr Sutcliffe can I just re-cap, do you or have you ever visited or used the services of prostitutes?"*

"*No,*" Mr Peter William Sutcliffe replied

The officers then asked Mr Peter William Sutcliffe for a statement of confirmation, and asked Mrs Sonia Sutcliffe for a statement, confirming her and her husband's whereabouts on specific days and dates. Neither could recollect a visit to Manchester, but Sonia remembered their visit to Leeds. Both complied without a fuss.
"*What blood group are you Mr Sutcliffe,*" Detective-Constable Graham Greenwood, asked.
"*I dunno,*" Mr Peter William Sutcliffe replied. "*Would you be willing to provide us with a sample of your blood?*" Detective-Constable Graham Greenwood asked.
"Yes," Mr Peter William Sutcliffe replied.

The two officers then searched his car and the garage but found nothing incriminating. They also obtained a sample of Mr Sutcliffe's handwriting and found out his feet were size 8½, and he wore soft crepe soled boots. 16:30 hours the officers concluded their questioning and left the Sutcliffe's in peace.

However Laptew and Greenwood didn't feel so peaceful. They both found the interview heavy going, the officers asked their questions, Mr Peter William Sutcliffe deliberated, procrastinated, he did not avoid the answers but answered without emotion. Softly spoken slightly high-pitched local accent, Sonia, didn't seem quite right, but for what reason, they just couldn't quite put their finger on it. What an odd couple, a lorry driver and a teacher the plastic covers on the settee and chairs, the pristine appearance of the property, unnaturally sterile, too clean, too tidy, clinical, un-homely, strange?
"*What do you reckon, shall we take him in?*" Detective-Constable Graham Greenwood suggested.
"*What arrest him on suspicion? That's a big call, I don't know, we'd need Oldfield's say so. Let's leave it but file a report with our concerns, that'll more than cover it. Agreed?*" Detective-Constable Andrew Laptew, retorted.
"*Agreed,*" Detective-Constable Graham Greenwood agreed.

Under suspicion, on the ropes, up against the wall, uncomfortable, caught off guard. Dour, unnatural, unnerving, disconcerting
Sutcliffe's vehicle had been sighted some thirty-six times in the red-light area and across all three areas. Already in the system but key information unavailable due to an overloaded system, delays in updating and the curse of human error. Laptew and Greenwood partially blind unaware of previous cross area sightings of Sutcliffe's red Corsair and the five pounds note inquiry.

He was in the frame, his body frame was the right build, his body was the right height according to Maureen Long and Marlyn Moore, two women who'd had first-hand experience of the Yorkshire Ripper. Sutcliffe had a Jason King style moustache and beard, dark complexion and black collar length hair, if not the Marilyn Moore photo-fit of the Yorkshire Ripper, not far off. The gap toothed 'Terry Thomas' cad, his bite mark a clue to his identity, like Jimmy Tarbuck but even less funny, another clue from the grave. He was a lorry driver, this was a possible suspected occupation for the perpetrator. He had a foot size 8½, Size 7 boot prints were found at the scene of the latest Halifax murder, boot that could be comfortably worn by a person with a shoe size of anything up to size 8½. The worn right shoe could suggest a lorry driver. Detective-Constable Andrew Laptew and Detective-Constable Graham Greenwood had interviewed hundreds of men throughout the Yorkshire Ripper investigation, both felt he, Mr Peter William Sutcliffe was the best they had seen by far. Something was not quite right.

The officers left Garden Lane with a to do list, a visit to T & W.H. Clark Limited, to check out Mr Sutcliffe in more detail, on contacting T & W.H. Clark Limited, it became obvious that Peter Sutcliffe was in their eyes the model employee. Timesheets were obtained and further samples of his handwriting were procured, all were in order.
Checking Sutcliffe's previous convictions via the Regional Criminal Records Office, Detective-Constable Andrew Laptew was not surprised to hear that he had been previously convicted for 'going equipped to steal'. However, in hindsight if he had checked with the Criminal Records Office at Scotland Yard, the details would have surely seen Laptew bursting through the doors of the Idle incident room demanding Sutcliffe's arrest; the important anomalies were the burglary tool had been an hammer, (the Yorkshire Ripper's signature weapon) and the fact that he had earlier been arrested in a stationary car in the red-light district. But this was not to be!

THE REPORTING OFFICERS ARE NOT FULLY SATISFIED WITH THIS MAN.

Detective Constable Andrew Laptew prepared a two page report highlighting his and Detective-Constable Graham Greenwood's concerns, he handed it over placing his trust in the system, where nine months later, approximately April 1980 CE it was read and marked to file, no further action.

Chapter 23
Babs

Unbeknown to Peter William Sutcliffe someone (other than God) was on his side, another missionary working in tandem on the Holy mission, another prophet, a disciple of the Lord. Someone else working tirelessly relentlessly to eradicate the filth and scum stagnating, impregnating and undermining society. The letters and tape were in the public arena, they were also manna from heaven for a hard-working Peter William Sutcliffe. Peter saw this as an opportunity and adopted an approach that helped muddy the waters. Unbeknown to Peter, the 'hoaxer' in his audio affront had hinted at an attack in September or October, the dull monotone voice from the cutting-edge technology of D.I.Y. (Do It Yourself) northern England, circa 1979 CE.

Barbara Janine Leach was twenty years old and a student at Bradford University, she was originally from Kettering in Northamptonshire but had come to Bradford in 1977 to study for a degree in social psychology. Barbara lived in a shared house at 20 Grove Terrace, Bradford, BD7, with fellow university students. Barbara had an older brother called Graham who was twenty-two years old and had successfully achieved a degree from Cambridge, her parents David (aged fifty-three) a clerk at Barclays Bank and Beryl (aged forty-eight), a school teacher at one of Barbara's former schools, the Henry Grotch primary school, lived in the three bedroomed semi-detached family home at Hazel Road, Kettering, NN15.

Barbara was commonly known around campus and the Bradford area as Babs and had immersed herself in all aspects of university life. She was part of the university's equestrian club and often travelled by bus to the Tong village stables, in the south east boundary of the city to pursue her hobby. She was popular in the student house in which she resided due to her sociable nature, this popularity was enhanced by her willingness to muck in with cooking and cleaning chores and generally act as a mother hen to the co-habitants at Grove Terrace. Her brother Graham (or Crow, as she often called him), described Barbara's take on life as a unique brand of 'Cosmopolitan Feminism', this was endorsed by her interest in Greenpeace, Canine Defence League, and the RSPCA (Royal Society for the Prevention of Cruelty to Animals). In her lust for life, Babs was popular, an extrovert and amiable, she was well known and liked within the university student community, but also the wider Bradford community and of course she was loved and adored in her Kettering 'home'.

Initially she resided in the university's halls of residence, however followed the usual rites of passage moved into the large Victorian terraced houses (at the time owned by the university) adjacent to the university but in the big wide world of Bradford city centre. A type of half-way house for students. Cutting the apron strings, encouraging independence.

Saturday the 1st of September 1979CE and the students in Barbara's cohort were on countdown to the start of the third and final year at the university and possibly the city itself. Bab's rang home from the public telephone box at the end of Grove Terrace to wish her father (David) a happy birthday, she apologised for forgetting to send him a birthday card and whilst on the phone arranged for her mother (Beryl) to book her an hair appointment (Bab's was adamant she needed to renew her perm), for Monday the 3rd of September when she planned to return to the family home in Kettering. The conversation ended. *"Bye mum, I'll see you on Monday".* In the afternoon, Barbara went into Bradford city centre shopping for a suitable present for her father, ironically she chose a mug bearing the dedication 'Life is too short not to live it up a little'.

Saturday the 1st of September was a bright hot and sunny day, autumn had arrived however summer was the season that was to the fore. The bright daylight gave way to a pleasant night and saw Babs and her friends decide to descend upon the Manville Arms public house, 31-33 Great Horton Road, BD7; a regular haunt for their group and other university students. They walked through the doors of the Mannville Arms around 21:00 hours. The Grove Terrace ensemble, team Bradford, Barbara, Paul (Smith) aged twenty-one, Alison (Hillman) aged nineteen, Gabrielle (Rhodes) and their flatmate Rob. The group while away the remains of the night listening to the music from the jukebox, the Mannville Arm's was quite renowned for the choice and variety of its jukebox. Similarly it was also known for its Tetley Bitter. The group also played a game of darts, Rob and Paul would help Roy Evans (the Mannville Arms jovial and friendly landlord) behind the bar if it became busy, or collect glasses for him and generally help out. Last orders were called by Roy Evans at 23:00 hours, however he'd decided to prolong the evenings ambience by allowing a lock in. Among the people who remained in the hostelry was Barbara who along with her fellow friends and students enjoyed the rest of the evening. Sunday the 2nd of September 00:45 hours and the participants of the private party had begun to disperse and make their way into the fresh night air. The balmy night remained warm and agreeable although a light drizzle had begun to fall, the five strong group thanked Roy for his hospitality whilst Roy thanked them for their help, company and their custom.

Having consumed two pints of cider and one steak and kidney pie, Barbara declined the idea of a curry nightcap but was prepared to go along with the common consensus of the group. After a brief discussion and a straw poll it was decided the group would call it a night. Barbara asked Paul if he fancied accompanying her on a brisk walk, he declined this offer, however agreed to wait up for Bab's at the flat, to let her in. Bab's had lent her key to Gabrielle (Rhodes) who had been attending Grove Terrace to feed JC a black and white stray cat adopted by Bab's. Such behaviour supported the trust and community present in this inner-city enclave, within a mile geographically of the city centre but a million miles away aesthetically and in its morality from the rest of the city centre. Two different worlds that were about to collide.

"I won't be late". Explained Barbara in what were to be her last worldly words. The main group peeled off, turning left onto the wide expanse of Grove Terrace, whilst Barbara continued to walk slowly up the ascent that was Great Horton Road, past Mannville Terrace, Back Manville Terrace, Claremont and Back Ashgrove, she took her fifth left turn into the wide expanse of Ash Grove, Barbara had a habit of taking late night walks, she liked to collect her thoughts and take in the night air.

Peter ever the amateur mechanic had spent the evening tinkering with his relatively new toy, 1971 CE ROVER P6B 3500 S (synchromesh) Saloon; the 0 to 60 mph in 9 seconds and a maximum speed of 117 mph, this type of performance bolstered Peter's ego, like the state of the art Ford Transcontinental HGV he got to drive at work, 'Wee Willie', Peter revelled in the prestige and the power when at the wheel of the quarter of a million pounds worth of advanced engineering with its easily recognizable by its high cab, it was an extremely advanced vehicle for its time offering a high standard of driver comfort and a high power output for its time.

Peter decided to test run his personal pride and joy to assess his evenings work. He also decided to cruise the streets of inner-city Bradford in an attempt to supress the urge or feed the urge that was now his constant companion. Urges to kill were continual and out of control a remote-control automaton of God. There was an ulterior motive to his mechanics and wheeler dealing in the used car market, he needed to keep one step ahead of the police. Peter was clever, but his alter ego the Yorkshire Ripper was really clever and really special to be able to avoid detection. He seemed reinforced by an almost supernatural power that aided and abetted his nocturnal outings, showing his incredible nerve, his incredible strength and his amazing courage to continue his superhuman crusade. But with God as an ally what else would you expect.

A precursor to the deplorable deeds that were to follow, a perverted piece of fore play, preparing Peter for his own type of debased fornication, he retreated to the toilet in his sterile clean home, the home he shared with his wife. In the house that underlined his success and the success of his marriage. In the house of his dreams where he hid the truth that his life was a sham. He removed his trousers, his underpants, put his feet through the sleeves of the V-neck sweaters arms and into his gimp leggings. Obviously aroused he knew what he had to do. He had fought the good fight and finally lost the battle after a five-month struggle. Peter had lost the battle his will broken, God had won. No clues, this was a vital mission. The battle finally lost, Peter consigned to his fate he was an instrument of God. God the victor. No dialogue just death, Peter was all talked out, he was certain that he could not be caught and this had been proved time after time. His killing urges his compulsion to kill in remission, but still he had to fulfil his mission. Who was God going to send him next?

Peter Sutcliffe was driving the streets of Bradford, he drove up Great Horton Road and chanced upon a group of young adults of mixed gender, his attention as ever was drawn to the females amongst the group, the urge was within him and this was possibly the opportunity at which it could be sated. He drove past them slowly in an attempt to further assess the situation, the slope of the road being no match for the powerful engine of the large brown Rover 3500 V8 saloon with a black vinyl roof registration FHY 400K. The crowd seemed in good mood, he decided to turn left and park up on Ash Grove, one of the many tributary roads to the left of Great Horton Road when travelling uphill out of the city centre. He pulled his car over on the left hand side of the road, which was bordered by large stone built terraced houses, their appearance once proud, grand and ostentatious was now a little down at heel, care worn having seen better days. Peter opened the driver's side car door and stepped out into the road, on exiting the vehicle he saw Barbara who had peeled off from the larger group, which had proceeded up the slope of Great Horton Road. Barbara turned left onto Ash Grove and was now strolling slowly towards Peter and his parked car.

Peter let her pass by and then quickly grabbed the large screwdriver and ball peen hammer from under his driver's seat and placed them safely in his jackets inside the false breast pocket, the lining cut to allow him to hide his implements of death. Swiftly Peter surveyed his surroundings looking up and down Ash Grove, this rushed reconnaissance gave the green light to his intended actions. He was happy that there was no one there to witness his imminent attack. He quickly manoeuvred onto the same pavement as Barbara reached into his pocket and pulled out his trusty hammer, he held it tight into his leg to obscure its obviousness and stealthily he closed in on his victim. He savoured the moment, compared himself to the power of his car, his HGV, he was at one with God, he was full of the spirit of the Lord. He had crossed over into the hinterland his morality heightened and diminished at the same time, he sensed Barbara's mortality. When he was in striking distance of Barbara he swung his left arm, which was in possession of the ball peen hammer, his swing was halted by the soft hair, flesh and hard bone that constituted the back of Barbara's head. Instantly Barbara collapsed to the hard floor of the pavement. Peter hurriedly dragged Barbara's limp body by the ankles to his left and down the side of number 13 Ashgrove, BD7. A dividing wall of Yorkshire stone separated the gardens of number 13 and 15 Ashgrove and also helped to obscure Peter's actions from possible prying eyes, whilst the gable end of number 13 also contributed to the seclusion, creating a ginnel/alley type affect.

The throbbing noise of a house party broke the calm of the night air, 16 Ash Grove, the windows were open the house was full, the welcome back to Bradford party in full swing. A house full of witnesses, a house full of revellers, a house full of hedonism self-centred embroiled in their own enjoyment, too busy to notice, too busy to care. For ignorance is bliss and bliss is in short supply when the grisly Yorkshire Ripper comes to call.

He pulled into the open back yard area of the property on what was now the cobbled and more isolated Back Ashgrove, Barbara's army style shoulder bag fell to the floor. Now intent and focussed on the job in hand Peter got down to work, he pushed up her cheesecloth shirt and bra to reveal her breasts and pulled down her denim jeans. Peter unzipped the front of his jeans, his gimp leggings allowing him the access he craved, these depraved actions aroused him. Barbara moaned in the shadows, but she was obscured from prying eyes. Quickly Peter satisfied his urges, then turned his attention fully onto Barbara whose moaning continued, Peter put an end to that by producing the large screwdriver from his breast pocket and stabbing Barbara in her central stomach, her chest and to the side of her trunk, skewering her vital organs and extinguishing her life. The moaning stopped. Barbara suffered eight entry wounds to her body, however Peter had indulged the urges of the beast within and had stabbed through the flesh, he recoiled his weapon partially then deviated the angle and thrust the implement repeatedly into her body. Re-insertion, sexual deviance and a Catholic crusade, this superhero world of Peter William Sutcliffe was debased and out of control, but he was on a roll, unable to stop. The urge dissipated, exhausted and spent, a sickening parallel to Barbara's young life. The time was 1:00 hours, the date was Sunday the 2nd of September 1979CE.

He now had to hide the evidence, the evidence that was Barbara Leach, he needed to buy some time to cover his tracks, and he appraised his surroundings and looked for a convenient place to hide Barbara's body. There was a dwarf wall to his left, scooping up her body he placed it in a jack-knife position in an area that was usually used to house the dustbins. Peter then picked up a tatty piece of discarded carpet, sodden and smelly from its prolonged exposure to the extremities. He draped it over the body and then weighed it down with the loose pieces of Yorkshire stone that adorned the yard. Discarded like rubbish in the place reserved for rubbish a final ignominy.

1:30 hours at Grove Terrace, Paul Smith retires to bed, leaving the door on the latch awaiting Barbara's return. He thought nothing of her 'no show' and assumed that she'd dropped in to see friends at one of the many parties that were ongoing in the student area. Little did he know that approximately two hundred metres away his housemate lay dead.

1:30 hours and Peter had finally completed his body posing, he returned to the pleasant tree lined suburban setting that was Ashgrove, he quickly returned to his parked car and decanted the tools from his pockets, replacing them under the driver's seat, before setting off on the short journey home. Right onto Easby Road, up to Dirkhill Road, right onto Horton Grange Road onto Ingleby Road, following the road around to the right onto Whetley Lane, left at the junction where Whetley Lane meets Whetley Hill meets Carlisle Road meets Toller Lane up Toller Lane, right onto Heaton Park Drive, then left onto Garden Lane, then left up the incline and onto the driveway of number six. The three-mile journey home was unremarkable and took less than ten minutes.

1:50 hours, the weather changed for the worst, the steady drizzle turned into a monsoon, a downpour, Mother Nature offering him a helping hand, destroying any valuable evidence. Proof if proof was needed that God was very much on Peter William Sutcliffe's side.

Peter unwittingly honoured the promise of his theological friend, the 'Geordie' Ripper tape was truly a message from God. The urge a catalyst was reinforced by the validity that the police place on the oral horrors promised by north east dialect narrative that was produced for the delectation of the police, who in turn had decided to unleash it on an unsuspecting public. His threats against northern women were recorded for posterity for an uncaring world to receive, retrieve and read into it what they may. Peter was clever, his timing was lucky, but seemingly influenced by the tape maker. The voice on the tape his anonymous co-conspirator, his long-distance accomplice, his right-hand man.
"Sorry it wasn't Bradford". Like a cat bringing dead animals' home and leaving them proudly for their owners. Peter delivered on 'Wearside Jack's' promise of time and place. To exonerate Peter from his deeds and to validate the content of the letters and tape. Opportunity knocked and both men opened the door widely and invited the imposter even further into their lives, with arms wide open. The tragedy in the process of being played would suffer an encore, an encore ultimately sponsored by 'Wearside Jack'. The oaf that George Oldfield was becoming type cast as, stuck with the hand he had been dealt, ultimately he was to be the scapegoat for West Yorkshire's keystone cops.

As ever the Yorkshire Ripper's timing was impeccable. The forces of the West Yorkshire Metropolitan Police Force were depleted, the hierarchy of the Ripper Squad on holiday, sick or compassionate leave. But Peter had little compassion and the Ripper had none. Life still goes on as does death. Prompted aided and abetted by the mystery benefactor, his literary accomplice Peter's alter ego struck once again. He struck at his earliest possible opportunity, as if to add extra authenticity to the letters.

The roll call of the Ripper Squad oligarchy showed a sparse attendance: - Assistant Chief Constable (West Yorkshire) George Oldfield. Absent. This was due to a heart attack he suffered in August 1979CE.
Detective Chief Superintendent (Leeds Area) James Hobson. Absent. This was due to an accident his wife had suffered, DCS Hobson was at his wife's Chapel Allerton Hospital bedside who had suffered a fractured skull after a fall at home.
Detective Superintendent (Bradford Area) Dick Holland. Absent. He was away on a caravan and fishing holiday in Glenrothes, Fife on the East coast of Scotland.
Detective Chief Superintendent (Bradford Area) Peter Gilrain. Present.

A big reason why Bab's had returned to the University of Bradford early was to participate in the social life which she had enjoyed for the past two years, but also to prepare herself and her attic flat for the third year of her degree. Bab's had chosen Bradford way back in

1977CE because she wanted to live with common people, real people and see how the other half lived, to witness northern wit, humour, hospitality, hostility and HORROR; in the raw and at first hand. In effect to live the course and study it practically and also theoretically. She was not afraid of hard work, having worked at Boots the Chemist (in Kettering), Prime Cuts factory, (Stamford Road, Kettering) and also in handbag making factory (in Desborough). She used the money to finance a girls holiday to Greece in the summer of 1979CE with her friend Lauris, they were saving up and planning to repeat the holiday experience in Crete in the summer of 1980CE, a trip that Barbara would now never make.

Mid-morning on Sunday the 2nd of September, Barbara's housemates discover that her bed has not been slept in. They spent the rest of the morning searching for Bab's asking around the university networks, all to no avail. They called into the Mannville Arms at twelve noon and drew another blank, it was then that they decided to contact the police, with their concerns and reported Barbara as a missing person.

18:30 hours Barbara's housemates contact the police and notify them of their concerns at her disappearance.

20:00 hours the Bradford police ring Mr and Mrs Leach at their Kettering home to check that she has not returned home unannounced and without telling her flatmates. This possibility had to be ruled out in case she was safe, sound, oblivious of all the fuss she'd inadvertently caused. Therefore any need to search for Barbara would be negated, unfortunately Barbara had not returned. The couple had been settled watching the long running BBC drama the Onedin Line, the telephone call and conversation left them distraught and unsettled, their minds racing, both were immediately concerned that an ill deed had been done, both thought and fought with the idea of the Yorkshire Ripper, for Bradford was one of his (un)happy hunting grounds, the Leach's were shell shocked, in a state of limbo, all they could do was sit, wait, worry and hope.

Monday the 3rd of September, 12:30 hours, Gabrielle (Rhodes) attended the Bradford Interchange Student Centre to keep her date with Barbara. Gabrielle had been a part of the group and the decision the Bradford university students made to contact the police with their concerns; she had also told the police of her scheduled meeting with Bab's they asked her to keep the appointment in the hope that Barbara would turn up, they asked Gabrielle to inform them immediately of the outcome. Barbara of course did not show up, Gabrielle of course notified the police, who duly intensified their search. Gabrielle in hope or in desperation also visited the Shoulder of Mutton 28 Kirkgate, BD1, where she and Bab's had spent a carefree afternoon talking, drinking and laughing on Friday the 31st of August, only three days ago, but it seemed like a lifetime ago. Unfortunately it was to prove a lifetime away and this fact was soon to be confirmed by a young police constable.

15:55 hours, police constable Simon Greaves was searching for Barbara in the Little Horton area of the city, he walked down the cobbled street that was identified as Back Ashgrove by the large DIY white painted arrow and the words ← BACK ASH GROVE on the Yorkshire stone of the wall that formed the edge of the cobbled road and marked the perimeter of the garden of number 1 Ashgrove. The cobbles were uneven, some sunken, soiled with dirt and debris with occasional tufts of grass poking their way through. The edge of the cobbles gave way to rough grass that clung to the base of the garden walls that formed the narrow road. These walls then gave way to open yards. He meticulously searched through the open yards of each property. Eventually he arrived at number 13 Ashgrove, it was here where he saw a discarded piece of carpet covering a small wall that was used for storing the dustbins, and he looked closer and saw the toe caps of Barbara's red boots poking out from underneath the carpet. The carpet was weighed down by stones to ensure it hid the grisly secret wrapped within. It was then that he saw a part of Barbara's head peeking out from under the cover. He pulled back the carpet and revealed the pale distorted figure of Barbara Janine Leach, semi crouched in the jack knife position that Peter had posed her. Police constable Simon Greaves reached for his police issue radio and immediately radioed in his find.

19:30 hours, wracked with concern and at his wits end, David unable to deal with not knowing, rang Bradford police station. He briefly explained his predicament, hoping that at any minute the officer with whom he was conversing would reassure him that it had all been a big mistake, a misunderstanding and Barbara had been found, larger than life. The police officer explained and promised that they would ensure that they would notify David and Beryl immediately there was any news about their daughter.

19:40 hours Detective Chief Inspector George Smith rang Mr and Mrs Leach to put their minds at ease and reiterate that the police would contact the Leach's as soon has there were any developments.

21:15 hours, Hazel Road, Kettering, a police Sergeant accompanied by a woman police constable rang the doorbell of the Leach family home. The visit confirmed Mr & Mrs Leach's worst fears, Barbara was dead. Kettering to Bradford. One hundred and forty-three miles, a journey of two and a half hours, one hundred and fifty minutes. Beryl and David, passengers in the police car transporting them to the mortuary that housed the body of their daughter. The parent's minds racing faster than the Hillman Avenger that conveyed them to their unwelcome destination. Hoping above hope that it wasn't their Bab's, hoping not their daughter, but not wishing this claustrophobic intense feeling of emptiness, inadequacy and hurt on anyone else. A sombre journey a prelude to the nightmare that was to overshadow their lives. Numb, clinging to a false hope, knowing the terrible truth, but not wanting to believe it. The torture and turmoil caused directly by the murderer was unspeakable, however the indirect suffering caused by the police, in their mismanagement of the situation was unacceptable. Their inept mishandling contributed towards the living nightmare that Barbara's parents had to suffer.

Tuesday the 4th of September 1979CE, the parents were greeted in Bradford by Detective Chief Inspector George Smith who then asked them to identify the body of their daughter. David did the thankless deed, half in a dream, but it wasn't a dream, it was a nightmare. They were then taken to an hotel, where they spent a sleepless night unable to comprehend what was happening to them. In the early morning the couple were collected and taken to Bradford police station. The couple worked with the police to build up a picture of Barbara in the hope that this may help them with the inquiry. In the afternoon they asked to be taken to Barbara's flat. The police drove Beryl and David up the hill up Great Horton Road to, Grove Terrace which was ironically bustling with life, police officers abounded and Barbara's shell shocked flat-mates offered their heart-felt condolences. David and Beryl refused to meet the press and maintained a stoical silence requesting through the police that their privacy be respected. Their day from hell was finally completed when they were chauffeured back to Hazel Road, Kettering by police constable Simon Greaves, the officer who had had the misfortune of unearthing Barbara's body.

Tuesday the 4th of September 1979 CE, Detective Chief Superintendent Peter Gilrain addresses a press conference and sends out a plea to the public of Bradford for further information.
"I appreciate that it was after 1 a.m. on Sunday when Barbara was attacked, but someone must have seen the killer. Disco dancers, late-night diners, folk going home by taxi in the area, might all be able to help".

Similar footprints to those found at Savile Park, Halifax, the scene of Josephine Whitakers murder was located at and around 13 Ash Grove, but this only confirmed what the police already knew.

Barbara's solitary, lone, solo walks, helped to clear her head, helped her study and were not an issue in Kettering, the civilised south, however Barbara had been warned against such behaviour by her parents and brother, for everyone knew, everyone was aware of the beast that stalked amongst the shadows in the heathen Badlands of the north, uncivilised, uneducated but always there. Bab's reassured her parents that she would not undertake her solo starlight walks whilst she was in Bradford. Typical of the arrogance of youth, Barbara would do her own thing, it could never happen to her, not in the fun and friendly tight knit student community, an enclave of Bohemia, free from the usual restrictions and bigotries of Bradford. A utopia that did not exist a dystopia waiting to happen, a dystopia encouraged into existence by the bloodlust of the Yorkshire Ripper.

Ashgrove sub-urban Bradford in urban Bradford, an oasis of middle England in a desert of inner-city squalor. University bed sit land. The Ripper tape had promised another victim in September or October, this had heightened the hysteria that abounded all around, it burnt brightly and with extra intensity in the red-light areas of Bradford, Leeds and Manchester. Women in West Yorkshire specifically the epicentre of this murderous maniac. The public gets what the public wants, Peter was just providing a service. Caught in the crossfire of a hoax tape and letters, he had no choice other than to take advantage of the situation on every possible level.

Poetry in Motion Jealous of George Oldfield's newfound pen pal Peter William Sutcliffe put pen to paper and his first attempt at poetry was duly published. This new poetic champion from the north of England went under the pen name of 'The Streetcleaner'. Thursday September 6th 1979, the Sheffield Star receive an anonymous poem called Clueless, it read:- *Poor Old Oldfield, Worked in a Coldfield, Hobson has no choice, Misled by a voice, Release of Drury, Arouses fury, Bradford was not me, But just wait and see, Sheffield will not be missed, Next on the list. The Streetcleaner (T.S.)* Peter's considered opinion was that his stuff was better than the low brow rubbish the police kept comparing/contrasting, his handwriting too, long may it continue. The review of his poetry was not good, not the real deal, it was denounced as a phoney. Irony rules in the world of the Ripper, where fake is real and real is fake, good is bad and bad is good, wrong is right and right is wrong, yes means no and no means yes.

Saturday the 8th of September 1979 CE saw three hundred feminists march on Bradford police headquarters in an attempt to reclaim the night from the Yorkshire Ripper's grasp. The tinted glass carbuncle that was the Bradford police headquarters, sited in the city centre at the Tyrls, Bradford. BD1. They were angered and aggrieved by the police inability to catch the Yorkshire Ripper and kicking back at the crass police comments to the women folk of West Yorkshire *"Don't go out at night alone"*. Unintentionally proposing a female curfew on the streets of Bradford, Leeds, Huddersfield, Halifax, Keighley and the surrounding areas. Anne Mason was the leader of these protests and made a statement on behalf of Bradford Women's Action Group, to the massed media.

"This is a protest to show our feelings about the Ripper, and a protest about the curfew the police have put on woman. They told us it wasn't safe to go out at night. But they have done nothing to make it safer".
"Yes means yes, no means no, however we dress, where ever we go. Yes means yes, no means no, however we dress, where ever we go. Yes means yes, no means no, however we dress, where ever we go. Yes means yes, no means no, however we dress, where ever we go. Yes means yes, no means no, however we dress, where ever we go".

THE FUTURE IS FEMALE, A WOMANS RIGHT TO SELF DEFENCE, CURFEW ON MEN, ALL MEN ARE POTENTIAL RAPISTS, WHY NOT A CURFEW ON MEN? RECLAIM THE NIGHT, WE ARE ANGRY, WE MOURN ALL THE VICTIMS, END VIOLENCE, MACHOISM = VIOLENCE TO WOMEN, CUT OFF MALE POWER, END MALE SUPREMACY, WOMEN ARE ANGRY, WOMENS VOICE WOMEN UNITE – RECLAIM THE NIGHT, NO MEANS NO, ENOUGH MALE VIOLENCE, MEN OFF THE STREETS NOT WOMEN.

"Yes means yes, no means no, however we dress, where ever we go. Yes means yes, no means no, however we dress, where ever we go. Yes means yes, no means no, however we dress, where ever we go. Yes means yes, no means no, however we dress, where ever we go. Yes means yes, no means no, however we dress, where ever we go".

Friday the 14th of September 1979 CE, twelve days after the murder of Barbara Leach police constable Keith Mount was manning the police incident room in Sunderland, the telephone rang as he sat prepared to answer and take notes, his pad and pencil at the ready. He picked up the receiver.
"Hello police incident room Sunderland".
Then came the chilling reply in the voice that he felt was straight from the tape, the voice he knew to be that of the Yorkshire Ripper. *"Tell him it's a fake".*
"Can you repeat that I can't hear you it's a bad line," Mount cagouled.
"Tell him it's a fake," abrupt.
"What's a fake?" (Hold him on the line).
"The tape recording".
"What one is this, the one he's just received?" (Hold him on the line).
"The Ripper tape recording".
"How do you know that?" (Hold him on the line).
"Just tell him".
"Just tell him". (Hold him on the line).
"The one in June".
"Pardon?" (Hold him on the line).
"The one in June".
"I'm sorry it's a bad line you're going to have to repeat it". (Hold him on the line).
Then the phone went dead.
Police constable Keith Mount reported the unnerving call he'd received which added weight to the view supported by an ever-growing group. In effect the 'No' camp that believed the Ripper tape was a hoax.
Police constable Keith Mount's report fell on deaf ears, this possibly contributed to the deaths of at least another two women and a further two life shattering attacks.

Tuesday the 18th of September 1979CE, a police 'Special Notice' was circulated. Victims, murders, attacks, tyre tracks, letters, an audio tape, shoe sizes, birth dates, blood types, accents, dialects and skin colour. The Yorkshire Ripper is: - Aged between fifty-five and twenty-year-old. Is a Caucasian. Wears size 7 to size 8½ footwear. Speaks with a 'Geordie' accent. Has type B blood coursing through his veins. The confidential eighteen-page report, commissioned by the West Yorkshire Metropolitan Police Force and headed 'Murders and Assaults upon Women in the North of England', was distributed to all other police forces. It contained handwriting samples, the narrative of the tape and a breakdown of the sixteen attacks (including Joan Harrison) now attributed to the 'Yorkshire Ripper'. More importantly it stated that a suspect can be eliminated from the enquiry if they do not meet one or more of these requirements.

(a) Not born between 1924 and 1959.
(b) If he is an obvious coloured person.
(c) If his shoe size is nine or above.
(d) If his blood group is other than B.
(e) If his accent is dissimilar to a North Eastern (Geordie) accent.

Thus discounting one Mr. Peter William Sutcliffe of number 6 Garden Lane, Heaton, Bradford. The Yorkshire Ripper!

Monday the 24th September 1979CE Barbara's funeral takes place, a wreath inscribed 'Our bright star' from Barbara's parents a poignant reminder of their loss and the loss of Barbara to all, Canon Frank Pearce led the service.

Out of sight out of mind, what you don't know, won't hurt you. West Yorkshire Metropolitan Police officers were surprised at how few people had heard the tape prior to them following the Northumbria Police lead, in taking the voice of 'The Ripper' into the public arena. This new tact was instigated by the murder of Barbara Leach.

Friday the 28th September 1979 CE as the police search steps up throughout West Yorkshire and the north of England, for the multi-murderer dubbed 'The Ripper', police chiefs warned women. *"Don't go out at night alone. This man could strike anywhere. Women should not go out in dark places at night unaccompanied and if they do they should keep to well-lit and frequented areas"*.

The Keighley News made a page one comment supporting the police, *'The Ripper could next kill in Keighley, in Silsden, in Haworth, in Sutton, in Cononley. The beast's threat is as close as that...The message is clear. The cost of ignoring it could be a hideous assault ending in death"*. Along with this plea were banner headlines 'Ripper plea by police', 'Page one comment', 'Murder victims' and 'Pubs hear killer's voice'. Menacing headlines from a threatening time which saw the tape hoax being played in pubs, clubs and factories. The red herring tape playing operation was a saturation policy and was undertaken in the hope that it would unearth the mass murderer. The size of the operation was highlighted by the 'warning' that it may take two weeks to process and check on any information. The police also emphasised that all information would be treated in the strictest confidence, highlighting that *"People who do give us information need not feel they are going to get anyone into trouble or incriminate an innocent person. People who may appear to fit the identity of the Ripper are usually only too pleased to come forward and clear their name"*. 'Project R' had been initiated and was now in full swing.

Twenty/Twelve
Bradford, Sunday 2nd September 1979 CE. (01:00 hours) *Fuelled by the urge and totally out of control Peter was now absolutely under the charge of the voice. His loss, God the victor. Hesitant he questioned the source of the voice, "I hated to think it was the devil". Peter suffered anguish and upset at this time but was reassured by the voice, "...the voice told me Whitaker and Leach were prostitutes. God knew best". Peter hated to think the voice was the devil and comforted himself safe in the knowledge that "God wouldn't have punished them. Prostitutes are not innocent. God couldn't make a mistake". Remorse racked his being anguished by his actions, but unable to stop killing. "I never wanted to kill anybody at all, I just had to get rid of all prostitutes whether I liked it or not".*

Barbara Janine Leach, born the Monday the 5th of January 1959CE, murdered Sunday the 2nd of September 1979CE.

Wearmouth Suicide Attempt

A guilt-ridden John Humble decided the only way out was to end his life, to stop the misery and end the turmoil. To dis-associate the blame from being on his shoulders. On Monday the 25th of November 1979CE John (then twenty-three) took himself to the Wearmouth Bridge with the intention of ending it all. He filled his pockets with stones, ballast to pull his body further into the murky water. John threw himself off the bridge into the abyss, a 100-foot plunge into the waters of the River Wear, he almost struck a passing boat and suffered minor injuries from his self-inflicted predicament. Two policemen pulled him from the waters unaware of their catch unaware that they had Wearside Jack in their grasp. The red herring. By default the Yorkshire Ripper had almost claimed another victim.

Tuesday the 26th of November 1979CE and the Sunderland Echo proclaimed the incredible luck of one John Humble, was it a suicide attempt or was it an unfortunate accident? They reported the event but did not report the reason for his desperation. John remained tight lipped at his earlier actions, however he was not to be deprived of his fifteen minutes of infamy, but it would take a quarter of a century for the truth to out.

Chapter 24
Flush out the Ripper - privately financed police publicity campaign

The Ripper roadshow, coming to a town, pub, club, factory, job centre, prison, probation office, DHSS (Department of Health and Social Security) office, supermarket, library; no venue too small. Roadblocks! Flush Him Out. West Yorkshire Metropolitan Police present in association with Nationwide Flush out the 'Ripper' Campaign at a shopping centre near you. 14th May 1979 - 11th May 1980 Flush out the Ripper Exhibition, Arndale Centre, Bradford.

WHO IS HE? DO YOU RECOGNISE THE WRITING? COULD YOU REGONISE HIS VOICE? THE YORKSHIRE RIPPER, WE DON'T KNOW WHO, BUT WE KNOW WHAT, HE'S DISLOYAL, FLUSH HIM OUT, HE DOESN'T DESERVE YOUR PITY.

Suspects were eliminated from the inquiry if their voice or handwriting did not match that of the letter writer, cassette message maker. But what if the writer was not the killer, what if the writer was not the Yorkshire Ripper, what if the author of the Sunderland letters and tape was a hoax? The red herring would lead to crimson red blood being spilt by Peter William Sutcliffe. The red herring would lead to red faced police officers. Was this turn a turn for the worse? Not in Peter's eyes he just believed God was paving the way for him to continue, to complete his mission. In God we trust. Misgivings and concerns were raised at this crash course or coarse form of investigation that was to prove either a fast track to solving and capturing Britain's most wanted, or a fast track path to oblivion, elongating the process, the suffering and death, these misgivings and concerns fell on deaf ears.

Northumbria police top brass attempted to capture the culprit whose hand had created the correspondence. Hoping above hope that when the person was apprehended he would be the Yorkshire Ripper, one and the same as West Yorkshire Metropolitan Police adhered, endorsed, enforced and re-enforced. This gung-ho approach of the West Yorkshire Metropolitan Police, tired, taunted, feeling the pressure of four years of the manhunt adopted an abrupt, crass and ultimately flawed interpretation to the Ripper Tapes and letters. If a suspect did not have a Geordie accent or his handwriting did not match the author of the letters, they would be eliminated from the investigation. Such a system was flawed, it relied on the fact that the author was who he purported to be, the killer, the so called 'Yorkshire Ripper'. If the letters were a hoax, fraud, a swindle then the writer would be able to provide cast iron alibis for his whereabouts on the night of the attacks or murders. A blemish, shortcoming, error, fault, flaw, failing that would return to haunt the police and cost the lives of three further women.

This personal, private, particular, individual, special, petty innuendo allowed to interfere and undermine professional objective thought and fact. But all men are fallible, frail, fickle; all but one. Peter William Sutcliffe, but his time would come. Aided and abetted by God, Peter lapped up this side show, this irrelevant circus, this sham and took full advantage, after all as the police propaganda stated 'The Ripper is an opportunist' and the police are always right aren't they?

Chaos reigned supreme and was counter intuitive, the flood of information swamped the Millgarth nerve centre, hiding clues in plain sight, hiding the clues that would identify the killer, out of sight out of mind; amongst a myriad of mis-information given with good intention.

FLUSH OUT THE RIPPER (Continued)
A four-page police appeal was printed and distributed throughout the North of England, page one had the West Yorkshire Metropolitan Police insignia at the top left-hand corner of the page and then had the following prose: -

For the past four years a vicious killer has been at large in the North of England. There have been to date 12 horrific murders and four brutal attacks. The evidence suggests that the same man may be responsible for all them. If so, he has struck 13 times in West Yorkshire, twice in Manchester and once in Lancashire. Large teams of police officers, including Regional Crime Squads are working full time in West Yorkshire, Sunderland, Manchester and Lancashire to catch him. His original targets were prostitutes but innocent girls have also died. You can help to end this terror...**HELP US CATCH THE RIPPER**

- HAVE YOU SEEN THE HANDWRITING? (If you haven't it's on the back page).
- HAVE YOU HEARD THE TAPE? (If you haven't ring the nearest of the following telephone numbers LEEDS (0532) 464111 MANCHESTER (061) 2468060 BRADFORD (0274) 36511 NEWCASTLE (0632) 8075

DO ANY OF THESE QUESTIONS DESCRIBE SOMEONE YOU KNOW?
- Has a Wearside (Geordie) accent?
- Is physically fit and reasonably strong?
- Travels between or has connections in the Yorkshire, Lancashire and Sunderland areas?
- Perhaps shows disgust for low moral values?
- Is a manual worker or has access to tools?
- Possibly lives alone or with aged parents?
- Is prone to sudden outbursts of emotion?

- Owns a car of his own or has access to one?
- Sometimes stays out late at night?

BUT DON'T DISCOUNT ANY SUSPICION BECAUSE OF THE QUESTIONS. IF YOU HAVE ANY DOUBTS AT ALL, CONTACT THE POLICE AND HELPCATCH THE RIPPER.

IF YOU ARE AN EMPLOYER.
- Does your firm possibly have business connections throughout the North of England, especially in the Yorkshire, Lancashire and Sunderland areas?
- Have you an employee who was available in Sunderland to post an envelope on the following dates?

> March 7/8, 1978
> March 12/13, 1978
> March 21/22, 1979
> Shortly before June 18, 1979

THROUGH HIS DUTIES OR BEING ABSENT FROM WORK WAS AVAILABLE TO ATTACK THE 'RIPPER' VICTIMS (SEE CENTRE PAGES) ON:

July 5 1975	April 24 1977	January 31 1978
August 15 1975	June 26 1977	May 17 1978
October 30 1975	July 10 1977	April 5 1979
November 20 1975	October 1 1977	September 2 1979
January 20 1976	December 14 1977	
February 6 1977	January 21 1978	

Page two and three, (the centre pages of the four-page newsletter) had a photograph of a lone woman, standing on the pavement, (obviously suggesting she is soliciting) under a streetlamp in a dark secluded area with a cobbled road. The text to the top right-hand corner of the picture read: - The Ripper is an opportunist. This is an opportunity.

IS THE KILLER WE WANT KNOWN TO YOU?

FOUR VICIOUS ASSAULTS

LEEDS (a pen picture of) WILMA MCCANN, October 30 1975. PRESTON (a pen picture of) JOAN HARRISON, November 20 1975. LEEDS (a pen picture of) EMILY JACKSON, January 20 1976. LEEDS (a pen picture of) IRENE RICHARDSON, February 6 1977. BRADFORD (a pen picture of) PATRICIA ATKINSON, April 24 1977. LEEDS (a pen picture of) JAYNE MACDONALD, June 26 1977. MANCHESTER (a pen picture of) JEAN JORDAN, October 1 1977. BRADFORD (a pen picture of) YVONNE PEARSON, January 21 1978. HUDDERSFIELD (a pen

picture of) HELEN RYTKA, January 31 1978. MANCHESTER (a pen picture of) (a pen picture of) VERA MILLWARD, May 17 1978. HALIFAX (a pen picture of) JOSEPHINE WHITAKER, April 5 1979. BRADFORD (a pen picture of) BARBARA LEACH, September 2 1979.
£30,000 Reward
HOW TO CLAIM IT

Page four had a sample of handwriting, *Dear Officer Sorry I havn't written, about a year to be exact, but I hav'nt been up north for quite a while. I was'nt kidding last time I wrote...That was last month, so I don't know when I will get back on the job but I know it wont be Chapeltown too bloody hot there maybe Bradfords Manningham. Might write again if up north. Jack the Ripper PS Did you get letter I sent to Daily Mirror in Manchester.*

below it was written: - DO YOU RECOGNISE THIS HANDWRITING? The handwriting above is an extract from a letter received by West Yorkshire Metropolitan Police. It was posted in the Sunderland area on March 22, 1979. Look at it carefully and if you think you recognise it or think you have any information which might help to trace the man, ring the police now.

Below is part of the macabre tape-recorded message from a man who claims to be the 'Yorkshire Ripper'. It was addressed to the man leading the hunt, West Yorkshire Assistant Chief Constable (Crime) Mr George Oldfield. The mocking voice was recorded on a cassette tape and sent to the Police Headquarters in Wakefield. It was an open gesture of defiance, could it be his big mistake? His downfall? For his warped sense of cat and mouse does not take YOU into account. He believes that no one can or will identify his Wearside (Geordie) accent. He believes that you don't care enough to report your suspicions to the police. He is prepared to bet future lives to win his bet. You can prove him wrong and save those lives. The police in conjunction with the Post Office have got the voice on the other end of a telephone line. If you haven't heard it, or even if you have, then ring whatever telephone number on the front page refers to your area.

Listen to it and think of the 12 girls and women for whom this voice was perhaps the last thing they ever heard. The killer has also written three personal letters. Two were received direct at Police Headquarters. One was forwarded on by the Daily Mirror. They were posted in the Sunderland and were postmarked March 8, 1978, March 13, 1978 and March 22, 1979. The cassette tape was also posted in Sunderland shortly before June 18, 1979.

Police do not believe that he necessarily still lives in his native Sunderland with his detailed knowledge of West Yorkshire suggests he probably lives in West Yorkshire but occasionally visits 'back home'. A sample of the handwriting is reproduced. Study it and see if you can recognise it. The hand that wrote it has killed 12 times and will kill again until he is caught. **That much is certain will you bet a girl's life that he won't.**

I'm Jack. I see you are still having no luck catching me. I have the greatest respect for you, George, but Lord, you are no nearer catching me now than four years ago when I started. I reckon your boys are lettin' you down, George. They can't be much good, can they? The only time they came near catching me was a few months back in Chapeltown, when I was disturbed. Even then it was a uniformed copper, not a detective…At the rate I'm goin', I should be in the book of records. I think it's eleven up to now, isn't it? Well, I'll keep on going for quite a while yet. I can't see myself being nicked just yet. Even if you do get near, I'll probably top myself first. Well, it's been nice chatting to you, George. Yours, Jack the Ripper. No good looking for fingerprints, you should know by now it's as clean as a whistle. See you soon. 'Bye. Hope you like the catchy tune at the end. Ha-ha.

LARGEST MANHUNT EVER UNDERTAKEN The hunt for the 'Yorkshire Ripper' in the largest murder investigation ever undertaken in British police history. The workload is enormous but the dedication is awesome. Determination is the keyword not only in West Yorkshire but throughout the North of England and nationally allowing Police forces who are contributing varying degrees of manpower and expertise.

There is no attempted one-man band by West Yorkshire Metropolitan Police has many critics have suggested. From the early stages of the investigation West Yorkshire has worked closely with the head of Lancashire Constabulary CID Detective Chief Superintendent Wilf Brooks and the man in charge of Manchester Central CID Detective Chief Superintendent Jack Ridgeway and more recently with the head of Sunderland CID in Northumbria, Detective Chief Superintendent Peter Docherty.

Chapter 25
Ilkley (Hidden History)

Yvonne Mysliwiec was a twenty-one-year-old reporter who worked for the Ilkley Gazette, she also worked part time in a local night club. She lived with her parents John (Jan) and Helen (Ellen) and had two other sisters, Suzanne and Janette. It was Thursday the 11th of October 1979 CE, 20:50 hours, and Yvonne left her Trivoli Place home in order to walk the quarter of a mile to work. She was cutting it fine and had to be there by 21:00 hours, so she decided to take the short cut across the railway footbridge to save some time. The short walk across Springs Lane over the black and white painted stripes of the pelican crossing, a bar code, with details and information that will be hidden by the West Yorkshire Metropolitan Police Force. Details and information that would be overlooked and blamed on the actions of a local man. A local man who would never be found, because he didn't exist?

Peter was in Ilkey, he was driving towards Ben Rhydding when he suddenly pulled up and parked the Clark Transport six-ton rigid back lorry on Spring Lane (B6382) opposite the junction with Trivoli Place. He quickly bundled a hammer, screwdriver and knife into the internal breast pockets of his khaki green coloured car coat he climbed down out of the cab, this was because he'd noticed the figure of a young woman heading from Trivoli Place; she was walking along Spring Lane towards the town centre. Peter pulled up for the urge was upon him and no woman was safe, Peter was in Yorkshire Ripper mode.

She walked onto Ilkley railway footbridge an elevated metal and wooden structure that traversed the car park, railway sidings, waste land and quadruple tracks of the Wharfedale Line and formed part of Ilkley railway station. She crossed the footbridge walking under the interspersed metal archways that formed the framework of the edifice and was beginning to descend the steps that led to Railway Road. Unbeknown to her she had become the focus of some unwelcome attention.

Sixteen year old Bryan Copping, a friend and neighbour was returning home after visiting Derbyshire's off licence come convenience store, 31 Railway Road, Ilkley LS29. His little sortie to the shop resulting in the purchase of a veritable feast of snacks, crisps, peanuts, pop and a Ritter chocolate bar. He strolled across a deserted Railway Road, retracing his earlier journey entering the recess in the wall that formed the access to the stone steps that formed the ascent and entrance to the railway footbridge. Bryan edged to the left as he ascended the stone steps, then continued to climb the two flights of wooden stairs that formed the access/egress route to the railway footbridge. About halfway up the second flight of stairs Yvonne appeared at the head of the footbridge travelling over the footbridge

in the opposite direction. Yvonne adjusted her gate in descending the stairs on the opposite side to Bryan. Bryan and Yvonne exchanged pleasantries.
"Hello, are you alright". Bryan asked gulping for breath close to the 'summit' of the footbridge steps.
"I'm fine, I'm just off to work and I'm running a bit late" Yvonne pleasantly responded, stepping to her left to begin he descent of the steps and avoid bumping into Bryan, blissfully unaware of impending doom.
"See you later". They both said almost in tandem.
The pair parted on the wooden stairs unaware of the horror that was soon to unfold. Yvonne to continue her journey to work, Il Tovatore, ('the Trav') 46-50 Leeds Rd, Ilkley LS29, the friend to make his way home. Bryan turned left and began to walk over the footbridge he walked a few paces when his gaze was attracted to a man walking towards him, walking in the same direction as Yvonne, he was on the near side of the bridge walking following the path of least resistance towards the stairs, towards Yvonne, towards his destiny. The two men continued on their course Bryan veering towards the centre of the footbridge, his foot fall firmly fixed onto the middle of the weather worn wooden foot planks; as they passed both looked up, their eyes met, Bryan saw that the man had dark features, black hair and a beard, which he attempted to hide by keeping his head bowed to the floor of the footbridge and turned towards the lattice railings that bordered the footbridge avoiding further eye contact, discouraging recognition and possible identification. Bryan continued his journey home, Peter continued his mission.

20:55 hours, Peter followed Yvonne down the two flights of stairs, he soon fell into step with the hapless woman, his bulging right breast pocket struggling to hide the weapon within, Peter labouring with his excitement, Yvonne oblivious. The pair were on the stone steps, just shy of the exit leading to Railway Road when he pounced. The hammer struck home hitting Yvonne on the crown of her head, she fell and stumbled. Peter was disturbed by a passer-by, he had failed in his mission.

Bryan walked away oblivious to Peter's attempt to send Yvonne to oblivion. Unbeknown to Bryan he was walking away from the crime scene he descended the single flight of wooden stairs and accessed Springs Terrace, he paid little heed to the wagon parked on Springs Terrace/ Lane. He walked along the desolate Springs Terrace, the railings forming the perimeter of British Rail owned land to his left, dividing the pavement from the wasteland of the railway sidings, the illicit adventure playground of the young children of Ilkley.

Peter heard their footsteps and fled back up the footbridge steps, retracing his steps of minutes earlier, back to the safety of the six-ton rigid back lorry and his means of escape.

Over the bridge left onto Springs Lane and then the one hundred metres to his escape vehicle. Peter walked briskly not wishing to draw attention to himself.

Bryan's isolation and the silence of the night was disrupted by the hefty boot clad foot fall of someone behind him, the cadence of the strides suggested urgency, Bryan alarmed turned in reaction to the noise. He observed the man he had passed minutes earlier on the railway footbridge. 20:58 hours, Bryan crossed the road towards his 38 (Springs Terrace, LS29) home literally at the same time Peter strode past hurriedly heading towards the cab of his wagon. Again as the pair passed both looked up, their eyes met for a fleeting instant, Bryan recognised Peter as the man from the footbridge, Peter quickly averted his eyes, turning his head down and to the left and the metal railings of the railway sidings, obscuring his visage in an attempt to avoid identification.

Jonathan Davies, his girlfriend and her brother were walking down Golden Butts Road, making their way to the pub, when they inadvertently disturbed Peter. They found Yvonne at the foot of the steps in a pool of her own blood. Quickly they raised the alarm, running to Derbyshire's shop to call for an ambulance.

High walled Yorkshire stone formed one side of Railway Road, fourteen foot high fortifications, unrelenting forboding, an industrial-esque carbunkle that had been seemingly dumped into this pleasant West Riding back water. Above the high level of the stone wall the railway footbridge loomed, overseeing proceedings, witnessing all. The other side was made up of a patchwork of terraced houses, town houses, the occassional shop and a row of garages. The concealed entrance to the stairs was opposite (and at the top of) the junction with Wellington Road. In the town centre busy during the day but also a lonely and isolated place after dark.

Bryan paused at the threshold of his garden and turned to his head to the left so he was looking up Springs Lane, observing the dark stranger disappear into the distance, toward the lorry, that was parked almost opposite to Tivoli Place, the home of his latest victim, just past the entrance to Railway Terrace. He climbed the stone steps to his garden and used the elevated position to observe the exaggerated urgency of the stranger. He pondered the slightly surreal situation a parked vehicle on the main roadside of any kind was unusual, let alone a twenty plus foot lorry. From his elevated position he witnessed Peter climb into the cab of the lorry and start up the engine and drive off towards Ben Ryhdding.

Along Springs Lane onto Bolling Road and then turned left onto Wheatley Road, leaving his usual devastation in his wake, heading to Bradford via Benn Rhydding and his anonymous run of the mill unmemorable mild-mannered hen-pecked husband persona.

For he was the man you never saw. Under the railway bridge and further under cover. The police seemingly actively supported him in his adventures, ignoring the elephant in the room, ignoring the obvious negating Yorkshire Ripper links and creating the scape goat of a non-existent local man. A green light to continue his mission, a red-light at the junction with Wheatley Lane and Leeds Road, brought Peter back to his senses, his life was unravelling he had taken a risk, maybe he wouldn't be so lucky next time?

Police constable Gordon Eddison was the first police officer on the scene, initially he was responding to reports that Yvonne had tripped and fallen down the steps that led up to the footbridge which traversed the quadruple railway lines.

Yvonne was rushed to hospital where she spent four to five weeks recuperating from the injuries sustained in the attack.

Peter returned to Clarks haulage yard on Hillam Road but not before his precursory body check. There was no signs of his earlier escapades his matching khaki slacks and coat were free from any evidence. So he paid his previous activities no mind, the Yorkshire Ripper went into sleeper cell mode.

The Yorkshire Ripper had visited the quiet market town of Ilkley the Ripper walked amongst them. Ilkley a former Victorian spar town and home to well-off professionals. The Ripper was certainly off-piste in this environment. His unwelcome encroachment into the life of the great and good of West Yorkshire, did not go unnoticed in the corridors of power. An enclave of affluence light years away from the darker recesses ordinarily occupied by the Yorkshire Ripper. Unsavoury, unwelcome and unacknowledged. This visit did not exist, what were the good people of Ilkley to gain from their town being tarnished by the Yorkshire Ripper. Nothing! And that is why it never happened. This attack was imitation Ripper, possibly a crazed local man. The Yorkshire Ripper had NOT visited the quiet market town of Ilkley.

The police once again seemed incapable or unwilling to see these connections between similar description by previous survivor's as the list grew longer especially Marcella Claxton, Marylyn Moore, (Tracey Browne), (Ann Rooney), (Yvonne Mysliwiec), Marguerite Walls and Doctor Upadhya Bandara. However police still refuted these claims, following the party line, keeping a lid on the pressure. The police official line was that this attack was non-Ripper. For this was another local incident. The Ripper had gone away, women of the north were free from his threat. The Ripper had gone nowhere, the West Yorkshire Police Force were in denial. Apparently Yorkshire and the Wild West Riding had a proliferation of local men who were hell bent on imitating the actions of the Yorkshire Ripper!

Tuesday the 6th of January 1981 CE. Truth unravels lies disentangle, clarity lost and found, memories slot into place a strange synergy of recollections lead people to ponder upon past actions and events. Bryan sees the first public picture of Peter Sutcliffe a Bradford lorry driver, the Yorkshire Ripper. The dark striking features stir an uncomfortable home truth, an Ilkley home truth, a hidden truth, a truth that grows into certainty, a link between past and present, a search for justice, reassurance. The image depicting/identifying the Yorkshire Ripper is on the front pages, on the television, the image is the face of Peter William Sutcliffe. The man that Bryan saw over a year ago. Incriminatingly just prior to the vicious attack on Yvonne, then minutes later hastily exiting Ilkley in an attempt to distance himself from his actions.

Bryan pondered soul searched he'd seen those dark unforgiving/unnerving eyes on another occasion.

Twenty-one /Twelve
Ilkley, Thursday 11th October 1979 CE. (20:55 hours)

INTERVIEW WITH A SERIAL KILLER NUMBER SIX:
Tuesday 23rd October 1979 CE

Tuesday the 23rd of October 1979 CE, two Yorkshire detectives call at 6 Garden Lane, Heaton, Bradford, West Yorkshire BD9. The door is answered by Mrs Sonia Sutcliffe with the words, *"Oh, not again, this is the third time. He's not in, you'll have to come back".* (Sonia seemingly unaware of the other occasions that the police had interviewed her husband in relation to the Yorkshire Ripper murders).

The two Yorkshire detective constables return at a pre-arranged time when they know that Mr Peter William Sutcliffe will be present. Mr Peter William Sutcliffe is questioned by two Yorkshire detective constables who pay particular attention to his Sunbeam Rapier, they pay even more attention to the fact that it has been seen in various red-light areas over 36 times.

Mr Peter William Sutcliffe was also asked to provide a sample of his handwriting, (again). Whilst he is writing the detectives dictated transcript, Mrs Sonia Sutcliffe interjects the proceedings. *"My husband is not the Ripper".*
"Well I think he is," retorted the officer.
Mr Peter William Sutcliffe stopped writing, stared at the officer impassively and then continued to write.

***

Monday 7th January 1980 CE, a new year, a new decade, a new start; Chief Superintendent Jack Ridgeway, Chief of Manchester C.I.D. in charge of the Jordan and Millward murders, addresses the officers, highlighting expectations in a half day briefing. Officers who were to interview suspects in 'Britain's Biggest Murder' enquiry were instructed that no one was to be eliminated due to their accent or on handwriting samples. The briefing covered in detail all the information the police had about the 'Yorkshire Rippers' crimes. Officers were told that suspects vehicles, garages and houses were to be thoroughly searched, if the investigating officer was not happy, was not satisfied, the sentiment encouraged was to 'bring them in' to the police station and conduct a more rigorous, more vigorous interview. To require elimination required a verifiable alibi.

INTERVIEW WITH A SERIAL KILLER NUMBER SEVEN:
Sunday 13th January 1980 CE

Detective Sergeant Boot (of West Yorkshire Police) and Detective Constable Bell (of Greater Manchester Police) visited 6 Garden Lane, Heaton, early in the afternoon, approximately 13:25 hours, Mrs Sonia Sutcliffe answered the door in her night clothes, she ushered the men into the living room then shouted her spouse. A dazed, drowsy and somewhat dishevelled Mr Peter William Sutcliffe appeared in the living room. The police question Mr Peter William Sutcliffe about his whereabouts on Saturday night, Sunday morning 1st and 2nd of September 1979 CE. Mr Peter William Sutcliffe could not recollect his whereabouts. Mr Peter William Sutcliffe told them he'd provided a handwriting sample previously, *"Way back in October or November".* This was news to the two detectives, Detective Sergeant Boot was intrigued, his sixth sense prompted him to note on his paperwork, *'Strange Runner'* in relation to their interviewee. He was later to check out Mr Peter William Sutcliffe's handwriting claim at the incident room at Idle police station. They also asked about his work, they later examined his boots, searched the house and garage, taking special interest in the tools in his garage. Peters 'working' boots were left undiscovered in a cupboard close by, God provided an alibi, 'hidden in plain sight'.

INTERVIEW WITH A SERIAL KILLER NUMBER EIGHT:
Wednesday 30th January 1980 CE

Detective Sergeant McAlister & Detective Constable McCrone made a visit to Kirkstall Forge Engineering Works, Abbey Road Kirkstall Leeds, West Yorkshire, LS5 3NF to interview Mr Peter William Sutcliffe who was in the process of loading his lorry. The police officers are particularly interested in the multiple sightings of his car in red-light districts and his whereabouts on Saturday night and Sunday morning 1st and 2nd of September 1979 CE. Of course he said he was at home on both the nights in question. This was later corroborated by Mrs Sonia Sutcliffe.

He saw they had a photograph of a boot print, his boot print salvaged from a despicable deed dated Wednesday 4th April 1979 CE, salvaged from Savile Park, Halifax. Detective Sergeant McAlister asked Mr Peter William Sutcliffe if he has any objections to the two officers searching the cab of his lorry, Peter does not. In fact he climbs up onto the wagon via the mesh steps, the mesh steps that allow full view of the boots sole, full view of the boot print, full view of the boots he wore on Wednesday 4th April, 1979 CE. But Peter is as soulless as the police are clueless, Peter stayed dead calm and laughed inwardly, *"They can't see what's in front of their own eyes'* he scoffed to himself.

D.C. McCrome followed Mr Sutcliffe into the cab, Mr Sutcliffe climbed out across the passenger seat, whilst D.C. McCrome painstakingly examined the interior of the cab.

Another fruitless day, another waste of police time, the calendar boys cab (Peter had recently posed for photographs for a calendar advertising his place of work and was now the public face of the company) was clean as a whistle. They'd found nothing incriminating here Detective Sergeant McAlister and Detective Constable McCrone have a brief discussion, they decide not to waste further police time, they decide not to search his car and home, but decide to put down in their report that they have.

INTERVIEW WITH A SERIAL KILLER NUMBER NINE:
Thursday 7th February 1980 CE

An incident room inspector not wholly satisfied with the previous interviews action report, ordered two detective constables to question Mr Peter William Sutcliffe about his whereabouts on the night of Wednesday 4th April 1979 CE. Detective Constable Jackson and Detective Constable Hannison visited T & W.H. Clark Limited, Perseverance Works, Hillam Road, Bradford, West Yorkshire, BD2. He also wanted further information on Mr Sutcliffe's vehicles and their continued sightings in various red-light district. Peter proffered his usual reasons for the sightings and of course he was at home on the night of Wednesday 4th April 1979 CE, this was later corroborated by Mrs Sonia Sutcliffe.

Drink Driver

Thursday the 26th of June 1980 CE, 23:30 hours. Grosvenor Road, Manningham, Bradford police static observation point, manned by two uniformed officers, police constable Doran and police constable Melia. Both men kept watch, whilst sitting in an unmarked police car. The need for speed, the need for excitement. Peter William Sutcliffe is at the wheel of his Rover, which is travelling at a speed of eighty miles per hour, on a road where the speed limit is thirty miles per hour. Peter had been to the Royal Standard, his old stomping ground for a few pints. The police sprang into action and followed Sutcliffe the short distance home. Peter was arrested outside his 6 Garden Lane abode by PC Bob Doran and PC Graham Melia. There was a brief altercation and voices were raised before Peter was finally co-opted into providing a sample of his breath, has he breathed into the breathalyser he hoped for the best, but knew that he was on sticky ground. Peter was arrested and taken to the police station to be processed and charged with 'drink driving', his world was beginning to unfold, was God deserting him. This action was to lead to the ultimate demise of the Yorkshire Ripper.

Chapter 26
Margo

Marguerite Walls was a forty-seven-year-old civil servant, she worked at the Department of Education and Science, 44-60 Richardshaw Lane, Pudsey, West Yorkshire LS28. She was born in Dunston in Lincolnshire in 1943CE, the family comprised of Thomas (her father), Kathleen (her mother), who now lived in Worcester in the West Midlands. Marguerite also had a younger brother Robert some ten years her junior and also a younger sister.

Her family moved to Northern Ireland when she was still a young schoolgirl. At twenty she joined the army and served in the Royal Army Corps attaining the rank of sergeant. She was demobbed at the age of twenty-two and became a civil servant firstly in Northern Ireland and then transferring to London, subsequently she left to try her hand at different careers, although Marguerite returned to the civil service taking a post in Basingstoke, Hampshire. In 1972CE Marguerite transferred to the customs and excise department and moved to a post in Leicester. She worked in the VAT (Value Added Tax) office until 1978CE, when she finally transferred to Leeds as an executive officer and once again switched departments.

Marguerite was commonly known as Margo to her family, friends and work colleagues. Margo lived alone in a detached house which she purchased on her move from Leicester at 7 New Park Croft, Farsley; at the time this was a new build estate. She was a keen member of the Leeds and Bradford Fell Walking Club and was due to take ten days annual leave, starting Thursday the 21st of August 1980CE; she was due to attend a former colleagues funeral in Newcastle on the Friday and then travel west to the Lake District for a walking holiday. These commitments were never fulfilled due to the intervention of a certain Mr Peter William Sutcliffe.

Wednesday the 20th August 1980CE, Marguerite went to work on this her final day before her well-earned holiday, Margo had her own set of keys for the office and had decided to work late, she was somewhat aloof from her fellow colleagues, a reserved and private individual. Earlier in the evening she had ordered a Chinese takeaway which she ate at her desk whilst she continued to work.

Diligent, hardworking, conscientious, industrious, work proud assiduous and attentive work colleagues knew her on a professional level but few if anyone knew the real Margo. Career minded, focused, she worked over in order to clear the backlog of work that had accrued to ensure her work affairs were in fine fettle and pristine order prior to embarking on her imminent holiday to the lake district.

Margo left the office and locked up at 22:45 hours she began her walk home. Margo walked to and from work every day, a journey of approximately a mile, she believed it kept her fit and complimented her fell walking. She walked forcefully down the incline of Richardshaw Lane, at the junction with the Bradford Road (B6157) quickly covering the four hundred metres before turning right onto New Street, she continued to walk up New Street for a further four hundred metres, however she did not realise that she was not alone.

Peter never wanted to kill anybody, it was his duty, and it was his mission to get rid of prostitutes. It did not matter whether or not he wanted to do it, he simply had to do it. The media stigma of all things Yorkshire Ripper, the name adopted by the Fleet Street hoards, billboards just didn't ring true with Peter, he felt if he used an alternative mode to murder, a more sanitised approach that softened the deed. However he would require his trusty hammer, he always required his trusty hammer; to stun and incapacitate his victim. He would then produce the ligature and strangle the life force out of her body.

It would also throw another red herring into the equation. He hoped it would further muddy the waters and contribute to the contrite catalogue of mistakes, misinformation and misdirection openly promoted and supported by the West Yorkshire Police at Millgarth Police Station, (Millgarth St, Leeds, West Yorkshire LS2).

Sonia had a night shift at the Sherrington Nursing Home, Heaton. Always an ominous omen as to the safety of women in the north of England. Peter ever the dutiful husband gave his spouse a lift on the short journey to drop her off just before her shift started.

Peter was quite pleased because now Peter had an opportunity to meet his needs and the needs of the Lord. He returned home to prepare for his missionary work, he got his ball peen hammer and placed it under the driver's seat, for easy access. He then went to get a knife, but changed his mind, should he use a screwdriver on this one he thought, no he would try something different. He picked up a length of blue and pink cord, that'll do he thought and placed it in his jacket pocket. It was around sixty centimetres in length with knots tied in it to aid his grip.

Now for his own self-indulgence, he retired to the toilet, removed his brown cords and underpants and placed his legs into his DIY gimp leggings, for as ever if he was doing God's bidding he saw no reason not to take full advantage, what harm could it do. The stigma the police had attached to the 'Yorkshire Ripper' and in return the media, society and the general public, in Peter's eyes he was much maligned and misunderstood. But it was a cross he had to bear in solitude, but he knew that the women he killed had been chosen by God for a purpose. He thought a more personal type of killing may make his work more acceptable, if only they could understand his depressions the burden he had to carry alone. They were not the ones who had to kill with their own hand, they did not have to suffer the stigma. He could not confide, he could not betray his special mission. Brown car coat, brown cords, black boots and black deeds, Peter was dressed to kill. Suitably attired and pumped up with the thought of what was to come, he left Garden Lane with a spring in his step. Poor Peter he thought. *"Let the Lord's will be done,"* he mumbled to himself.

Peter drove to Leeds predisposed to his intentions of premeditated murder, a 'prostitute' was going to die. He was driving through Farsley on Bradford Road (B1657) on his way to his usual hunting grounds of Chapeltown. He was in his brown Rover. When he saw a lone figure some fifty-five metres away, Peter realised it was a woman and she was walking towards him, the woman he would later discover to be Marguerite Walls, and she was soon to become his twelfth murder victim. Peter slowed down indecisive as to his next move, this was possibly an ideal opportunity. Marguerite continued to walk towards Peter she then turned right onto New Street. This right turn helped Peter to make a decision, Marguerite had left the main road for the quieter New Street. Peter duly drove forward and turned left, following his would be target.

The rage grew within him, his ire was up. The intense pretence of respectability had worn him down once more. He pulled his car over and parked outside the gable ends of the terraced houses on New Street, he fumbled under his seat and grabbed the wooden handle of his ball peen hammer, (his weapon of choice, his constant) quickly placing it in his inside breast pocket and jumped out of his car and scurried to the pavement and began to follow Marguerite his rancour soaring with each individual footstep. As he walked behind Marguerite awaiting an opportunity, surveying his surroundings, he felt slightly naked without his knife or sharpened screwdriver, but he could feel the hammer bulging in his pocket, encouraging him to proceed emboldening his resolve. With each stride he narrowed the distance between him and Marguerite, each step a death knell, tolling the bell to her impending doom. Still the anger surged - it was now out of control, too late to worry about the prying eyes of would be witnesses who'd intervene, contravene, report the scene onus in on any indiscretion he made in the heat of his hunt, to plot his downfall. Only he and she existed it was unfortunate for Marguerite but God must have a sacrifice, for Peter read Abraham, for Marguerite read Isaac, for Pudsey, Leeds read the Temple Mount, Jerusalem.

The urge surged once more he would soon have to unleash his pent-up violence and silence Margo for good. Past the enticing open expanses of Westroyd Park, he was undecided whether or not to launch his attack, but he held back, Peter tracked her for four-hundred metres and then he was upon her, 'Kill, Kill, Kill', the distorted inner hatred, rage, anger, horror and satisfaction of the voice inside sang in exaltation. As his killing instinct took control in the final few moments he'd felt inside his brown jackets breast pocket and liberated the hammer, brought it to his trusty left hand and swung the hammer of (in)justice with all his might. His five-foot eight-inch West Yorkshire frame had undertaken a metamorphosis into a six-foot Geordie, spring heeled Jack a supernatural creature of the northern night.

Peter was now fevered by missionary zeal. In Peters mind he saw Marguerite lift her left leg up and place it down, slowly almost in slow motion, he saw Marguerite lift her right leg up and place it down provocatively displaying her body. Peter struggled to hold his contempt it was 23:00 hours.
"You filthy prostitute," he shouted at the stunned Marguerite who fell face first onto the hard Leeds pavement. The voice jolted him out of his fever it sounded vicious, angry far from Peter's meek, mild, meagre and restrained mannerisms. His senses partially back in place he now thought it might be a good idea to check if there was anyone else about, any witnesses to his sacrifice to the Lord. No there wasn't, however, he knew that this would be the case for Peter operated in a protective bubble, the inner sanctum of a Holy order.

Peter moved to phase two of his would be sacrifice, he dragged Marguerite's unconscious body through the tall stone pillars that formed the gateway of the big house and into the spacious surroundings of the garden, into the darkness, into seclusion. He dragged her further into the garden, Peter half heard footsteps and sensed that somebody else was close by, but he had no choice but to continue. He dragged Marguerite by the heels, Margo's shoes fell off at this stage. Unconcerned his attention was drawn back to the gateway of the garden that just seconds earlier they had passed through to escape the glare of the open road. He turned in time to see a silhouetted figure stop midway across the house driveway pause mid crossing and peer into the garden, into the shadows, into the active crime scene. Peter did not panic the distant figures inquisitive indecision alleviated they continued on with their journey home and reprimanded themselves for letting their imagination run away with them. Confident that there were no further spectators Peter bludgeoned Margo again with the hard steel of the hammer head, he dragged Marguerite off of the driveway, across the rockery and into a wooded area to the left hand side of the driveway.

Peter continued with his crime, exploring new boundaries, he felt for the pink and blue cord in his pocket and kneeling down onto Marguerite's chest, could hear her ribs splinter under the weight of his frame. He wrapped the cord around her neck and pulled the cord tighter and tighter, ensuring all signs of life had expired. Peter then began to undress Marguerite, he pulled off her blue mackintosh with its tartan lining, he then tugged off her purple wool cardigan and her purple blouse, he threw her violet wrap - around skirt and pulled down her fawn tights, as he pulled down Marguerite's knickers he indulged himself, inserting his fingers into her vagina, his finger nails inadvertently scratching the soft tissue of the external walls of her vagina, leaving the tell-tale signs of this intrusion. She was stripped naked with the exception of her fawn coloured tights. Had the halo dropped from our holier than thou killer yet again? His rhetoric intrinsically flawed, his logic ill or illogical, only time would tell.

He undid the zip on his jeans - his penis fell out. He dropped to his knees, the DIY knee pads cushioning his kneecaps, his weight weighing down on Marguerite's naked body. Excited by his actions he ejaculated into the tissue he had brought to aid his crusade and help avoid detection. Still in the throes of murderous excitement, he pushed the tissue in his jacket pocket, he replaced his penis and zipped up his jeans. He had a subconscious idea to pose Marguerite, to leave her body in an obvious place and an obvious position. But his rage had dissipated along with his sexual urge, coupled with the increased traffic on the thoroughfare where he had first attacked Marguerite and therefore an increased chance of detection, Peter decided to go home, but first he flung grass cuttings which were piled to the side of the driveway over Marguerite's body to obscure his sacrificial art.

His humility returned during his journey home, upset at his actions but unable to control them. His actions were not his own he was under the control of God, a one-man religious terrorist. Tormented by his deeds, he knew he just had to get rid of all the prostitutes, whether he liked it or not. Upset at his actions but relieved at their necessity Peter returned home to Heaton hill. He calmed down during the fifteen minutes it took him to travel the short distance, he felt pangs of guilt but corrected himself, it was God's will. Unimaginable anguish and upset but a slave to God's will and the mission. Blessed by God, chosen by God, he could not let down his Lord and creator. In a fix, caught in a cycle of depravity, caught up in the mission to rid humanity of the scourge of prostitution. Peter had no say in this role he just did God's bidding.

Thursday the 21st August 1980 CE 08:50 hours, the gardens of Claremont, New Street, Farsley LS28 8ED; the gardeners arrived for work, walking through the stone gateway and onto the driveway that approached the house. The morning walk to work nearly completed was prematurely cut short, interrupted by the remnants of Peter's nocturnal antics. Startled, puzzled, their walk interrupted by a pair of discarded woman's shoes, approximately ten metres into the driveway. They proceeded, however their gaze was caught by a discarded violet tattered and torn wrap - around skirt, which was to their left on the lawned area. A rockery separated the driveway from the grass. Close to the skirt lay a leather shopping bag and Marguerite Walls cheque book.

The couple had seen enough and the police were called and Marguerite's body was found at 08:55 hours she lay almost naked in a prone position next to a stone garage that was sited to the left of 'Claremont' the main house, Marguerite was partially covered by her black Mackintosh raincoat and some grass cuttings that had been taken from a heaped pile that was against the garage. Various items of Marguerite's clothes were strewn around the wooded area, these too had been obscured by the grass cuttings.

In an ironic twist Claremont was owned by a local Magistrate, an upholder of law and order. Mr. Peter Hainsworth, he was also the managing director of Hainsworth and Son's Limited that owned many mills in and around the area. The house and its gardens grandeur dated back to 1858 CE when another mill-owner Benjamin Waite decided to show his material wealth and build the large house. At the time Waite named the property Springfield House. Waite ran into financial difficulties and in the 1880's CE, Abimelech Hainsworth, bought the house and eighteen acres of land, renaming it Claremont. The house was then passed down through the generations, Peter Abimelech's Grandson moved into Claremont in 1960 CE, with his wife Eileen and their four sons, Timothy, Robert, Richard and Roger.

This area was a step up in class from the usual districts in which the Yorkshire Ripper operated, this was upper middle class, middle England (albeit transferred to the north). Suburbia, not the spit and sawdust down at heel localities where the locals were downtrodden, glum, care worn, down in the mouth. The area was full of professionals, the upwardly mobile, and people with money, historical wealth and power. There was no such thing as gentrification, because it wasn't needed. Things like this were not meant to happen here, this was not meant to happen in Farsley, a small town to the East of Bradford and the West of Leeds, it came under the jurisdiction of Leeds. There was a less salubrious area to the West of the district where council tower blocks could be located, however this was still no Chapeltown, this was no Manningham, this was no Moss Side. Like a fish out of water, a snowman in the dessert, this was not the place for the Ripper, or was it? The police came to the same conclusion and were looking for a local man.

His master plan seemingly successful the police initially didn't link this killing with the Yorkshire Ripper murders.
"I am satisfied the woman's death was in no way connected with the Ripper killings. We do not believe this is the work of the Yorkshire Ripper…My feelings are that it is a local man who did this murder. I have a team of detectives at Miss Wall's house looking for addresses of male and female friends," said Detective Chief Superintendent James Hobson as he faced the media scrum, to all intents and purposes the Ripper Squad/Ripper Task Force, (a media name for the team of detectives investigating the murders) were fooled by Peter's change in style, the ligature had served him well, just as he had served the Lord well.

Robert Walls, Marguerite's younger brother commuted to Leeds from his Lye home, near Stourbridge, Dudley in the West Midlands with the thankless task of identifying Marguerite's body.

Twenty-two/Thirteen
Leeds, Wednesday 20th August, 1980CE. (23:00 hours) Voices in his head, "Kill, kill, kill". I'm responding to Gods orders I have the divine right to do this. "Kill, kill, kill". A

trip to Leeds with the intention of killing a prostitute, in a rage and centre stage, in the wrong place at the wrong time, in his eyes it could only end one way; "You filthy prostitute". A third person voyeur, angry, filthy and detached. Peter does not get angry, this was out of character, this was not Peter, but it was Peter. Peter was helpless, unable to control his urges, *"I couldn't do anything to stop myself. I were suffering inner torment and just wanted to get rid of all prostitutes...I knew it was me who had done what I had done with my own hands, and when I get into the depression this happens".*

Chapter 27
Upadhya

Saturday the 1st of September 1980 CE saw the Yorkshire Ripper's supposed inactivity 'celebrated', although mutedly. The whimsical wisdom of the West Yorkshire Metropolitan Police believed and promoted the fact that the Yorkshire Ripper had gone to ground. He had apparently gone one year without inflicting an attack on an unsuspecting innocent. This inactivity detracted from their ineptness and reassured the general public whose fear faded as the media mayhem moved onto the next headline, the next scandal, the next nightmare. For time waits for no man and now the Yorkshire Ripper was yesterday's news, yesterday's man: out of fashion, out of time and out of the news. Out of sight, out of mind, left behind obsolete, antiquated, old hat and aged.

Unbeknown to them Peter had remained active, or were the police aware and unwilling to add to the hysteria the Yorkshire Ripper had created, aided and abetted by the police. What had become of the man they had hunted for five years they surmised and devised a whole array of possibilities in denial of the truth and the facts that were at their disposal.

Psychologists, police and the press speculated about his homicidal hiatus, his killing drought. Suicide is painless, it leads to many changes? Found love and settled down? His murderous actions were just a passing phase, which he had now grown out of? He had been imprisoned and was unable to commit further attacks while being held at Her Majesty's pleasure? Ill health had prevented him from adding to his heinous crimes? He had been sectioned, hospitalised for his own safety and that of others? A false celebration of misinformation, God's smokescreen to protect the mission, God's smokescreen to protect Peter William Sutcliffe and his mission. His mission to end the low morals that offended his morality and created his duality that triggered the perpetuation of the mission. A necessary cull to reduce their numbers and control their behaviour.

By killing one woman and saving her soul, Peter saved many more. Sometimes the world doesn't need a hero, sometimes the world needs a monster. A monster for the greater good an ideological, theological killer, tormented by his actions, made to suffer for his cause, but ones suffering serves all. *"Never in the field of human conflict was so much owed by so many to so few"*. In this case one man. Peter knew resistance was futile and willingly complied, for Peter was a true altruist. Intent on homicide the goal and objective of his mission was to get rid of all prostitutes, he was actively coerced if not forced by God to participate in this process.

Doctor Upadhya Anadavathy Bandara was thirty-four years old and had arrived in England in August 1979CE from her native Singapore, after successfully winning a scholarship from the World Health Organisation and was studying towards a post graduate course in Health Service Studies at the Nuffield Centre for International Health and Development at the University of Leeds. She was the youngest in a family of twelve siblings, she had eight sisters and three brothers. In Singapore she worked for the government's health ministry as a doctor in an outpatient's dispensary.

Peter, ever the dutiful husband took Sonia to work at the nursing home, he was in a hurry. God had given him the word that tonight was the night to recommence his mission, to rekindle his killing ways, to warn the women of West Yorkshire their immoral actions would not go unpunished. Time was of the essence, prior to giving Sonia a lift, Peter had retired to the bathroom of 6 Garden Lane, to equip himself with his gimp leggings. Personal gratification was a key element of Peter's wayward and twisted mission, ultimate power corrupts. Peter thought he had ultimate power, but God wanted to let Peter know that only God had ultimate power. However ultimate power corrupts, had ultimate power corrupted God. Peter quickly removed his underpants and placed them into his jacket pocket, he first placed his left leg through the green silk of the DIY gimp trousers and then his right leg. Anticipating his actions he smiled with glee, a glint entered his dark eyes, as he put on his trousers, ready to take Sonia to work, ready to go to work, ready to take the life of an innocent victim. He looked in the mirror, his manicured reflection stared back at him, "Thy will be done," he said calmly, a smile came to his lips. He washed and dried his hands then went downstairs, alerting Sonia to the fact that he was ready to take her to work.

The six or seven miles to Leeds passed quickly, uneventful, his mind was not on the road, his mind was on the mission. Leeds, but not Farsley, not Chapeltown, he'd try a new hunting ground. Fresh blood, fresh misery, fresh flesh. Indiscriminate killing, but not on an empty stomach. 22:05 hours, Peter thought he'd sample the delights of Colonel Sander's finest and parked his car in the small car park just off Wood Lane, to the rear of Kentucky Fried Chicken, 'It's finger lickin good'. He bought two pieces of original recipe chicken and a portion of fries for the princely sum of one pound and ten pence. Then sat at a window seat table to eat his meal and also to pick a suitable candidate to kill, staring into the Otley Road bustle and the Headingley night. Walking slowly like a prostitute, slow strolling, she must be a woman of the night, slow strolling, strolling slowly to her demise.

Wednesday the 24th of September 1980CE, it was 22:15 hours when Dr Bandara began the one kilometre walk home after visiting friends in Cottage Road, north Headingley, she left their house and embarked on her journey to the flat she called home, a walk she had undertaken many times before without incident, through the pleasant gentrified middle class streets of student Leeds. She walked on the bustling bohemian streets of Headingley, Otley Road, after walking approximately eight hundred metres Upadhya reached the

Arndale Centre, she walked along the full frontage of the 1960's CE American influenced shopping centre. As she continued to walk homeward bound she walked past the "Kentucky Fried Chicken" franchise on the southern fringes of the Arndale Centre, her attention was captured by the brightly lit interior and within the glass façade she noticed a dark haired man inside KFC (Kentucky Fried Chicken, Otley Road, Leeds, LS6). Even at this distance she felt slightly intimidated by his open stare, she quickened her step and forgot about the strange little dark-haired man and continued on her journey and walked on past where Otley Road becomes North Lane.

The slight figure of Upadhya had caught his eye, she was walking slowly displaying her wears, she was walking like a prostitute, so he vacated the warmth of the KFC shop and followed the petite, slim, dark haired figure of the woman he had seen walking solo past the window. Upadhya then turned right into St Michael's Street and past the Skyrack public house 2-4 St. Michaels Road, Leeds, LS6 3AW, along the busy streets under the shadow of St Michael and All Angels church and then under the lesser shadow of the white stone of the Headingley cenotaph to her left and turned left onto St. Michaels Lane and then left again on Chapel Lane. All the while Peter followed.

Chapel Lane was a cobbled back street that connected St Michaels Lane with Cardigan Road a main thoroughfare, it was quite narrow but became progressively narrower after the first corner. Peter continued to stalk his prey as she walked down Chapel Lane, they rounded the corner as the snicket narrowed further Upadhya suddenly became aware of footsteps to her rear, sensing their owner was close at hand she used her Singaporean etiquette, stopping and therefore allowing the faster walking stranger to pass by.

However 'spring heeled Jack', Peter Sutcliffe was walking at such a pace for a reason, a reason that would soon become evident to both parties. Upadhya glanced to her side and caught a glimpse of Peter, his distinct short trimmed beard and moustache and his dark staring eyes, this was the man that she had seen earlier in KFC.

22:28 hours as the lane narrowed further he felt happy that the time was now right and he was upon her. Peter leapt into action, he slammed his hammer into her head - the first blow provoking a shriek, he repeated the process, he swung the hammer, Upadhya again felt the blow, her body crumpled to the cobbles the second blow rendering her partially unconscious. As she fell to the cobbled stone floor of the snicket he then crouched down and dropped the blue and pink plaited cord over her head, before pulling it tight. Then she felt the rough cord of the rope digging into her neck, restricting, constricting her windpipe, her air supply, her life. Upadhya fought back, managing to get her fingers between the cord and her neck, in the seemingly vain attempt of preventing the inevitable.

Peter deceptively strong as he had proved continually throughout his murderous reign continued to cross the cord, increasing the pressure he dragged her along the cobbled road.

Happy now that she could no longer struggle he loosened the ligature as she dropped to the floor. Happy that his anticipated kill was unable to protect herself or attempt an escape, Peter paused to think. Upadhya lay bleeding. Peter celebrated his cunning, his intellect, his deception, his power. But Peter was unsure whether or not he had the stomach for this close quarter killing. So he formulated a plan, which was to drag her off the cobbled road and into the dustbin storage area to continue his work. He began to drag her, his arms holding Upadhya under the armpits and dragging her towards the more secluded bin store servicing adjacent properties. The noise of her shoes dragging on the cobbles unnerved him, he stopped in his tracks and pulled her beige cardigan up, it got caught on her head, he paused again and removed the offending article from her feet and also picked up her discarded handbag.

This disjointed effort was proving disconcerting to Peter, he decided to hide her shoes and handbag and took them several metres away close to the bin storage area he had targeted for her final resting place, the bin storage area was shielded from the cobbled street by a wall. Lifting up the circular shield like dustbin lid, he placed the handbag and shoes into the bin and replaced the lid. He returned to Upadhya's listless body and grabbed hold of the ligature around her neck again it was then when he was disturbed, the silence of the night was broken by the sound of footsteps. The footsteps belonged to a resident of St. Michaels Crescent, a row of properties that backed onto Chapel Lane. 22:30 hours the footsteps belonged to Mrs Valerie Nicholas who had heard the noises of the initial attack, the noise of the dragged heels on the cobbled floor and the dustbin lids being disturbed so she had gone out to investigate.

Startled, Peter heard her footsteps and loosened his grip on the cord, as the cord loosened the attack lost all momentum, he tried to rekindle the flames with a cheap shot kick to the head catching her a blow to the rear of her left ear with his left leg. A true left footer, once a Catholic, always a Catholic, but not for Peter, Peter was different, Peter was always different. Once an Altar boy Peter could not alter his killing ways, or could he?

Abort, abort, abort something inside other than the beast was preventing him from continuing. It was as if the crescendo of violence he was expected to release after the hammer blow just plateaued, he then lost all momentum and he regained his composure and could not see the deed through. The intimacy and hard work of strangulation was not for him, he made a conscious decision to return to the hard metal of knives and screwdrivers.

Mrs Nicolas rang the police uncertain of what the commotion was all about. Better safe than sorry she thought.

Echoes of forgiveness, echoes of Marcella, the black girl, echoes of Soldiers Field, echoes of Bingley Cemetery, we be echo, echoes of echoes of echoes of echoes… Inept attempts, disconcerted, averted, apologises. Excuses for failings, lost opportunities and lack of bottle. 'STOP' boomed the voice in his head. Peter duly concurred, his heart wasn't in it. This was not spontaneous. It was forced. Peter left the scene to continue his inner conflict, "Sorry," he mumbled and strolled off into the Headingley night

Hurriedly he retraced his steps, adopting a brisk walk, wanting to extricate himself from the situation, but not wanting to court undue attention. Chapel Lane, Saint Michael's Lane, Saint Michael's Street, Otley Road, Wood Lane and back into the Rover, another attack over, although not concluded satisfactorily. Home to reassess, self-assess and read the press, no doubt God would send him a message, a sign the next time his services were needed. 22:35 hours Peter started his car engine and carefully drove home, his frustrations unresolved.

22:40 hours a white police Ford Escort patrol car that was in the area enters Chapel Lane, from St. Michaels Lane alerted by the telephone call from Mrs. Nicholas, they slowly drove down the cobbles and manoeuvred round the corner, where they saw the slumped body of Upadhya blocking their path. One of the officers got out of the patrol car to investigate further. Upadhya was lying unconscious on the cold cobbles her head in a newly formed pool of her own blood. The policeman unsure if she was alive checked to make sure they weren't too late and hoping he would be able to offer his assistance or get medical assistance.

Upadhya was comforted by the police until an ambulance arrived to take her to a nearby hospital. Before she was rushed away Upadhya described her attacker to the police, she explained her assailant was aged twenty-five years old, approximately five foot four inches tall, he had a moustache, full beard and black hair. A very similar description to previous survivors' photo fits, especially Marcella Claxton, Marylyn Moore and Tracey Browne.

Police dismissed this latest attack from the 'Yorkshire Ripper' series, for similar reasons to the killing of Marguerite Walls. The use of a ligature but no stab wounds. Although they did link it to the Farsley murder of Marguerite Walls and were concerned once again that two separate killers were working in tandem. Mary Gregson a thirty-eight-year-old part time cleaner at Salt's Mill in Saltaire had been murdered on the towpath of the Leeds/Liverpool Canal on Tuesday the 30th of August 1977CE at approximately 17:20 hours, the modus operandi of the murder involved strangulation through garrotting. The police were once again concerned that a copy-cat killer was at large and active in the area and had now reached the serial killer status. Saltaire, Farsley and Headingley; police alluded to a possible link to the press, but they did not believe it was a 'Ripper Job'.

Twenty-Three/Thirteen
Leeds, Wednesday 24th September, 1980CE. (22:30 hours) *Walking slowly like a prostitute, unprepared, no real tools to ply his trade. Improvisation make do and mend. Up close and personal, too personal, the blue and pink cord was not his weapon of choice. A sick Indian rope trick, it was exceedingly horrible, strangulation did not sit well with Mr Sutcliffe. Peter's penitence, atonement an apology, overwhelmed he relented. He stopped mid show asked for forgiveness and left her there.*

Upadhya had recently successfully completed her course and was due to go on holiday, she cancelled her ten city European holiday to recover from her attack and to assist the police with their enquiries and take part in a police reconstruction

In Singapore Upadhya's family were completely unaware of her ordeal, she forbade her employers in the Singapore health ministry to tell her family what had happened. She eventually returned home in December 1980CE and when quizzed about the scar on her forehead, she explained it away as a minor accident. It wasn't until February 1981 CE that the family found out about the attack.

Chapter 28
Leeds (Hidden History)

Saturday the 25th October 1980CE, Maureen (Mo) Lea was out preparing a night of fun and frolics to celebrate her twenty-first birthday. She met a group of friends in Headingley's student area for a quiet drink and to formulate plans for the big day. Maureen was born on the 26th October 1959CE in Liverpool, where she grew up, she eventually moved to Leeds in 1977 CE to study art at Leeds Polytechnic. Mo was in the third year of her degree course, she was a happy go look character, gregarious, confident and outgoing person. Enjoying the freedom of student life and the vibrant counterculture of the city, its music its art and its people. The group split up around 22:00 hours, Mo briskly walking hoping to get into Leeds city centre and catch her bus and prior to the pubs closing and thus avoiding the gauntlet of Leeds late night revellers and drunks. The atmosphere was upbeat. The cold Leeds night doing little to dampen the mood. Indirect victims of a self-imposed curfew due to the nocturnal activities of a certain Mr. Sutcliffe, it had only been six weeks since his callous attack of Uphadya Bandaras the Headingley student and the 'hangover' of her attack haunted the north of England. This feeling was exaggerated in Leeds which was the epicentre of the Yorkshire Ripper's attacks. A feeling that was endorsed and supported by the Yorkshire Evening Post, that provided a constant reminder of the Yorkshire Ripper and his reign of terror. The Yorkshire Evening Post was the paper that Mo wrapped her etchings and artwork in whilst transporting them to and from university. The media stories were a constant reminder of the very real danger that was a malevolent threat to the women folk of Yorkshire.

Mo walked down the side of the park, a huge swathe of grassland situated in LS6, the well-lit wide-open road offered little fear and Mo walked unconcerned towards her destination. Focussed on her destination oblivious to her unfolding predicament on a crash course with evil. Mo's concern grew has she entered the university grounds, has the streetlights grew dimmer and further apart and the mulling crowds faded out. Mo felt a little uncomfortable but was more concerned with the passing time than the eerie surroundings. Mo can't have been too concerned for her safety, when she finally passed through the university grounds, marked by the iconic University of Leeds Parkinson building clock tower. Faced with a decision to turn right and continue her short cut trip to Leeds, or turn left and take the longer Woodhouse Lane route. Fatefully Mo decided to pursue the path of least resistance, the quickest route as the crow flies and began to walk down Hillary Place.

22:50 hours, has she walked down the hill a man walked out of the shadows from behind her, she realised that she was not alone, she realised that Hillary Place was poorly lit, she realised how quiet the street was, she realised how vulnerable she was. Suddenly the silence of the night was broken by a soft and unassuming male voice.

"Hey you, don't I know you?" Peter asked, wanting to gain the confidence of his victim, wanting to see his victim's eyes, wanting to manipulate the situation to his advantage. Mo turned to greet the friendly voice. By her very nature Mo was a popular person and knew various people in and around Leeds through her studies and her social life. But the face of the man who had greeted her partially obscured by his upturned coat collars was not one of them.

"How are you?" Peter mumbled realising his plan was back firing.

Frozen in time, static unmoving she surveyed the man once again. There was no recognition, no recollection of his dark features, he was a stranger.

"Do I know you?" She responded glibly. Intrigued by his posture filled with trepidation at the way he held himself, as if feeling his body, hugging his arms into his body. As if struggling to conceal something.

"I'm sorry I don't know you". Mo turned to continue her journey, hopefully free from further molestation. Mo felt awkward, uneasy, this unwelcome stranger unsettled her. She continued to walk down the road, but with each passing step her unease grew. Her walking pace quickened into a jog, the strangers footsteps quickened behind her. The jog turned into a sprint, Mo sensed danger the dark high sided narrow street cast in shadow, lonely uninviting, awkward and dangerous. She could see the bright well-lit relative safety of Woodhouse Lane only yards away.

Peter lunged at Mo striking her from behind with the full force of his ball peen hammer. Mo fell stunned unconscious to the hard-unforgiving floor. Peter despatched a further hammer attack two, three, four more blows to Mo's defenceless head. Peter the whirling dervish wasted no more time. He grasped at his pocket and clasped the handle of the oversized sharpened screwdriver and released his anger, sinking the D.I.Y. weapon deep into the base of Maureen's neck, not once but twice. Just missing severing her spinal cord by millimetres on both occasions. Now crouched over Maureen's helpless figure, Peter was about to obliterate his victim, but he was disturbed by the intervention of two concerned Samaritan's

Lorna Smith who was walking with her friend Michael down Woodhouse Lane, the well-lit, well used main through fare to the city centre. The pair were walking across the junction where Hillary Place meets Woodhouse Lane when they were alerted by Mo's muffled scream which drew their attention to a commotion that was unfolding in the shadows of Hillary Place only yards away. As they approached the distant figures, the dominant figure turned and made good his escape. Lorna rushed to Mo's aid, Michael rushed to the student union building some four hundred metres away to raise the alarm and get help. Mo was lying in a pool of her own blood and kept falling in and out of consciousness.

Peter made good his escape, back to the Rover, back to his home, back to normality. His life was unravelling, his mission faltering and his life spinning out of control.
The attack left Mo fighting for her life with a fractured skull, a fractured cheek bone, a broken jaw, and stab wounds to the base of her neck, cuts and abrasions to her legs, knees and face.
Mo woke up in Leeds Infirmary unable to talk, her tongue was swollen and the inside of her mouth was sore, her broken jaw was wired. Her parents visited from Liverpool and were initially unable to recognise their daughter due to her injuries.

The police once again seemed incapable or unwilling to see these connections between similar description by previous survivor's as the list grew longer especially Marcella Claxton, Marylyn Moore, (Tracey Browne), (Ann Rooney), (Yvonne Mysliwiec), Marguerite Walls and Doctor Upadhya Bandara. However police still refuted these claims, following the party line, keeping a lid on the pressure. The police official line was that this attack was non-Ripper. For this was another local incident. The Ripper had gone away, women of the north were free from his threat. The Ripper had gone nowhere, the West Yorkshire Police Force were in denial.

However like all the Yorkshire Ripper survivors Mo suffered from long term post-traumatic stress a legacy that would never fully disappear. Maureen went public with a campaign in 2010 CE using her art for something positive, reclaiming the agenda. Like her attacker using art as therapy. Selling her artwork and donating money to 'Victims Support'.

She speaks candidly about her attacker being Peter William AKA the Yorkshire Ripper.
"It's an open secret, I know, the police know, we all know. But it has never been documented and acknowledged formally".

Mo is an artist, academic and campaigner.

Twenty-Four/Thirteen
Leeds, Saturday 25th October, 1979CE. (22:50 hours)

Chapter 29
Theresa

Theresa Simone Sykes lived at 35 Willwood Avenue, Oakes Huddersfield, HD3 with her partner Jimmy Furey, a twenty-five year old millworker and their three month old son Anthony, in a two bedroomed semi-detached council house that overlooked the playing fields between Willwood Avenue and New Hey Road. Theresa was sixteen years old and prior to having her son had formerly attended Deighton High School. The newly formed family had recently been allocated their family home by Kirklees Council. The couple planned to marry in the New Year and the future, their future looked bright but that was all to change.

Wednesday the 5th of November 1980 CE, bonfire night. A cold and icy November night, mid-week and mayhem was to be unleashed. 17:03 hours saw Peter clock off from work at Clark's Yard on Hillam Road, but Peter wasn't for going home to his showroom clean, cold and clinical marital home and the nagging dominion of Sonia. Although it was his home it lacked that homely feel, it was sterile, cold and uninviting, more a house than a home. Maybe he'd take in a bonfire or two, a firework display, sample some pie and peas, eat some Yorkshire Parkin, and have some bonfire toffee. Or maybe he would murder someone. His life was unravelling, starting to spin out of control, the pressures had mounted up, he needed a release, but Peter's release had become the all-important life consuming, life ending mission. He only felt alive when he was on the hunt for his next victim, he only felt alive when he was in the midst of death.

Peter called Sonia, his premeditating mind working overtime as he lifted the receiver on the public telephone, his finger laboriously dialled his home telephone number, his index finger on his left hand winding the dial clockwise to register the digit, then extracting his finger from the dial, releasing it, the mechanics of the dial whirring as it returns to its original location. The mechanics of 1970's CE technology. He repeated the process five times in total. He could hear the dialling tone, this was then broken by the voice of his wife Sonia.
"Hello". The voice was surrounded by the urgent beep beep noise emitting from the receiver demanding that the caller inserted his payment. Peter responded to Sonia's voice, Peter responded to the beeps, Peter inserted a ten pence piece into the slot on the main body of the telephone unit and began to speak.
"Hiya love, am gunna be a bit late toneet, I've bin stuck in traffic". He lied in order to open up an opportunity for the Yorkshire Ripper to destroy another life.
"Alright Peter, don't be too late," came Sonia's reply.

Peter replaced the receiver and returned to his car, God had told him Huddersfield, so Huddersfield it must be. He travelled south along Canal Road, Wakefield Road, A6177, M606, M62 West, Hartshead Moor Service Station, Peter pulled the Rover into the parking bay of the westbound service station. The West Yorkshire night sky sporadically broken by the yellow, red and orange of bonfires, skyrocket fireworks illuminating the plot night air were the background to Peter's journey.

A prelude to the non-sexually motivated sex attack, sweetening the proceedings. Latent anger simmered within, resentment of womankind, mad, bad and dangerous to know. The lengths that Peter would go to for God's mission, the trials and tribulations he would have to suffer to attain sexual gratification. Peter had found his way to the public toilets in the heart of the service station, inside a cubicle, isolated from the hustle and bustle of the evening outside, in his own world, he pulled down his trousers, took of his underpants and placed them in his jacket pocket. He then stepped into the DIY gimp leggings that underlined the fact that he was a DIY pervert. Aroused again the freedom to kill re-charged his fading libido. A woman would die and he would be satisfied and God would be satisfied as well. Peter now focused on the task in hand, he replaced his trousers and checked his clothing before re-entering the fray of everyday life and death. Peter returned to his Rover, his mobile abattoir and set off on the second phase of his mission.

He drove off the slip road and back onto the M62 West, Junction twenty-three onto New Hey Road, on to Huddersfield. After almost a three-year hiatus the Yorkshire Ripper was going to make a return to the West Yorkshire market town. This time the crime scene was two and a half miles west of his original atrocity and this time his attempt at murder was to end in failure. He drove east down New Hey Road towards Huddersfield town centre for about a mile and a half, before turning left up Acre Street at the roundabout. 19:45 hours, Peter parked his car in the car park of the Bay Horse public house, 1 Acre Street, Lindley, Huddersfield HD3, an area of wide pavement that saw the pub setback from the roundabout that fed New Hey Road to the east and to the west, Acre Street to the north and Reinwood Road to the south.

Theresa and Jimmy were settling down to watch Coronation Street, however they were running low on cigarettes, Theresa asked Jimmy to go, hoping he would and she could watch the rest of the Manchester based soap opera. Jimmy refused, he didn't much fancy a walk out into the wet and windy night. Theresa perplexed at Jimmy's selfish and unchivalrous behaviour, exited the property in a mood, this low-level lovers tiff, was a prelude to the stormy waters that would hit their relationship in the very near future. Theresa had just nipped out to the local convenience store, she visited the Jeco off-licence and grocers on 22 Acre Street HD3, where she purchased a packet of cigarettes, the time was 19:50 hours. She then began the ten-minute walk home, her mission accomplished, well partially, oblivious to the oncoming storm. The night sky often illuminated by the bright sparks and explosions of an array of multi-coloured fireworks, the still night disturbed by the noise of the traffic and the explosions of the rockets and bangers.

An intention that had to be acted upon, Peter had a deal with God, he was going to attack the first woman he saw, that was to be the trigger, he would need no time to decide, to identify her, he already knew inside his head, his mind was made up. God was his witness, his benefactor and his provider? God was ensuring that Peter had a conveyor belt of readymade victims. She was the one, the first person he saw that night. He needed no time to decide if she was a prostitute or not. God would not have chosen her if she was not suitable, he could not be held responsible. After all he had an inbuilt ability, a gift and something just clicked inside when he saw them. It was a trait, an attribute, a mannerism that went with the mission, complemented his motives validated his actions. A gift from God.

Peter quickly assessed his surroundings and headed towards the red phone box outside 80 New Hey Road, Lindley, HD3 where he stood and further assessed the situation. The traffic island of green grass ensured there was good visibility and the glass and steel sides of the red phone box protected him from the elements.

Theresa crossed the busy New Hey Road and walked past the petrol station which was on her left, she then turned left down the three hundred metre long concrete flagged pathway that connected New Hey Road with Willwood Avenue, to her right the lush green playing fields, to her left the cul-de-sac endings of Bay Close, Peckett Close, Millfield Close and Raynor Close. The open fields to her right were obscured on occasion by the leafless trees however the darkness of the night covered the field like a black velvet cloak. The streetlamps interrupted the murky shadows, to her right darkness, to her left darkness, behind her was a certain Mr Peter William Sutcliffe in front of her the sanctuary of home. Theresa looked around and saw the dark-haired figure of Peter about ten feet behind her, their eyes met and time seemed to stand still as she looked into his dark piercing eyes. Then as quickly as she had realised he was behind her, he disappeared into an alley down to Raynor Close.

Theresa was relieved that the stranger had gone, she was about twenty metres away from the relative safety of Willwood Avenue, with its street lighting and a road bordered by houses and the eyes and ears of their occupants. Theresa relaxed and continued towards her final destination, relieved she reached the penultimate lamppost on the pathway when she saw the shadow of her stalker had reappeared. It seemed to sneer at her from the concrete flagged floor. She tried to run but froze with fear, her sixth sense seemed to anticipate the shadow belonged to somebody that was up to no good.

Theresa veered to her left and the gate of a garden, a garden to a house, a house with inhabitants, and a house of safety full of denizens of dependable civilization. Secure, warm, safe, away from this uncouth follower intruding into her life with designs on causing her death. Peter positioned himself quickly, his left hand brandishing the ball peen hammer swiping through the night air and smashing it down onto Theresa head.

The first blow felled her, she grasped and grabbed at the garden gate, the second blow snapped her from the subconscious to the conscious and a scream shattered the still night, louder than the Standard fireworks illuminating the Huddersfield skyline. Huddersfield was home to the Crosland Hill Company which was a major employee in the district. He hit her one more time but was aware of an ever-increasing audience which had been alerted by Theresa's screams. His flawed attempts meant he decided that discretion was the better part of valour and casually walked away from hapless Theresa, retracing his earlier steps. He then heard footsteps and raised voices and his walk burst into a sprint as he fled the scene.

Jimmy Furey was a fitness fanatic had been looking after Anthony their son and was looking out of the living room window at the fireworks in the night sky, he was also watching dutifully for Theresa to return from the shops; he heard the commotion caused by Theresa's screams and initially thought it was two youths fighting, he went to the front door to investigate the source of the noise. From here he could survey the playing fields and the footpath, he heard a second scream which was a result of Peter's third hammer blow. He left the house barefoot running towards the origin of the hullabaloo.
"Theresa!?" He yelled. The dark shadowy figure of a man was walking away from the scene, away from the fracas, on hearing Jimmy's shout he lurched into a dash. Theresa screamed holding her head trying to quell the blood, she heard the footsteps of her assailant briskly walking away from his victim.
"Won't someone help me?" She heard voices in the distance comforting, reassuring, and abusive. In the opposite direction the brisk footsteps turned to a sprint. Mrs Rita Wilkinson a neighbour alerted by the commotion also ran from her home to aid, care and comfort the blood covered Theresa. She cradled Theresa in her arms and comforted her, trying to take her mind and her gaze off the pool of blood that surrounded Theresa's head.
"Won't someone help me? Please!" Jimmy hurtled passed the prostrate figure of Theresa who was slightly obscured by Rita; he only had one objective in mind to capture the suspect, the shadowy attacker. Peter ran a hundred metre sprint pursued by Jimmy, he turned right and rushed down Millfield Close, he hurtled the seventy or so metres down Millfield Close and careered around the corner taking a right into Reinwood Road. All the time he could hear the muffled barefoot steps of Jimmy behind him.
"I'll fucking kill you", Jimmy shouted. Fight or flight, Peter preferred to fight when the odds were stacked firmly in his favour, with weight advantage, the element of surprise and access to an array of weapons that his adversary did not, flight was therefore his only option. However he was fast becoming fatigued from his exertions, he used the distance, the time and the fact that he was out of view of his chaser to hide. The tumult he'd created only metres away had not yet been transmitted to this street. He hastily ran diagonally, following the most direct course, following the path of least resistance and shot diagonally

across Reinwood Road, then down Adelphi Road. Peter then ran a further fifteen metres and turned right into the darkness of a dirt track/lane that ran on the back of Adelphi Road.

Jimmy came to the end of Millfield Close and stared into the darkness of Reinwood Road, he looked around, up and down the street, but drew a blank, he muttered under his breath and realised his bare feet were cut and grazed due to the chase, he then thought of Theresa and turned on his heels and ran back to be by her side.

It was then that God intervened instructing Peter to hide behind a garden wall, Peter duly complied. He jumped over the dry-stone wall and ducked down out of sight, slipping into the shadows like a supernatural sorcerer. He took deep breaths recapturing his composure, expecting his tormentor to re-appear. When this did not happen Peter dusted himself down climbed back onto the dirt track, adjusted his clothing and strolled out nonchalantly like nothing had happened, he crossed Haywood Avenue and continued on the disused dirt road, finally reaching Wellfield Road, where he turned left and headed towards New Hey Road and the sanctuary of his car. A distance of approximately four hundred metres, whilst Peter made good his escape, concerned neighbours had carried Theresa into their home and raised the alarm dialling 999 requesting police and ambulance. Theresa sat in a chair blood flowing furiously from her head wounds, the panicked teenager became hysterical and once more began to subside into a fit of screams.

Soon the area was swarming with police, ironically the police station was only three hundred metres away on New Hey Road, Oakes, Huddersfield, HD3, Theresa and Peter had both passed it on their journey down the footpath. A police dog handler team were employed in a reconstruction of Peter's previous visit to Huddersfield under the guise of the Yorkshire Ripper. This time the trail was still hot, the Alsatian quickly picked up the attacker's scent, following its trail along Raynor Close, onto Reinwood Road, down Adelphi Road and then the dirt track, where the Yorkshire Ripper had hidden only minutes earlier. Then the trail went cold, fate intervened once more, fortune favoured the felon. Had God intervened to ensure the integrity of his mission to save society from the scourge of prostitution and loose morals?

Detective Superintendent Mr Dick Holland lived at Birchencliffe a village located near to Ainley Top and the M62 motorway was immediately notified of the attack. He quickly drove the short distance of less than a mile to the scene of the attack and straight into the thick of the hunt and the ongoing investigation. In doing so he drove past the house that his daughter lived in along with three other nurses, only a stone's throw away from the crime scene. Just showing the audacity of the Yorkshire Ripper striking in the backyard of the senior police hunting him and also highlighting that with this maniac at large no woman was safe.

The police were on the scene at about 20:10 hours at the same time Peter was driving his car north on Market Street, turning right onto Lower Gate then onto Luck Lane (although Peter knew he didn't need luck with God on his side). The driving soothed him, eased his mind, distracted him from his deeds and the self-doubt that they invoked. Peter continued to drive, to distance himself from the scene of the crime, manoeuvring his car onto Reed Street, left onto Westbourne Road right into Thornhill Road and left onto the A629 Halifax Road, then the M62 East, Peter pulled the Rover into the parking bay of the eastbound service station. Peter turned on the car's interior light and checked over his clothes and body for the tell-tale signs of his earlier exertions. His once over inspection confirmed his suspicions, he had been clean and clinical, and there had been no time for knife work which minimised the likelihood of blood. His hurried escape also meant that he had only been in close proximity of Theresa for a brief and fleeting moment. Happy at his appearance he disembarked from the car and walked the short distance to the Hartshead service station building.

He bought a cup of tea and sat down and reflected on the evening's events, it had been a close call, and he had nearly been caught red handed. Had God deserted him, was this a sign? Peter slowly sipped at the overpriced soulless brown dishwater tea, lost in his thoughts. He thought of the Geordie hoaxer on 'Dial a Ripper' and the prophetic words it had contained. *I reckon your boys are lettin' you down, George. They can't be much good, can they? The only time they came near catching me was a few months back in Chapeltown, when I was disturbed. Even then it was a uniformed copper, not a detective...I can't see myself being nicked just yet. Even if you do get near, I'll probably top myself first.* He fought back laughter with incredulity at the stupidity of the police investigation.

Eventually he sought the sanctuary and the seclusion of the toilet cubicle, for he had a job to do, a trail to hide and a secret to maintain. Frustrated again he reassured himself that next time he would be successful. He undressed and replaced the offending garment, with the correct attire, he placed the DIY gimp leggings in his pocket and finally vacated the public convenience and returned into the public arena. It was getting late and he decided to make tracks. He braved the cold night air and opened the boot of his car, he took out a black bin bag, felt in his pocket where minutes previously he had placed the leggings. Hurriedly he fumbled the leggings into the black receptacle then he took the refuse bag and placed it safely out of site in the refuge of the dark reclusive area of his Rovers spacious boot.

Theresa was rushed to Huddersfield Royal Infirmary, Acre Street, Huddersfield and then transferred to Chapel Allerton Hospital, Chapeltown Road, Leeds where she underwent neurosurgery on her head wounds. It was around thirty-five days before she was finally released from hospital.

He climbed into the seat of his car and set off on the slip road, entering the motorway M62 East, then the M606 and back to Bradford. Back to normality, or Sonia's version of it. Under the radar until his next wrecking mission. Back in Bradford he headed home northeast to his domestic troubles, to his domestic bliss. 22:00 hours Peter returned home to 6 Garden Lane. He was the Yorkshire Ripper no more, he was Peter William Sutcliffe, Sonia's Peter.

The media blackout was working, it was helping to flush out the killer. Unfortunately there had to be some collateral damage, but if the next attack was the one that helped capture the beast, if the next murder led to his imprisonment then the sacrifice would be worthwhile, wouldn't it? An altruistic murderer, an altruistic police force, an altruistic victim in an egotistical society. The police were aware of the risks, it was a risk they were prepared to take in order to bring justice to the streets of the north.

The 5th of November was already synonymous with an infamous Yorkshireman, Guy Fawkes, intriguingly both were Catholics with a strangely similar appearance, the beard and moustache. Guy Fawkes was born in York on the 13th of April 1570 CE and was a major part of the Gunpowder Plot of November 1605CE, when he was arrested 'red handed' in an Undercroft underneath the House of Lords guarding the stock piled explosives he was dutifully taken to The Tower of London where he was tortured until he signed a full confession, he was later executed for his troubles on the 31st of January 1606 CE aged thirty five. The failure of the Gunpowder Plot has consequently been commemorated throughout the British Isles since Guy Fawkes and his cohorts attempt to assassinate the Protestant King, ever since his effigy has traditionally been burnt on a bonfire alongside the obligatory firework display. Due to an outbreak of The Black Death/Bubonic Plague the opening of Parliament was delayed from its intended date of Thursday the 28th July 1605CE to Tuesday the 5th of November 1605CE, the plotters had prepared for the original date but had to hold on until the re-scheduled State Opening of Parliament

An anonymous letter was also integral to his story, but unlike his twentieth century counterpart this led to his incarceration and demise, Peter benefited from his written and recorded hoaxer maintaining his freedom. In his grave digging days Peter spent many a day in the half world of the underground within the crypts and mausoleums of Bingleys great and good, just as Guy had done when guarding the gunpowder. The Black Death or the Great Plague, Peter saw himself as the avenging Angel of the North, his special brand of medicine fighting against the plague of prostitution. Although separated by three hundred and seventy-five years, they were the two kindred spirits?

The observance of the 5th of November Act 1605CE was brought into law on the 23rd of January 1606 CE, also referred to as the 'Thanksgiving Act', that celebrated the deliverance of King James I; this Act was subsequently repealed in March 1859CE however its traditions had moulded themselves in the very fabric of folklore, ritual and custom. Unfortunately like his Tudor counterpart, or his Victorian equivalent Jack the Ripper, Peter's alter ego the Yorkshire Ripper had also reached mythological status.

Twenty-Five/Thirteen
Huddersfield, Wednesday 5th November, 1980CE (20:00 hours) *Peters prostitute radar was faulty; initially it took no time to decide which women were prostitutes. A straight skirt with a slit in it represented a green light. An amber gambler in disarray 20:00 hours is far too early for this shit. Out - sprinting a physical fitness fanatic, Peter was faster than fast, an English Allan Wells. Jim Furey was fast, but Peter was faster, possibly God had once again intervened. It was a close call, the Yorkshire Ripper had almost been caught quite literally red handed. But Peter was not the Yorkshire Ripper; Peter was Peter, the mild-mannered janitor/lorry driver. The stigma attached by the pseudonym did not rest well on his shoulders, Peter did not like it, it was not him, and it did not ring true.*

Monday the 1st of December, Theresa underwent further surgery on her injuries at Pinderfields Hospital, Wakefield nearly a month after the attack, eventually she was released home over five weeks after Sutcliffe's attack.

Bonfire Night attack 'not Rippers work' ran a headline on page three of The Yorkshire Post on Tuesday the 2nd of December 1980CE. She was the last victim to survive the Ripper - although at the time police refused to publicly link the attack with the Ripper and insisted they were looking for a local man. When asked about a connection with this attack and similar attacks in the area to the 'Yorkshire Ripper', Detective Chief Superintendent Mr Jim Hobson (Leeds Area), explained that
"They have found no indication of a connection yet".

Theresa's parents Mr Raymond and Margaret Sykes did not agree with the police in this matter. Her father who was the landlord of the Minstrel Inn Public House, Cross Church Street, Huddersfield, HD1, believed that there were too many similarities between his daughters attack and that of other 'Ripper' victims and claimed that Theresa was the monsters latest victim. '***I know it was him***' ran the headline in the Daily Mail. However police refuted these claims, following the party line, keeping a lid on the pressure, Detective Superintendent Mr Tony Hickey reiterated that he believed, *"This was a local incident".*
Time was to prove Raymond Sykes theory correct, however the fact was not confirmed for a further month. For Peter's mission was drawing to a close, God was preparing to draw the final curtain on this unholy alliance. Peter the ever-faithful follower could only let destiny run its course.

Haunted by his eyes unnatural, staring, very dark and piercing. Holding her in his gaze, making a couple of seconds seem like an age. A shadow like figure with dark hair and a neatly trimmed beard. The Sulphur yellow light of the streetlamps creating an impression that his black beard and moustache were ginger tinged. Police seemed incapable or unwilling to see these connections between similar description by previous survivors especially Marcella Claxton, Marylyn Moore, (Tracey Browne) and Doctor Upadhya Bandara.

Peter read the news or the medias personal reviews of his work, but news was scarce. The scarcity acted to reassure him of the fact that the police or media had failed to attribute his last few attacks to be the work of the Yorkshire Ripper. He felt safe and protected, he believed that God had assigned a guardian angel to watch over him, a guardian angel to protect him. Or then again was it a double bluff, lulling him into a false sense of security, whilst the police net was tightening and his capture was imminent.

A trio of NHS hospitals, Huddersfield, Leeds and Wakefield, as a result of a trio of hammer blows that Peter felt of no consequence, however Theresa would have to deal with the consequences of his actions for the rest of her life. Theresa was unable to settle back into her old life, the skull shattering blows to her head, were life shattering. She lost all confidence around men, became paranoid feeling that all members of the male sex might attack her. Theresa changed from a happy go lucky young woman to a difficult and tortured victim, always ill at ease in the company of men. The Yorkshire Ripper inadvertently added another victim, another unenviable skill to his portfolio, that of a relation wrecker. Theresa moved out of Willwood Avenue with Anthony and back into the Minstrel Inn and the security of her parent's home. She was convinced that her assailant was the Yorkshire Ripper and he would return to kill her and finish the job he had started.

Chapter 30
Jackie

The 17th of November 1980 CE a cold wet, rainy mundane Monday, Peter completed his last job of the day a delivery of engineering equipment to Kirkstall Forge, in Leeds, 19:00 hours he returned to T and W H Clark (Holdings) Limited, Hillam Road depot and swapped his lorry for his 1971 CE registration brown Rover 3500. He set off in search of a public telephone box and rang Sonia.

"Hiya love I'm in Gloucester, I won't be back till late". Peter lied ensuring he had an opportunity to indulge his fixation.
"Don't wait up". He replaced the handset excited, awkward at what lay in store. He then set off on his journey, his latest fling with his fantasy alter ego; the cold wet and rainy day became a cold wet and rainy evening. Peter drove to Headingley, Leeds in his brown Rover on the Leeds/Bradford Road through Kirkstall, past the abbey and then up the hill to Headingley. Peter stopped at the KFC attached to Headingley Arndale, he parked in the car park to the rear of the establishment, just off Wood Lane in a re-enactment of the prelude to his September attack on Doctor Upadhya Bandara. He then went into the shop to sample some southern fried chicken and hospitality, he purchased his food a carton of chips and fried chicken for the princely sum of £1.10 and retired to his car, to avoid prying eyes and possible recognition. His Rover was to act as his dining carriage for the evening

Jacqueline Hill, commonly known as Jackie was twenty years old and had come to Leeds to study at the University of Leeds, where she was in the third year of an English degree. Originally from Ormesby near Middlesbrough where she was actively involved in the church working as a Sunday school teacher at Ormesby Parish Church. Jacqueline's family home was a four-bedroomed detached house in Lealholme Crescent, Ormesby, Cleveland, TS3, where she lived with Jack, her father (aged 48), a retired plant mechanic; Doreen, her mother (aged 46), a teacher and her two younger siblings, Adrian (aged 16) and Vivienne (aged 15). Her parents were concerned for Jackie's safety in light of the continued attacks of the Yorkshire Ripper and had persuaded Jackie to return to the 'safety' of the halls of residence during the university term where she resided in the student apartments in Lupton Hall, ironically it was this considered move to a safer climate that contributed to her death.

Jacqueline a volunteer probation worker seeking a career in social work often attended a probation officers' seminar in Leeds city centre. On Monday the 17th of November she attended her last seminar on the fateful evening, she left the seminar and caught the Holt Park number one green and white Metro Bus, which was a double decker on Cookridge Street in central Leeds (LS2) at 21:00 hours, she had less than half an hour to live. Jackie alighted the bus at the bus stop/shelter on Otley Road, close to the junction with

Dennistead Crescent and opposite Woolworths that made up part of the Arndale Centre (Headingley, LS6). The time was 21:23 hours. Jacqueline looked for a gap in the traffic and crossed the busy Otley Road, she had her hood up on her check pattern coat protecting her against the elements, she walked under the shadow of Arndale House, her path was lit by the shop fronts and the street lights with the addition of the passing traffics headlights.

Peter finished his meal and then set off to cruise the area for a suitable victim. Peter was unable to turn right onto Otley Road and had to drive across the junction where Wood Lane meets Otley Road, he then drove onto North Lane turning right onto Chapel Place and then right again onto Chapel Street, and he then turned left onto Otley Road, (the A660). He edged out onto the road and drove slowly along the main road, his attention focused on the margins it was then that fickle fortune sealed the fate of Jacqueline Hill who was walking on the pavement of Otley Road to his right in front of him and walking in front of the shadow of the Headingley Arndale centre. Peter clicked into Ripper mode, he correctly assumed from Jacqueline's demeanour and body posture her anticipated direction of Alma Road. It was at this point that Peter thought to himself 'she looks a likely victim,' but now to put the theory into practice.

Peter turned right onto Alma Road, driving past Jacqueline, he pulled his car to a standstill approximately 5 metres along Alma Road just shy of the striking Yorkshire stone of Carlton House 3-5 Alma Road, Headingley, Leeds LS6 and scurried to collect and conceal his wooden handled ball peen hammer in the inside breast pocket, along with his large yellow handled screwdriver, back to the tried and tested methods of murder no namby-pamby ligatures, no pink and blue cord, just brute force and pre-meditated violence, a self-medication on Peter's behalf, an horrific heinous crime in the eyes of society.

He quickly extricated himself from the Rover and became part of the foot fall on the Headingley high street tributary of Alma Road. As he did this he scanned up and down the road, his thought process had served him well and Jacqueline had followed the route he'd anticipated, she was walking up Alma Road dwarfed by the small brickwork, concrete and glass that constituted the Arndale Centre. She began to cross the access point to the service area at the rear of the ground floor shops, she then crossed the road that gave access and egress to the Arndale Centre car park. Peter crossed the narrow road diagonally taking the path of least resistance, he walked at a pace, failing to notice the one way road signs standing sentry to the rest of Alma Road, his attention fixed on the figure of Jacqueline in front of him and to his right. He continued towards his goal and put in the extra physical effort to ensure he positioned himself so he was just behind Jacqueline as the pair proceeded up Alma Road.

Peter reached what he adjudged to be an appropriate distance, so as not to unsettle Jacqueline, but also within striking distance. In synch some three metres shy of Jackie, step for step it was then that he noticed the opening in the chain link fence on the right-hand side of the pavement. The inner demon needed no further invitation and spring heeled Jack jumped into action as Jacqueline drew level with the gap less than a hundred metres short of the sanctuary/safety of her flat in the Lupton Flats Hall of Residence, Alma Road, HeadingleyLS6.

Peter pulled the ball peen hammer from his jacket pocket and struck Jacqueline a sickening blow to the back of her head, Jacqueline dropped to the ground from this blow a gurgling noise exited Jackie's mouth. He hauled Jackie through the gap in the chain link fence and onto the waste ground, away from the public pavement into the private wasteland that was to be his killing fields, pulling her by the hands further away from safety, further into the darkness. Peter focussed on his work in a different world, a parallel universe where light and dark forces were in conflict. He was fulfilling his mission in his altered reality Jacqueline taunted him, turning around adjusting her skirt and her stockings, flaunting herself. His delusional interpretation, his invention fuelled his intention, his premeditated need to kill. For God had invested in the mission and God had invested in Peter ensuring he had the opportunity and the means to kill. God protected him, hoodwinked the police and of course God had a hand in the hoax tape and letters. Peter's destiny was in God's hands, Peter was unconcerned for his fate for he knew that God would steer him clear of trouble. In respectable Headingley where curtains twitched, sex wasn't allowed, 'No Sex Please, We're British' the great and good of the area protested. Peter scoffed at their inability to accept the truth, prostitution in Peter's head was rife, and prostitution in Peter's Headingley was rife. His altered perception changed Jacqueline's determined walk home in a slow strut where Jacqueline tried to grab the attention of two passing motorists. Where she loitered on the street corner of Otley Road and Alma Road. Vengeance is mine, I will repay. Peter the moral barometer, Peter the cold-blooded murderer, Peter the Yorkshire Ripper.

Reality was not a million miles away, in fact reality was seconds away in the shape of car headlights driving up Alma Road illuminating him and his latest crime scene, and he threw himself on top of Jackie to avoid the glare of the headlights. The car and its occupant past by oblivious to the oblivion that was ongoing, again Peter baffled at the fact that he had not been seen felt reassured, he knew that God was working to protect him. His false reality fortified he continued his interrupted onslaught. Jacqueline confused, distressed and in shock, her body mechanised, struggling to contemplate what was happening. Peter hit Jackie once, twice with the hammer, targeting her head in an attempt to further incapacitate her, to control her. Her resistance negated he heaved her body further into the wasteland, further into the abyss. However in fact reality was fifty metres away and literally seconds away in the shape of 19 year old Andree Proctor, a fellow student also returning home to the sanctuary of Lupton Hall, returning home walking in the recent footsteps of Jacqueline Hill, walking in the footsteps of Peter Sutcliffe. Peter froze in the darkness, Andree urged by a sixth sense turned to her right and looked into the darkness of the wasteland, she thought she saw something move in the shadows, her suspicions slightly aroused, however she decided it was her mind playing tricks with her, it had been a long day and she couldn't wait to get out of the cold and the wet. She walked past Jacqueline's glasses that had fallen from her face when she was attacked, she walked past Jacqueline's handbag, she walked past Jacqueline's single discarded Fair Isle knitted mitten, but she didn't see any of them. The sound of her footsteps disappeared into the night and Peter seized the opportunity to continue his work.

Peter pulled at Jacqueline's clothes, when he had removed most of them he pulled out the sharpened screwdriver and stabbed at the trunk of her body in the hope of stabbing her lungs. He then noticed Jacqueline's face and her eyes, they seemed to stare at him, a judgemental gaze, an accusing gaze *'why have done this, why have you done this to me?'* Peter unnerved and phased by the gaze and her/his imagined narrative decided to remedy this situation in his crass northern diplomacy. In an act of despair, desperation and desecration he plunged the screwdriver into Jacqueline's unprotected left eye. The wound an attempt to despoil her dignity failed, Peter recoiled as Jacqueline's gaze remained upon him. It unnerved him all his movements being scrutinised by the mocking reproach of Jacqueline's death stare. Like an English Mona Lisa! Peter could not hide from her discerning gaze, the rage sated the inner demon defeated, any further need or desire to progress his misdemeanour were discarded and he knew it was time to leave his chaos and return to the sanctuary of 6 Garden Lane.

Don't look at me, I don't like it, the inner insecure child that was Peter came to the fore, he became self-conscious, in effect his style cramped, the fire of frustration and hate was extinguished. He stopped, re-grouped collected his clutter (one wooden handled ball peen hammer, check, one yellow handled screwdriver, check). He placed them safely in his pockets and regathered his composure.

21:30 hours Peter left Jacqueline lying on her back her gaze to the stars, her feet pointed the way to his exit, and he climbed through the gap and back into the everyday, away from the make-believe. He returned to the car, drove up Alma Road to the top of the incline, he then turned around and drove back down Alma Road towards Otley Road, when he was just past level with the entrance to the Lupton Hall, a pedestrian gestured to him that he was driving the wrong way down a one way street, Peter continued down the road and turned left onto Otley Road and then proceeded to drive home as if nothing untoward had happened.

21:55 hours Amir Hussain, a 31 year old Iraqi postgraduate student at the University of Leeds was walking on Alma Road and he found Jacqueline's forcefully discarded cream raffia handbag with a red handle, he checked inside the handbag to see if he could discover to whom the mystery bag belonged. Inside he found a small amount of money and a Barclaycard in the name of Miss J Hill. He called in at the reception area in the students hall of residence in Lupton Halls just off Alma Road, unfortunately he was unable to locate anybody to hand over the handbag to, so he returned to his student flat at Lupton Court with it still in his possession, where he shared his discovery with his flatmates.

The group discussed the discovery and decided that they would report their find first thing in the morning. However Amir unable to sleep returned to the shared kitchen where he had left the handbag, his mind was racing with intrigue trying to work out what the handbag was doing abandoned on a Leeds street and he wondered what had happened to its owner. The group reconvened. Tony Gosden a 49-year-old flatmate and fellow postgraduate a former Hong Kong police inspector picked up the handbag emptied out its contents and examined it closely under the bright kitchen light. It was then that he saw the fresh blood stains on the exterior of the cream handbag. Tuesday the 18th of November 1980 CE., 00:03 hours Paul Samson rang 999 and explained the concern at their findings. Paul explained that they knew the bag belonged to a Miss Jacqueline Hill and he suggested that it may be prudent for them to check if Jacqueline was in her flat. The telephone call was logged, 'Found handbag with blood on it'.

00:12 hours two uniformed officers were dispatched from Ireland Wood police station and attended Lupton Court, they arrived in a police panda patrol car and on gaining access to the flat they showed no real urgency and seemed disinterested in the students repeated suggestions to check Jacqueline's whereabouts and her safety. They seemed more intent on completing the lost property paperwork and drinking their coffee than beginning their investigation into the matter in hand. Only after they'd finished their drinks did they arrange to drive Mr. Hussain to the location where he found the handbag. They collected the bag and inspected it with continued disinterest, then returned to the Panda car with Mr Hussain and drove under the guidance of Mr Hussain approximately one hundred metres down Alma Road.

00:27 hours Amir Hussain showed them where he had first found the handbag. The two officers conducted a three-minute torchlight search of the surrounding area 9 Alma Road, LS6, a derelict detached house which was unfortunately across the road from where Jacqueline's body lay. They walked past Jacqueline's glasses that had fallen from her face when she was attacked, they walked past Jacqueline's single discarded Fair Isle knitted mitten, but they didn't see them.

00.30 hours the two uniformed officers were called away and left to attend a burglar alarm call, Mr Amir Hussain returned to his Lupton Court address and explained that the police had seemingly gone through the motions and undertaken a rushed and fruitless search.

Tuesday the 18th of November 1980 CE, the poor weather persisted, if anything it deteriorated, the rain occasionally turning to sleet. 9:00 hours Jacqueline's mitten and her intact glasses were found on the pavement close to the gap in the chain link fence on Alma Road, her partially naked body lay some twenty-seven metres away still undiscovered.

It wasn't until 10:10 hours that Donald Court a shop manager at the Arndale Centre discovered the lifeless body of Jacqueline Hill, he was walking up the ramp which led to the car park at the rear of the shopping centre after banking the previous days takings. Slightly struggling with the weight of a big bag of silver coins he stopped to swop the weight from one hand to the other, in doing so he looked over the concrete wall onto the rough ground, amidst the wild grass, rubbish, young saplings and leafless trees he saw Jacqueline's hastily covered body. The police were called immediately.

Wednesday the 19th of November 1980 CE, George Oldfield released a statement to the press, *"This man is obviously very mentally ill and has got this sadistic killer-streak in him. He can flip at any time. We hope fervently we can catch him before any more lives are lost".*

Peter reflected on the ramifications of his Monday evenings outing. Insane in the membrane, insane in the brain - all hope lost, unaware, and unable to care, the tumult and turmoil abated the section papers lodged, signed and dated. A killing zombie on a holy mission, a war of attrition, good versus evil sees collateral damage, brain damage and despair, but too mad to care. If only the police weren't so inept, their inability to see through the falsehoods and fallacies, dishonesties, deceptions, denigrations, defamations and deceits. Their incompetence, ineptitude and ineffectiveness had contributed towards his killing spree, his suffering, would it ever end? He felt sorrow for himself, feigned sorrow for the tragedy his actions had created, he believed he needed to be stopped, he believed God should and would shortly release him from his Holy mission, the Holy mission that was destroying him and the lives of many others.

Twenty-Six/Fourteen
Leeds, Monday 17th November 1980 CE. (21:25 hours) *Fast food outlets still in their infancy Peter was on the prowl in search of a likely victim. False reality, in another world, a world of his own, completely out of touch with reality. Adjusting her skirt surely the actions of a prostitute. "God invested me with the means of killing. He has got me out of trouble and I am in God's hands. He misled police and perhaps God was involved in the tapes so the police would be misled. In God we trust.*

A reward of £25,000 was initially offered, this was increased to five pounds0,000 after Jacqueline Hill's murder for information leading to the arrest and conviction of the person (or persons) responsible for the above-mentioned crimes.

"The sponsors are the West Yorkshire Police Authority who are offering up to £20,000 and Yorkshire Post Newspapers who are offering up to five pounds,000. The full terms under which this money is offered are as follows: -
Anyone with any information for the police should dial 100 for the operator ask for FREEPHONE 5050 or give details direct to a police officer.
There is no need to disclose your name and address immediately if you want to help and eventually claim the reward.
If you wish to remain anonymous – for the present – give a personal code word and a six-figure number. This will be your identification should you wish to claim the reward later. The police will keep a record of your identification code.
Should your information lead to the conviction of the killer you will be able to claim your reward by identifying yourself with your personal code word and number.
Anyone wishing to give information in writing should send it to Mr. G. A. Oldfield Assistant Chief Constable (Crime), County Police Headquarters Wakefield, West Yorkshire.
An identification code and number as suggested above should be included in the letter. You should tear off and retain a corner of the paper on which the letter is written as an additional safeguard.
Any reward will be paid at the discretion of Mr. Ronald Gregory, the Chief Constable of West Yorkshire".

Tuesday the 25th November the formation of a 'super squad' –a think tank of senior officers drawn from other forces, is announced. As a direct result Assistant Chief Constable George Oldfield was effectively taken off the case, although he remained head of West Yorkshire CID. Then Hobson, in a statement that was almost clairvoyant (if not obvious), announced that when the Ripper is caught 'it will be by an ordinary uniformed copper, going about his normal duties'

Forever friends Trevor Birdsall and Peter Sutcliffe shared lives, shared aspirations, shared failures, shared jobs, shared dreams, shared dilemmas. Trevor was concerned and he had misgivings that Peter was the Yorkshire Ripper, Peter was concerned that he was the Yorkshire Ripper and that the police net was closing. You can't buy friendship and Trevor wasn't one to split on a mate, but £50.000.00 (worth £225.000.00 in 2015CE terms) was a nice incentive to break the unwritten northern code of male friendship, maybe he could split on a mate after all. Peter was distraught, distressed, his drink driving court case was looming and he felt he was not in control, his life was a mere whim, that God could do with it what he wanted.

Tuesday the 25th of November 1980CE Trevor decided to cash in his chips, to sell out his best mate and confidante, if Peter was Jesus, Trevor was Judas and he hoped to cash in on the thirty pieces of silver offered by the police and media.

"To whom it may concern
I am writing to inform you that I have a very good reason to believe I know the man you are looking for in the 'Ripper Case'.
It is an incident which happened within the last five years. I cannot give any date or place or any details without myself been known to the ripper or you if this is the man. It is only recently that something came to my notice, and now a lot of things fit into place. I can only tell you one or two things which fit for example, this man has had dealings with prostitutes and always had a thing about them. Also he is a long-distance lorry driver, collecting engineering items etc. I am quiet sure if you check on the dates etc., you may find something. His name and address is:
PETER SUTCLIFFE
CLARKE TRANS, 5 GARDEN LANE, SHIPLEY, HEATON, BRADFORD"

The police response to Trevor's anonymous letter came from Detective Sergeant Boot 'Action to trace/interview Sutcliffe'. This act triggered an action form to be sent to the department where the index clerks worked, police constable Sue Neave was working as an index clerk and received the action form, and she checked the filing system for the name Peter Sutcliffe and found three index cards relating to Mr. Sutcliffe; all three index cards contained information about Sutcliffe's vehicles continually being sighted in the red-light areas under police surveillance. Sue summarised the contents of the index cards onto the action form.
'Gap in teeth – h/w neg, but officer interviewing not happy'. Police constable Sue Neave her part of the process complete placed the action form into the appropriate filing basket. The action form remained in the filing basket awaiting additional copies of paperwork relating to previous interviews to be attached before an interview could be undertaken, these copies were never attached and no interview resulted from this action form, the system had broken down (again) due to human error, neglect and lethargy, or was this another act of God?

The band of brothers replaced by a band of gold. Time to cash in, time to milk the cash cow, time to get his just reward and Sutcliffe to get his just deserts. Wednesday the 26th of November 1980 CE, Gloria Conroy harangued her boyfriend Trevor Birdsall and after a few drinks accompanied him to the Bradford police headquarters, at the Tyrls, in Bradford city centre. Only fourteen months previously the scene of a feminist protest to reclaim the night from the Yorkshire Ripper. The pair arrived at 22:10 hours and were greeted by a fledgling police constable manning the reception desk, Trevor encouraged by Gloria did his best to impart his suspicions and reasons for them. Through the pound signs that appeared in his alcohol infused eyes he told the police constable of all things he thought to be Yorkshire Ripper, all things Peter Sutcliffe. He spoke of Halifax, Olive Smelt, August, 1975CE, nights out and Telegraph and Argus reports. All ears, the young officer took out his trusty police issue pocket notebook and began to write. As Trevor attempted to right the wrongs from four years of silence, of guilt through neglect. Trevor and Gloria finished their tale, all they could do now was wait, sit back and wait for Peter's arrest and the windfall it would bring. The young police constable dutifully captured the information from his notebook and submitted a formal memorandum of his impromptu revelation about the would-be identity of the Yorkshire Ripper to the Ripper incident room, Millgarth police station, Leeds. LS2.

Wednesday the 10th of December 1980CE Trevor picked up the handset of his rotary dial telephone and dialled 23422, he explained his reason for ringing and asked if there was any news on the information he had supplied. A polite police officer took down his particulars and made notes, Trevor received no return call and assumed his misgivings about Peter were misguided and forgot the incident. He'd have to think of a new way of making his fortune.

It was later disclosed that after Peter's arrest, Trevor Birdsall had entered into a financial agreement with the Sunday People newspaper being paid five hundred pounds and a retainer (receiving sixty-five pounds per week). This meant that by Peter's Old Bailey Trial Trevor had accrued sixteen weeks at sixty-five pounds = one thousand and forty pounds. Trevor's hotel room for the duration of the trial was financed by The Sunday People this included the full tab he racked up inclusive of drinks etc. Whilst Gloria Conroy his girlfriend received two thousand pounds for the exclusive rights to her story.

Chequebook journalism, blood money, the Press Council, hotel bills, personal expenses, News of the World, Sunday People, the Sun, the Star, the Sunday Mail

Chapter 31
Ava

A New Year a new beginning, but Peter's New Year resolution was the same one he'd had for a number of years, since his epiphany in a Bingley graveyard in the late 1960's CE. His epiphany manifested itself into a mission, Peter's deal with God, that got off to a stuttering false start in the later stages of 1969 CE, however this was a false dawn, the time was not quite right for Peter William Sutcliffe to take on the mantle of the Yorkshire Ripper. His resolution had successfully been applied with the murder of Wilma McCann, in November 1975 CE, his alter ego had been born out of his nocturnal handy work and officially received the moniker, The Yorkshire Ripper, in February 1977 CE. The mission was well under way and the myth surrounding the Yorkshire Ripper was looming large in the subconscious of northern England. A New Year a new beginning, Peter's New Year resolution remained unfaltering, to rid the world of the scourge of prostitution, he was zealous in the pursuit of his resolution/mission and had put his theological theories into practice for the past five and a half years.

Olivia St. Elmo Reivers aged twenty-four, was born on the Caribbean Island of Jamaica and as a child in the early 1960's CE dreamt of becoming a singer or a nurse, having money for life's luxuries not having to self herself to make ends meet. Olivia's father moved the family to England in 1969 CE. He found work as a factory labourer in Birmingham that lay claim to being the second city of the United Kingdom. Olivia left school at the age of fifteen in 1971 CE and worked in various shops as a salesgirl. Olivia eventually moved from Birmingham in 1973 CE and settled into her harsh Industrial South Yorkshire surroundings of the Steel City of Sheffield, where her two children were born, Louise in 1975 CE and Deroy in 1980 CE. Her childhood dreams in Jamaica failed to materialise and she cut her cloth accordingly becoming resigned to reality and her lot and stoically dealings with the reality of her every day, day to day predicament. 1976CE saw Olivia turn to prostitution for the first time, struggling to support her young daughter on her own. The absent father of her children lived in London and was not overgenerous with providing for his offspring, exasperating Olivia's woe's, Joe her live-in boyfriend was at least there. Olivia's family and friends referred to her as Ava. The young family came to settle on Wade Street, Firth Park, S4; to the North of Sheffield city centre.

16:05 hours, Friday the 2nd of January 1981CE Peter William Sutcliffe prepares to leave his matrimonial home on Heaton hill.
"Sonia am just off to ger our Janey's car keys, Mini's broke darn agen".
It is the first Friday of the New Year and Peter is lying to his wife, because he had no intention of going to Bingley to collect his sister's car keys, Peter had a more sinister reason for this escapade. Peter set out with the intention of murdering a woman. Peter drove the

eleven miles to Cooper Bridge Spares, Brighouse Road, Mirfield, West Yorkshire WF14. Whilst in the scrapyard Peter found a number plate that had fallen from a Skoda, the registration plate read HVY 679 N, he took this as another message from God and went on to detach the other from the vehicle, he knew now what he must do. 18:00 hours Peter leaves the scrapyard with the stolen number plates and heads off into the night.

He drove up the A644 Wakefield Road, up onto the M62 and north to junction 24-25, and Hartshead Moor Service Station, Brighouse, West Yorkshire HD6. Sheffield, South Yorkshire it was to be, as he had foretold in his September poem to the Sheffield Star. Peter felt usurped by his Sunderland rival so he'd penned his own poetry and forwarded it to the Sheffield Star the post room received the poem entitled Clueless, it read: -

> '*Poor Old Oldfield,*
> *Worked in a Coldfield,*
> *Hobson has no choice,*
> *Misled by a voice,*
> *Release of Drury,*
> *Arouses fury,*
> *Bradford was not me,*
> *But just wait and see,*
> *Sheffield will not be missed,*
> *Next on the list*'.

The Streetcleaner (T.S.).

Sheffield will not be missed, he thought to himself. 21:00 hours Peter rings Sonia from the Hartshead Moor motorway service station.
"Hiya love, cars still playin up, al see ya when I see ya".
Thus creating an opportunity to attempt to chalk up his fourteenth victim. Thus creating an opportunity to disappear to the toilet cubicle and remove his brown corduroy trousers and his underpants, he placed his discarded underpants in his blue plastic jacket, in the same side pocket that housed the pink and blue cord he'd used to strangle Maureen Walls and attempted to kill Uphadya Bandara. He took his DIY gimp pants out and pulled them onto his body. 'Sheffield will not be missed,' he thought openly excited at what was to come. But not now he must wait, he must wait until the death throes. He regained control and adjusted his clothing. He tucked his blue shirt into his trousers flushed the toilet then returned into the male public area of the urinals and wash hand basins. He washed his hands and looked into the mirror, his dark staring eyes, his manicured moustache and neatly trimmed beard, he wondered whose unlucky night it was going to be. He drove

down the M1 to Sheffield. 21:50 hours Peter pulled over removed the stolen number plates from the boot and taped the stolen registration plates over his existing registration plates with some black electrical tape he had in a toolbox in the boot of his Rover.

Sheffield, South Yorkshire, circa 20:00 hours; Olivia put Louise and Deroy to bed, tucked them up in bed, gave them a goodnight kiss. She then prepared herself for the cold night air and donned her work coat, a fur coat, similar to Helen Rytka's fun fur that she had worn on the night her path and Peter's crossed, her memory now preserved with a makeshift wooden cross on a Bradford hillside in Scholemoor Cemetery.

She then set off out to brave the elements on this cold and blustery evening. Her fur coat helped ease the discomfort of the ice-cold wind that chilled her to the bone, taking away her breath, but Olivia remained focused and purposely strode out into the dark night air. Her dark Afro-Caribbean complexion was undermined by the acne scars she suffered on her cheeks and forehead. However in the dark night light, in the soft sulphur diffused street lighting these became difficult to see and complemented her youthful looks. The cold night air was countered by the heat provided by the bus ride south to Havelock Square. Two buses later and one connection Ava found herself in the red-light district and automatically adopted prostitute mode.

21:00 hours Olivia Reivers met her friend and fellow prostitute Denise Hall, (aged nineteen) and they began to ply their trade along Wharncliffe Road, (S10 postcode). Like Olivia, the younger woman was of Afro-Caribbean descent. In another quirk of fate, from a distance, in the half light of the Sheffield winter night the couple resembled the Rytka twins, with their slim figures and Afro hairstyles.

Havelock Square (abode to the have nots) and its adjacent streets (the Broomhill area) were once a fashionable district in the city of Sheffield, unfortunately the district had fallen on hard times, there were still signs of its former glory, tall once impressive houses, offered a glimpse of its former glory. However time had taken its toll on this area, it had become run-down and fallen into disrepair and had gained a bad reputation. Now its large houses and cheap house prices encouraged private landlords to enter the area and cash in on the need for affordable housing. This period also saw an influx into the area of West Indians, Asians and Arabs, who complemented the indigenous white working-class residents. A truly multi-cultural hotch-potch of humanity a cosmopolitan district.

This saw a marked increase in the number of low-income households and the demography of the area transform into single parent families, low earners, high unemployment and multiple/over occupation of the properties in the area. The changing and transient population impacted on the social cohesion of the community. Along with the deprivation came the prostitution, crime, drug abuse and the reputation of the area declined further. In the mid to late 1970's CE Havelock Square was labelled Sheffield's red-light district. The Broomhall high rise flats and the Viner's cutlery factory were landmarks on the landscape that at times it seemed law and order had forgotten.

Saint Silas church was sited in the area. Reverend Alan Billing the vicar of this Church often prayed for his flock who lived in the area, part demolished, moderately despondent, wholly distressed, an unholy alliance of degradation, exploitation and poverty. Cavendish Street, William Street, Wharncliffe Road tenement buildings, popular with Afro Caribbean residents and the police who often raided the properties active brothels. Havelock Street, Holberry Gardens, Brunswick Street (that leads onto Wharncliffe Road), Broomspring Lane. Transient residents, illegal drinking dens of iniquity, ill virtue, prostitution and pimping. A shelter for Sheffield's great unwashed, the lost souls, life weary and those who prey upon their misery and misfortune.

Olivia and Denise were victims of a society that didn't care, but they didn't care. Denise was targeted as a victim by the Yorkshire Ripper, Olivia was very nearly a victim of the Yorkshire Ripper. Selling sex for 'easy' money, selling sex for 'accessible' money, selling sex through necessity. Young mothers, teenage mothers with babies to feed, nappies to buy and bills to pay. The sex trade seemed an ideal solution, however it did have its' downside for the voiceless prostitutes from the high rise tower blocks of Low Edges, to the one night stands, on remand, court dates, sink estates, the prison spells and of course the emotional and economical oblivion. Noise annoys, anti-social, social security, damp and mould, cold flats, cold uninviting streets, incomplete lives, frigid wives, half a person. Freedom, debt collectors, loan sharks, brothels, saunas, street walking, vice, skint, de-sensitised, benefits, nameless faces, victims, martyrs. But society didn't care. Olivia had four years' experience on the game and was known to the police. Olivia didn't care.

Peter drove to Havelock Square, in the Broomhill area, the heartbeat of the Sheffield's red-light district, 22:05 hours he pulled up on Broomhall Street and propositioned Denise Hall, a coffee coloured Afro Caribbean woman.
"Are yer doin business?" he asked nonchalantly.
For Peter William Sutcliffe worries had disappeared, the confines of his small humdrum existence of little or no concern. He was the 'Yorkshire Ripper', 'Spring Heeled Jack', 'Jack the Ripper', the servant of God. His Rover was hallowed ground, a mobile confessional where he practiced the Lords work.
"Sorry," came her mumbled reply as she walked away from the open window of his Rover 3.5, the powerful car that compensated for Peter's sexual short comings. Denise disappeared into the night air. Un-phased at this rebuff, Peter simply wound up his

window and drove off, down Broomhall Street into Broomhall Road. She was not the one, God would select the right one, God would ensure the mission was successful. God his master, his confidante, his patriarch, his creator. Peter was unconcerned for he had seen another woman that had tickled his fancy, it was natural selection, evolutionary biology, selective breeding, Darwinism, religious Darwinism. The selection process, God ensuring that Peter his theological weapon was given a conveyer belt of appropriate and deserving victims. In the Lord we trust, back onto Broomhill Street. *They never learn...I can't be held responsible*, he thought.

"Are yer doin business?" he asked.

"Yeah" came Olivia's quiet and mumbled response.

"A tenner?" he suggested.

"A tenner with a rubber". she agreed as she got into the warmth of his car.

Along Broomhall Road he drove, a right turn into Park Lane, a left turn into Clarkehouse Road, then a right turn into Newbould Lane, then a left turn onto Melbourne Avenue.

Melbourne Avenue was a public through fare camouflaged to look like a private drive to the passing motorist however the Sheffield locals knew differently. The twin stone pillars that adorned both ends of the avenue, marking the beginning and the end of Melbourne Avenue, also acted to give the false impression of private ornate wealth similar to Claremont House in Farsley where Peter had murdered Marguerite Walls. He still had the cord with him that he had used to kill her and attempted to kill Uphadya Bandara, but he was erring away from strangulation/garrotting, he had decided to get back to basics, back to the ball peen hammer, knife and DIY killing tools for this one. The blue and pink cord was to remain in his coat pocket next to his discarded underpants. The fine surroundings lead to a false impression of wealth, however Olivia knew the locality and knew that there was little prosperity in the area, Olivia and the other prostitutes also knew that it was the ideal location for undisturbed sex with a client, if the price was right of course. Unfortunately for Peter, unfortunately for Olivia or fortunately for Olivia, the police were also aware of this city centre enclave a drive through brothel. This local knowledge was to contribute towards the end of Peter Sutcliffe's reign as the Yorkshire Ripper and his ultimate downfall.

"I'm Dave. What's your name? he introduced himself.

"I'm Sharon," Olivia lied and replied.

Peter carefully reversed his car into the parking bay revealing his expert driving skills, his dexterity but also his predatory nature and premeditation, he may need to make a speedy exit he thought. The car came to a slow and controlled halt and the driver dimmed his headlights to make the vehicle less conspicuous and fade into the background.

"Do yer mind if I talk to you a bit?" he asked then continued without waiting for a response.

"No," came Olivia/Sharon's response.

"Why are you frightened?" asked Olivia/Sharon, confused at his behaviour.

"Sonia my wife is highly strung, she thinks she's better than everybody else, she's a social snob, who can radiate disapproval by her very presence. Bossy, badgering, boring, controlling, detached, disapproving, domineering, reserved, weird, emotionless, but I love her. The unworldly daughter of strict Ukrainian/Czechoslovakian parents. Keeping up appearances the façade of respectability although in reality tears and tantrums behind closed doors. The nagging wife, baron, infertile. Dutiful sex unemotional and open resentment. Miscarriages, nervous breakdowns, nervous meltdowns, but I love her. I'd make a great father. Obsessive compulsive disorder, OCD scrubbing, cleaning, sterile, obsessed, but I love her. Cracking up, schizophrenia, agitated states and unprovoked outbursts of rage and rancour. But the pretence of respectability all encompassing, all important, but I love her. Kicking, punching, teasing, pinching, nipping, provoking. I never lifted a finger, never raised my voice, never mind my hand, because I love her. I've packed my bags wanting to leave but failed because I love her. Domestic bliss a living hell that must have some release. But I love her and I'm so generous, loving and thoughtful. I'd do anything for anybody, nothing is too much trouble". (I'm too good to be true, I'm going to kill you, he thought).

Peter/Dave continued to unload his personal angst on Olivia/Sharon, who was stoically listening allowing him to unburden his problems, to bare his soul. However money is time and time is money and Olivia/Sharon was in the business of making money, not making friends. Her business was her displeasure, an evil necessity to provide for her family. His pleasure would be her displeasure, her death, gimp trousers and sadistic necrophilia pleasure.

"Have you got that tenner?" She asked and passed him a condom, Peter/Dave handed over a ten pound note to Olivia/Sharon who passed him the durex and took the ten pound from his hand in one fluid movement, Olivia/Sharon placed the money into the packet and then put it in her bag. On receipt of the money Olivia/Sharon went into prostitute mode, removing her knickers and pulling up her skirt, for easy access.

"Yer better than my last punter," Olivia/Sharon small talked.

"Why's that?" enquired Peter/Dave.

"He wor a big fat taxi driver who stank of sweat," came Olivia/Sharon's matter of fact response.

"Can wi do it' in't back? Dashboard'll ger in't way," Peter/Dave protested. His protests and attempts to control the situation fell on deaf ears.

"No it won't," Olivia/Sharon politely disagreed, *"Taxi Tom had no trouble".*

Peter limply reacted to her voice, although thought with the power of gentle persuasion and God's assistance, he'd be able to manipulate the situation to his advantage. All he needed to do was bide his time.

Peter/Dave removed his black plastic car coat and carefully placed it on the back seat of the car in the hope of enticing Olivia/Sharon onto the back seat, for this was where he wanted her to believe he wanted her. Playing for time in an attempt to coax her into the open, into the killing zone. He wanted her to believe that this was his intention, to feel at ease, to lull her into a false sense of security, to concentrate on the back seat and access to the rear of the car. It would be then that he'd spring into action. To ensure control of the situation and the moment, he grabbed the gear lever with his left hand and placed his right arm on the headrest behind her head, to give him purchase as he straddled her body. He began to go through the motions, the sex mechanics, Olivia/Sharon repositioned her contorted body in the confined space of the car to allow Peter/Dave to manoeuvre into her. But it wasn't access that Peter required. (I'm so generous, loving and thoughtful. I'd do anything for anybody, nothing is too much trouble. I'm too good to be true, I'm going to kill you, he thought). His ire was rising he just needed to orchestrate the opportunity.

Peter/Dave remained immune to Olivia's/Sharon's well-rehearsed efforts of sexual gratification, after about ten minutes effort, Olivia/Sharon came to the conclusion that her efforts were wasted, the punter remained flaccid, he was unable to obtain an erection through 'normal' sex.

"I don't think we'll be able to do it," she suggested, cushioning the blow of his failure by sharing the blame. Massaging his ego, ever the professional, she stayed calm wanting to close the deal with the least possible hassle.

"It looks like it," Peter/Dave responded, his thoughts elsewhere with his intentions. He needed to lure her out of the car and into the open then he could continue his mission unperturbed and undisturbed. The pair revisited their earlier chat.

"I carn't go wiv me wife, I just carn't". Peter/Dave explained, his words lost on Olivia/Sharon, she feigned interest to try and appease her situation. The situation was becoming too protracted, his lingering excuses, his lengthy ramblings. Delaying, coaxing, manipulating Olivia/Sharon began to feel ill at ease, suspicious of the punter beside her, or was she just being stupid.

Sergeant Robert Ring and Probationary Constable Hydes were going to become synonymous with the Yorkshire Ripper, however this was unknown when the pair clocked on for their 22:00 hours night shift. Sergeant Ring was a forty-seven year old officer, he had served in the force for twenty-six years and was an ideal candidate to impart some of his vast knowledge and skills to probationary constable Robert Hydes who was a thirty-one year old probationer, seven months into his probationary period.

Probationary constable Hydes, had successfully completed his police driver training in November 1980 CE, he had subsequently undergone various other aspects of his ongoing training, including foot patrol, plain clothes and the Force Intelligence Unit. Tonight was his first day back in uniform after his CID training, it was also going to be his first time on mobile patrol.

22:20 hours the pair set off from Hammerton police station on what was to be a history making patrol. Sergeant Ring instructed probationer P.C. Hydes to drive directly towards Melbourne Avenue some two miles south of the police station onto Bessingby Lane, Walkley Lane, Walkley Road, Northfield Road, Crookes, Crookes Road, Fulwood Road, Glossop Road, Westbourne Road, Southbourne Road and then Melbourne Avenue. The sergeant had an idea in mind, he thought he'd teach his probationer how to deal with, arrest and process a prostitute and her punter.

22:30 hours and sure enough it seemed the opportunity had presented itself, the pair noticed a box-shaped dark car parked on the driveway of the Light Trades House, the car was parked in a little bay on the right hand side of the driveway, with space enough for two cars to park side by side, the pair also thought they'd recognised the reason why the car was parked there. 'Nudge, nudge, wink, wink, say no more. A nods as good as a wink to a blind bat'. Their assumption was to prove partially correct, however the true sinister purpose of this tryst, this tête-à-tête, this dangerous liaison was one they could not foresee.

In the interior of Peter/Dave's Rover, the pair were disturbed by the sound of the engine of Sergeant Ring and police constable Hydes patrol car, the white Vauxhall Chevette front bumper almost kissing the front bumper of Peter's brown Rover V8, ensuring that Peter could not use his vehicle to execute an escape. Bumper to bumper nose to nose, toe to toe; where would this interaction go? The punter and prostitute (murderer and victim, imaginary boyfriend and girlfriend) startled by the noise of the police patrol car's engine. They were further caught unaware when the interior of Peter's car was illuminated by the beam of light emanating from the torch held in PC Hydes hand. Peter/Dave turned to Olivia/Sharon and whispered.
"Leave it to me. Your me girlfriend".

Olivia/Sharon remained calm, if a little disgruntled and did her best to relax into the passenger seat of the Rover. She took on the role of onlooker, a spectator in a verbal game of cat and mouse that realistically was only ever going to have one winner. Her punter (would be murderer and pretend boyfriend) was not it. Peter wound down the window in response to this interruption and confronted his would-be accuser.
"Are you the registered keeper of this vehicle, do you own it?" asked probationary police constable Robert Hydes under the watchful eyes of his mentor and accomplice Sergeant Ring.

"Yeah," replied Peter in his slight soft West Riding voice.
"What's your name and address?" came Hydes retort.
"John Williams, 65 Dorchester Road, Canklow, Rotherham". Peter lied.
"And who's she?" Sergeant Robert Ring interjected in full old school police fashion.
"Me girlfriend". Came Peter's audible but feeble reply. The conversation, the interrogation, the verbal joust falling away from his favour.
"What's her name?" Sergeant Ring quickly questioned.
"A don't know, I h'ant known her fer that long," Peter responded and quite literally crumbled inwardly at how the conversation was going. (Love's young dream, Dave and Sharon make a pair, split them up if you dare).
"Who are you trying to kid. I haven't fallen off a Christmas tree?" came Sergeant Ring's rather festive response.
"I'm not suggesting you have," Peter stuttered grasping for an opportunity to turn the tables. Turning to the woman sat in the passenger seat Sergeant Ring directed a question to her.
"What's your name love?" he asked gently, openly ignoring Peter's lies.
"Olivia Reivers," came her aggravated response.
Sergeant Ring went to the rear of the vehicle to get the registration number so he could do a police check. The police officers returned to their patrol car leaving Peter/Dave and Olivia/Sharon. *"Carnt yer mek a run for it?"* Peter/Dave asked in his low soft voice.
"No, I can't. The police know me," Olivia/Sharon replied.
Peter/Dave sighed, raised his eyebrows and resigned himself to a long night.

Fractured minds constant voices, stay calm, they'll keep you free from harm. He no longer had rancour with Olivia all hostility had gone. Vengeance depleted, the wrath of God exhausted, an opportunity to flee, to make good his escape allowed to close, Peter stayed put and made no attempt to manoeuvre his vehicle away for it would be futile, he must let fate play out, God had allowed the patrol vehicle to block him in to prevent his exit. But Peter could not be bothered. Lies and deceit, but still the tipping point had not been reached, Peter needed to hold out in the hope that God would advise, dictate his course of action, however until that point had been reached he must play the waiting game, verbal chess with the boys in blue.

Ring and Hydes conferred at the open doors of the Ford Escort police patrol car; after some consideration Sergeant Ring radioed divisional headquarters to verify the details proffered by the odd couple, the occupants of the brown Rover saloon parked for a quick getaway in the driveway of Light Trade House, 3 Melbourne Avenue, Broomhill, Sheffield, S10.

"Control, Sierra 5809, can I have a vehicle check on a Rover, registration number Hotel, Victor, Yankee 679 November," crackled Ring's South Yorkshire accent across the South Yorkshire airwaves.

The Police National Computer (PNC) check was duly consulted by the control room officers, *"Its showing a Skoda saloon, registered keeper Mr Aslam Khan"*, came the operator's response.

Hydes and Ring returned to their suspect's vehicle, leaning into the open window of Peter's car, one of them said *"There seems to be a problem with your number plates?"* Sergeant Robert Ring then grabbed and removed the car keys hanging from the ignition keyhole in the steering column and placed the confiscated keys safely in his uniform pocket. Peter remained calm at this new turn of events, although the situation was rapidly deteriorating, spiralling out of control. He was aware of the hammer and knife under the driver's seat and the knife in the pocket of his car coat. Would God intercede? How would God intercede?

Meanwhile police constable Robert Hydes was closely inspecting the tax disc on the windscreen, the tax disc disclosed the information that the vehicle taxed was a brown Rover V8 and the registration number was FHY 400K. Unhappy at the strange story coming from the odd couple, Sergeant Ring and police constable Hydes happily cautioned the twosome and decided to take them into the station for further questioning. Olivia had had enough, and vented her frustration on the two officers of the law - (unbeknown to her the unwanted attention from the police officers had saved Olivia's life a fact that she was soon to be made aware of) - they were the enemy a necessary evil an unwelcome disruption to her attempts to make a living. (Without their intervention Olivia would have joined an unwelcome list, Olivia was a very lucky lady. *"If those cops hadn't arrived I feel I'd be dead".*). But that was taking into account hindsight.

Her actions almost allowed the Yorkshire Ripper to maintain his freedom. Almost! The two police officers distracted by Olivia's antics focused on the female and escorted Olivia Reivers to the rear of their patrol car, leaving Peter alone in his own company for a brief moment, this was his opportunity, God had created an opening, a window of opportunity. Never one to miss an opportunity, he seized the moment and seized the knife and ball peen hammer from under his seat and sprung from the vehicle, there was still life in spring heeled Jack and he walked purposely towards the relative shelter and cover of the far side of the large ornate stone built entrance porch, uncontested, unmolested he strode across the car park with one sole purpose in mind.

Light plays tricks on the mind, it illuminates and blinds vision, eases sight and eases flight. At the rear of the patrol car and therefore the remaining car park was at sea of darkness, the Rover an irradiate island of as yet undiscovered ambiguity. The tranquil sea of the car park devoid of vision, bereft of evidence, impossible to see in the dark. The dusky, murky, black and gloomy figure disappearing into the darkness, becoming obscure, becoming opaque. A gift from God, an alibi, freedom? Unopposed he strode into the night. Unabashed he strode into the night, unrestrained, unconstrained, his luck couldn't hold, or could it? Immoral, immodest, dissolute, depraved, debauched, degenerate, dissipated; Peter strode out.

Should he make a run for it, no he thought, they'll be able to trace me by the car, keep calm and carry on, became his mantra. At the far side of the porch out of sight of the police, he found an oil tank that provided the fuel for the central heating for the building, this abutted the exterior of the building and provided an ideal hiding place for his hammer and knife, his murder weapons, the evidence. He took out the offending articles and dropped them amongst a pile of leaves that had accumulated on the floor between the oil tank and the external wall of the building and arranged the leaves to further hide the weapons, the noise they made seemed to resonate seemingly amplified by the predicament Peter found himself in.

Sergeant Ring's attention was grabbed by the solo fracas that disturbed the silence in the near distance behind him. He turned to the noise, he faced the noise and his eyes began to decipher the night scene that was unravelling in front of him. The morphing outline merging with the night and coming into focus, circa twenty metres away and decreasing. Approaching, returning at a healthy walking pace attracted back to the light of the patrol cars headlights. Behind the figure loomed the masonry of the Light Trade House, the porch jutting into the tarmac that formed the car park. At the side of the porch, the rectangular metal mass of the oil tank, seemingly elevated further by a surrounding wall. Sergeant Ring placed little significance on the scuffling sound he heard, he was more concerned in ensuring that their suspect did not disappear.
"What are you doing there?" Ring demanded.
"Hav fallen off that fuckin wall," came a disgruntled reply. *"I wanted a piss".*
"Go over there if you need to urinate". The policeman pointed towards the side of the Light Trade House building.
"I'll leave it," Peter replied inwardly happy that his quick-fire plan seemed to be bearing fruit.

Little more was thought of the incident at the time, however it was to prove crucial to the demise of the Yorkshire Ripper. Sergeant Ring chaperoned his prisoner, he had been caught out once and did not want a repeat performance; Ring allowed Peter to return to the Rover and collect his car coat from the back seat and in doing so it allowed him to take control of the knife within its breast pocket. No search, little care, a second error of judgement from the police sergeant perhaps? Sergeant Ring then ensured that the suspects Rover was securely locked up. Peter was then escorted by Sergeant Ring to the back seat of their patrol car and positioned in the back seat beside Olivia. Sergeant Ring checked that the Rover was locked up once again for good measure and returned to the patrol car and then the patrol car headed north onto the confines of Hammerton Road Police Station, Hillsborough, Sheffield, S6 2NB.

Chapter 32
Hammerton Anarchy

The group of four arrived at the station and entered the building to a scene of disarray. Ever the opportunist Peter saw this as a sign from God, a chance to conceal incriminating evidence that may link him to the Ripper murders and curtail his mission. Organised chaos greeted the ensemble, pandemonium was the order of the day. Other officers had undertaken a police raid on an illegal drinking den and made a number of arrests. The situation was compounded further by the ongoing prison officers' industrial action, which meant that additional prison inmates were being held at police stations throughout the country. The station was full to capacity with every room in the building overflowing with various people. It was to this backdrop that Peter and Olivia were introduced to police custody and it goes a long way to explain the lack of a thorough search, whilst they were being processed.

"Can I use the toilet?" Peter asked in his unassuming mild manner. He was immediately taken to the toilet by Sergeant Ring, where he was left unsupervised, a third error by the South Yorkshire police. Once inside the cubicle he grabbed the knife from the inside pocket of his car coat, standing on the toilet pan to gain the height necessary to access the high-level cistern. He lifted the lid and dropped the knife into the water filled cistern. He heard the splash, replaced the cistern lid and climbed down off of the toilet pan. Relief flushed through his body and his confidence surged, it reaffirmed his trust in God and the importance of the mission, he urinated, then flushed the toilet and returned to the chaos of the police station. He felt he was on the home run, straight to freedom.

It was during this process that Sergeant Ring noticed the grease, the grime and the dirt of industrial labour under his suspects, and soon to be prisoners, fingernails. His patience was all but expended and the pair were soon to be charged. A miscreant, a pair of miscreants. A member of the hoi polloi, two members of the hoi polloi.

He was unkempt, unclean, uncouth and debase, small in stature, however his high hairline and its black tight curls standing high atop his forehead, giving the silhouette of a taller man.
She was a common whore, he'd seen it all before, desensitised to the situation under enthused at their shallow, sallow, pallid washed out lives. The odd couple, now uncoupled, separated at the police station and interviewed separately.

This saw Dave become John William, become Mr. Khan, become Peter William Sutcliffe. Sharon become Ava become Olivia Reivers. The Rover HVY 679N, become a Skoda, HVY 679N, become a Rover FHY 400K, the webs of deceit they weaved began to unwind and unravel. The truth will out. Olivia Reivers remained Olivia Reivers, a convicted prostitute currently on a suspended prison sentence for soliciting. For Peter William Sutcliffe the verdict was out.

Peter admitted his true name and address, Peter William Sutcliffe of 6 Garden Lane, Heaton, Bradford. Date of birth 2nd of June 1946CE. Peter opted for a co-operative approach, he thought give them a little bit of information to appease their questioning, take the rap for a small misdemeanour thus avoiding the awkward questions in relation to the Yorkshire Ripper, thus avoiding capture. Peter also admitted to the theft of the number plates from a Skoda car in the Mirfield scrapyard. The reasoning behind the theft he explained was his imminent court appearance on a drink drive charge. His car insurance had only just expired and he had failed to renew it because it was inevitable he was going to lose his driving licence. A plausible story Peter thought that the police would accept, he could then be charged with theft of the number plates, valued at fifty pence, and quite possibly released on police bail, however if not and more importantly the alleged theft was deemed to have taken place in West Yorkshire, this would then see him handed over to the West Yorkshire Metropolitan Police, because the theft had taken place on their patch. Out of sight out of mind. He could also return to Light Trade House and remove his discarded weapons of murder.

On the wall in the police station was a photo fit of a man wanted in connection with the Yorkshire Ripper attacks and murders, Sergeant Arthur Armitage looked at the photo fit, then looked directly into the dark soulless eyes of Peter William Sutcliffe, with the dark black hair, beard and moustache. There was a distinct similarity. The rotund Sergeant proclaimed.
"Tha's the Yorkshire Ripper, thee". Peter William Sutcliffe remained motionless and stared back at his accuser emotionless and silent.

Too many questions, false number plates, false name, prostitution, Bradford, a metre-long length of blue and red nylon cord.
"What's this for?" Sergeant Ring asked holding the three-foot length of cord, with strategically placed knots.
"Repairing cars," Peter gesticulated.
"What can you use this on cars for?" Ring continued to question.
"Just lifting things, things like that," Peter explained.
"What are the knots for?" Ring doggedly continued.
"To grip I suppose," Peter lied. *(And choke the life out of the bitch whores!!!!* he thought*).*
Sergeant Ring turned his back on his prisoner and walked out of the room. He left Peter in the company of probationary constable Hydes, maybe he could crack this nut?

Sutcliffe was fidgeting, unhappy at the situation fraught with worry, wanting his freedom.

"Yer all the same you coppers. Yer did me for speeding in Bradford, saying a were doing fifty in a thirty-mile zone. A few weeks later they upped the speed limit to fifty, tell me where's the sense in that". Peter almost incoherent protested, his mind seemingly elsewhere.

"I can't comment on that Peter, is there anyone you'd like me to call?" Probationary constable Hydes suggested. But Peter had other things to get off his chest.

"NO. Last June I got breathalysed by your lot and now am gonna lose me licence and me job".

"Sorry to hear that Peter, are you sure you don't want me call anyone?" Presented Hydes.

"NO. Just let me out and I'll be home in an hour".

"Do you want me to call your wife and let her know your alright," offered Hydes.

"NO. How long is this gonna take?"

"It's just procedure, red tape. It'll take as long as it takes. Now give us that number".

"No..., oh alright, if it'll shut you up and get me out of here. It's Bradford 0274......," he lied ensuring Sonia would remain unmolested and his secret would remain a secret. Once Peter had finally acquiesced to Hydes perseverance and volunteered the number, the dialling code plus the six digits stammered from his lips, almost whispered begrudgingly. Hydes wrote the number down carefully, he told Peter of his intention to contact Mrs Sutcliffe and put her mind at rest. Peter seemed aloof, despondent and was unresponsive. Hydes left the room and dialled the number Peter had provided.

Unfortunately the number was incorrect and Hydes had to apologise to the owner of the false telephone number that Peter had supplied, for the early, early morning call and disturbing the household from their slumber. The Pakistani man who answered the call half asleep was unimpressed by this unwelcome disturbance and returned to bed. Maybe it was Aslam Khan's house, the former registered keeper of the Skoda saloon from which Sutcliffe stole the number plates. That would be a strange quirk of fate, a coincidence too far? It seemed Peter had a penchant for false names, false number plates and also false telephone numbers, Hydes thought to himself we've definitely got a strange one here, a strange one with possibly something to hide, but would they unearth the strangers dark secrets.

Sergeant Arthur Armitage and Constable James Tune were intrigued by the prisoner, who was fast becoming the talk of the nick. The circumstances of his arrest, his attitude, his appearance. They offered to bring Sutcliffe's Rover back to the confines of the Hammerton Road police station car park. Sergeant Armitage and constable Tune had a hunch that there was far more to this prisoner than met the eye when they called in at Melbourne Avenue, the arrest location to check out the vehicle further. The Light Trade House was well known as a firm favourite with prostitutes and their punters, both officers noted the unusual way the Rover V 8 was parked up, with its front end facing towards the open road. Most, if not all of the cars that parked there on an evening parked with their front's facing away from the open road, affording their occupants enhanced privacy from prying eyes. The couple completed their allocated task and brought the vehicle to the safety of the police station garage. Their suspicions raised, fuelling the furore around the mysterious prisoner.

Sergeant Ring returned to the room and escorted Peter to the police station garage, carefully removing the black gaffer tape that held the stolen number plates onto the Rover's real number plates. Sergeant Ring opened the boot to reveal a toolbox, there were also other tools scattered on the floor of the boot space. On closer scrutiny there was no hammer, there were tools that required a hammer, specialised tools that required a hammer, but no hammer.

"Why isn't there a hammer?" Sergeant Ring challenged.

"I dunno, I just keep loads a tools in me car," Peter half-heartedly offered.

Sergeant Ring lifted the drift punch – a drift punch used to aid and align rivet or bolt holes before inserting a fastener. The drift punch is a tapered rod and requires a hammer blow to the large end of the taper. - and asked Peter again.

"Why isn't there a hammer?"

Peter just shrugged. On the back of the Rover lay a filthy brown woollen Army surplus cap, it replicated the unkempt appearance of its strange owner.

They returned inside the police station, where a detective asked Sutcliffe.

"Have you been questioned by the Ripper squad?"

"Everybody has been questioned. They are always questioning. It makes you sick," Peter turned to face his inferred accuser and replied nonchalantly. However he couldn't hold the gaze and sheepishly turned his head. (Liar, liar, your bums on fire. Your nose is bigger than a telephone wire).

Probationary constable Robert Hydes and Sergeant Bob Ring held an impromptu conversation about their peculiar prisoner, with Peter William Sutcliffe sitting behind them, they retreated to the corner of the room and turned their backs on the subject of their discussion. Their voices lowered to whispers. Hydes explained his misgivings to Ring, Peter's irrational lies, his inability to tell the truth, he didn't even try to hide his lies, his words and actions were unreasoned, almost out of control. Peter was a strange one, his stories didn't ring true. He'd say one thing then contradict it in the very next sentence. Lying, misleading, a pathological liar with something to hide, but what? Very strange indeed. Ring agreed, it didn't add up, talk and banter was rife in the Hammerton nick and the joke of the moment was that Sutcliffe was the Yorkshire Ripper.

Ring turned suddenly and looked Sutcliffe in the eyes, testing for a response, looking for a tell-tale sign a give-away.

"If you are the Ripper, why don't you just admit it? All you have to do is admit it, are you?" Peter sighed his indifference and turned away from Ring's gaze. Perturbed and unhappy with the response, Ring decided to push the matter further, he placed the palms of his hands flat on the police station walls, either side of Peter's head and slightly above the seated Sutcliffe's shoulders. He then leant forward pushing his face forward into that of Sutcliffe's. Sutcliffe the rear of his head pressed against the police station wall, had nowhere to hide. Ring leant in further to Sutcliffe their noses millimetres apart.

"I think you are". Stillness, calm, unroused Peter seemingly unfazed. Ring was still unhappy with Sutcliffe and the circumstances of his arrest, there was something wrong, something Bob could not put his finger on. Another detective in the room asked Peter directly.

"Why do you use prostitutes".

"I don't know any prostitutes. I've never been with any," Sutcliffe snapped back.

The bemused detective shook his head in disbelief, Sutcliffe remained unmoved.

In the light of the Jaqueline Hill debacle Along with the poor press this incurred and the political interference and the inception of the Ripper Super Squad, Chief Constable Mr. Ronald Gregory had issued an order to all police officers. *'Any man found with a prostitute in suspicious circumstances was to be held and referred to the Ripper Squad for checks'.*

Sergeant Ring and his colleagues weighed up the situation and made what was to prove a monumental decision. Faced with two distinct options, two distinct courses of action, this decision was going to alter criminal history. The suspects, one a punter who had stolen a set of number plates from a Mirfield scrapyard and adhered them to his vehicle and two a known prostitute who had been caught red handed whilst on a suspended sentence. Mirfield became an important factor, this seemingly minor incident, this small misdemeanour in a Mirfield scrapyard became the fulcrum on which the scales of British justice were to balance in relation to the Yorkshire Ripper case. Which way were they going to tip, who were they going to favour good or evil? Sergeant Ring had every right to bail the male punter, Mirfield came under the police jurisdiction of the West Yorkshire Division of Dewsbury, therefore Sergeant Ring and probationary constable Hydes could just bail Mr. Peter William Sutcliffe to return to 6 Garden Lane, Heaton, Bradford to be questioned at a later date by the West Yorkshire police force.

OR charge Mr. Peter William Sutcliffe, with the theft of number plates to the value of fifty pence to appear before Dewsbury Magistrates Courts. If these two options had been pursued Mr. Peter William Sutcliffe, the Yorkshire Ripper would have been duly police processed and be free to take the Sheffield air and walk the Sheffield streets and possibly take another life, if it was his wont.

OR they could hold Mr. Peter William Sutcliffe in custody at Hammerton police station

A joint decision, a group discussion, a coming together of minds, divine intervention. The police decided to hold onto their catch, let him sweat a little in the cells. A decision that would change history and especially Mr. Peter William Sutcliffe and his story. Mr. Gregory would have his way, due process would be applied and adhered to.

Saturday the 3rd of January 1981CE, 0:00 hours, in light of this information Sergeant Ring rang Dewsbury Divisional Headquarters and explained they had a certain Mr. Peter William Sutcliffe in their custody. Ring continued explaining the facts surrounding the arrest and the theft charge. He explained that Sutcliffe's Rover was in the garage at Hammerton police station. At 1:00 hours, Sergeant Ring, rang to inform the Ripper Incident Room (as was Mr. Gregory's directive) of his arrest and the nature/circumstances of this arrest. He spoke to Detective Sergeant Rob Bennett and basically repeated his earlier telephone call. He identified the suspect as a Mr. Peter William Sutcliffe of Garden Lane, Bradford. Ring also explained the background of the arrest and the prostitute link. Detective Sergeant Bennett diligently took notes, explaining he would investigate further, to ascertain if there was any record of Sutcliffe in the Ripper Incident rooms index system at his end, and then telephone back.

In the quiet of the almost empty rooms and corridors of Milgarth police station and the infamous Ripper Incident room, Detective Sergeant Bennett's investigations showed that Sutcliffe was in the system, it also showed that he had been interviewed in relation to the five pounds note inquiry, it indicated that there were 'Cross Area Sightings', there were also other unresolved questions and question marks in relation to the information in the index system on Mr Peter William Sutcliffe. His shoe size was eight and a half, (the same as the Ripper), and the gap in his upper front teeth, (the same as the Ripper). Sutcliffe had previously been rejected as a potential suspect on his handwriting alone, Detective Sergeant Bennett decided that this was insufficient, an inconclusive elimination. This prompted him to delve deeper into the information relating to Sutcliffe in the system. His 'digging' uncovered further interesting information, the suspect was a lorry driver, (a likely Ripper job role) the suspect denied using prostitutes, and the suspect had previously only ever supplied generalised alibis from his wife. Furthermore a number of the interviewing officers had noted their concern and dissatisfaction with the suspect's responses at the time of the initial interviews. Detective Sergeant Bennett concluded that Mr Sutcliffe was a suitable candidate for re-interview in relation to the Ripper murders and must remain in custody until this could be arranged. 02:15 hours, Detective Sergeant Bennett rang Sheffield to impart this information and spoke to police constable Hydes, all seemed quite routine, low key but unbeknown to all parties the net was beginning to close in on the Yorkshire Ripper, would the good Lord intervene on Peter's behest, only time would tell.

02:30 hours, Olivia St. Elmo Reivers is released on police bail annoyed at the expense and the inconvenience, unaware that their unwelcome interruption had saved her life.

02:30 hours, Peter went to sleep oblivious of the ongoing investigations, confident that God was watching over him, he knew that if he wanted to he could extricate himself from the situation, unconcerned he knew he was in control. God was coaching him, reminding him of the ongoing mission. God was still feeding Peter instructions about the mission, God must have had second thoughts about the Sheffield prostitute. Friday had been a setback, in fact 1980 CE had been a series of setbacks, however life is all about dealing with adversity, although his kill ratio was down and the police were choosing to deny his handywork this reinforced the fact that his mission was a success, the message was as clear as his conscience, it was a dirty job but somebody had to do it. All was well, the South Yorkshire Police had placed a spanner in the works, it was a mere blip, and pretty soon he'd be placing a hammer in the head of an unsuspecting hooker. God kept in contact with Peter through the 'voices' which instructed him on how best to continue the mission, he'd sit tight and wait for the 'voices' to instruct him on his next move, after all the police were fools and he had an answer for everything.

His mantra to keep Sonia in the dark, for she need never know he'd been arrested, she need never know he'd been arrested in the company of a prostitute, he remained calm, he repeated the mantra, keep Sonia in the dark. He would remain amiable and obliging, knowing he just had to ride out the storm, sit tight, God would do the rest. Keep Sonia in the dark. Keep Sonia in the dark...don't go to the light.

05:12 hours and various phone calls between Sheffield, Wakefield, Bradford, Leeds and Dewsbury determined what charges Mr. Peter William Sutcliffe would be facing and where he would be dealt with. The police in Dewsbury were going to send some officers to collect Sutcliffe and his car once the 6:00 hours shift started. The seamless logistics of inter force police work.

Chapter 33
Dewsbury Police Station

Saturday the 3rd of January 1981 CE, 06:00 hours, three officers were despatched by West Yorkshire Metropolitan Police Force, from Dewsbury police station, to collect the prisoner held at Hammerton police station in the Hillsborough district of Sheffield. A boring mundane job on a boring Saturday morning that was under the cloud of a festive hangover after the New Year festivities. Why three officers? One officer to drive the police car, one officer to accompany the prisoner in the back seat of the police car and one officer to drive the prisoners impounded Rover back to West Yorkshire.

West Riding meets South Yorkshire. Hands are shaken and pleasantries and small talk are made, hatred and mistrust simmer openly. Thinly veiled contempt poorly hidden. A statement is made by Bob Hydes, outlining the context of his earlier arrest. Formalities completed, then on with the task in hand.

07:40 hours Peter William Sutcliffe and his entourage depart Hammerton police station car park. This strange cavalcade left Sheffield bound for Dewsbury, under the watchful eye of probationary constable Bob Hydes who was about to leave the station for his home in Parson Cross in the North East part of the city, it had been a long night and his bed was calling out to him.

The West Yorkshire officers performed their duty with aplomb, such a menial task that brought the Yorkshire Ripper closer to his possible freedom, but also closer to his possible capture. At the time, these four police officers were unaware of the identity of the infamous cargo they were shipping up the M1 North to the West Riding. All that is except for that cargo - a certain Mr. Peter William Sutcliffe, responsible for thirteen murders and numerous attacks under the guise of 'The Yorkshire Ripper'.

The journey back from Sheffield had been strange and sombre. Neither the two police officers nor their prisoner having much to say for themselves. An uncomfortable journey for the suspect and the officer in the rear of the patrol car, thrust together through (mis)fortune, now intrinsically one, joined at the wrists, by a pair of police issue handcuffs. Discomfort, unease and mistrust. A silent journey, the brinkmanship of silence, or tiredness or disinterest. The missing conversation, chit-chat, saw a reasonably short journey made longer. Every minute measured, every moment lingering. SHHHHHHH!! Calm, hush, stillness, keep Sonia in the dark. (In God we trust).

08:00 hours at Dewsbury police station the duty sergeant contacted the Ripper Incident Room at Millgarth to inform them that Sutcliffe their promising prisoner was pending and the suspect would be arriving at the Aldams Road station shortly, where he would then be available to be interviewed as and when required.

08:55 hours, Peter William Sutcliffe arrives at Dewsbury an insignificant individual on another insignificant day. The police car carrying this forlorn figure pulled into the Dewsbury police station car park (the new building/style was state of the art, cutting edge). The Yorkshire Ripper facet of Peter had diminished, disappeared into the shadows of his troubled mind. The Yorkshire Ripper was so much more cutting edge, there was so much more to his portfolio, slashing, stabbing, stamping, strangling and bludgeoning. Would the Yorkshire Ripper recede in the pretence of respectability purveyed by Peter or would this be his last stand, his final curtain call. Only God could decide.

The third officer arrived at the police station shortly after the Sutcliffe et al, having brought the suspect's vehicle back from South Yorkshire. 08:59 hours, Peter William Sutcliffe is processed, the desk sergeant logs him in. He is searched then taken to an interview room in a basement room of the station. The police in West Yorkshire incorrectly self-congratulate themselves and celebrate their division, their patch, their force, scoffing at their South Yorkshire rivals. The reason for this 'back slapping' was the fact that their search uncovered money that had gone unnoticed by their South Yorkshire rivals. Unfortunately Peter's DIY gimp leggings remain in 'situ', they will not be discovered until later, much later and seem of little or no interest to West Yorkshire's finest. Why ever would they, is this, was this the expected attire of every red-blooded Yorkshire man.

The prodigal son returns home from the distant 'shores' of South Yorkshire and is offered breakfast, it is the start of a roller coaster ride of cat and mouse that will eventually lead to the full and frank confession of the suspect. But there is many a slip between cup and lip, you can't make an omelette without breaking eggs; you can't be the Yorkshire Ripper and kill women without splitting heads.

And so it begins, again. Interview number ten, would it be normal service resumed? (And that was to exclude an unrelated interview on Tuesday the 15th of October 1975CE, which resulted in Peter being sacked from his job as a driver for the Common Road Tyre Company. At this stage the Yorkshire Ripper label had yet to be coined, however Sutcliffe was already four attacks in, although he was still to kill. The subsequent appearance at Dewsbury Magistrates Court in early 1976CE saw Peter found guilty.

- Interview one, Wednesday the 2nd of November 1977CE, twelve attacks in, six murders, six survivors.
- Interview two, Tuesday the 8th of November 1977CE.

- Interview three, Sunday the 13th of August 1978CE, sixteen attacks in, nine murders, seven survivors.
- Interview four, Thursday the 23rd of November 1978CE.
- Interview five, Sunday the 29th of July 1979CE eighteen attacks in, ten murders, eight survivors.
- Interview six, Tuesday the 23rd of October 1979CE, nineteen attacks in eleven murders, eight survivors.
- Interview seven, Sunday the 13th of January 1980CE.
- Interview eight, Wednesday, January 1980CE.
- Interview nine, Thursday the 7th of February 1980CE.
- Interview ten, (ongoing) Saturday the 3rd of January 1981CE, twenty-three attacks in, thirteen murders and ten survivors.

Hindsight dictates ineptness, ineptness induces hindsight. The Keystone cops throughout blunder, through their lines and fluffed their chances. An exaggeration of incompetence, or the will of God? Sutcliffe's extreme guile, cunning, calculating, wily, sly and Machiavellian persona; or inept, maladroit, clumsy, ham fisted, bungling of the investigation by the police? Or a little of all interspersed with workload, context, politics, finance and luck or wretched luck. You are the referee, you decide?

In the interview room, the interview environment Peter seems unusually at ease oblivious to the oncoming storm, why would you worry if God was your protector, your ally, your partner in crime. Such an insignificant, trivial transgression, why all the trouble? For Peter had a track record in the art of evading detection in a police interview situation. During the process of processing their prisoner the 'interview' was hours away, but also started, for no conversation with the police goes un-noted, (and possibly used in evidence against you).
"Name?"
Revisit the mantra, prepare for any eventuality, (keep Sonia in the dark).
"Peter William Sutcliffe".
"Address?"
"6 Garden Lane, Heaton, Bradford".
"Date of birth?"
"The 2nd of June 1946CE".
"Occupation?"
"Am a lorry driver". Their ears prick up, their eyes open wider, their attention grasped, he lives in Bradford, he drives a lorry, it's on the list as a possible occupation.
"Do you have any links with the North East?"
"I drive an arctic, thirty-two tonnes and make regular deliveries to Sunderland".
Coincidence or not. Sunderland, letters and tapes, he's ticking the boxes. Chit chat/thinly veiled interrogation continued apace.
"What car do you drive?"

"A V8 Rover P6B 3500 S (synchromesh) Saloon. I like me cars".
"What's all this about the Ripper?" Asked the police officer amiably.
"I've been interviewed before, loads of times, twice for the five pounds note inquiry and also due to me car driving through Manningham". (Keep Sonia in the dark). Amiable soft voiced unimposing but somehow inappropriate. Peter's attitude, his answers, his deportment, his disposition; but that would be for other individuals to uncover. If there was anything to uncover, other than number plate theft totalling fifty pence. The police were intrigued by the man in custody, there did seem to be some startling links with him and the murders, but they had been here before. A promising suspect, a promising candidate who failed to become Britain's most wanted man. Only time would tell. Only God will decide if the mission, their mission had run its course?
10:00 hours, Dewsbury police station call the Ripper Incident Room again at Millgarth to reiterate their concern and flag up the fact that they have a man in custody whom might be of interest with regards to their investigations into the Yorkshire Ripper murders. Peter's appearance, the gap in his upper front teeth, the dark beard and moustache, his jet-black hair, his shoe size and even his general demeanour, didn't sit well with the Dewsbury police. The Dewsbury police felt that Peter William Sutcliffe needed to be interviewed by the Ripper Squad, as soon as possible (A.S.A.P.), they had major concerns about the man in their custody. An officer relayed the information to their prisoner.
"You'll remain in custody until you've been interviewed by the Ripper Squad". Peter seemed wholly indifferent to the gravity of the situation. Keep Sonia in the dark. The calming mantra disassociating himself from reality.

Fate introduced Detective Sergeant Desmond Finbarr O'Boyle into the scenario, he was a thirty-five-year-old officer and was formerly a serving detective in the Manningham area of Bradford who had a good working knowledge of the Ripper Murders. Senior Ripper Squad detectives chose and despatched him on what was to be a historic appointment, he had to assess, investigate and interview the Dewsbury prisoner.

However at the time it seemed anything but historic, it was just a run of the mill inquiry, a task he had undertaken on umpteen occasions previously, a task he fully expected to be repeating with future suspects for the foreseeable future. He drove into Millgarth to prepare himself for the task ahead and read the file on Peter William Sutcliffe, once he'd acquainted himself with the file he was fully aware of the boxes Sutcliffe ticked: -

1. worked in engineering industry,
2. five pounds note inquiry employee,
3. red-light sightings Bradford,
4. Leeds
5. and Manchester.

Desmond felt it wasn't anything to write home about but then again you never know, there definitely were questions that required answering. He automatically checked the high-profile list Sutcliffe wasn't on the high profile 'wanted' list produced by the West Yorkshire Police Force. (This list consisted of the most likely suspects in relation to the Ripper murders, the D-62 file would automatically trigger interviews with the suspects listed when a new attack occurred). Peter William Sutcliffe was not considered worthy of this ignominious accolade, therefore weakening his Yorkshire Ripper credentials in the eyes of O'Boyle.

12:00 hours and Detective Sergeant O'Boyle arrived at Dewsbury police station with a colleague, Constable Rod Hill, prepared to go through the motions, tick the appropriate boxes and mark the file *'NO FURTHER ACTION REQUIRED'*. The first task they undertook was to examine the suspect's soft brown back Saloon car, registration number FHY 400 K, with a fine-tooth comb. They found something in the glove compartment to feed their interest, three screwdrivers.

Simultaneously to O'Boyle's arrival, a phone call was made to Sonia Sutcliffe explaining that he was being held in police custody in Dewsbury where he was currently being questioned in relation to the theft of a pair of number plates. Sonia Sutcliffe was informed of her husband's arrest. The mantra was broken, when he found out Peter was unnerved, however he soon refocuses. Keep Sonia in the dark, there was no need for her to know about the prostitutes, what good would it do?

Eventually the time arrived for the different parties to be introduced. A strange atmosphere saw the strangers thrown together, strange strangers each with a common knowledge of their adversary; 15:05 hours and the suspect Mr. Peter William Sutcliffe is brought to the interview room, where O'Boyle and Hill await.
"Hello, I'm Detective Sergeant O'Boyle from the Ripper Squad, I'd like to ask you some questions relating to your recent arrest". Gesturing to his colleague.
"This is Detective Hill he'll being taking notes and keeping a record of the interview". A low key start to seemingly insignificant conversation, a succession of ice breakers allowing O'Boyle to build on his initial view of Peter William Sutcliffe and the information in his Millgarth file, allowing O'Boyle to formulate a picture of the man sat in front of him. Family background, childhood, school days, employment, employment record, married/single divorced? Home life, social life, what, why, when, who, where and how? Is he a killer? The suspect remained calm, co-operative, pleasant and amiable.

"Why did you go to Sheffield?" Asked O'Boyle.
"I left our house at abart four o'clock and went looking for spare parts for me Rover and me sisters Mini. I'd had a row with our lass abart drink driving a court case. How were we gonna manage without me wage from Clark's an stuff like that. Sonia was going off on one so I got outta road," came the prologue to his tale, the scene setter, a quite candid and straight

forward introduction. Money, or lack of it is the root of all evil in the Sutcliffe household, not mass murder. Or that is what Peter would have you believe. The verbal jousting continued.

"*Cos I were due to get banned, I never bothered to renew me car insurance, it ran out on Thursday, what were point? When I were in't scrap yard I saw a number plate laid on't floor so I picked it up. I pulled other plate off of the Skoda an thought I could use them on't Rover an avoid payin me insurance. I left't scrap yard abart six o'clock withart payin for't plates. Then't exhaust blew on't Rover, so I had to sort that. Abart seven o'clock I went to Hartshead Moor service station for somert to eat. It were there that a met three people who wanted a lift, from Bradford to Rotherham an Sheffield. They said they'd give us a tenner to take em home".*

Into the realms of unreality, into the realms of fantasy fiction, still detained, still on the radar. Fantasy fiction sprung to mind as Sutcliffe unravelled his ever-varying tales, Sutcliffe the storyteller saw blatant lie upon lie revealed, his actions re-visited and reinvented in an attempt to avoid the finger of suspicion. An adult version of the BBC children's TV show Jackanory. *'I'll tell you a story of Jack a Nory, And now my story's begun, I'll tell you another of Jack and his brother, And now my story is done'.* (I'M JACK)!!! 'Tales of the Unexpected' meets 'The Twilight Zone'. Stephen King meets John Ronald Reuel Tolkien and beyond.

An 'insane', inane narrative. Soon after arriving in Sheffield a woman flagged down his Rover, ever the Good Samaritan, ever the gentleman, ever the helpful upstanding citizen, Peter stopped.

"*I thought she were in trouble so a stopped. She asked us if I wanted business. I were took a back. I was surprised. I dint know she were a prostitute. I thought about things and realised I had ten pounds burning a hole in me pocket, an thought I might as well use it. The first girl had disappeared, so I drove on an saw another girl and stopped. She asked me if I wanted business. She got into't car an told me where to drive. I paid her ten pound, I did not want sex, I just wanted to talk about me problems at home. I did not want sex at all".*

LIES, DAMNED LIES AND STATISTICS. Peter William Sutcliffe is a fine figure of a family man, he does not require the services of a prostitute! The suspect had given O'Boyle, an opportunity to explore the bedroom antics of Peter William Sutcliffe.

"*What about your sexual relationship with your wife, is it normal? Is it regular?*" The policeman probed.

"*The last time were four days ago,*" Peter replied giving short shrift.

"*What about all the rows?*" O'Boyle pressed home his doubt.

"*We forget are rows when we go to bed,*" came Peter's terse response. (Keep Sonia in the dark, there is no need for her to know about prostitutes, he thought and concentrated on the mantra).

O'Boyle changed tack, he threw in a curve ball.

"Where were you on bonfire night?" Detective Sergeant Desmond Finbarr O'Boyle was part of the Ripper Squad investigation into the recent attack on Theresa Sykes, the Huddersfield teenager. He like many a West Yorkshire police officers, found it strangely disconcerting (and also highly questionable) that the senior officers were quick to dismiss a plethora of hammer attacks on the women folk of the West Riding as non-Ripper. Were there multiple mass murderers out and about in northern England? Was murder as rife as domestic violence, in these parts? O'Boyle for one thought not. Political pawns, puppets or police, he pondered to himself, awaiting a response?

"At home with me wife," came Peter's stock reply.

Detective Sergeant Finbarr O'Boyle was also part of the Ripper Squad investigation into the Sunderland letters and tape. He was also part of the growing number of Ripper Squad detectives who had reservations and questions about the authenticity of the Sunderland letters and tape and was the source of them really the murderer. Political pawns, puppets or police? He pondered. Grassroots unrest, senior ranks denying the truth, due to pressure from politicians, the press and the public. This was the context, blame, fear, guilt, self-accusation, counter claim and fear and loathing. Fear and Loathing in West Yorkshire. West Yorkshire police forces very own version of Hans Christian Anderson's classic fairy tale, 'The Emperor's New Clothes'.

17:00 hours, O'Boyle decided he'd get his suspect to do a handwriting sample.

"Ave already done on,". protested Sutcliffe.

"Then we'll do it again," instructed O'Boyle.

"I also need a blood sample, will you give me your consent? This could help eliminate you from our inquiries," intimated the officer.

"What if it's the one yer wantin?"

"Are you the Ripper!"

"NO".

"Well what have you to fear?"

"Alreight then but let me know't result oft test as soon as you ger it".

The police duty doctor then attended. Peter sat in front of the doctor and rolled up the right sleeve on his jacket. The doctor produced a syringe from his bag of medical tricks and proceeded to take a sample of blood from Sutcliffe's right forearm, just shy of the internal side of the elbow joint. Uncomfortable and unflinching Peter watched the syringe fill with the claret coloured fluid, his blood. Peter remembered the bright red blood of Tina Atkinson's during the last few hours of her life, some three years and nine months previously. Peter was taken out of his comfort zone, after all he was the Yorkshire Ripper, the apex predator. It should not be his blood that was being spilt. It should have been that whores! The 'police' doctor also took a sample of Sutcliffe's hair, to compliment the saliva sample that had been taken when he was initially processed. The samples were packed and rushed to the pathology laboratory at Saint James Hospital, Leeds for analysis. (Keep Sonia in the dark, spluttered the mantra in his head, more out of habit than help, he thought). The tables had turned, the tide had changed, he wondered whether God had forsaken him.

17:30 hours the 'expressed' blood sample results were complete, by 18:00 hours they were with Sergeant O'Boyle. The findings were quite conclusive, it showed that Mr. Peter William Sutcliffe had blood group B coursing through his veins, however it also showed he was a non-secretor. The person responsible for the killing of Joan Harrison, in a garage on Berwick Road, Avenham, Preston, Lancashire on Tuesday the 20th November 1975CE which was unlinked, but at the time was incorrectly presumed to be a part of the Ripper series of murders, was blood type B. The (as yet unknown 'hoaxer' Wearside Jack) author of the 'I'm Jack' letters and tapes was a blood type B. However both were blood type B secretors. O'Boyle felt this was as good a place to end his interview and more than likely his investigation. *'NO FURTHER ACTION REQUIRED'*. The blood type non-match was an end to a promising line of inquiry and again outlines the harm and havoc that the hoaxer caused, and it could have continued without the intervention of a senior Dewsbury police officer.

Chief Superintendent John Clark, the senior officer at Dewsbury police station felt that Peter William Sutcliffe had become a good candidate to be revealed as the Yorkshire Ripper. Detective Sergeant Desmond O'Boyle felt differently, the dead end on the blood sample had been the final nail in the coffin of the belief that Sutcliffe may be the Ripper, another false dawn. O'Boyle should have clocked off at 16:00 hours, but felt compelled to continue with his investigation, the reason for this was because he thought he had a keeper. Each passing word of the interview seemed to confirm his suspicions. However the blood test results undermined his convictions, he didn't feel that Peter William Sutcliffe would be convicted for the crimes of the Yorkshire Ripper. O'Boyle spoke to his Dewsbury colleagues outlining his *'NO FURTHER ACTION REQUIRED'* stance. When Dewsbury Chief Superintendent John Clark heard this, he disagreed and ordered Detective Sergeant O'Boyle to express his displeasure to his Millgarth colleagues in the Ripper Incident Room and more importantly the duty officer, Clark felt that his Leeds counterparts had paid his officers request for a Ripper Squad interview lip service, sending a mere Detective Sergeant rather than a higher ranking officer that he thought it required. Big city contempt for the rural back waters of Dewsbury, police snobbery of the highest order?

18:00 hours Detective Sergeant O'Boyle contacted the Ripper Incident Room and spoke to Detective Inspector John Boyle who was the duty officer, he relayed **CHIEF SUPERINTENDENT** Clark's concerns, unsurprisingly the Detective Inspector concurred with his superior ranked colleague. As a result of Clark's direct intervention Boyle ordered O'Boyle to persevere with his interview. Police politics at play, O'Boyle a puppet, a pawn in the melodrama of the political hot potato that the Yorkshire Ripper had become.

O'Boyle reconvened. *"Where were you on the night of Monday the 17th of November 1980CE? The night of Jacqueline Hill's murder"*.

"I reckon al a been at home wit wife". Peter's repeated his stock answer.
"Just to make you aware I'll be checking your story tomorrow with your wife". O'Boyle stated nonchalantly. Sutcliffe's mood markedly changed. (Could his mantra be completely broken? Keep Sonia in the dark, no need to mention prostitutes).
"NO. Don't tell Sonia a were caught with a pro". Peter pleaded. He repeated the mantra in his head, keep Sonia in the dark.
"You got yourself into this. As far as I'm concerned you are a regular punter". O'Boyle jibed hoping for a further reaction. Peter shook his head in disagreement.
"Am not, have never been with another woman," Peter protested a little too loudly.
"If you don't use prostitutes why has your car been seen so many times in the red-light districts?"
"I pass through Lumb Lane on me way to an from work".
O'Boyle decided to throw in the 'cross area sightings', *"Your cars been spotted in Chapeltown, Manningham and Moss Side all red-light districts, how do you explain that?"*
"Me car broke down in Bradford city centre and I had to leave it in't car park behind Bradford Central Library. All I can think is someone must a used it to go to Manchester and put it back on't same spot".
"What was wrong with the car?"
"The electrics".
"So you expect me to believe that your car was stolen, driven to Manchester in the night with defective lights and returned to exactly the same place where you'd originally left it?" O'Boyle responded mockingly to this incredulous answer.
"Yeah, that's what must have happened," Peter verbally fumbled.
"Your car has been seen in the red-light districts of Bradford, Leeds and Manchester. Last night you were caught in a car with a prostitute in Sheffield and you paid her ten pounds. I don't think that's a coincidence?"
"It's true! I am NOT a punter".
"You have been previously interviewed about your car being seen in prostitute areas and you were adamant that you weren't a punter, but having said that you may well be telling lies when you were asked previously".
"Am not a liar," protested Peter vehemently.
The second bite of the cherry seemed to wield a positive result for the police. 22:00 hours, Dewsbury police station Detective Sergeant Desmond O'Boyle draws his interview to a close for the day. This is to allow him a rest from the intensity of the interview room, but also to enable the police to verify his suspect's 'suspect' stories.

O'Boyle rang Detective Superintendent Dick Holland at his Birchencliffe home to update him about their now 'strong' suspect. A pathological liar who seemingly couldn't tell the truth even if his life depended upon it. Peter retired to his police holding cell, courtesy of Her Majesty's Government. Would the police unearth his dark secret, for after all the truth needed to be found because women's lives throughout northern England may well depend upon it? Food for thought indeed. O'Boyle notified Holland of his intention to call at the suspects Garden Lane address, to interview his wife and search the property on Sunday morning. O'Boyle then returned to Millgarth, Ripper HQ to place the blood and saliva samples safely in the station fridge. Food for thought, food for thought indeed, Detective Sergeant Desmond Finbarr O'Boyle was in for a sleepless night, his suspect Mr. Peter William Sutcliffe had given him a lot to think about.

Chapter 34
Sheffield

Sergeant Robert Ring returned to work after a restless day's sleep and was informed that yesterday's arrest, was still under the scrutiny of the Ripper Squad. It was uncanny but he had felt uncomfortable with Sutcliffe and the circumstances of his arrest, his demeanour, manner and disposition. The prisoner's momentary disappearance also troubled Ring, the charade he'd purveyed and the cloud of the Yorkshire Ripper.

22:00 hours, Hammerton police station, Hillsborough, Sheffield and back on duty Sergeant Ring was uneasy with certain aspects of the initial arrest. Sergeant Ring felt compelled to re-visit the scene. A police man's hunch, as innocuous and run of the mill as it was, something didn't sit quite right with the whole situation, he remembered the scuffling noise and recalled where he was at the time of the incident, but more importantly where the suspect was. Sergeant Ring decided to retrace the previous evenings movements and drove directly to the Light Trades House on Melbourne Avenue, he parked in a similar position to where he had parked just less than twenty-four hours ago.

He picked up his police issue radio and his police issue torch and strode out into the darkness, walking to the far side of the porch and the oil tank that abutted the building. There was a dwarf stone wall that surrounded the oil tank and formed a bund (an overspill tray for excess oil). Sergeant Ring ungainly climbed onto the stone wall, like Peter William Sutcliffe had done, less than twenty-four hours earlier and began to shine the beam of the torch randomly around the area, edging along the wall moving towards the main building itself. At ground level between the oil tank and the main building was a grate and a gully. This was a natural gathering place for the windswept leaves, a heaping enclave where a pile of decaying detritus accumulated and also a natural hiding place maybe? He shone the torch into the leaf filled gully the light glanced back off the metal head of a ball peen hammer, gleaming in the torchlight. He bent and instinctively grabbed the handle, touching the wood, then he recoiled, realising his schoolboy error and the possibility of the enormity of his find.

Struggling to control his excitement Sergeant Ring edged his way back into the open, walked back to his Vauxhall Chevette patrol car and breathed deeply in a slow and purposeful manner to help gain his composure and allow the realisation of his find to sink in.
"Control, Sierra 5809 requesting Inspector Hopkirk and police constable attend Light Trades House on Melbourne Avenue immediately," came his clear and cryptic message crackling across the airwaves. Inspector Paddy Hopkirk was stirred and in response instructed another officer to contact probationary constable Hydes. He radioed police constable Bob Hydes who was on foot patrol in the Hillsborough district of Sheffield and arranged where

the Inspector would pick him up on the way to answer Sergeant Ring's request. Hydes was initially a little concerned at the call and wondered what an Inspector wanted with him, what was possibly wrong?

Saturday the 3rd of January 1981CE, became Sunday the 4th of January 1981CE, Hydes and Hopkirk were greeted by Ring in the car park of Free Trades House. Ring bubbling with excitement could hardly contain himself asking the men to follow him and then led them to the oil tank at the side of the building. Ring showed them his find using the beam from his torch to outline the ball pein hammer.
"Do you think it's the handyman's?" he half-heartedly suggested. Hydes decided to take a closer look and mounted the wall, the younger more agile man shone his torch down into the gully. The blade of a knife glinted in the beam of light emanating from his police issue torch. His stomach jumped somersaults, as his eyes struggled to realise what they were seeing and what it meant.
"The hammer might belong to the handyman, but who does the knife belong to?" Came the retort from the relatively 'green' officer.
"Oh, Jesus Christ!" Said Sergeant Bob Ring now fully aware of the magnitude of the find and a little concerned that he had allowed his prisoner to conceal these items whilst under his custody. The group regathered their self-control at the enormity of the situation and the realisation of what their find meant. Eventually Sergeant Ring walked to the patrol car radio and picked up the handset, he turned and looked at Inspector Hopkirk who nodded his head to affirm the intention and approve the deed. The significance of this historic moment was starting to sink in as the trio stood almost dumbfounded in silence.
The trio returned to Hammerton Road to contemplate their next move, their conversation and imagination running away with the endless possibilities that their actions had unearthed.

Approximately 01:00 hours, Sergeant Ring picked up the phone and dialled the telephone number for Dewsbury police station, he gave them an update relating to the new evidence they'd uncovered.
"Hello Dewsbury police station".
"Hello, this is Sergeant Ring of South Yorkshire police, we've found incriminating evidence regarding the prisoner we arrested yesterday, his name is Peter William Sutcliffe. He was transferred to Dewsbury on Saturday. I need to notify you that a ball peen hammer and a knife have been found hidden at the scene of his arrest. Could you please inform the Ripper Squad immediately?" Ring couldn't believe what he was saying. The duty Sergeant dutifully noted down the details, in almost speechless awe, he mumbled a thank you to his colleague and told him he would contact Millgarth and the Ripper Squad immediately. The tide seemed to have finally turned. This triggered the amazing chain of events that eventually resulted in the end of the mission and the admission by Peter William Sutcliffe that he and the Yorkshire Ripper were one and the same.

The phone rang at The Ripper Incident Room, the duty officer at Millgarth police station was detective inspector Mr. John Boyle who listened intently to the voice on the other end, the voice that was relaying information, the voice that was relaying information that was music to his ears. It seemed that the nightmare may have ended. Filled with hope, exaltation, exhilaration, joy and rapture, but covered by a self-control that this may be another false alarm. Detective inspector John Boyle dialled the digits that made up the home telephone number of Detective Superintendent Dick Holland to inform of this new and important news. Holland remained impartial and quickly took stock of the situation, delivering clear and concise instructions to Boyle. The wheels of the West Yorkshire police force were finally clicking into motion. Detective inspector John Boyle then called Detective Sergeant Desmond Finbarr O'Boyle to inform him of the development. *"Are you dealing with a guy at Dewsbury?"*

"Yes". Replied Desmond tired and irritated but aware of the rank of the voice on the other end of the phone, ensuring a professional persona was portrayed.

"What have you got him in for?" Curt and direct.

"Theft of number plates".

"Well what are you doing with him?"

"I've left him at the end of a pack of lies and have bedded him down for the night. I am going to search his house in the morning".

"We have just had a phone call from Sheffield, the two fellows who dealt with him last night found out you have got him in, they have panicked and gone back to the scene, and searched and found a ball-peen hammer and a knife hidden in grass near where his car was parked".

"BINGO! We have got him". As he responded all sleep deprivation washed away from him, adrenalin shot through his body, as the hairs on the back of his neck stood to attention and a strange tingling emanated down his spine?

Dick Holland directed operations from his bedside phone, he'd been here before and was not one to count his chickens before they hatched. He went into automatic pilot, delivering orders to secure the Light Trades House area and maintain the integrity of the site in order to maximise any clues there may be. Cordon the area off and place a police guard around the cordon. Place the suspect on suicide watch, he ordered around the clock supervision. No way were they going to lose their man to his own hand, as he had inferred in his audio correspondence, *'Even if you do get near, I'll probably top myself first'*. He ordered Boyle and O'Boyle down to Sheffield to interview Hydes, Ring and Reivers. He set the wheels in motion for full mobilisation of the West Yorkshire Ripper expeditionary force to be bussed into Sheffield to take control of the investigation. Optimistic he went to bed, if the initial signs were right, they may just have their man and he'd need all the sleep he could get, if not well he'd just keep trying.

Time was of the essence any hope of sleep had been abandoned; detective sergeant Desmond Finbarr O'Boyle dutifully left his Bradford home and set off for Sheffield's Hammerton police station. Detective Inspector John Boyle left Millgarth police station for the same destination as his colleague. They arrived at Hammerton and were then escorted to 'Light Trades House', where the drone of an industrial generator could be heard, powering the floodlights which illuminated the once dark car park, there were no shadows to hide in now.

An inter police sparring match was about to ensue, Ring had prompted Hydes to let him do the talking due to his probationary status. Blame could be apportioned and blame could be laid at their door, the Sheffield pair did not want to be scapegoated, the Sheffield police force did not want to be scapegoated.
Boyle and O'Boyle had no time for pleasantries, no time for excuses. They needed facts, cold hard facts not platitudes and prevarications from a probationer. Curt, terse, blunt and brusque Boyle established the facts.
1. Hydes and Ring had not planted the weapons,
2. Hydes and Ring had allowed a prisoner in their custody to discard the weapons.

Not an ideal set of circumstances for Hydes and Ring, but Rings eventual conscientiousness had paid dividends and offered some redemption. As did the fact that they had possibly arrested Britain's most wanted man, the so-called Yorkshire Ripper. However their imminent concern was for their jobs due to their earlier error. For Detective Inspector John Boyle was not from the 'how to win friends and influence people' cohort of police officers and the police culture of that was prevalent at the time was one of narrow mindedness, small minded bigotry and blame; therefore these fears were very real.

Unconcerned, uncaring Boyle and O'Boyle then returned to Hammerton police station, their eyes firmly focussed on their prize. Olivia St. Elmo Reivers had been sought and brought, Ava the victim that never was, but still remains. Haunted by what ifs, wheres and why - fors. Brief introductions and a pretence of concern, then employing the tact of a bulldozer they began. *"You would have been the fourteenth. You're a very lucky girl"*. Desmond O'Boyle explained to Ava, who puffed nervously on the cigarette in her hand. These were familiar surroundings although the circumstances were unfamiliar. On this occasion she found herself on the 'right' side of the tracks and thanked her luck and the policemen she had readily cursed less than twenty-four hours earlier.
Detective Inspector John Boyle interrupted the silence with his take on the situation. *"Right now I could easily be at the morgue, looking at your body on a slab"*. Pleasantries exchanged the West Riding duo continued their conversation with the luckiest, unluckiest prostitute in South Yorkshire.

Hydes and Ring or Boyle and O'Boyle, not quite Starsky and Hutch or Bodie and Doyle, but men who cast by fate were thrown into the spotlight of a real-life police drama. Boyle and O'Boyle returned from Sheffield, back to Dewsbury. After a quick brew, O'Boyle went down into the bowels of the police station where Sutcliffe was being held under the scrutiny of his newly assigned personal police guard.

"Did you get a good night's sleep?" Asked Desmond trying to make light of the unnatural situation the pair found themselves in, but also allowing for him to broach another subject, one to which he was keen to see the suspect's response.
"No I dint get much sleep," came Peter's response
"Neither did we, we've been up all night. Guess where?"
"Where?"
"Sheffield". With this the colour faded from Sutcliffe's face.
O'Boyle mission accomplished left Sutcliffe to consider the implications of this information, he and his newfound shadow who sat at the open door of his cell and watched his every move. Peter was left almost alone and to his own devises to ponder what the police knew and their possible next move. (Keep Sonia in the dark, no need to let her know about the prostitutes, he hoped. The mantra clearly fading, his mission faltering, maybe he would have to reconsider).

Chapter 35
6 Garden Lane

Meanwhile in Bradford, circa 9:30 hours Sonia answered the door of 6 Garden Lane, Heaton to the pre heralded police officers, Mr. Smith had rung and spoken to Mrs Sutcliffe earlier that day. This phone call initiated the intention of the police to call and collect Mrs Sutcliffe and transport her to Bradford central police station. Sonia was under the impression that Peter had been arrested over his cars. He was always tinkering about in the garage or driveway up to his elbows in oils and grease. Sonia was already wearing a coat, the police assumed she was eager to proceed, the police intuition was wrong. The unwelcoming Yorkshire winter weather leaving a light covering of sleet come snow on the ground, was replicated by the unwelcoming greeting from Mrs Sutcliffe. A plethora of police officers, four number in total.

Number one, Dick Holland, the Hillman Hunter driving Detective Superintendent (Bradford Area), who was in possession of a certain ball peen hammer and a certain kitchen knife that had been found in the grounds of the Light Trades House. Both items were 'housed' in sealed plastic forensic bags, to prevent further contamination.

Number two Detective Chief Inspector George Smith an upwardly mobile officer, destined for great things. He was a leading light in the Ripper Squad who had investigated the Barbara Leach murder.

Number three Detective Sergeant Desmond O'Boyle circumstances had made him and the fate of the Sutcliffe family intrinsically linked.

Number four, Detective Constable Jenny Crawford-Brown, the token woman, a 1981CE attempt to play lip service to political correctness and gender awareness.

The uninvited guests were ushered into the front room of the house, where Sonia returned to her Sunday morning television. Sonia sat down writing pad and pen in hand ignoring the intrusion of her unwelcome guests continued to watch Kontakte, a German language TV show. The police officers surveyed their surroundings, show house clean (plastic covers protected the chairs and sofa), operating theatre sterile (unhealthily clean) but the most notable impression was the cold chill in the air. It was colder inside the house than outside, hence Sonia's coat.

She seemed distant her attention focused on Kontakte, which translated means: - CONTACTS, DEALINGS, RELATION and RELATIONS quite appropriate for the situation. Sonia sat enthralled, using it has a barrier to deflect the police attention. Dick Holland known for his northern no nonsense approach spoke to break the human silence.

"We're holding Peter at Dewsbury police station, where he is helping the police with our inquiries". Engrossed in Kontakte grasping at the false reality to avoid the harsh truth, an attempt to avert the oncoming storm. Oblivious to the obvious.

"What do you think of this situation?" **SILENCE!**

"How long have you and Peter been married?" **SILENCE!** Detached, disengaged, disconnected from reality, impassive, impersonal and ill-mannered to this unwelcome imposition.

"Where were you on bonfire night of Wednesday the 5th of November 1980?" **SILENCE!** Holland not a man to mess with had had enough, he stormed to the telly and switched it off. *"Turn the telly off!"* His raised voice grabbing the rooms attention, his action underlining his intentions and frustration. (What discourteous and coarse behaviour so inappropriate for a high-ranking police officer, thought Sonia, but kept her thoughts to herself, because she was better than that and so was Peter, her Peter. Why were they being victimised by the police. She later decided to report Chief Superintendent Dick Holland to more senior police officers. Irony rules for in affect Holland prevented Sonia from learning German, how very European, how very BREXIT).

KONTAKTE BROKEN CONTACT MADE. *"Where were you on bonfire night of Wednesday the 5th of November 1980?"* He repeated, resilient, slowly, solidly and stoutly. Ignorance is bliss, unawareness on the brink of being shattered. Sonia stuttered a reply, the realisation of the gravity of the situation descending upon her.

"We were due to go to a party, but Peter rang to say he couldn't make it, because he had to work over. I stayed in and Peter came in later".

The weight of the West Yorkshire police 'machine' had been 'kick started' into action, Holland had already ordered an officer to Clark's Transport to crosscheck, reference this information, information that seemingly conflicted with Peter's version of events. The officer's findings destabilised Sutcliffe's defence even further. For he clocked off work at 17:00 hours. This information had already been relayed to Mr Holland to whom this information was manner from heaven, an epiphany, a revelation, a realisation a moment of truth. BINGO!! His mind worked overtime, his rough calculations suggested that Sutcliffe should have returned home circa 17:30 hours, however he did not, he went off the radar un-alibied for approximately two hundred and seventy minutes, more than enough time to travel to Huddersfield and attack Theresa Sykes and then return to the cold family fold. Sonia un-phased, detached was now forced to face the facts and faltered, Holland instructed Detective Constable Jenny Crawford-Brown and Detective Chief Inspector George Smith to sit with Sonia, whilst he and O'Boyle conducted a perfunctory unwelcome, unguided tour/exploration of Sonia and Peter's home.

In the kitchen on the work surface he found a wooden knife block set, the wooden knife block set had one knife missing, the wooden knife block set grabbed Detective Superintendent Dick Holland's attention. On closer inspection the knives in the box set were exactly the same style and colour as the one that Holland held in his hand in the plastic forensic bag. The one that Peter had attempted to hide at the Light Trades House, Sheffield. The one that Sergeant Robert Ring had retrieved from Peter William Sutcliffe's hiding place outside the Light Trades House, Sheffield.

Spotless, spic and span, shiny new paintwork, pristine and perfect. Broken by seventies high fashion kitsch wallpapers yellow and caramel in colour, floral pinks, pale blue bathroom suite and pink pebbledash on the exterior, throughout this process Sonia remained detached like her house. Checking the garage that stood at the head of the steep driveway; at the rear of the garage was an adapted workshop, with tools hung on nails for easy access, it was here that Holland found the piece de resistance, the icing on the cake, a hacksaw, he cringed and thought of Jean Jordan and the turmoil of her broken body. At this moment Smith walked into the garage to explain that they were about to take Sonia down to Bradford police headquarters to question her further and build up a profile of Sutcliffe, his life, loves, works and whereabouts. Holland ordered him to place the hacksaw into a forensic evidence bag, Smith looked confused, nonplussed, but acted upon the instruction. He carefully placed the hacksaw into a forensic bag and sealed it for evidence. Holland also ordered Smith to bag up various ball peen hammers and a large yellow handled screwdriver.

The police obtained a key from Sonia and explained to her that a full forensic search would be undertaken by the police, whilst she was to assist police with their inquiries at Bradford police headquarters. The house was quickly under intense scrutiny, whilst officers undertook a thorough search of 6 Garden Lane, the garden and an adjacent playing field. The officers who conducted the search were unnerved by their unnatural findings and echoed their colleague's earlier assessment. The property was pristine, with nothing out of place. It was over fussy, finicky and meticulous, there were crochet-covers over the covers on the living-room suite. Nothing was out of place and it was clear the occupier/s had some type of obsessive-compulsive disorder, facecloths, old clothes and shoe rags were all folded and creased neatly. The house was also exceptionally cold.

10:00 hours, Sonia was taken to Bradford police headquarters, sited in the city centre at the Tyrls. Only sixteen months ago women had marched on this very station in a cry for help about the unchecked antics of her husband; a cry for help which was largely ignored. Sonia spent the next few hours under police investigation/protection. Seemingly unwilling or unable to assist or resist the police questions. The police set out to utilise their interview with Sonia to build up a profile of Peter and Sonia, their home life, their relationship and also to determine if Sonia had colluded with Peter and assisted him in avoiding detection. Why had she repeatedly offered false alibis for Peter, was she implicated? Surely Sonia suspected her husband of something? Detective Constable Jenny Crawford-Brown and Detective Chief Inspector George Smith conducted the interviews, when Smith showed Sonia the kitchen knife that Sergeant Ring and Constable Hydes had uncovered in Sheffield she confirmed that it was a part of the set she had purchased for her marital home. The interview was eventually concluded at 20:00 hours and it was decided to transfer Sonia to Dewsbury police station ten miles away and half an hour drive. South East along Channing Way past Norfolk Gardens Hotel, that would soon be doing a thriving business with the massed hordes of the world's media encamped within its many bedrooms, left onto the Hall Ings and right into Shipley Airedale Road. Past Bowling Back Lane, past the gypsy camp, past the place where her husband had attacked Maureen Long and left her for dead way back in 1977CE, over three years ago. They continued to follow Wakefield Road/A650 along Tong Street then onto Bradford Road/A651, through Birkenshaw and onto Gomersal and a left turn onto Church Lane, right into Muffit Lane then White Lee Road then Common Road, where Peter had worked before he got his job at Clark's, in fact there was a strange symmetry to Sutcliffe's appearances at Dewsbury Magistrates Court. Then a left turn onto Halifax Road, through Staincliffe and onto the Dewsbury ring road and into Dewsbury, where Helen and Rita Rytka once lived with the well to do foster parents. Left onto Webster Hill and left onto South Street to the police station.

In the subsequent detailed search undertaken at 6 Garden Lane by the police, various articles were confiscated, Peter's wellington boots, evidence in the murders of Emily Jackson and Patricia Atkinson.

Chapter 36
Dewsbury Police Station Revisited

Pre- interview Peter ate toast and drank coffee in preparation for his next spell in the hot seat. Simultaneously Boyle and Smith reviewed the facts and evidence they had at their disposal, the knife and the ball-peen hammer that had been found at the scene of his arrest, his use of prostitutes. The fact that he actively pursued the service of another prostitute after his first rebuke reinforced his habitual use of prostitutes and emphasised his habitual lies. There was no alibi for the Theresa Sykes attack in Huddersfield on bonfire night, Sutcliffe was fast becoming a 'keeper'. There was a major discrepancy with Sutcliffe's alleged version of events and the truth of his whereabouts and actions. It was their task to ensure that Peter William Sutcliffe would be kept at Her Majesty's pleasure for a considerable duration of time.

12:00 hours, Sutcliffe was escorted to the makeshift interview room that was normally the Detective Sergeant's office. However O'Boyle was not there to greet him, this time Detective Inspector John Boyle and Detective Sergeant Peter Smith were awaiting the prisoner. Dick Holland had decided to change tack, deploying two new faces, this approach was to further unhinge, unbalance, disturb, unsettle and confuse the suspect, their suspect, the man they believed to be the Yorkshire Ripper. Holland's tactics employed Detective Inspector John Boyle for his forthright no nonsense approach and to maintain consistency due to his experience, knowledge and input into the Ripper investigation. Boyle was to be ably assisted by Detective Sergeant Peter Smith (who had interviewed Sutcliffe way back in August of 1978CE).
The two police officers introduced themselves to the prisoner and then it was straight into the questioning.
"Every time you have been seen, you always seem to have the same alibi. That you were at home with your wife. I find that rather strange. How can you be sure that's where you were?" Boyle tried to force the issue by laying down a marker.
"Am allus at home on a night when am not on a overnight stay". Peter put forward his best defensive statement in the style or manner of Geoffrey Boycott opening batsman for Yorkshire County Cricket Club and England, his famous forward defensive stroke seemed almost impenetrable. And of course the mantra keeps Sonia in the dark, no need for her to know about the prostitutes. They then re-capped on the O'Boyle/Sutcliffe interview of yesterday.
"I understand you were interviewed yesterday by Detective Sergeant O'Boyle about your movements during last Friday afternoon and evening up until the time you were arrested at Sheffield," came Boyle's synopsis of O'Boyle's previous work. (Hitchhikers, motorways, Bradford, Rotherham, Sheffield, prostitutes, punters, false names, false number plates, blah, blah, blah, blah).
"Yeah I told em whar happened". Forward defensive stroke. (The mantra keeps Sonia in the dark, no need for her to know about the prostitutes).

"I am not concerned with the allegation of theft of car number plates. I want to speak to you about a more serious matter, concerning your reason for going to Sheffield that night," came Boyle's blunt home truths.

"A told em all abart that neight". Here we go again thought Peter.

"I've spoken to Sergeant O'Boyle and I'm not satisfied with your account of that night". Boyle tried to get on the front foot and provoke a response.

"What do yer mean? I give three people a lift to Rotherham and Sheffield from Bradfud. They stopped me on t M606 and offered me tenner to take em home, so I did". It was his version of the truth and he was sticking to it.

"Why did you go to Sheffield that night? I think you went to Sheffield with the sole purpose of picking up a prostitute," came Boyle's forthright assessment.

"NO". Sutcliffe kept a straight bat. "That's not true. It were only after I got to Sheffield and turned down an offer to go with a prossy then a decided to use t money I got from the hitchhikers and go with one," explained Peter implausibly on the back foot.

"I believe you've concocted the story as a ruse". Boyle pried.

"NO". Again a la Boycott the fellow Yorkshireman, he batted away, the mantra intact for the time being.

"I reckon you put false number plates on your car to help avoid detection, to conceal your identity if you were spotted in a red-light area".

"NO". A straight bat, Boycott was set for a long innings. Peter was here for the distance. Although inside he was faltering, forty hours in the corridor of uncertainty had taken their toll. It was time to follow a different approach. It was God's will.

"No, that's not reight. To be honest wiv yer, ave been so depressed that I put em on because I was thinkin ov committing a crime wit car".

"I believe the crime you were going to commit was to harm a prostitute". Boyle kept the pressure on, kept pressing the buttons.

"No, it's not true". A good bowl, a slight edge, but dropped in the slips.

"Do you recall that before you were put in a police car at Sheffield you left your car and went to the side of a house?" Hinting further at the fact that the police knew what he had done.

"Yes, I went to urinate against t wall".

(An ending fitting for the start, a false dawn in the grand scheme of the life of The Yorkshire Ripper, a life changing revelation, where the world is introduced to the character and not only his handy work. But what will become of this strange looking man, sitting in a Dewsbury police station. This was the beginning of the end).

"I think you went for another purpose". Teasing, enquiring, suggesting and inviting a riposte.

No response from Sutcliffe. The silence spoke volumes, this was the time. This was the time to come clean. Peter realised that this was the time to tell them, to draw a close to this nonsense. The police, 'they' were suggesting, inferring, extrapolating that the ball peen hammer and the knife had been discovered in Sheffield. I acknowledged the signal from God, he was talking through the police. Now was the time to admit that Peter William Sutcliffe and the Yorkshire Ripper were one and the same.

"Do you understand what I am saying? I think you are in serious trouble," came his baited statement.

(*Thy will be done on earth, And forgive us our trespasses, As we forgive them that trespass against us. And lead us not into temptation, But deliver us from evil. For ever and ever and ever and ever*). Divine intervention the truth will out.

"I think yer leading up to it". He looked dead pan, matter of fact. His soft Bingley twang showing a hint of relief.

"Leading up to what?" Pressed Boyle who needed to link Peter to the knife and hammer and get him to admit to it being him.

"The Yorkshire Ripper," gifted Sutcliffe, he felt that the Lord wanted him to come clean, to deliver himself to the mercy of the British justice system. The time for him to fulfil the mission was over, the baton (or ball-peen hammer) would have to be taken up by another missionary. Peter was tired, Peter was glad to hand over to the young bloods, relief, tangible relief flowed through his body. A great weighed was lifted from his shoulders, praise the Lord God Jesus Christ.

"What about the Yorkshire Ripper?"

"Well it's me". An anti-climax, the anticipation had far outweighed the actual deed. The two policemen stood dumb founded had they really heard the almost whispered words that emanated from Peter's mouth.

"Peter, before you say anything further I must tell you are not obliged to say anything unless you wish to do so but what you say may be put in writing and given in evidence. Do you understand?" Mouth slightly agog Boyle stated.

"Yeah, I understand". Peter's response, slight of voice, pronounced and accepting.

"If you wish you may have a solicitor present on your behalf". Boyle offered partly to buy some time and partly to figure out what next. He also wanted to inform Detective Superintendent Dick Holland of this auspicious development.

"No, a don't need one. A just want to tell you what av done. Am glad it's all over. I would have killed that girl in Sheffield if A hadn't been caught, but I'd like to tell me wife meself. I don't want her to hear abart it from anyone else. It's her I'm thinking about, and me family. Am not bothered about mesen".

Peter confessed, feigning remorse, portraying the victim. Ever the gentleman protecting his family to the end. No thought for his victims' families, no thought for his victims, he was emotionally inept when it came to others. Peter thought why would I need a solicitor, God is my guide, steering me on my theological mission, why would I need a solicitor? God was aware, God was in control, Peter's destiny was in the hands of his maker.

Thinking on his feet Detective Inspector Boyle realised he needed to get some definite evidence to link the suspect to the weapons found in Sheffield and reinforce the as yet

unknown quantity/quality of the impending confession. He therefore focused on inextricably linking Peter to the hammer and knife. Boyle continued to force home his advantage.
"You didn't go to the side of the house to urinate, did you?"
"No, I knew what you were leading up to. You've found t hammer and knife, ant yer?" Peter replied impassively.
"Yes we have, where did you put them?" Calm collected Boyle said.
"When they took t girl to the Panda car A nipped out and put them near the house in't corner. I were panicking, A were hoping to get bail from there and ger a taxi back and pick em up. Then I would have been in the clear," proclaimed Sutcliffe matter of factly.

Bingo thought Boyle, full house, but now was no time to celebrate, it was time to deal with the matter in hand.
"Tell me, if you are the so-called Ripper, how many women have you killed?"
"Eleven, but I ant done that one at Preston. Ave been to Preston but I ant done that un". Candid coy.
"Are you the author of the letters and the tape-recording posted from Sunderland to the police and the Press from a man admitting to be the Ripper?" Asked Boyle.
"No am not. While ever that wer goin on A felt safe. Am nor a Geordie. I wer born at Shipley," explained Sutcliffe.
"Have you any idea who sent the letters and the tape?" Probed Boyle.
"No, it's no one connected wiv me. I've no idea who sent em".
"How did all this start?" Queried Boyle trying to fathom out Sutcliffe's reasoning, or lack of it.
"Wiv Wilma McCann. A didn't mean to kill her at first, but she wer mocking me. After that it just grew and grew until A became a beast".
Boyle then asked Sutcliffe. *"Do you know all the names of your victims?"*
"Yeah, A know em all".
"Do you keep any Press cuttings of them or make any records?" Boyle checking if Sutcliffe kept a record, kept trophies. Checking if Sutcliffe may have hoarded clippings that linked him to the crimes, checking for further evidence implicating Sutcliffe.
"No, they're all in me brain reminding me of the beast I am," declared Peter.
The murder count was soon to be revised after Detective Inspector Boyle inquired.
"You say you have killed eleven women. Just take your time and think about how many there are".
Sutcliffe thought and recalculated. *"It's twelve, nor eleven. Just thinking about em all reminds me what a monster I am. A know I would have gone on and on but now I'm glad ave been caught, and I just wanna unload the burden".*

A reinvigorated Detective Sergeant Desmond O'Boyle left the Dewsbury Detective Sergeant's office to collect the appropriate statement forms, leaving the newly identified Yorkshire Ripper in the capable hands of Detective Sergeant Peter Smith. O'Boyle's sleep deprivation disappeared he had shackled the Yorkshire Ripper. Immediately he sought out Detective Superintendent Dick Holland and Detective Sergeant Desmond Finbarr O'Boyle, from within the maze of rooms within the police station his excitement, his urgency belies his professionalism.

"He's coughed". Colloquial police jargon, an understatement, matter of factly, unfussy, and inconspicuous. No back slapping, just relief and a realisation that the hard work had just begun.

Detective Inspector John Boyle eagerly approached Superintendent Dick Holland, *"Hey Boss, he's just told us he went back to Manchester to Jordan and tried to cut her head off with a hacksaw".*

Holland turned to Boyle and responded in a matter of fact way *"Yes I know. I confiscated the hacksaw from his garage this morning. Jack* (Ridgeway) *swore me to secrecy way back in 77".*

Detective Chief Inspector George Smith was within earshot and retorted in aghast, *"Well you kept that dark".*

The impromptu group dispersed, surrealism juxtaposed with reality, this strange situation impacted on the participants but unruffled they continued with the task in hand. There was also soon to be a very special guest who was intrinsic to this story Assistant Chief Constable George Oldfield. Nobody wanted to be caught coasting when Mr Oldfield arrived.

13:00 hours, Detective Superintendent Dick Holland instinctively acted upon his inquisitive nature and went into the interview room unannounced, to come face to face with his antagonist, the man he had been trailing for the past sixty-five months, five years and five months. He stood feet away from Sutcliffe and Smith who small talked nonchalantly almost unaware of this intrusion. Sutcliffe slight in stature and voice, with a womanish, unmanly deportment with effete mannerisms. (Holland would later recall his first impression of Sutcliffe was completely different to what he had expected. An image in his mind of a strong and powerful man, emanating overt evil, sinister, menacing, ominous, threatening, disturbing, disquieting and evil looking. Sutcliffe fitted none of these criteria, he was the polar opposite. The man next door, Joe Bloggs or John Doe to coin an American term. His appearance was normal. His appearance was every day, he was every man). Holland felt flushed with relief as he stood motionless he couldn't help but notice how much he looked like Marilyn Moore's photo fit. He was startled by the accuracy. Holland suddenly snapped back into police mode, this man's misdemeanours were going to keep him busy for quite some time to come. He also had to let his 'gaffer' know, a certain Assistant Chief Constable George Oldfield (West Yorkshire), the pair had made an agreement, a promise, a bond to inform one another of the capture of the man they had come to know as the Yorkshire Ripper.

13:15 hours, he dialled Huddersfield 0484 the telephone rang in a house in Grange Moor village, high on the hills on the outskirts of Huddersfield disturbing a family's Sunday roast dinner. The house was the residence of the Oldfield family. Assistant Chief Constable George Oldfield answered the phone. No niceties straight down to business.

"We've got the bugger!" A pregnant pause, silence for the words to sink into his psyche. A professional watershed a conclusion to over five years work.

"He's from Bradford. We've got him at Dewsbury nick". No pregnant pause this time from the Huddersfield end, just a blunt response.

"I'm coming straight down". Then as he put the handset down onto the receiver, he told Margaret the news, both seemed dumbfounded. 13:25 hours Oldfield then picked up the telephone handset and began to dial 0924 the Wakefield code, Mr. Ronald Gregory, Chief Constable of West Yorkshire Police Force.

"Fasten your seat belts, we've got him," proclaimed Oldfield with almost evangelical zeal. He then headed to his car and drove the six miles from Grange Moor to Dewsbury. 13:40 hours he walked into Dewsbury police station, his purposeful stride heading towards the first floor of the building and a makeshift interview room, where a very special interview was being undertaken. Assistant Chief Constable George Oldfield entered the room and sat at the table facing a nonchalant Sutcliffe, he looked him up and down. He introduced himself to the Yorkshire Ripper.

"I'm Assistant Chief Constable George Oldfield I'm the one you almost bloody killed as well". Peter staring forward remained silent, offering no response, no reaction.

Mr. Ronald Gregory arrives at Dewsbury police station and orders a cadet be despatched to buy a bottle of scotch whisky to help with their imminent celebrations.

But Peter was going to put his own slant on the confession, his own spin. Due to time constraints and counter dependencies, differing circumstances. Twelve murders and two attacks, the garrotting of Marguerite Walls omitted, denied. His thinking was to streamline the confession, sanitise it. He was hopeful to avoid adding Marguerite to his recognised CV (Curriculum Vitae), using the pretence that he was concerned it would muddy the waters, 'open lots of new lines of enquiry that were nothing to do with him'. He decided to just deal with the ones that had been accredited to his fair hand. This saw Peter passionately negate the accusation that he had murdered Joan Harrison way back in 1975CE.

The damp squib of an arrest was a disappointment, the link between Spring Heeled Jack the Victorian folklore villain who preyed on lone victims in the still of night, the midnight mystery. Throughout the generations, an urban myth or an urban reality, his legacy unresolved ongoing through the years. Then onto Jack the Ripper and his unsolved Whitechapel murders, the Canonical five and the From Hell letter, these tales gained credence with the passing years.

Jack the Ripper was followed by the Yorkshire Ripper, a regional incarnation that preyed on prostitutes like his Southern counterpart. The From Hell letters became letters from Sunderland as the murder mystery turned full circle. An arrest for the theft of number plates from a West Yorkshire scrapyard possibly truly gauged the moral barometer of the perpetrator, however Peter William Sutcliffe's (possibly) full and frank admission to the murder of thirteen murders and seven attempted murders may have ended his/the mission. The mystery and the malady lingered. Wearside Jack was finally uncovered in 2006CE, a Sunderland alcoholic would prolong the grief of the victims, their family and friends for a further twenty-four years. Dark forces had been at work, hopefully there was light at the end of the tunnel, at last. The Yorkshire Ripper was to prove a fallible, insignificant individual, unremarkable. Normal?

One in one hundred, or so the statistics suggest. But Peter knew differently, Peter knew he was the chosen one. Early adulthood onset schizophrenia or Gods personal telephone number. Peter was sane, Peter was insane, Peter was. No openly tangible positive symptoms, but Peter had been instructed to keep them secret. His so-called delusions, his hallucinations and unusual beliefs. Or were his belief's just an extension of the misogynistic society that had created him, was he an instrument of control? The negative symptoms were deemed as positive by the police and were probably manifested in the lapses of time between his attacks. The medical men suggest that lack of motivation and isolation were long term side effects of his condition. Peter knew it was God's will. He attacked to order, God led his hand, God controlled the hammer, they were a team. Abnormal or normal?

"God invested in me the means to kill prostitutes. Perhaps he has just put me in jail to give me a rest. The prostitutes are still there and my mission is only partially fulfilled. Perhaps another is ready to take my place".

"Tell them, tell everyone I'm sorry. I just did not know what I was doing. Something came over me that I couldn't control and I was made to do it, I'm sorry. I must have been possessed on the nights I did it".

He realised that now was the time, it was God's will, his involvement in the mission was concluded he would have to hand on the baton or more appropriately the ball peen hammer to the next missionary. He was the special one. He was in the system, the tragic irony of ten times interviewed Peter William Sutcliffe the lunatic lurking ritual sadistic murderer.

Chapter 37
Peter the Confessor

Peter's demeanour changed, it was as if a weight had been lifted off of his shoulders. Relief flooded through his veins, he felt the warm swell of gladness throughout his body. No more suffering in silence, no more pain and isolation, he felt unburdened.

Confessions of a Window Cleaner, Confessions of a Pop Performer, Confessions of a Driving Instructor, Confessions from a Holiday Camp, Confessions of a Plumbers Mate. The 1970's CE sex comedy films spanning from 1974 CE to 1977 CE that starred Robin Asquith with a twist. Confessions of a Serial Killer, the sequel/crossover drama that spanned from 1975 CE to 1981 CE, the sex tragedy starring Peter William Sutcliffe the twisted lorry driver from Bradford. A lapsed 'devout' Roman Catholic boy, ever the good Christian was to confess, but not to a priest, for he had no need, after all he was in league with God.

Not a small enclosed booth, but a small compact interviewing room, this would have to do as the sacrament of penance and the venue for the purposes of his confession. Confessions and reconciliation. Peter was to face up to his foibles, his indiscretions, acknowledging his actions, his sins and wrong doings, (well most of them).

Unable to absolve his sins, unable to provide healing of the tortured soul, for Peter to gain the grace of God, but then again he didn't need it. God was his work colleague, his line manager his friend and confidante.

14:50 hours, **(Sheet One)**. Peter the confessor :- I Peter William Sutcliffe, wish to make a statement and I want someone to write down what I say I have been told that I need not say anything unless I wish to do so and whatever I say may be given in evidence. *"Leeds, a pint or two, you tell me the date"*. Wilma McCann, lime green K registered Ford Capri with a black roof and rear louvre sun grill, hitchhiker, white trousers and a jacket. *'How far yer going?'* Business? Business! Scornful, derisory, hateful. Field, lonely, isolated.

Yorkshire Ripper confession plus twenty-eight minutes, Greenwich Mean Time (GMT) approximately 15:18 two hours. (Sheet Two), drunken, uncouth, fiver, cold, uninviting, unromantic. Swearing, taunting, toolbox, hammer concealed by my car coat. A hammer blow to the head.
Yorkshire Ripper confession plus fifty-six minutes, GMT approximately 15:46 hours. (Sheet Three), one, two, metal on bone, gurgling. 'Do you see, Ahab's dead but he beckons,' panic, toolbox, handyman, self-taught mechanic, toolbox, knife, blade, stab, silence. Lungs, throat, death, dead. Hush, still. Discarded clothing, (trademark pending), blind panic, silence, desperado, fugitive, escape.

Yorkshire Ripper confession plus eighty-four minutes, one hour and twenty-four minutes, GMT approximately 16:14 hours. (Sheet Four), bolt hole, forty-four Tanton Crescent, in-laws, in a trance. Fear and loathing, cover his tracks, clothes worn out, hammer and knife no recollection. TV news murder, paranoia the police will be calling to arrest me, anytime soon. Act naturally go to Common Road Tyre Services in Oakenshaw. Act naturally, no knock on the door, no arrest, no accusations. Scott Hall, scot free. It's never the same after the first time, I just hate prostitutes, self-justification. A drive to Leeds again in search of a prostitute. Inner compulsion to kill whores. Christmas plus one month.

Yorkshire Ripper confession plus one-hundred and twelve minutes, one hour fifty-two minutes, GMT approximately 16:42 hours. (Sheet Five) Capri, telephone boxes, big lass, how much, fiver, cheap perfume, sweat, hatred, unhinged, no sex just death. Working clothes, wellies, directions to her death. Cul-de-sac, cul-de-sac of life, premeditated, planned, fake break down, red warning light, mechanics assistant.

Yorkshire Ripper confession plus one-hundred and forty minutes, two hours and twenty minutes, GMT approximately 17:10 hours, (Sheet Six), cigarette lighter. Candle in the wind? No concert hall encore, just death. Hammer attack, accompanied by screwdriver stab wounds. Sexual revenge, echoes of Wilma McCann discarded clothes, (trademark still pending). Phillips frenzy. Dank yard, debris, detritus, flotsam and jetsam of life, the wreckage of her life, the wreckage of his life? Peter's ruin, hate always hate, seething uncontrollable hatred. Tangible hate, physical hate, palpable hate, perceptible hate. HATE. *"I stabbed her all over her body"*. HATE. Three-foot piece of wood, a piece of timber three inch by one inch in dimension. Strategically placed against her vagina, pushed up against her vagina. Her supine prostrate shell unresponsive, life extinguished. Disturbed by headlights, mentally disturbed, scared, caught like a rabbit in the headlights. Flight, bolt hole, Clayton, in-laws. Justification, satisfaction, vindication for his actions. Bloodless clothing.

Yorkshire Ripper confession plus one-hundred and sixty-eight minutes, two hours and forty-eight minutes, GMT approximately 17:38 hours, (Sheet Seven)
"I had no need to dispose of them". (Emily) Jackson/Wilma McCann was the murder weapon the same, was it the same hammer. Memory blank, however, I remember buying a new hammer from the hardware shop near Clayton roundabout. Claw hammer, forged steel flat head and nail extraction curved and split 'V', therefore forming the somewhat deformed classic 'T' shaped design associated with wood working. As opposed to the ball peen hammer associated with metal work and the Yorkshire Rippers predominant stun weapon of choice. *"The first two had a flat head on one end and a ball on the other"*. Next, red or white Ford Corsair, (red = PHE 355G), (blue = KWT 721D); can't recollect which I drove to Leeds after closing time to kill Irene Richardson. Chapeltown, walking alone, red-light district, vice estate, kerb crawling, find a prostitute and kill a prostitute. *"To make it one more, one less"*. I stopped the car and she climbed into the passenger seat. "You are not going to send me away are you?" Roundhay Park, big field on the left,

block of toilets, Irene went to use the toilets, they were locked. Placed her coat on the ground alfresco piss.

COMFORT BREAK GMT approximately 18:06 hours, INTERVIEW RESUMED GMT approximately 18:36 hours.

(Yorkshire Ripper confession plus two-hundred and twenty-six minutes, three hours and forty-six minutes, GMT approximately 18:36 hours, (Sheet Eight) crouched, woman, stealth attack. Ideal target, a hat trick of hammer blows to the back of the head. We all fall down. Discarded clothes, (trademark still pending), slash, stab and cut. Stomach and throat. Silence, silence, still and calm. Coat covered body posed, knee boots, drove off the field. Two pedestrians sat on a park bench unaware they'd nearly witnessed his third killing, unaware, uncaring, unknowing. Jeans, boots and no bloodstains. Stanley knife retained and lent to someone. Red or white car who knows? Sold the white Corsair to Ronald Barker, who lived at forty-six Tanton Crescent but the engine seized up, refunded Ronald kept it for a fortnight and sold it for scrap on Canal Road. Obsessed with killing prostitutes, *"I couldn't stop myself, it was like some sort of a drug"*. Two months later, Saturday night and a Bradford debut with Patricia Atkinson. Lumb Lane, Church Street prostitutes.

Yorkshire Ripper confession plus two-hundred and fifty-six minutes, four hours and sixteen minutes, GMT approximately 19:04 hours, (Sheet Nine). White or red Corsair, St. Pauls Road junction, a drunken scene, a drunken altercation with a motorist, hammering on the roof of his white mini with her hand, swearing like a trooper and erratic as a whirling dervish, out of control, out of time in my imaginary gun-sight. Spinning wheels, burning rubber, underlined the termination of this embarrassing altercation of these two unidentified protagonists, just every day on the everyday streets of red-light Bradford, with similar scenes replicated throughout the country. Nobody battered an eyelid, Peter kept his eyes firmly on his prey, unblinking, red-light, gunsight; he would batter her to death if the opportunity arose. He would attempt to ensure it did, pulling up alongside her, *"I've got a flat we can go there"*. Manningham Lane, Queens Road, Oak Avenue a flat. Solo living, solo dying. Clayton (hardware store) claw hammer, she closed the curtains for privacy (and to prevent witnesses). Made myself at home, it was warm in the flat (unlike my house) so I took my coat off and hung it on the hook behind the door. She removed her coat and sat on the bed with her back to me, beginning to remove her jeans, an opportunity to attack the back of the head with his hammer. She fell onto the floor, red blood on the bed and red blood on the floor, lots of red blood. Repeat the process attack the head with the hammer, (gurgle) lifting her limp body onto the bed.

Yorkshire Ripper confession plus two-hundred and eighty-four minutes, four hours and forty-eight minutes, GMT approximately 19:32 hours, (Sheet Ten) I undressed her further, (trademark still pending) I proceeded to gouge, (gurgle) hit, (gurgle) scuff and (gurgle) cut her bare flesh using the claw part of the hammer, the flying vee of the woodworking trade made strange indentations upon the canvas of her body. A shy artist I covered my handy work using the bed clothes. Face down on her side, I left her face down gurgling. *"I knew she would not be in a state to tell anybody"*. Back home to Heaton and the privacy of my garage, the cursory check of my clothes, blood on my jeans, remove and rinse in the kitchen cold tap and hang up to dry. Blood on my brown Doctor Marten's boots which I wiped off with a sponge. I think I kept the claw hammer to use on another woman. I know I threw it away, over a wall in Cottingley near Sharps Printers. Young girl, Jayne McDonald I felt terrible, awful, appalling and abysmal. I recently read about her dad dying of a broken heart, thanks to me. I felt dreadful it brought it all back to me, the monster, fiend brute of a beast that I had become. *"I believed at the time I did it that she was a prostitute"*. Saturday night, Leeds, I'm 99% sure it was the red Corsair.

Yorkshire Ripper confession plus three-hundred and twelve minutes, five hours and twelve minutes, GMT approximately 20:00 hours, (Sheet Eleven). The urge to kill prostitutes filled my head constantly, I was out of my mind. Solo slow walking lass, Hayfield pub, Chapeltown. Anticipation, car park, claw hammer, kitchen knife black ebonite handle. Cut her off at the pass, cut her off in her prime, follow, follow, and follow. Attack, claw hammer to the back of the head she fell, drag her behind a fence, and hit her again. Undressed her further, (trademark still pending) exposed her chest stabbed her body. Left her for dead and returned to my car.

(MEANWHILE) 20:00 hours, a telex message (a similar system to a telephone network, but not with vocals via text messages and paper, via tele printers) from the West Yorkshire Metropolitan Police Chief Constable Mr. Donald Gregory was received by South Yorkshire Metropolitan Police Chief Constable Mr James Hilton Brownlow, it read:-

'Will you please convey to your Sergeant Ring and Constable Hydes my sincere personal thanks for their outstanding policeman ship on Friday evening the 2nd January 1981. They are a credit to the Police Service, and in West Yorkshire we appreciate their efforts very much indeed, well done'.

A trio of press conferences were to be held over the next eighteen hours. Off the cuff unorthodox, unprofessional (questionable), but under the circumstances who would begrudge such events. An unholy triumvirate, the holy trinity, not to be undone, our press conference is better than your press conference. A necessity out of requirement, media clamour, Hammerton Police Station under media siege, Dewsbury Police Station under media siege, the eyes of the world on Dewsbury and Sheffield, not New York, London, Paris or Munich, but DEWSBURY and SHEFFIELD. Both parties wanted their fifteen minutes of fame, the praise for their actions or redemption for their inactions. Fickle fate and infamy, fortune and misfortune walking hand in hand.

(One, two, three; you're back in the room).

Yorkshire Ripper confession plus three-hundred and forty minutes, five hours and forty minutes, GMT approximately 20:28 hours, (Sheet Twelve) returned home to an empty house, Sonia was working at Sherrington Private Nursing home, Bradford, she worked predominantly Friday and Saturday nights. Hence a lot of my attacks are on a Saturday night. No blood, I think I washed the knife and think I left it in the Corsair when I took it to scrap, the claw hammer was the one I discarded at Cottingley. I felt inhuman when I read that McDonald was only sixteen and not a prostitute, I realised it was the Devil driving, dictating, guiding, forcing my actions against my will, "I was a beast". Work, pubs, clubs and if the Ripper murders became the topic of discussion, I could blank out the fact that it was me, amazing, astonishing and astounding. What a man I am being able to detach myself from reality. Next Maureen Long. *"I saw Maureen just a couple of weeks ago I was in the Arndale Shopping Centre with my wife when I came face to face with her. I recognised her immediately she seemed to look at me but she obviously didn't recognise me".* Manningham Lane, Saturday night July 1977, I spy with my little eye, maxi dress wearing, Mecca night club departing, Maureen walking towards the city centre.

Yorkshire Ripper confession plus three-hundred and sixty-eight minutes, six hours and eight minutes, GMT approximately 20:56 hours, (Sheet Thirteen) I offered Maureen a lift, she offered directions Leeds Road, ex-boxer, terraced house, 'do you fancy me', lies and deceit, instructions, drive past whilst Maureen does a reconnaissance mission. Plan 'B' adopted Bowling Back Lane, cobbled street. NARRATIVE. Maureen needs to relieve herself on the wasteland I need to hit her on the head with a hammer, this seems like an ideal occasion. I hit her, silence. I pulled her into the night.

(MEANWHILE) 21:00 hours, Chief Constable Mr. Donald Gregory addressed the press, they had been ushered into a large room in the Dewsbury police station, and the press conference began with Mr. Gregory explaining. *"On Friday evening last, a man was detained in Sheffield by the Sheffield Police in connection with a matter which was identified as theft of number plates of a motor car and the number plates had been stolen from the West Yorkshire area.*

He was brought to West Yorkshire and as a result of discussions between the South Yorkshire Police and the West Yorkshire Police further inquiries were made and this man is now detained here in West Yorkshire and he is being questioned in relation to the Yorkshire Ripper murders.

It is anticipated that he will appear before the Court in Dewsbury tomorrow. I cannot say where he is at the moment because a lot of inquiries have to be made. Mr. Oldfield and Mr. Hobson and other senior investigating officers have to make a number of inquiries tonight, but I can tell you that we are absolutely delighted with developments at this stage".

One of the many photographers made a request, questions galore sprung from the floor, Mr. Gregory became a media whore.

The press questioned, interspersed by Mr. Gregory's responses.

"Can you all smile, please? Can you move in together, please and keep smiling? Smile everybody please. Can you give us any details at all about the man? Can you tell us whether he has a Geordie accent? Can you give us any details of the arrest, Mr. Gregory? The circumstances of it, not actual details. Are you scaling down the operation, the general hunt for the Yorkshire Ripper from this moment on? Do you know what he'll be charged with in the morning? Will it probably be the motoring offence? Can you say if these two officers were on foot or in a vehicle? Would that be on foot or in a vehicle? Could you say what time? PM? Can you tell us where? Was it near the motorway? Could you say if there was any violence of any sort? Can you tell us whether it was a red-light district? What's happening to the lady he was with? You mentioned a lady. Is she helping with your inquiries? Does that mean she is under arrest? Was it a woman he was with? Was she an acquaintance of long standing? Was his car being sought because there had been any sort of incident earlier? Did the officers first stop him because of the false.... because of the questionable number plates or because of the lady? Would it be fair to say it was an indelicate position? At this stage was the lady with him injured in anyway? Was he injured? Were they in a state of undress? The car was at a standstill, it wasn't flagged down? Can you tell us what sort of car, Mr. Gregory? Was that the old style or the new style? What colour was it? Getting down to the really important things, are you able to tell us the man's, well presumably, will you be giving his name tonight? What about his age? And is he a bachelor? Has he got a North East accent at all? Is he a married man? Is he a family man? As far as you know, Sir, is he or has he been, until the arrest, been living with his wife? Do you know his occupation? Do we have an occupation for him sir? Can we just have you all smiling again, please, gentlemen? Can you all smile, please, Sir?"

Mr. Gregory centre stage his now debunk out of favour former deputy to his left, still officially on sick leave, (what about the health and safety implications) brought back into the media circus to oversee the final throes of a one thousand nine-hundred day investigation, a two thousand one hundred day man hunt. The loyalty of Dick Holland in tipping his boss the wink and ensuring he was in on the finale would lead to a severe reprimand and the rest of his career in uniform. Mr Hobson of the tyre investigation, their grey suits belied the air of relief that was tangible, for this was a celebration in all but name. Mr Gregory spoke interspersed by press questions.

"I said at Dewsbury, but it may not be Dewsbury, it may be at another Court, but he will appear in West Yorkshire sometime later tomorrow. No, not at this stage because the man is being interviewed at this very moment in time, but indications are that there will be a charge later tomorrow. I cannot tell you that because I have not heard him speak. All I can say is

that he was detained in Sheffield. He was with a lady. He was detained in relation to an incident in Sheffield and he was detained, let me tell you, two outstanding officers, Sergeant Ring, of the South Yorkshire Police, Robert Ring and Constable John Hydes, H.Y.D.E.S, of the South Yorkshire Police. They are uniformed officers who have my heartfelt thanks, who made the original detection, and as a result of questioning later on by West Yorkshire Police we have reached the present stage. It is just the initial stages and I thought you should know now before we go any further. Yes right. I can't tell you what the charge will be at the moment, but it may be a serious charge. The South Yorkshire officers? I think they were on anti-vice patrol. Vehicle. About eleven o'clock on Friday evening. P.M. In Sheffield I'm sorry I'm not certain of the area. Near the centre of Sheffield. None at all. I cannot tell you that, I don't know. She has not come to any harm. She is, yes. No, she is not under arrest. No. He was with a lady, yes. No. No. They came upon him in a certain position and they looked at the car, checked on the number plates, found they were false. I cannot say what it was, I don't know what the position was at all. None at all. Not at all, No. No. I don't think so. I can't say. I don't know. I have not seen...you see all the statements have not come through yet. No. Standstill. It was a Rover motor car. Bearing false plates. I don't know what style. Dark coloured V.8 George says. His name will be disclosed tomorrow. His age will be disclosed tomorrow. He's about thirty odd and he comes from Bradford. I think he's a married man. I don't know about that, I don't know yet, I've not spoken to him. He is a married man. I don't know. I don't know. It's too early to go into detail and if I could I would tell you, but he is helping police with their inquiries at this very moment in time. I don't know his occupation. No".

"I can tell you that we're absolutely delighted with developments at this stage, absolutely delighted, really delighted, George is delighted as well, yes, absolutely delighted".

21:30 hours and the curtain comes down on 'The Mr. Gregory Show'. Gregory, Oldfield, Hobson and Holland retired to the sanctuary of the inner sanctum of the police station and small talked around their success. Eventually the group began to disperse there was much work to do and time was of the essence. Gregory and Oldfield also make plans to pop in and see their prisoner, the so-called Yorkshire Ripper.

(One, two, three; your back in the room).
Yorkshire Ripper confession plus three-hundred and ninety-six minutes, six hours and thirty-eight minutes, GMT approximately 21:24 hours, (Sheet Fourteen) silence. I pulled up her clothes (Yorkshire Ripper registered trademark) and I stabbed her in the chest and back. Enlightened caravan, gypsy saviours, I thought I'd done enough to kill her, but I thought wrong.

Mr Gregory and Mr Oldfield make an impromptu visit to see their much publicised and prized prisoner GMT approximately 21:32 hours.

21:20 hours, the press conference completed, Mr Oldfield and Mr Gregory talk and decide to visit their prized prisoner, they decide to drop in and see O'Boyle, Hill and Sutcliffe. O'Boyle and Hill perception is somewhat different than that of their superiors. The duo have had a long-pressurised day that is far from over. They see this unwelcome top brass visit as an interruption and disruption to their work but they were powerless to protest. Ours not to reason why, ours but to do and die.
"Are you OK?" Asked Chief Constable Ronald Gregory. **A forced situation, abstract, surreal but real.** Flanked by Assistant Chief Constable George Oldfield who had popped in to see Peter earlier that afternoon.
"Yeah," replied Peter, looking around at Detective Sergeant Desmond O'Boyle and Detective Inspector John Boyle for their approval.
"Are my men looking after you?" Trying not to gloat in the circumstances, the arrest of Britain's most wanted man.
"Yeah". Replied Peter, looking around at Detective Sergeant Desmond O'Boyle and Detective Inspector John Boyle for their absolution.
"Do you need anything?" Offered the Chief Constable, oblivious to the unsettling affect his actions were having on his officers and their prisoner in attempting to complete his statement.
"Am alreight thanks," Peter responded quietly.
"Would you care to see your wife?" asked Gregory.
"Yeah, please," Peter thanked.
The duo then left, leaving their subordinates to pick up the pieces.

INTERVIEW RESUMED GMT approximately 21:42 hours.
Into the city then home. Sonia was working I did a self- inspection and could find no signs of the attack on my clothing. Soon I got a nasty shock, I heard, read and saw that the woman, Maureen was still alive. Was this the end of the line for the Yorkshire Ripper? I just knew she would recognise me if she saw me again she would be able to identify me and distinguish me from a crowd of would be murderers. In a panic I threw the claw hammer over Sharp's wall. Then I read that she was suffering from memory loss and this eased my worries of detection. You could say I was long gone, but Maureen proved she wasn't going anywhere. I wanted to kill more prostitutes and the craving to do so engrossed me. I wanted to come clean admit my deeds and pay for my actions, but then I thought how it would affect Sonia and my family. I didn't care about myself, it was the others. It became apparent that the police hunt was intensifying in Leeds and Bradford. The press had labelled me the Yorkshire Ripper, therefore I decided to take a trip over the Pennines to Manchester

Yorkshire Ripper confession plus four-hundred and thirty-four minutes, seven hours and fourteen minutes, GMT approximately 22:02 hours, (Sheet Fifteen) to murder a prostitute in cold blood. The idea was triggered by an article I read about a Manchester priest preaching blood, fire and rebuking the prostitution in and amongst his parish. October 1977, Saturday night, red Corsair, Road Atlas, road-trip, Manchester, Moss Side. NARRATIVE. City centre, Princess Street, university, Moss Side degradation, dilapidation and deprivation. Street walking girls punting for business. Kerb crawling, trawling for fresh flesh, *"Do you want business?"* Bonny looking, slim, light haired destined for death. Two hundred yards, three-point turn, another offer from a punter in a fawn car, but not a better offer, *"the biggest mistake she ever made"*. One English five-pound note, one crispy brand-new English five-pound note. Directions to an allotment, my uncle's greenhouse what a coincidence.

Sonia is allowed to see her husband GMT approximately 22:30 hours, Sonia is ushered into the interview room. The duo attempt to find some privacy some solitude in the confines of the small room. Abstract, unnatural, surreal; business as usual for the Yorkshire Ripper.

"What on earth is going on, Peter?" came Sonia's startled opening. The pair had last seen each other over two days ago.
"It's all those women. I've killed all those women," came the hushed confession from her husband's lips.
"What do you mean?" Unable to grasp, as if talking at crossed purposes. Incredulous.
"It's me. I'm the Yorkshire Ripper. I killed all those women". His soft response, calm, composed, collected and unruffled.
"Is it, is it really". The emotion of the situation stifled by the gaze of onlookers, Sonia held back her tears.
"What on earth did you do that for, Peter? Even a sparrow has a right to live". She trembled with feeling, trying to grasp the enormity of his words.
"Did you do it with them?" The jealous irrational human aspect of the whole situation entered into the formal environment. An attempt to personalize this hell.
"Only once and it was mechanical". Peter ever the gentleman exonerated himself to lessen the blow to his wife. Rationalising the irrational.

Sonia is escorted away and billeted in an annexe to the rear of Dewsbury police station and chaperoned by Detective Chief Inspector George Smith and woman police constable (WPC) Jenny Crawford-Brown. Protective custody, to hide their possible star witness away from the media glare that was shining brighter than a super nova.

INTERVIEW RESUMED GMT approximately 22:40 hours.

Yorkshire Ripper confession plus four-hundred and seventy-two minutes, seven hours and fifty-two minutes, GMT approximately 22:40 hours (Sheet Sixteen), I engineered her moves through deception into the allotment. One English five-pound note, one crispy brand-new English five-pound note. Blue is the colour. Uncle, greenhouse, people in glass houses should not throw bricks, straddle the fence, no defence, time for my offence, hammer blow to the back of the head (Yorkshire Ripper registered trademark). Moaning, groaning, grunting ear splitting moaning. Bang, bang, bang...silence, hush, calm. Headlights, panic, hide under the bushes, hide from the glare, hide from the stare of others. Threw her handbag away to the right on a diagonal trajectory, lay low survey the scene wait for the car to go, wait for the coast to clear, the car eventually left, but as it did, it was replaced by another vehicle, another prostitute and punter combination. I was concerned I'd get caught.

Yorkshire Ripper confession plus five-hundred minutes, eight hours and twenty minutes, GMT approximately 23:08 hours (Sheet Seventeen) so I hid behind the red Corsair waited for the other car to park, then I decided to extricate myself from the unwelcoming situation and set off back to Bradford. I used a hammer I found in the garage at 6 Garden Lane, it must have been left there by the previous owner Mr. Rahman. Halfway home I realised I had paid using a crisp new five pound from my wage packet, a clue the police would cherish. Should I return and attempt to retrieve it and risk capture or should I leave it and my freedom to chance. Sonia was working or in bed, when I finally arrived home. I sat and waited and watched and wondered, no newspaper report, no television report, nothing. What had become of her, I finally decided the body laid where I had hidden it and I would return to recover, regain, rescue, re-claim and repossess my property. A week or more had elapsed when I had a chance to return to Manchester. Housewarming party, lifts home mother, father, sister and brother. Manchester via Bingley in the red Corsair to the allotment.

Yorkshire Ripper confession plus five-hundred and twenty-eight minutes, eight hours and forty-eight minutes, GMT approximately 23:36 hours (Sheet Eighteen) I discovered the body still in its original resting place, I wrenched it from the bushes and undressed the corpse (Yorkshire Ripper registered trademark), in search of my money. It was then that I realised it's not in her clothes it's in her bag but where is her bag? Frenetic and in a frenzy, swearing, cursing and cussing at the girl's body, my luck and my inability to find the money, the clue, my possible ticket to prison. Time to vent my frustrations on the body. Broken pane of greenhouse glass, slash her stomach cut open, the stench of putrefaction spilt out and unravelled my senses, the repugnant reek hit the bile in my stomach and I heaved the contents of my gut puking out the bitterness. I forgot to mention the hacksaw I'd brought a hacksaw from my garage to remove her head, so I started to saw through her neck, but the blade was blunt and was making little or no headway through the pale skin, flesh and sinew of her neck. I gave it up as a bad job. The plan was to remove the head, cut it off and then abandon it somewhere else, to create a big mystery. Roll up for the tragical history tour, not quite the Beatles, four lads that shook the world, Peter William Sutcliffe one man who shook the north. Time to leave, I'd spent long enough on this time-wasting exercise, no fiver, and no time. I returned home unfulfilled, unhappy, unsatisfied, unease.

Yorkshire Ripper confession plus five-hundred and fifty-six minutes, nine hours and sixteen minutes, GMT approximately 00:04 hours Monday the 5th of January 1981 CE, (Sheet Nineteen) at the small amount of blood I had on me, a little bit on the back of my hand and a little bit on the bottom of one trouser leg, I went to bed. FASHION STATEMENT. Old grey casual trousers, (not the Whistle Test), dark brown slip on shoes. I wiped the shoes clean but could not eliminate or expunge the blood, the evidence, I decided to expunge the trousers and hid them in the garage, and I burnt them later. I read the newspaper story that the body of Jean Royle had been found and I waited for the unavoidable knock on the door, the inescapable five pound note investigation that would follow, with all roads leading to Bradford. Or maybe Shipley, where the trail led to the Midland Bank, the listening bank, the bank that Clark's used for their banking, the bank that was used to supply the wage money, the wage money that he'd used to pay a Manchester prostitute. Local enquiries but although questioned I escaped detection. I have been the 'proud' owner of three hacksaws at least and I have no idea which one I took to Manchester. I disposed of the blade in the rubbish and one of the hacksaws broke so I threw it away. The urge to kill was all encompassing and I was a slave to it. December 1977 a trip to Leeds to try once more. Red Corsair PHE 355G, Chapeltown red-light district, I found Marilyn Moore walking the streets looking for business. Spencer Place telephone boxes I witnessed her reject a punter.

Yorkshire Ripper confession plus five-hundred and eighty-four minutes, nine hours and forty-four minutes, GMT approximately 00:32 hours (Sheet Twenty) I manoeuvred the vehicle, I manipulated the situation, I lured her into a false sense of security, I lured her into a trap. I parked at the corner knowing full well she would walk around it any second, I stage managed a jovial and friendly good bye to a non-existent girlfriend all for the benefit of tricking her into the passenger seat of his vehicle. "Bye now see you later, take care". The amateur dramatics his father pursued must be in the genes, my actions comforted Marilyn allayed her misgivings. Top timing she fell for it hook line and sinker and when he broached the subject of business, she was in and away. NARRATIVE. I became Dave and began to drive, directions to a place that resembled Flander's Field at the height of the First World War, an oasis of mud. Let's get into the back to utilise the extra space available, she concurred, this was my chance to hit her with the hammer, I bailed out of the car hammer in hand and hit her with it at the first available opportunity, I slipped and lost my footing in the quagmire of mud. The hammer hit home but with reduced affect, Marilyn screamed in terror, pain and panic. I hit her again, her screams seemed to get louder, I caught her full square with the second shot and she fell into the mud but her screaming continued, it seemed louder than bombs. In the distance two figures, time to make good my escape, I attempted to depart post haste but the laws of physics would not allow it, Speedway, Odsal Top, Bradford Dukes, The Shay, Halifax Dukes; wheel spins and hare pins.

Yorkshire Ripper confession plus six-hundred and twelve minutes, ten hours

and twelve minutes, GMT approximately 01.00 hours, (Sheet Twenty-One)
Slower on the accelerator let the wheels grip get some purchase and make good his escape eventually. Homeward bound, an old brown car coat, brown Doctor Marten boots and blue denim jeans were the catwalk order of the day.

Detective Chief Superintendent Jack Ridgeway, head of the Manchester CID drove across the Pennines to view the prize, Peter William Sutcliffe who was fast becoming a human freak show. Mr. Ridgeway was in charge of the handling of the investigation into the two Manchester 'Yorkshire Ripper' murders of Jean Jordan and Vera Millward. Mr. Ridgeway was also responsible for the two five-pound note investigations conducted, which brought police officers face to face with the man who had become known as the 'Yorkshire Ripper'. Ridgeway surveyed Peter William Sutcliffe, he pulled the interviewing officers to one side and ordered caution. He instructed O'Boyle, Boyle and Hill to pause the interviewing process, he was concerned that if they continued to interview Sutcliffe it could be counter intuitive and could be used by Sutcliffe and his legal team at a later date, to undermine the case for the prosecution. He instructed them to err on the side of caution to ensure that this criticism could not be levelled against the police investigation. O'Boyle, Boyle and Hill duly closed down the interview/confession on Monday the 5th of January 1981CE at 01:12 hours. The band disband, Peter taken to his chaperone cell, O'Boyle and Hill off home to capture some must needed sleep and to attempt to get their heads around the situation that they were central to.

I have read the above statement and I have been told that I can correct alter or add anything I wish. This statement is true, I have made it of my own free will. SGD: P W Sutcliffe Witnessed: J Boyle DI P Smith DS 368 D.A.P O'Boyle DS 4169I, PETER WILLIAM SUTCLIFFE wish to make a statement and I want someone to write down what I say, I have been told that I need not say anything unless I wish to do so and that whatever I say may be given in Evidence. SGD: P W Sutcliffe Witnessed: J Boyle DI P Smith DS 368 D.A.P O'Boyle DS 4169.

(Meanwhile) 01:00 hours in the annexe to the rear of Dewsbury police station, where Sonia is billeted the gravity of the situation suddenly overpowers her, Sonia comes over all queer, feels faint. The realisation that this living nightmare was happening, this whole sorry, sad, sick state of affairs was true. Sonia finally settled, all be it under surreal circumstances.

They were all friends in this room, be it through duty or necessity, they were all friends of sorts. But with friends like these who needs enemies. Interviewer, interviewee, interrogator, interrogated, 'friend', confidante, informer, carer and victim? Sonia bursts into a flood of tears and is consoled by Jenny. Sonia, tears streaming down her face nestles into Jenny's shoulder, attempting to hide her upset from view, struggling to keep the truth from penetrating into her fallacy of domestic bliss and failing. George hands Sonia a glass of Scotch whisky, to fortify her constitution, to take the edge off as the reality bites. The West Yorkshire Police Force had scotched the Yorkshire Ripper and brought an end to his reign of terror, they now 'scotched' his wife to dull the reality of her husband's actions.

George Oldfield and Dick Holland swing by the annexe, they slip into the ether unnoticed by Sonia but seen by their work colleagues. They delay the inevitable and return briefly at a more appropriate time. 01:15 hours, George joins the group of 'friends' and strategically sits next to Sonia on the settee. Turning to Sonia he confronts/introduces himself to her in a fashion that only an Assistant Chief Constable in the context of the early 1980's CE *"You know who I am don't you?"* in his best agony aunt demeanour in an act of fake concern. The conversation stuttered, stifled, progressed painfully. Sonia distant, detached, unresponsive, stared into the near distance, aloof and unable to engage in eye contact.
"My priority is to let my parents know". Sonia showing her self-centred concern for her family. Also showing the strange dynamics of the Sutcliffe family and the surreal situation. Talking to the fresh air in the near distance.
"Oh no I wouldn't advise you to do that. The press will get you". George reasoned.
"What on earth are you talking about? What do you mean?" Sonia's attention suddenly focussed on George's face, his sixty-one harsh years etched onto his face.
"We've had a press conference. They're all waiting outside," explained George.
Sonia was left flabbergasted at this hammer blow, George made his excuses, distancing himself from the predicament that was his making. Sonia eventually settled down, overcome with the emotion and drama of the day.

The room was left illuminated, the one-hundred-watt light bulb having to work overtime. WPC (Woman Police Constable) Jenny Crawford-Brown was Sonia's constant companion, for Sonia was also a priceless commodity that may be of use to the West Yorkshire Police Force. Although a second WPC is brought into the fray to chaperone Sonia and allow Jenny to rest. And her life like that of her husbands would never be the same, ever again.

Tear(ful) and not from Wear (side), luck had enhanced his self-belief, this also reinforced and reaffirmed his belief in God's influence. Peter reflected and looked back at the sequence of events, he had handed the Yorkshire Ripper to the police on a plate. Without his assistance, his confession, the police would have only issued Peter William Sutcliffe with a minor driving offence and not charged him with multiple murders of women throughout the north of England, Britain's most wanted man would still be at large. The joke police were only interested in motoring offences he thought to himself. What a fine upstanding citizen I am, I surrendered, I called time on the façade, the circus, the mission. Ring and Hydes, the backwater South Yorkshire country 'bumpkins', they didn't realise I was what/who they were looking for, who everybody was desperate to capture. They didn't have a clue, they were clueless. He found them pathetic, beneath his contempt. He closed his eyes and soon fell fast asleep.

Peter slept well, under the watchful eye of his police shadow, his conscience seemingly cleansed, his tryst with God fulfilling its natural outcome. He woke refreshed still slightly startled, in shock at the significance that was being placed upon his arrest. Detached, disconnected, disenfranchised. The centre of attention, but fast becoming old news. Peter inwardly buoyed by the fact that he was the centre of attention, the fulcrum on which this investigation centred. Peter knew he would have to introduce his connection with God, his mission; but Peter also knew he would have to wait until he was sign posted to do so. Until then he would make the most of his time in the limelight.

Monday the 5th of January 1981CE, 09:05 hours, when he awoke he was greeted by his police shadow, he eased the sleep from his body, as only a thirty-four-year manual worker can. The unfamiliar, unfriendly surroundings had been unkind, the situation had begun to unravel. Peter cut a forlorn figure, he was almost friendless only God could truly understand his position. *"What do you want for breakfast?"* he grunted half police mode, half prison officer mode.
"Coffee and toast, please".
"Is that all, you've got a big day today".
"I'll be reight".
The officer passed on Peter's order and remained with his charge. He was under strict instructions not to let him out of his sight, no way was he going to be allowed to avoid justice, by taking his own life.

09:15 hours, the continental breakfast is served. Peter prepares himself for the day ahead, he begins to contemplate his fate. This solemn mood was shortly to be lifted. Meanwhile Boyle, O'Boyle and Smith prepare to continue their interview, planning, cross referencing, re-examining. Peter is brought to the first-floor room in the Dewsbury police station, the makeshift interview room, where the Yorkshire Ripper had been identified. He sat waiting in forced silence, the silence was broken by a surprise of some unexpected news. Peter William Sutcliffe the star suspect, Peter William Sutcliffe the Yorkshire Ripper was receiving preferential treatment. Woman Detective Constable Jenny Crawford-Brown entered the small room, escorting the petite dark-haired figure of Sonia, it was a fleeting 'meet and greet, a possible police tactic to unsettle their prisoner, or an act of kindness for a sick man.

Boyle, O'Boyle and Smith entered the room Sonia was chaperoned out of the interview room, Let the interview commence.

Yorkshire Ripper confession plus one-thousand, one hundred and forty-two minutes, nineteen hours and two minutes, GMT approximately 09:50 hours ((Sheet Twenty-One) continued). Yvonne Pearson in Bradford followed Marilyn Moore. I saw her as I was driving my red Corsair on Lumb Lane. I had to slow down because a car was reversing into the road, it was at that moment that I saw the blonde girl that I later found out to be Yvonne Pearson. Fate, fate, fatal fate, Yvonne saw a possible punter in Peter and asked if I wanted business?

Yorkshire Ripper confession plus one-thousand, one hundred and fifty-two minutes, nineteen hours and twelve minutes, GMT approximately 10:00 hours (Sheet Twenty-Two) I was honestly going home, murder wasn't on my mind. But the chance arose and a hammer was under my seat, Yvonne told me where to go, Lumb Lane, Drummond Mill, White Abbey Road, a street behind Silvio's Bakery, to the end of the street and wasteland. CONVERSATION, banter and barter, five or ten pounds. Yvonne Pearson, the good time girl, Yvonne Pearson the more than good time girl, if the price is right come on down. Yvonne Pearson a woman of few words "Shall we get in the back?" We got out of the car to get into the back when I hit her on the head with Mr. Rahman's walling hammer twice, this hammer is still in my garage. Down she went onto the floor, soon she would be no more. Whining, whimpering, moaning groaning noisily. Peter drew the police a sketch of the hammer he had used, it was a walling hammer. Mid attack I was disturbed by the headlights of a car. The seemingly ear-splitting noise that originated from Yvonne's mouth seemed deafening and I had to quell the noise. I used the filling from an old settee to gag her, I also used the settee to hide behind. I pinched Yvonne's nose and this stopped the noise, however if I released my grip the noise returned.

Yorkshire Ripper confession plus one-thousand, one hundred and seventy-seven minutes, nineteen hours and thirty-seven minutes, GMT approximately 10:25 hours (Sheet Twenty-Three) I tightened my grip on her nose once again. Time stood still, eventually the car drove off. Fear was replaced by rage, senseless rage, sadistic and savage, brutish rage. I pulled her jeans off, I kicked her in the face, the head and the body. I started to act weird and said that I was sorry, but the damage was done, Yvonne was dead. I began to cry as I covered her body with the settee. On my way home I pulled over and contemplated what I had done, trying to decipher why I had committed this off the cuff murder. I was confused, my mind was in uproar, uncertain, unsure, unsafe and unstable. Time passed and I kept an eye on the newspapers but Yvonne's body hadn't been found. One newspaper said that Yvonne had gone to Wolverhampton. I never returned to her body, why would I? Before Yvonne's body was found I had killed again, I went to Huddersfield and attacked Helen Rytka. One afternoon I had to make a delivery to Huddersfield and I came across the red-light.

Yorkshire Ripper confession plus one-thousand, two hundred and two minutes, twenty hours and two minutes, GMT approximately 10:50 hours (Sheet Twenty-Four) district near the market. I returned a couple of nights later driving my red Corsair to Huddersfield under the uncontrollable influence of an impulse to kill females. When I drove into the red-light district I saw two street walking girls, I stopped and had some dialogue with one of them she was a half caste I asked if she was doing business. She replied in the positive but explained she would have to service a regular (punter) who was due to pick her up shortly. A lifesaving appointment, I drove around the corner and saw another half caste girl, I approached her and stopped the car and she climbed in and agreed to sex in the car for a fiver. She directed me to a nearby timber yard. Into the strange dark comforting yard, into the shadows of row after row of stacked timber. Prostitute sisters sharing a flat? When I read in the newspaper I remembered I had seen them before, they were familiar, I had seen the girls in Clayton. Helen unfastened her jeans and began to remove them. Helen stopped and suggested it would be better in the back of the car. I concurred, because it was what I was after anyway, it fitted my modus operandi, my style. We exited the car and she went to the back-passenger side door. Hammer in hand I walked around the front of the car and met her as she was about to enter the car.

Yorkshire Ripper confession plus one-thousand, two hundred and twenty-seven minutes, twenty hours and twenty-seven minutes, GMT approximately 11:15 hours (Sheet Twenty-Five) I attempted to smack her on the head with the hammer, but the door frame deflected the full force of the blow, top sill, fairy tap, shock and horror. Helen jumped from the car her jeans dropping to her ankles, *"What was that". "Just a small sample of one of these"*. Another attempt another hammer blow, but more success this time an uncompromising jolt from the hammer blow saw Helen free fall to the floor. Two would be witnesses, two taxi drivers, two men deep in conversation, two men oblivious to the obvious that was unfolding under their eyes. I dragged rag dolly Helen further into the wood-yard pulling off items of clothing, her groans had ceased but she was not deceased. Helens eyes flickered and moved, and she raised her arms in an attempt to shield her head from further attack. "Don't make any noise and you'll be alright". I lied. I was sexually aroused *(because I am a sadistic necrophile killer on a mission from God to FUCK over the prostitutes)*. I undid my trousers, parted her legs and did it. It was over and done within a matter of minutes, the sex mechanics. Her eyes stared into mine but she was limp and just laid there, like a sack of spuds, did she think of England or her imminent demise. I got up and Helen began to groan again. The two taxi drivers were within earshot, this forced my hand.

Yorkshire Ripper confession plus one-thousand, two hundred and fifty-two minutes, twenty hours and fifty-two minutes, GMT approximately 11:40 hours (Sheet Twenty-Six) I was trapped and scared, frightened that I would be caught, captured and castigated. Helen continued to sound off, Helen forced my hand into my pocket so I produced the knife and sunk it into her ribs and heart, six times in total. I hid Helen's body behind some bushes, between a wall and a woodpile and covered in a piece of asbestos sheet. I remained in the wood-yard for a half hour, thirty minutes, three thousand six hundred seconds and the next time I checked the coast was clear to make my exit, my escape, my bid for freedom, my move to distance myself from this atrocity, the taxi drivers had gone. I was soon homeward bound, I rinsed Helen's blood from my fawn shoes in the comfort of my kitchen, other than that I was as clean as a whistle, spic and span. Helen's lifeless body lay in the dark and dirt of a cold Huddersfield night, some fifteen miles away. The urge to kill controlled my actions, the urge when it descended transcended all other needs, it was my raison d'etre. It returned, so I returned to Manchester in my blood red Corsair, a few months after Rytka. The red-light area was deserted so I scouted around, night club, a maze of terraced houses.

Yorkshire Ripper confession plus one-thousand, two hundred and seventy-seven minutes, twenty-one hours and seventeen minutes, GMT approximately 12:05 hours (Sheet Twenty-Seven) I drove around and eventually found my next victim. My fix of premeditated murder was to be satisfied, *"Are you doing business?" "Yes. Car sex only. Five English pounds".* I picked up Vera Millward and she directed me to MRI, (Manchester Royal Infirmary), I parked in the car park and went into kill mode, the tried and tested method. Suggest the back of the car and use the 'mechanics' of the task to prepare and put into practice. Hammer stun attack as Vera attempts to open the rear passenger side door, hammer blow again drag into the darkness, remove clothes and stab and slash and cut and thrust. A diagonal incision opened up her innards, Vera's stomach spilled onto the car park tarmac. My nights work finished I drove back home across the Pennine hills. No blood on me, I was wearing my brown car coat, which I believe you now have in your possession. The urge faded only to return with even stronger cravings.

Yorkshire Ripper confession plus one-thousand, three hundred and two minutes, twenty-one hours and forty-two minutes, GMT approximately 12:30 hours (Sheet Twenty Eight) more random, undiscerning, arbitrary any woman was fair game. Surely this would lead to my downfall my apprehension and incarceration, but maybe that was my goal, my objective, my target, my destiny. I believe it was what I wanted, now. Next up Josephine Whittaker in Halifax, I drove there in my black Sunbeam Rapier registration. NKU 888H. All the eights eighty eight, in hindsight 666 (the number of the beast) would have been more fitting. I'd offloaded my red Corsair to a bloke in Eccleshill because the gearbox was a bit hit and miss. The urge was upon me, my ire was up and no woman was safe. I drove the seemingly empty April streets of Halifax. Bulls Head Roundabout, Halifax Building Services cruising the streets, nothing doing, no one anywhere nothing to kill nothing to despoil no life to extinguish. I then chanced upon the green, green, grass of Savile Park, Halifax. I drove around and around until I saw Josephine Whittaker walking purposely up the incline. I parked up and set about springing the trap that would result in Josephine's murder. Our paths crossed. I tagged along, I knew she was not a prostitute, but I didn't care. *"Do you have far to go?"* I asked in an effort to formulate the logistics of her death. The if's, the but's, the where's and why for's. The inter dependencies and intricacies of her death. Callous, calculating, in-human, in too deep and out of control.

COMFORT BREAK GMT approximately 12:50 hours, INTERVIEW RESUMED GMT approximately 13:15 hours.

Yorkshire Ripper confession plus one-thousand, three hundred and forty-seven minutes, twenty-two hours and twenty-seven minutes, GMT approximately 13:15 hours (Sheet twenty-nine) *"Why don't you learn to drive?" "I prefer horse riding, I find it a more satisfactory mode of transport".* We approached the green, green grass of Savile Park and Josephine explained she usually took a shortcut and walked across the grass on her way home. Grandmother, horses, sleep overs, you can't trust anyone these days (sick, evil the beast I am) and onward the odd couple went. My jacket bulging with a hammer and extra-large Phillips screwdriver that had been lovingly sharpened especially for the inevitable entry into human flesh, into the human body. *(Because I am a sadistic necrophile killer on a mission from God to FUCK over womankind).* "What time is it?" I asked. Josephine craned her neck towards the church clock tower and replied, I cannot remember her response. *"What good eyesight you've got".* I went all amateur dramatic and over exaggerated my movements and gestures make-believing I was looking towards the clock. I loitered, lingered using this ludicrous pantomime exhibition to conceal my dark intents. Then I unloaded the contents of my jacket and crashed the metal of the hammer into the back of her head. Once, twice. She groaned loudly in pain and fell to the floor and continued to moan. I then saw a figure in the night on the main road to my right. I remained calm and grabbed hold of Josephine's ankles and dragged her into the gloom filled darkness. Into safety (for me) into harm (for Josephine), more voices, behind to the left dog walkers. Five feet away almost within touching distance, loud moans, ignorance is bliss. I withdrew my screwdriver.

Yorkshire Ripper confession plus one-thousand, three hundred and seventy-two minutes, twenty-two hours and fifty-two minutes, GMT approximately 13:40 hours (Sheet Thirty) and removed some of her clothes. Grease lightning speed agility and dexterity, thrust, cut, jab, stab, gash, wound, injure and endure. Then walk away, as if nothing untoward had happened. Walk away without blame, what a lame excuse for a man, what a beast I am. Unsure and wishing to avoid detection I altered my escape route to avoid prying eyes, I returned unhindered to my Sunbeam Rapier. Home alone no blood stains but plenty of mud stains, goddamn the British weather, for your benefit I was wearing my black boots which have subsequently worn out and I have thrown them away. I was also wearing my old brown coat. The urge compelled me to kill again, intense, fervent and burning at my very being; I was out of control. Bradford and Barbara Leach was the next murder, September 1979. I was driving my new to me, Rover 3.5 car, registration FHY 400 K (still not 666), which I'd been tinkering with. It was a Saturday evening and I decided to take it out for a test drive. The urge was upon me, some poor unfortunates life was about to end. I went into town to see what I could find, a victim, a lone woman, unaware, unprotected, and unlucky. I drove up towards the University. Just passed the Mannville Arms and to my left, I saw her, Barbara Leach. I drove past her, turned left and lay in wait. Sure enough Barbara turned left and I realised it was destiny. Barbara walked, strolled slowly past my stationary car, I waited for her to pass then I got out of the Rover, I pulled out my hammer.

Yorkshire Ripper confession plus one-thousand, three hundred and ninety-nine

minutes, twenty-three hours and seventeen minutes, GMT approximately 14:05 hours **(Sheet Thirty One)**, I was also in possession of my big screwdriver. Barbara reached the entrance of a big house and I pounced, I hit her a flush blow succinctly delivered to the crown of her head. Barbara fell to the ground moaning. I dragged her out of the electric sulphur glare of the streetlights towards the rear of the property. Barbara moaned and groaned protesting at her molestation, grasping at life, gasping for air. I showed no pity, no mercy. I pulled out the large Phillips screwdriver and plunged it into her body. I concealed my work in the dustbin area in the back yard of the house, I covered her over, I was on auto-pilot going through the motions it was like a dreamscape semi-conscious half unconscious, aware but unaware. No real memory no recollection, I must have driven straight home. I do recall throwing the large screwdriver over an embankment at Hartshead Service Station westbound lorry park. My last murder was in Headingley, Leeds on a Monday night, the woman was Jaqueline Hill. I drove my Rover through Kirkstall and stopped at Headingley's Kentucky Fried Chicken franchise, it's finger licking good. I parked up and sampled their wares, I purchased a take a way fried chicken meal and retreated to my car. I ate my food in the Rover sitting in the car park to the rear of the Arndale Centre, then I set off and was forced by road signals to go straight on. I had wanted to turn right so I thought if I took my next right turn, I'd eventually end up in the direction I'd initially wanted to go, back onto the main road,

(Meanwhile) 14:00 hours, Superintendent Frank Morritt held a press conference at Dewsbury Police station. *"Can I first of all confirm information that I have no doubt many of you already possess and the man who is currently helping us with our inquiries is Mr. Peter William Sutcliffe aged thirty-five years, a lorry driver of 6 Garden Lane, Heaton, Bradford. If our current arrangements materialise, it is intended that Mr. Sutcliffe will be charged with offences and he will appear before Dewsbury Magistrates' Court, hopefully at 4:30 p.m. this afternoon. Can I also please take this opportunity of reminding various members of the media, that the lady who was with Mr. Sutcliffe at Sheffield and various other people who not unnaturally you are trying to interview; can I remind you please that those people are material witnesses to a prosecution which is now being launched, and I would ask you to bear that in mind when you seek interviews etc.*

Can I also please make one more point, I am given to understand and I believe I am right in saying, that again not unnaturally you have gained photos of the accused man.

Can I take this opportunity of saying to you again, that that man's facial features will form part of the prosecution case, and therefore any publications in that respect that you may or may not consider, I ask you to bear that aspect in mind when that decision is made by you and your editors". Cranking up the pressure, undermining the investigation, unwittingly unravelling other people's hard work.
"Are you asking us not to use these pictures? What would be the nature of the charges? Is the interviewing complete? How long do you think it will be before charges are made?"

"Where's he being questioned? Can you tell us whether the incident that you are talking about, the 'Ripper' are they likely to be one of the murder cases, as opposed to one of the others? Is Mrs Sutcliffe helping with inquiries? Will she face any charges? Is she in protective custody?"
"Not in protective custody. Is she in the same police station as her husband?"

Deflect, defend, suggest intend. *"It would be helpful if they weren't used. From my point of view"*. Discussions, decisions upstairs in Dewsbury. All's fair in love and law. *"Suspected stolen vehicle registration plates and one charge relating to the 'Ripper' series of incidents. No comment, no further discussion"*. Tongue tied harangued and berated but not silenced. But would silence have been the better option? Unprepared not prepared.
"I am not prepared to answer where people are at his moment in time, and on that basis, ladies and gentlemen, can I say thank you very much. It will be Dewsbury Court at 4.30 p.m., unless there is a hiccup in our arrangements".

An attempt to right the wrongs, undo the errors and retrieve the situation. Jim Hobson's assistant and confidante, his right-hand man. For Hobson read Morritt, for Oldfield read Holland. On the same side but on different sides. Losing the moral high ground. Highlighting inadequacies, continuing the catalogue of errors, continually pressing the self-destruct button.

(One, two, three, you're back in the room).
Yorkshire Ripper confession plus one-thousand, four hundred and twenty-two minutes, twenty-three hours and forty-two minutes, GMT approximately 14:30 hours (Sheet Thirty-Two), I turned left onto Otley Road. When I saw who I now know to be Jacqueline Hill walking to my right along what I now know to be Alma Road, she looked a promising victim. I drove past her onto Alma Road and parked up and awaited her next move. Jacqueline walked up on the right-hand side pavement of Alma Road, I slipped in behind her one, two, three yards behind. Jacqueline drew-level with an opening in the fence on her right-hand side. I grabbed my chance, removed the hammer from my jacket, grabbing the handle of my hammer and hitting her on the back of the head. Jacqueline fell to the floor groaning I had been transported into another reality, another world estranged from reality. Old faithful modus operandi I dragged Jacqueline into seclusion to despatch her life force, then an unwelcome interruption when car headlights illuminated the waste ground. I threw myself to the ground to avoid detection, unbelievably I went undiscovered. The lights disappeared and I erupted into a rage, Jacqueline was in the throes of terminal agitation. I struck again, once, twice hammer meets bone. I pulled her further into the darkness and further away from the possibility of prying eyes and illuminating headlights. A girl walked past, I stood motionless in an attempt to avoid discovery, she continued to walk up Alma Road, unmolested I took my vengeance on womankind, pulling, tugging, tearing away her layers of clothing, I pulled out the yellow handled screwdriver, the yellow handled

screwdriver with the bent blade, the yellow handled screwdriver that plunged into Jacqueline's body, the yellow handled screwdriver, with the bent handle that I would plunge into her staring eye.

Yorkshire Ripper confession plus one-thousand, four hundred and forty-seven minutes, twenty-four hours and seven minutes, GMT approximately 14:55 hours (Sheet Thirty-Three) The quizzical stare, why, why, why? Jacqueline's eyes remain open, this unsettled me, my disposition saddened. My job completed, my work done I departed the crime scene. I reached the Rover and drove up Alma Road I turned around and drove back down towards Otley Road, as I drove down a pedestrian waved indicating I was travelling the wrong way on a one way street, however I carried on regardless, I needed to be inconspicuous and away from that area post haste. The hammer and knife I used in Leeds on Jacqueline are the same ones I dumped in Sheffield, like I explained earlier.

I have read the above statement and I have been told that I can correct alter or add anything I wish. This statement is true, I have made it of my own free will. SGD: P W Sutcliffe Witnessed: J Boyle DIP Smith DS 368 D A F O'Boyle DS 4169I, PETER WILLIAM SUTCLIFFE wish to make a statement and I want someone to write down what I say, I have been told that I need not say anything unless I wish to do so and that whatever I say may be given in Evidence. SGD: P W Sutcliffe Witnessed: J Boyle DI P Smith DS 368 D A P O'Boyle DS 4169.

And so here ends the confession of Peter William Sutcliffe, (of Heaton, of Heaton in Bradford, formerly of Clayton, formerly of Clayton, Bradford, formerly of Bingley, West Yorkshire) also known as the Yorkshire Ripper, a serial killer and lorry driver, a religious zealot, an apologist, a missionary, a sick deviant necrophile killer, a poor excuse for a man, a loving brother, son, uncle, husband, quiet and caring leaving countless families despairing. An enigma, an unnerving mystery. Abhorrence, detest, odium, revulsion, disgust, dislike, animosity, aversion, distaste, loathing, Monday the 5th of January 1981CE, the soul is purged the task complete, the weight lifted, a marathon of endurance completed. Good and evil blurred, confused. Sentiment refused good and evil fused into one. What will become of this poor wretch? How did he become this poor wretch?

Pressure was building, it was 'eating' up Peter, chewing away at his sanity. The Yorkshire Ripper his alter ego, but also his nemesis and the theological mission weighed heavily on the lorry drivers blue collared shoulders. The mission had taken its toll, it had impacted on his family life, his work life and also his social life. It had engrossed every fibre of his very being for every waking moment. It had compromised his ability to function rationally. His inability to confide in others, his oath of silence had exasperated his consternation. His inner turmoil, his inability to confide in Sonia troubled him, because he'd never kept anything secret from her, apart from his use of prostitutes, his many infidelities and his many murders. The looming drink driving charge was the final nail in the coffin, it undermined his self-worth, his position, his status. Unravelling, spiralling into a cycle of uncontrollable angst, anguish and anxiety.

Bungled beginnings, inept investigations, why should the end differ from the previous five and a half years? Enforced time constraints, riding rough shod over policies and procedures, riding rough shod over the British judicial service. Slow and steady wins the day but doesn't oblige the necessity that the world's media has for sensationalism and copy. 'Cheque Book Journalism' was going to impact negatively on the final stages of the Yorkshire Ripper investigation. Sub judice seemed unemployed an archaic principle that no longer mattered.

Mr. Ronald Gregory, Chief Constable of West Yorkshire Police Force *"You have to get this man into court, I want him in court now".*

The baying hordes assembling at Dewsbury Town Hall, which at this time also housed the town's magistrate's court, were causing consternation with the risk of a riot to further undermine the West Yorkshire police standing in the eyes of the general public. This process could not go wrong it was to be a celebration, an opportunity to right the wrongs of the past five years. In essence Mr. Ronald Gregory's reputation was on the line, Mr. Ronald Gregory's reputation was not going to allow such a thing to happen. Any missed detail in Sutcliffe's confession could be gathered after the court appearance, after all Mr. Sutcliffe was going nowhere.

O'Boyle and Smith were to be the final victims of this case, left in an untenable situation. Sleep debt snatches through high workload and the intense nature of their work, sleep deprivation eroding, corroding their senses their sensibility. They were very definitely at the sharp end of the process and in hindsight should have been allowed carte blanche to allow the confession to develop at a natural pace and let it run its natural course. The officers should not have been pressurised to deliver the required results in an unrealistic and unrequired time frame. It was complete madness and underlined the amateur way that the entire investigation had been conducted. If Peter William Sutcliffe was going to hell in a hand cart, so too were the West Yorkshire police force for their incompetence and a 'gentleman' from the North East (but that was for the future).

Of course Mr Gregory was to win the day for that was how things worked. However at what cost?

After at least twenty two attacks that had resulted in the murder of thirteen women, this was the moment to dot the I's and cross the t's and not to worry about unnecessary time constraints, it was madness, but madness was to win the day. O'Boyle, Smith and Sutcliffe continued post haste, (pronto, pronto, pronto!) knowingly shortchanging themselves and

British justice. Skipping over important facts at this stage was to cost time at a later date, it was also going to make O'Boyle, Smith and the West Yorkshire Police look incompetent, a fitting epitaph for the bungling investigation that contributed to the Yorkshire Ripper's ultimate success. Ham-fisted, hopeless, heavy handed, inept police.

I'm late, I'm late for a very important date. Became the overriding backdrop to their work, wallpapering over key dates and facts, expunging survivors and attacks only from their interview, because of Gregory's enforced time constraints. 15:15 hours and Peter signed his final statement. Peter signed his freedom away. Peter signed his sins away.

The fifty pence number plate thief had undergone a metamorphosis, into Britain's most wanted man. Even at the time of the arrest and his subsequent transfer from Sheffield to Dewsbury, if they wanted the police could really push the envelope and charge him with witnessing the act of solicitation, not really a 'major league' crime.

Assumption is the cousin of consternation and leads to short cuts, misinformation and errors. All had been much too evident throughout this investigation. Overwork, overtime, low morale, inappropriate poor or non-existent supervision and lethargy all walked hand in hand along the course of the Ripper investigation. If a wrong choice was to be made, it was inevitable that it would be made. Unfortunate at best, criminally negligent at worst. How hindsight is a wonderful thing and resolves all riddles, alleviates all inadequacies. But retrospection cannot absolve, excuse or 'cover up' ineptness.

O'Boyle and Smith assumed that their suspect had been duly processed by their colleagues Boyle and Hill whom had assumed that their suspect had been duly processed by the Dewsbury officers whom had welcomed Sutcliffe to Dewsbury; the Dewsbury team that earlier flaunted the fact that they had meticulously searched their prisoner. Had their South Yorkshire 'friends', counterparts and colleagues failed to miss such items when they completed their arrest and or custody search? Could their prisoner have had an item that he may use in police detention or custody to cause physical harm to himself or others; or to damage government property, or to interfere with evidence? Maybe evidence relating to an offence or to assist in an escape. The West Yorkshire police officers chose to bask in their perceived glory of a false superiority complex. Did they also assume that the Sheffield officers had searched their suspect rigorously? As each occasion passed and time elapsed, it was quite clear that none of the police involved had acted in complete accordance with police policies and procedures. This was something that the police chose to overlook, to ignore. In essence the self-preservation or self-deprecation of Sergeant Ring in realising his earlier mistakes retrieved his earlier misconduct. Missing hammers, missing knives (plural, allowed to conceal/dispose of on two separate occasions), and small change (missed, but ultimately small change in the grand scheme of things).

Frustrated Detective Sergeant Desmond O'Boyle and Rod Hill their actions dictated by the clock, acting under orders from the detached reality of their superiors. The gravity of the situation was overtaken by the gravity of the situation. All their policing skills told them to take their time, collate and gain as much information as possible, 'Sutcliffe was singing like a canary' so surely it would be prudent to tap this rich seam of information whilst it was available, to make hay while the sun shines. Not to let UNECESSARY, inappropriate, unimportant, insignificant self-imposed deadlines compromise their work. However the eyes of the world were on this small West Yorkshire town, Dewsbury. A time and date had been given for the Yorkshire Ripper to be paraded in front of the world. Mr Gregory and Mr Oldfield were delighted.

"I can tell you that we're absolutely delighted with developments at this stage, absolutely delighted, really delighted, George is delighted as well, yes, absolutely delighted". Echoed the words of Mr Gregory, but O'Boyle and Hill were far from delighted, more like upset angry and slighted. The rhetorical cavalcade processing Sutcliffe through the justice system, would soon become a police cavalcade transporting Sutcliffe to Dewsbury Town Hall, the carnival had come to town.

15:15 hours, O'Boyle charged Sutcliffe with the unlawful killing of Jaqueline Hill on the 17th November 1980 CE. The paperwork was completed, the case was done and dusted. O'Boyle and Hill were confident that the confession and signed statement of Mr. Peter William Sutcliffe would enable the three magistrates to remand their prisoner to Armley Prison, where he would be held at Her Majesty's Pleasure. However there was one last hurdle to be jumped, one last task to undertake. Their prisoner was still wearing the clothes he'd been arrested in some forty-two hours ago, and now O'Boyle and Smith come to prepare their prisoner for his court appearance. Their actions are driven by the need to provide him with some fresh clothes, not by the need to preserve possible evidence and the fact that his clothes are primary evidence. The removal, tagging and bagging of Sutcliffe's attire should have been a formality. A formality that should have been triggered as soon as Sutcliffe had become a serious suspect for murder, but they were not. They should have been in sterile evidence bags awaiting forensic analysis. Unfortunately the police had been caught out!

Driven by triviality not professionalism, the keystone cops really do exist? But O'Boyle and Smith through sleep deprivation and coerced by the context, impelled by superiors have to ride with the wave, have to ride the runaway roller coaster, have to be eternally castigated for their clumsy handling, scapegoated due to others failings. Between a rock and a hard place, making history, becoming history, but creating mystery.

Chapter 38
Do It Yourself (DIY) Gimp Attire

On the first floor of Dewsbury police station in the Detective Sergeants office a strange and impromptu striptease was about to take place. A policewoman acting as a stylist for a mass murder, ordered into Dewsbury with Sutcliffe's sizes and ordered to report back with her purchases. A blue cardigan, grey trousers and other items of clothing were passed to Sutcliffe, this was qualified by a few words from the lips of Desmond O'Boyle.
"Put these on".
Sutcliffe hesitated as if in two minds, undecided, uncomfortable, he motioned to undress, then paused, then proceeded slowly in this stop start rhythm
'You have to get this man into court, I want him in court now'. The words still resonating in his ears the pressure still building in his. Post haste, (pronto, pronto, pronto!).
"Hurry up Peter we don't have all day".

Peter took off his jacket and placed it on the desk in front of him. O'Boyle leant forward and picked the garment up, he began to search through the pockets. The inside breast pockets were of particular interest, firstly he noted that the pocket linings had been cut out. He already knew the sinister and practical reason for this amendment. The inside breast pockets had their linings cut out to enable the wearer to carry and conceal the weapons of his trade, allowing easy access to the hammers, knives, screwdrivers and cords he used to hasten his victims death. O'Boyle's hand felt deep inside the linings into the aperture, he felt something his grasp tightened and he pulled out a pair of underpants. O'Boyle's face contorted into disbelief as he held up the offending articles at full arm's length away from his body, with only the very tips of his thumb and forefinger maintaining a grasp.
"What are these?"
"They're me underpants". Peter attempted to reply nonchalantly.
O'Boyle shook his head in incredulity and continued with the process, after all time was of the essence. Peter continued with his strange striptease, it was definitely different from anything he had ever witnessed in The Belle Vue on Manningham Lane. Sutcliffe removed his trousers and this action answered a lot of as yet unasked questions. He was wearing his gimp pants/trousers/leggings, these consisted of an adapted V-neck sweater where he had placed his legs through the arms, the V-neck allowed easy access to the wearer's genitals. O'Boyle and Smith stood mouth agape lost for words.
"What on earth is that?" a shocked O'Boyle blurted. Then silence, the pregnant pause forcing Peter to break the quiet to softly mumble a reply disingenuously
"Erm leg warmers".
"Oh leg warmers, eh".

This strange attire left nothing to the imagination and did nothing to hide his modesty, the V-neck 'skins' covering his legs. His shrivelled flaccid penis and testicles hanging on full display to an audience of two, Hill and O'Boyle incredulous carried on regardless.

Peter stepped out of the DIY 'gimp pants' and placed them on the desk. O'Boyle picked them up and began to examine the strange garment slowly and closely. Padding had been sewn into the knee area of the leggings (or the elbow area of the V-neck sweater), to protect the knee area of the wearer, like a gardeners mat, but these items of 'work wear' were not to be used for gardening. It proved that the murders were premeditated and suggested that he had created specialist clothing to enable himself to kneel for prolonged periods of time over the naked bodies of his victims and easily access his penis to masturbate and achieve sexual gratification.

This new line of inquiry was massive and a complete diversion from the story that Sutcliffe had attempted to engineer. This put a new slant on the crimes, his crimes, it was something he had chosen not to refer to, chosen to overlook. Could the fact that it implicated him as a sexual deviant *sadistic* necrophile killer have been reason enough not to mention it? It clearly suggested, emphasised and underlined the fact that Sutcliffe undertook these crimes for sexual gratification. Dress it up as you might, Sutcliffe could not hide the fact that his gimp leggings revealed far more about him than just his genitals, they gave an insight into the true nature of the man, the beast that O'Boyle and Hill had been compelled to deal with. Had such a fact been known at the outset of the interview it would have followed a very different path, but now time was against them, would they pursue the wrong path, would they cover up what had been un-covered? Was it too much work, would they be indifferent to the consequences and hope it would fade into non-existence thus exonerating them and the West Yorkshire Police Force?

'You have to get this man into court, I want him in court now'. The words still resonating in his ears the pressure still building in his. Post haste, (pronto, pronto, pronto!). *"Hurry up Peter we don't have all day".*

I'm late, I'm late for a very important date. Now dressed in a police supplied outfit, white shirt, jeans and blue polo-neck sweater. Peter prepared to be introduced to the world, Peter prepared to take his bow. Time was against them, so much to do, so little time to do it. No health and safety instructions, no risk assessments, no method statements, just an order. Just a time, just a date for a court appearance. Desmond O'Boyle handcuffed himself to Peter, the pair obviously exhausted, physically and mentally, one last scene to play in front of the baying British public.

Chapter 39
Dewsbury Magistrates Court

Dewsbury town centre not unlike any other town centre in the north of England. Dewsbury town, part of Kirklees Metropolitan Borough Council, to the South of Leeds and Bradford, nestled on the river Calder. Dewsbury town the largest of the towns that formed the Heavy Woollen District, comprising of Dewsbury, Batley, Heckmondwike, Ossett, Liversedge, Gomersal, Gildersome, Birkenshaw, Mirfield, Cleckheaton, Morley, Tingley, East Ardsley, Birstall and Horbury. Dewsbury town centre quiet and unassuming, Dewsbury town centre, for tonight, was the centre of interest for the world's media. The eyes of the world had descended upon Dewsbury town centre, along with a two thousand plus baying mob, here for the spectacle of unmasking the Yorkshire Ripper, here for the spectacle of public relief, to rejoice in the revelry and to celebrate, a shadow had been lifted. A more anticipated spectacle than the unmasking of the mysterious wrestler Kendo Nagasaki, a Japanese Samurai warrior; AKA Peter William Thornley from the Potteries, Stoke, whose December 1977 CE televised voluntary unmasking ceremony was viewed by millions on prime-time Saturday television.

HATRED, ANGER, OBSESSION.

Superintendent Dick Holland took control of the crowd control operation, which focused on Dewsbury Magistrates Court. Hatred funnelled into the streets of Dewsbury, nobody knew quite what to expect, except the unexpected.

16:30 hours, the designated time for Peter's appearance. *'You have to get this man into court, I want him in court now'.* The words still resonating in his ears the pressure still building in his. Post haste, (pronto, pronto, pronto!). *"Hurry up Peter we don't have all day"*. I'm late, I'm late for a very important date. The eyes of the world were upon West Yorkshire, West Yorkshire Metropolitan Police Force wanted to portray a positive image.

An entourage was assembled, a West Yorkshire Police Force cavalcade headed by the standard white police Ford Escort patrol car, the police van, registration KUA 97V, was sandwiched by a red unmarked police car, in which Sonia and her father were transported to the court rooms.

O'Boyle, Boyle, Sutcliffe and three uniformed officers cramped into the back of the police van, huddled in this confined space. Sutcliffe was pensive his fear and apprehension overtly on display for all to see - in preparation for a very strange journey. A peculiar backdrop. Weird atmosphere, odd, abnormal. Everybody unsure as to what to do, how to behave.

Bizarre in the extreme. The police van set off with its precious cargo. HATRED, ANGER, OBSESSION. Northern misogynist terrorist, inside the van, inside the man.

Blue flashing lights and wailing sirens broke the crisp night air, cold and uninviting streets were throng with humanity, this good-natured carnival of inhumanity teetered close to misrule. Quelled by the cold Yorkshire winds and the constant onset of snow, but possibly more by the threat of a heavy presence of uniformed police officers, but would the thin blue line be enough to protect the Yorkshire Ripper on his debut public appearance. Dewsbury Police Station, Aldhams Road, (WF12). South Street, left onto Church Street and right onto Wakefield Old Road. Dewsbury Magistrates, Wakefield Old Road, (WF12). The sirens heralded an oncoming storm, for they heralded to the crowd that the object of their contempt was soon to be amongst them. The cavalcade crawled forward through the town eventually arriving at its destination.

Missiles bombarded the Black Maria, coins, stones, cans and bricks filled the skies, abuse heckled from the frustrated crowd. The buffeting mob surged towards their target, the van that 'housed' the Yorkshire Ripper. As a thousand flashlights lit up the night sky creating a staccato sheet lightening effect adding to the surreal feel of the night. The police line broke and momentarily the mob spilled out onto the road, halting the van in its tracks. Men, women and children contorted with hatred slammed their fists into the light blue metal of the van, rocking it with the weight of the crowd, spurred on by the fever that swamped the rabble. The Yorkshire Ripper was a sitting target! HATRED, ANGER, OBSESSION. Superintendent Dick Holland joined the fray, his physical presence rallied the troops and the police regained control.

Hunched in the back of the van cowering under the realisation of the situation Peter was fazed, dazed, afraid apprehensive at the mayhem that unfolded around him. His official companions representing the interests of law, justice and order tried to portray an impression of calm and control. Peter mumbled a mildly incoherent sentence, *"What if there's an assassin, a man with a gun in that lot"*. Typical Peter it's all about Peter, too important to be murdered, for Peter William Sutcliffe a prominent person, a political figure, his murder would be an assassination.

HATRED, ANGER, OBSESSION outside the van HATRED, ANGER, OBSESSION filled the bodies, hearts and minds of the two thousand plus baying mob. Young punks in their late teens or early twenties courted the cameras. One holding up a hangman's noose in his right hand, a black leather wristband with silver studs complemented his black leather jacket and short black spiked hair. Another dressed in a bomber jacket, holds aloft a poster '*The Ripper HANG HIM* (added in free hand with a black marker pen) *IS A COWARD*'. These two were the focal points for photographers, they were flanked by a mass of humanity, young, old, male and female. People perched precariously on the windowsills of surrounding buildings to obtain a better view of the proceedings. Bobble hats, scarves, gloves, handbags, glasses and head scarves a festival atmosphere. Bodies eight deep, spilling out onto the roads, held back by good cheer and good luck, British Bobbies and consensus policing.

It was time to vacate the van and enter the court, it was time to run the gauntlet. The back doors of the van were opened by uniformed police officers, the hatred from the crowd spiked and the malicious, vicious intent unnerved the occupants. Fifteen metres to traverse, fifteen metres of atonement. A chorus of abuse. *"Fucking die you bastard! Die! Die! Die!"*

16:50 hours, the ensemble left the police van in a rush for sanctuary. Sutcliffe and O'Boyle manacled together, O'Boyle took the roadside and a uniformed Sergeant resplendent in custodian helmet took the other. O'Boyle was closely followed by a bearded Sergeant in his uniformed glory topped off with his flat cap, made a good body double for Sutcliffe, his beard and moustache very similar to Peter's. Peter who cowered below the blanket. Hooded in a strange shroud reminiscent of the Elephant Man Joseph Carey Merrick. Waiting uniformed officers formed what could have been misinterpreted as a guard of honour for the approaching group. This was through necessity to protect the hooded Sutcliffe from would be assailants.

Dewsbury Magistrates Court number one court, fleet streets finest, shoehorned into the ornate oak-panelled public gallery, but today this was not the public gallery, because no members of the public were allowed, because this was no ordinary court appearance. The public gallery became the press box.

Sonia Sutcliffe and Mr. Bohdam Szurma (Peter's father in law) sat at the front of the court room, Sonia was stoically weeping, her father attempting to comfort her. Silent, overwhelmed, everyone finding it difficult to fathom what is unravelling in their midst. The courtroom is called to order, three police officers chaperone Peter to the dock - unblinking, unerring and preparing to face justice. Mr. Dean Gardner (the Court Clerk) addressed the room.
"Are you Peter William Sutcliffe of 6 Garden Lane, Heaton, Bradford".
"Yes," replied Peter in a soft almost inaudible manner.
"You are accused that between November 16 and November 19, 1980 that you did murder Jaqueline Hill against the peace of our sovereign lady the Queen. Further you are charged that at Mirfield between November 13 and January 2, you stole two motor vehicle registration plates to the value of 50p, the property of Cyril Bamforth".
Mr. Maurice Shaffner, the prosecuting solicitor, rose and spoke to the room.

"The defendant is not legally represented, however due to the seriousness of the charges I think it would be beneficial for all concerned that Mr Sutcliffe is remanded in custody for a further eight days?" The magistrates agreed and Peter was then taken down the steps to the courts holding cells. A short but not particularly sweet visit for the Sutcliffe's, but a necessary evil, their lives could now progress and streets of the north of England would be a safer place. The fellowship reconvened, deep within the bowels of the courthouse. Each member taking deep calming breaths in preparation for a repeat of the walk of shame.

Another spike in the mob's vitriol as Peter is escorted from the relative safety of the Magistrates Court to running the gauntlet of the Dewsbury streets, a distance of ten to fifteen metres. A distance that none of the party relished. O'Boyle was handcuffed to Peter with his left hand shackled to Peter's right. Peter's head was covered by a grey blanket, his left arm was held by a uniformed officer, who along with O'Boyle guided their prisoner away from the court and back to the relative safety of the police van. A police Sergeant flanked the trio, walking on the far left of the wide pavement, two other uniformed officers followed close behind. Dick Holland followed behind them another uniformed Sergeant walked to his right, the fact that he wasn't wearing a helmet ensured he stood out from this strange entourage.

The right-hand rear door of the police van was already open, to minimise delay and ensure that the group could beat a hasty retreat. Boyle entered the van first crouching but ensuring that the sightless Sutcliffe did not bang his head on the roof of the van, O'Boyle followed attached to his prisoner, then the uniformed officers disappeared into the safety of the van. Another officer out of the group remained outside the vehicle and shut and locked the door before retreating to the pavement. Another officer possibly with OCD second checked the door handle and then withdrew to the opposite pavement.

Peter reflected when he had last attended this building it was under less auspicious circumstances and definitely with far less public interest. He remembered back to 1976 CE, it seemed a lifetime away. It was a lifetime ago for all his victims, Peter was already a double killer when he presented on Monday the 9th of February, Peter received a twenty-five pound fine after pleading guilty to stealing second hand tyres from Common Road Tyres, his then employers. He knew that the outcome of this appearance would be more drastic. The consequences of his actions had finally caught up with him.

Back to Dewsbury police station, back to safety, then a surreal sight-seeing trip. Boyle, O'Boyle and Sutcliffe toured Bradford city, visiting areas where he had previously secreted the murderous tools of his Yorkshire Ripper crusade. Detective Inspector Boyle acted as chauffeur, whilst Detective Sergeant Desmond Finbarr O'Boyle sat handcuffed to the Yorkshire Ripper in the back of the car taking in the surroundings. The roller coaster ride of emotion almost complete, the Boyle and O'Boyle duo had one last deed to do before they could return to something like normality.

A strange homecoming, a slight detour, taking Peter to his home at 6 Garden Lane for the very last time. The house was a veritable hive of activity, Sonia had returned home after the court appearance, various high-ranking police officers were also in attendance, most notably Superintendent Dick Holland and Detective Chief Superintendent Jack Ridgeway. Peter began to point out various items of clothing he had worn whilst committing his attacks.

The party were grouped in the master bedroom of the house, surveying items of Peter's attire. Sonia the mother hen, interrupted proceedings.
"Peter I've saved you some Christmas cake. You can't go to jail on an empty stomach and you're not leaving here until you've had a cup of warm milk and a slice of cake".
Peter looked at his captors as if to seek approval.
"Is it OK?"
O'Boyle instinctively looked to Holland his superior. Holland nodded his head to uphold the request, Holland also scratched his head in bewilderment. Having been given consent Peter dutifully complied for Sonia was domineeringly quiet, she wore the trousers in the Sutcliffe household. Peter the hen-pecked husband, passive, domestic frustrations building until they are allowed to escape. Silent disapproval, disappointment terse verbal admonishment. Peter the perfect husband, Peter the serial sex killer.

The company relocated to the kitchen, Peter sat at the kitchen table and his escort Desmond sat at the table to the right of him. Sonia true to her word appeared at the table with a cup of warm milk and a slice of Christmas cake. She placed it on the table in front of her husband. The finale a slap stick scene, Peter the puppeteer, raising his right hand and forcing Desmond's left hand into action. The protracted scene was odd to say the least and raised a wry smile amongst all present with the exception of Sonia, who seemed oblivious to the group's reactions.

Finally the last supper partaken Peter was taken into custody at Her Majesty's Prison, Armley. Boyle and O'Boyle took their captive to the car for the final journey, which ended with their very special cargo being delivered to the gates of Armley Jail. Peter lost his name, Peter became known as inmate G40203. This was a new venture, a new dawn in his life. Had the Beast of Bingley, the Yorkshire Ripper, Peter William Sutcliffe been tamed?

Chapter 40
HMP Armley

Tuesday the 6th of January 1981CE Peter William Sutcliffe was now free from his mission, free from the pressure and turmoil that went in tandem with all that the mission entailed. Here by the grace of God ready to adapt to his new lifestyle, ready to adopt a new role.

Because Peter was a remand prisoner he received certain privileges that convicted prisoners were ineligible to receive, for example more visits, visitors could bring him additional food and books.

Peter received star status, this high-profile captive was constantly chaperoned twenty-four hours a day, a group of hand selected prison officers were his companion. Watching, ensuring their detainee did not self-harm, did not take his own life. Observing their cell mate, ensuring the light was on and their attention was focused, for Sutcliffe had to face justice for his heinous acts. Peter was billeted in a special cell of his own in the Amley prison hospital. He had a single bed and access to a shower, possibly to ensure his safety from other inmates, but probably to safeguard any opportunity to collate further evidence against their prisoner and a daily log of his actions.

Peter settled in to his new surroundings, his fellow inmates nicknaming him JR, after his alter ego Jack the Ripper, also a play on the character JR Ewing played by Larry Hagman in the popular American TV drama series, JR was a TV baddie who had been shot and the tabloids in America and Britain were awash with the question, 'Who shot JR'.

Loose tongues cost life sentences! At visit time, eaves-dropping officers document every sentence. On Thursday the 8th of January 1981CE during a visit, prison officer Leach overheard and duly noted that Peter had admitted to Sonia that he had given police full details about his crimes and he was guilty of all the charges. A tearful Sonia caught in the eye of the storm, the magnitude of her husband's actions sinking in. Peter tried to play down the situation, reassure his spouse, save her from worry and protect her from the truth. *"Al be in here for a good while, thirty years, so don't be afraid to make a life for yerself".*
Sonia remained distraught and inconsolable, tears streaming down her face, Peter attempted to cheer her up. *"Not to worry if I can mek em think am mad I might only get ten years in a loony bin".* Sonia regained her decorum eased by Peter's throwaway words. Peter wiped the tears from her face, he then licked the salty tears from his hands.
"Why didn't you confide in me Peter I may have been able to help you with your compulsions".
"Leave it to Doctors to find owt,"

Doctor Hugo Milne a consultant psychiatrist with over twenty-nine years of experience in the role, paid eleven visits to Peter whilst he was held on remand in Armley jail, probing Peter for a sexual motive to the crimes of the Yorkshire Ripper. The police saw fit not to alert Milne to Sutcliffe's strange DIY gimp pants that his patient was eventually found to be wearing upon his arrest. Peter William Sutcliffe did not see fit to disclose this important information. Important information that was overlooked and omitted until 2003CE when the Yorkshire Evening Post ran the headline 'Killing Kit of the Ripper'. Doctor Milne came to the conclusion that Peter was and had been suffering from schizophrenia of a paranoid type since circa 1965CE.

Interview one, Wednesday the 14th of January 1981CE, Doctor Hugo Milne visits and so begins the thorough clinical examination of remand prisoner Peter William Sutcliffe.

Interview two, Tuesday the 27th of January 1981CE, Doctor Milne interviews Peter, during the interview Peter manifests paranoid notions with regards to prostitutes, uncontrollable yearnings concerning his actions in his early attacks. Milne is still cautious of his patient, suspicious that Peter was trying to hoodwink him into a false diagnosis. But this was a vocational pit fall of which Doctor Milne was all too aware and it was not a trap his experience was going to allow him to fall into. Milne knew Sutcliffe to be a liar, manipulating circumstances and individuals to his own ends. Sutcliffe had an IQ (intelligence quotient) of between 108 and 110, this suggested an above average intelligence. Was Doctor Milne certain that he had not been wilfully misled by Sutcliffes lies.

By interview three, Doctor Milne was 'confident' that Peter was a paranoid schizophrenic, however he held his counsel and questioned himself due to the gravity of his patient's crimes.

Thursday the 5th of February 1981CE, Doctor Milne interviews Peter for the eight time, and Peter finally divulges the secret of his divine mission to another person. Elaborate insights into an unhinged mind. Peter was describing his attack on Irene Richardson, his third official murder victim. It was then that Sutcliffe disclosed, *"Am on a mission from God to rid the world of prostitutes"*. God had allowed Peter to divulge his divine mission, God had given Peter a sign that now was the time.

Constantly aware that Sutcliffe could have been calling their bluff, they had the tools and know how to identify this Doctor Milne explained that the process of unwrapping his symptoms collating the signs and timelines reinforced his diagnosis. The interdependencies of his symptoms pieced together gave Milne no real alternative than to come to the conclusion that Sutcliffe was not simulating schizophrenia, Sutcliffe was mad and had been unwell for some time.

Proved by Sutcliffe's suspicious mind, untrusting, fractured through misinterpretation, misunderstanding and troubled interaction with others. His overpowering compulsions, obsession and mistrust aimed at all thing's female prostitution. Misconception that prostitutes are responsible for all the ills that beset society that they were to blame for everything. Notions of grandeur his self-perceived supernatural powers; hallucinations, external stimulus impacting upon his senses impacting on his actions, these were all telltale signs of his illness. This linked and interacted with Peters religious delusion compounding and accentuating his high opinion of himself. Depression, suicide and an inability to correctly interpret conversations and actions of others. Misidentification through bewilderment reality merges with fantasy. The fact that Sutcliffe was able to deal with stressful situations with great fortitude, able to control his emotions, his feelings, his behaviour, to detach himself from the horror of his actions. There was no insight into wrong from right, actions and reasons become vague, Peter was ill but he didn't realise it. Not to mention thought argument, the internal struggle and turmoil it caused, Peter tried to ignore the voice, resist its insinuations, its suggestions. Disorientated by the internal discussions unable to decide in a state of decision limbo. The abnormal became the norm and an outward veneer of respectability can eclipse the madness. Schizophrenic thinking, illogically using the thought process and formulating unreasoned conclusions. But more importantly not being able to recognise their irrational behaviour and thinking and therefore not able to determine, fathom or admit that their behaviour was wrong or even questionable. In essence Peter was unable to comprehend his behaviour was wrong it was acceptable to him and should also be appropriate to society.

Primary schizophrenic experiences are difficult to identify, buried in the past and hidden by other aspects of the illness but they are central to the diagnosis, they are the essential ingredient. The other symptoms are add on, they provide substance and corroborate the initial symptom. Over-exaggeration, sees fiction become fact, fantasy becomes a warped reality, a point of reference off line with the norm. A moral compass so corrupted his self-created consensus forcing him to misinterpret, allowing him to assume a woman was a prostitute. The indicators become more prominent, to the fore, regular. Premeditation a watchword, a self-determination to avoid detection; cold, calculating, cunning, emblematic of a fully blown paranoid schizophrenic. Doctor Milne was happy to state, *"In general terms this man has more than sufficient symptoms to make up a diagnosis of paranoid schizophrenia".*

Peter was an accident waiting to happen, his condition dictated this. The only issue was how it would manifest itself Milne stated that the primary schizophrenic experience was in Bingley Cemetery, a profound place to experience his first hallucination. It was then that life events played their part and set Peter on the path to becoming the Yorkshire Ripper. Fickle fate threw up the lover's tiff, the prostitute faux fuck, the wheels were set in motion and ultimately no woman in the north west of England was to be safe. The illness developed hand in hand with the circumstances and context of his life. His compulsions faded as he and Sonia grew together their relationship stabilised and the pair married in August 1974CE and the illness went into remission. In essence his urges sated by his environment his inner turmoil, his illness controlled.

Patterns of death, sporadic attacks, then clusters, finally a free fall, free for all killing season. A clinical culmination to match his actions. *'In the last few months he became much madder and one attack followed another'.* Cravings, triggered by hallucinations and morbid depression; cravings driven by madness?

Milne concluded that the attacks although containing some sexual content were not driven by a sexual motive. *"In simple terms, although his victims were female and it might be thought he might be a sexual killer, I am not of the opinion that he is primarily a sexual killer".* For Peter was a paranoid schizophrenic on a divine mission from God to rid the world of prostitutes. Peter robustly denied any sexual connotation to his crusade. Always mindful of what other people thought, Peter lied? Aghast at the title of serial killer and dynamically averse to insinuations of a serial sexual killer. Milne proffered arguments of accidental sexual content the fact that the victims were all female, however ultimately these were withdrawn or diminished when under the scrutiny of the court.

Milne dismisses the simulation of illness through ideas of reference theory, for Milne and his medical cohorts Peter William Sutcliffe was a paranoid schizophrenic. Serial killing and mental illness don't go hand in hand, but the health care professionals agreed that in Peters case it was a mitigating factor and Peter was acting under diminished responsibilities.

Doctor Malcolm MacCulloch was a consultant psychiatrist who also worked as a medical director of Park Lane special hospital Liverpool, he visited Peter on three occasions whilst he was held in Armley. Doctor MacCulloch concurred that Sutcliffe was suffering from schizophrenia of a paranoid type. In fact it was a diagnosis that he was confident in giving after thirty minutes such was his assurance.

Doctor MacCulloch said that Sutcliffe presented with four 'first rank signs', which aided the diagnosis of paranoid schizophrenia. There were eight 'first rank signs' in total. If a patient was to present with just one of these signs, it would be fair to say that they would be diagnosed as a paranoid schizophrenic.

1. Bodily hallucinations, internal feelings and sensations that Sutcliffe suggested felt like a hand gripping his heart.
2. Influence of thought, Sutcliffe felt his thought process was swayed by an external influence. Sutcliffe also revealed he could read other people's minds.
3. Delusional perception, where outside objects can offer insights or projections that only the sufferer can understand gleaming a secret and special message that are far from the reality of the situation.
4. Passivity, Sutcliffe claimed to be an empty vessel acting at the behest of God, he was controlled by God.

Doctor MacCulloch was also acutely aware that not only his professional reputation was under scrutiny but also the good name of psychiatry, therefore he was cautious with his diagnosis. The plausibility of Sutcliffe's paranoid schizophrenic disorder stood up to MacCulloch's questions, this was reinforced by his personal historical back story and by two other eminent medical professionals. MacCulloch had toyed with diagnosing a personality disorder that incorporated sadism and sexual deviancy but could find no evidence to corroborate this.

Doctor Terence Kay was a consultant forensic psychiatrist who worked in Wakefield and Armley prison, his bread and butter work was dealing with prisoners and this also included by default interacting with prison officers. Doctor Kay visited Peter on eight occasions whilst he was held at Armley jail. Doctor Kay concurred that Sutcliffe was suffering from schizophrenia of a paranoid type.

Doctor Kay was a familiar figure in Armley prison and had built up a good working relationship with the prison officers. The prison officers were adamant that the medical professionals had been hoodwinked by their patient. They firmly believed that Sutcliffe was lying, cheating, manipulating and deceiving his way to a lesser sentence. (Life story, background, family life and employment history... *'all prostitutes are scum'*).

"All prostitutes are scum...It was important to my cause that I had to carry on with the mission...I know if I was allowed out I would know it was all right. I'm here now but it might only be temporary. If I was out the feeling would come back. It would be wrong to say I wouldn't do it again. It would be difficult to say that I couldn't. I know it's wrong to kill but if you have got a reason it's justified and it's all right...I have no doubts whatsoever. I wasn't as rational then as now. If there were women around now it wouldn't take long to get these thoughts again. The prostitutes are still there, even more on the streets now, they say. My mission is only partially fulfilled. God gave me the mission to kill. He got me out of trouble. I'm in God's hands. He misled the police. Perhaps God was involved with the tapes...I were called to do it yer could say it wer my calling. Now I reckon God decided a should be caught to free me from the mental torment of all the killing. Maybe he's chosen someone else to

continue the mission. Have never seen God, but ave heard him often". "I know it is wrong to kill. If you've got a good reason, it's justified and all right...I'm glad to be here because of the innocent people. I am not glad really because of the trouble and the family. ...Near the end I began to think most women were prostitutes. At this stage I could have gone into town between nine and five thirty and attacked any woman...I wondered if God's purpose was to get me back into the Faith. I had been having Mass regularly and had been asked about confession".

Milne on Sutcliffe. *"I think he thinks we are all wrong and he is right".*
"His mental state fluctuates and so does his insight into his illness. Sometimes he would think he was mentally ill, and at times he would completely deny it".

On Tuesday the 14th of April 1981CE, a hospital prison officer and remand prisoner Sutcliffe were sitting together. An upbeat and openly tickled Sutcliffe claimed he was sane as the next man and scoffed at the medical professionals he had tricked into believing his pretence. Echoes of his disdain for the police and their ineptness, echoes of we be echo, echoes of arrogance, echoes of insanity?

Late April 1981CE Peter is transferred from HMP Armley to HMP Wormwood Scrubs Psychiatric ward G2, his makeshift home for the duration of his show case trial.

Wednesday the 29th of April 1981CE Peter William Sutcliffe appears in the dock at Number One Court, Central Criminal Court, "Old Bailey", London, for trial preliminaries. Tuesday the 5th of May 1981 CE, the trial of the century begins, Number One Court is packed to the rafters and the air is heavy with anticipation.

Friday the 22nd of May 1981 CE, the final day of the trial, after just under three weeks of court room drama at 10:21 hours, the Judge Mr. Justice Boreham emphasised that the jury must seek a unanimous verdict and decide whether Sutcliffe *"had been driven by a divine mission to kill prostitutes, or was a callous and brutal murderer, as the prosecution charged".*

15:28 hours, the jury return and inform the Judge that they are unable to reach a unanimous decision. Mr. Justice Borham says he will accept a majority decision, the jury retire to deliberate further.
16:13 hours, the jury return and deliver their verdict of guilty to 13 counts of murder with a majority of 10 to 2.
Doctor Terence Kay returned to inform the Judge that himself, Milne and MacCulloch felt that Sutcliffe should be locked up for the rest of his life.
Mr Justice Boreham delivered the sentence, *"I have no doubt that you are a very dangerous man indeed. The sentence for murder is laid down by the law and is immutable. It is a*

sentence that you be imprisoned for life. I shall recommend to the Home Secretary that the minimum period that should elapse before he orders your release on license shall be 30 years. That is a longer period, an unusually longer period in my judgement, but I believe you are an unusually dangerous man. I express my hope that when I have said life imprisonment, it will precisely mean that. For reasons that I have already discussed with your counsel in your presence I do not believe that I can make that as a recommendation in statute".

Chapter 41
HMP Parkhurst

Peter William Sutcliffe (PWS) is star sign Gemini, apparently freedom is fundamental to their mental wellbeing. This perhaps is not the best omen for an already fragile Mr. Sutcliffe.

Friday the 22nd of May 1981CE and Peter began his life sentence at Her Majesty's Prison (HMP) Parkhurst, Clissold Road, Newport, Isle of Wight, PO30 5NX, where he was housed in a maximum-security wing. He was transferred from HMP (Her Majesty's Prison) Wormwood Scrubs, Du Cane Road, London W12 0AE, where he was held during his show trial at the Old Bailey after previously serving over four months on remand at HMP Armley, Leeds.

Peter was not mad, or so the law had decided, however the doctors at Parkhurst felt differently. Parkhurst time is hard time and Sutcliffe was treated like any other lifer by the authorities. But Peter wasn't just any other lifer, Peter was the Yorkshire Ripper, Peter was infamous, even amongst the infamous. God gave him a mission to kill. He was in God's hands.

In prison Peter spoke clearly, coherently the shackles of his alter ego the Yorkshire Ripper, now broken, it had come to an end in somewhat of a damp squib in a Sheffield back street. Peter believed God had decided to call time on his nocturnal leisure pursuit, God had decided Peter should be arrested and convalesce; take time out from the mental torment that accompanied the killings. God had chosen someone else to continue the mission. His divine right wavered, his freedom lost, but like any good henchman he was only acting under orders. Peter explained, *"I couldn't do anything to stop myself. I were suffering inner torment and just wanted to get rid of all the prostitutes".*

Peter knew he was in good hands, God had not failed him, God had helped, God had helped Peter on a number of occasions whilst he undertook his mission. *"He got me out of trouble. I'm in God's hands. He misled the police. Perhaps God was involved with the tapes.... God has another disciple I'm fairly convinced. No tapes for a while. My mission is halted for a while. I might carry on shortly. The other fellow may send more tapes. God may have stopped."*

Peter continued highlighting his relief it was over; *"I know if I was allowed out I know it was all right. I'm here now but it might only be temporary. If I was out the feeling would come back. It would be wrong to say I wouldn't do it again. It would be different to say that I couldn't. I know it's wrong to kill but if you have got a reason it's justified and it's all right. I have no doubts whatsoever. I wasn't as rational then as now. If there were women around* now it wouldn't take long to get these thoughts again". The Yorkshire Ripper, the beast inside then interjected. *"The prostitutes are still there, even more on the streets now, they say. My mission is only partially fulfilled. God gave me the mission to kill"*. This was truly fucked up shit.

A time to reflect, for Peter had plenty of time on his hands. Bingley cemetery 1966CE Peter's primary delusion or his cunning excuse. This was the birth, the onset, the inception the origin of the Yorkshire Ripper. If the founding moment of the Yorkshire Ripper was the epiphany at Bingley cemetery, the trigger point was the 1969 CE five or ten pounds prostitute scam in Manningham.

The voices that communicated the messages to him spoke in Old Testament prose, evoking resentment and hatred *'Prostitutes are scum and must die, they are an evil upon the world that must be destroyed'*. They spoke to him about a divine mission to clean the streets.

Peter reflected upon his actions and showed no remorse, he felt aggrieved and unique in equal measures and argued to himself that such a thing could have happened to anyone, any impressionable young man who was a Catholic with an unshakeable, steadfast, staunch and unswerving belief in God. Try walking a few steps in my shoes, then you would understand how this necessary mission took over my life. I was a vessel for God, a vehicle for good, the scene was set. I was at a low ebb, my Grandmother Coonan had recently passed away and her body lay cold in the ground feet away from where I was working. Around this time a friend's mother had also committed suicide, the lines between life and death were blurred. In this emotional state and at a young age I was susceptible, this divine intervention offered an insight into a better life, gave me a purpose. It was an enlightening spiritual experience, although one that had to remain a secret and on hold, under strict instructions from God.

How can I be guilty, of course I am not guilty. I was acting as an instrument of God, acting upon his behest, acting for the best, how could I be held responsible for these actions. It was as if someone else was doing, not me. Anybody who knows me, knows that I wouldn't hurt a fly. How could I be held responsible, *'let he who is without sin cast the first stone'*. Someone else, not me; I wouldn't hurt a fly. I didn't know any of the women, the 'none-prostitutes' were misidentified by God and ended up being collateral damage. I'm sorry that they weren't all prostitutes, but the buck stops with God, he is the one to blame! They were not meant to be part of the mission but God implicated them, God chose them, God killed them.

His bland emotionless face, expressionless, stern, methodical, in control, neat and tidy. Fragments of reality. Fragments of life, fragmenting defaulting from the regimental constraints of control, fragmenting into madness and mental anguish control lost. Fractured broken unhinged.

He misled the police, the courts and the doctors Peter Sutcliffe, (the 'Yorkshire Ripper') Christian, serial prostitute murderer. He believed he'd pulled the wool over their eyes during his pre-trial psychiatric interviews, now he was to become the model prisoner. But time spent in the solitude of his cell further unhinged Peters already fragile mind. Peters behaviour deteriorated, his reasoning diminished, his symptoms became more pronounced. Peter was suffering a severe case of paranoid schizophrenia, controlled madness in mind, undetectable, hidden.

Schizophrenia, ill not evil. Parkhurst doctors supported the claims of the Old Bailey trial doctors Milne, MacCulloch and Kay et al who unsuccessfully argued that Peter was suffering from paranoid schizophrenia. However the prison doctors attempts to have Peter admitted to a secure Psychiatric unit fell on deaf ears. Peter was therefore housed on F2 at Parkhurst. F2 (F-wing, second landing), the hospital wing, it was isolated from the rest of the prison and was used to house and observe the psychiatrically disturbed prisoners amongst others. It was here that Peter confided in his doctors that Emily Jackson his second murder victim often visited him in his prison cell. *'I feel her presence in my cell. Emily Jackson, her ghost visits me in my cell'.* This was the backdrop to Peter's incarceration, left to rot and decay, like one of his victims. One of the Yorkshire Ripper's victims. Peter was now suffering at the hands of his alter ego.

Tuesday the 2nd of March 1982 CE Sonia Sutcliffe, nee Szurma, obtains a judicial separation from the London Divorce Court, she cites her custody estranged husband on the grounds of 'unreasonable behaviour'. An understatement if ever there was one.

Monday the 24th of May and Tuesday the 25th of May 1982 CE, Sutcliffe's lawyers appeal to the Court of Appeal requesting that the thirteen murder convictions are quashed and replaced by a verdict of manslaughter on the grounds of diminished responsibility. The Court of Appeal deny this application.

September 1982CE, the Parkhurst prison medical office recommended that Sutcliffe should be transferred to a high security mental hospital, under Section 72 of the Mental Health Act. Section 72 enables a transfer from prison to hospital, however it requires the approval of the Home Secretary, a long and drawn out process.

Monday the 13th of December 1982CE, Home Secretary William Whitelaw declined the transfer request, claiming it was in the public interest that their prisoner remained in jail.

The Home Secretary did not want to be seen as a soft touch, the infamous Yorkshire Ripper must be punished for his crimes.

Chapter 42
Peter meets James

Monday the 10th of January 1983CE; blanking out The Sun, DIY censorship from cell eleven, but this is a communal paper and other inmates are none too pleased with what they perceive to be preferential treatment for Peter Sutcliffe. Peter dreaded articles about the Yorkshire Ripper, his crimes or any associated articles, they always resulted in a backlash of sorts, heightened resentment, increased hatred, especially amongst the prison population who openly loathed him. Peter took a black marker pen to specific articles that raised his ire. This did not go down to well with other inmates. His makeshift defacing of the daily red tops did little to promote his popularity.

05:55 hours and Peter's cell (number eleven) had been unlocked, he was using a plastic bowl to collect water, filling the bowl from a sink that was situated in a recess off a prison corridor. Peter turned off the hot water tap and turned to return to his prison cell, he felt the presence of a fellow inmate nearby but paid it no heed. He saw a man was also occupying the recess, the man was James Costello. Costello seems to have decided to follow Sutcliffe's lead. Instead of blacking out the eyes of newsprint images he was going to obliterate the eyes of the protagonist of this story, a certain Peter William Sutcliffe. Hopefully this would black out the Sun on all levels for Sutcliffe.

James had an idea to attack his adversary and decided that the relative obscurity of the recess would provide a perfect opportunity. Unaware Peter proceeded, one step, two step. James used his tee-shirt to obscure the makeshift weapon, when he was about to pounce he dropped the tee-shirt to reveal the gleaming glass swinging towards the swaggering Sutcliffe, the demon, the Yorkshire Ripper. The attack was over almost as soon as it had begun, seven seconds from inception to end. James, the assailant held a broken coffee jar in his right hand and swung it towards Peter's left eye. Peter caught a fleeting glance of the shards of jagged glass as it accelerated towards his face, then he felt the impact. Peter reeled at the first strike, the glass on flesh causing a slicing wound from the top of his left eyelid to the top of his left ear. James repeated the process causing another gaping wound to Peters face. The second strike causing a five-inch-long injury from his neck to the centre of his left cheek. Blood spurted from the wounds, splattering onto the walls and floor, leaving an arcing form of red artwork on the white prison walls. Peter reacted by pushing his arms out forcing his attacker away. The glass weapon fell to the ground and shattered, a possible symbolic metaphor to plethora of shattered lives left in the wake of the Yorkshire Ripper's reign of terror. Peter was now getting a taste of his own medicine. The plastic bowl fell into the sink and Peter used his arms to fend off James. Two hospital orderlies reacted to the commotion and separated the men from their scuffle. Peter roared in pain like a wounded animal.

Oh how the tables had turned, oh the incredulity and the affront, how had such a thing been allowed to happen and why would anybody be so evil as to initiate such a nasty unprovoked attack. Oh the irony. Peter was distraught and believed he'd been the victim of a vicious and premeditated attack, glass was a prohibited item on the wing, in an attempt to prevent inmates from harming themselves or others, after all this place was quite popular with the criminally insane. Peter picked up James's discarded tee-shirt and pressed it to the left side of his face to stem the blood flow. Shocked, exhilarated, ecstatic, adrenalin pumping through his fast emptying veins. The hunter became the hunted, the tables turned. Peter's wounds also included two lesser injuries, a cut below his left eye and a cut to his left eyelid, in total he required thirty stitches. As a result of his injuries Peter lost about a pint of blood. He later required an operation to patch up cursory damage to muscles in his face. Worst things had happened to women on the streets of Leeds, Bradford, Manchester, Huddersfield, Halifax and Keighley. (Silsden, Horsforth and Ilkley).

James Costello was thirty five, two years the junior of Peter, he was a career criminal, his first court appearance being 1963CE, he hailed from Glasgow, had served time on a number of occasions receiving bed and breakfast from her majesty. In total he had appeared in court a total of twenty-eight times between 1963 CE and 1980 CE. Nine of Costello's twenty-eight court appearances had been for violent offences, whilst fifteen had resulted in jail terms. His 1980CE conviction was for possessing a firearm without a certificate, possessing a firearm with intent to endanger life/resist arrest. Costello was sentenced to ten years' incarceration. Whilst in Parkhurst Costello was diagnosed as suffering from mental illness and was placed in the prison hospital until he could be transferred to Broadmoor. Costello had attempted to black out the eyes of Sutcliffe with his D.I.Y. weapon, no D.I.Y. gimp pants here. Just good old-fashioned Scottish ingenuity and extreme violence.

Tuesday the 11th of January 1983CE the prison doctor David Cooper and professor John Gunn (who was a consultant forensic scientist) sectioned Sutcliffe under the Mental Health Act and continued the process of having him transferred to a high security hospital with a specialist psychiatric unit, Broadmoor Hospital. Unfortunately for all concerned, all things Peter, all things Yorkshire Ripper, were political and therefore under the microscope of public scrutiny. A public who subconsciously believed the 'free' press, The Sun, The News of the World, The Mirror and The People and therefore could not suffer any injustice.

Thursday the 14th of April 1983CE, Newport Magistrates Court, Isle of Wight both Costello and Sutcliffe made an appearance, the Director of Prosecutions, Graham Grant-Whyte put forward the case. Sutcliffe had been attacked by Costello, two hospital officers had partially witnessed the scuffle and separated the fighting parties. Costello claimed that Sutcliffe had attacked him. (As some people say the best form of defence is attack).

The voices were still with Peter, a constant companion giving him advice when he felt depressed, offering him support and solace, boosting his morale. In Parkhurst, he was an unpopular prisoner, an unpopular person. He rose above it, didn't let it affect him, because he knew that they were ignorant and didn't understand. Their taunting and provoking were wasted on him. He never took any notice, but on occasions he did feel sorry for them, unable to understand their ignorance, unwilling to stoop to their level, their lack of knowledge, their small mindedness unable to comprehend his reasoning. Anyway he did not crave nor need their company. The moral high ground was his. He would not succumb to the sin of avarice, he would openly oppose it, like he had done the sin of lust, 'that is what is wrong with society today the greed immorality and depravity. All they think of is finance. There are no moral values at all' he thought, and the voice in his head agreed. There is a lot wrong with society today. It is depraved. 'Hasn't anyone got any morals anymore?' People don't understand, it is difficult being called nasty names. But Peter was the bigger man, he didn't harbour any grudges.

Wednesday the 3rd of August 1983 CE, a receiving order was made against Peter Sutcliffe to Bradford County Court, this was done by solicitors acting on behalf of Irene MacDonald (Jaynes mother). A receiving order was the first step to making Sutcliffe bankrupt. It would possibly enable those who had suffered at the Rippers hand, directly and indirectly to receive financial damages owed by Peter.

Thursday the 27th of October 1983 CE, Peter's attempt to avoid bankruptcy fails after a written plea submitted via his solicitors to rescind the receiving order is rejected.

Monday the 31st of October 1983CE Newport Crown Court, 1 Quay Street, Faulkner Rd, Newport, Isle of Wight, PO30. Judge Lewis McCreery was presiding over the trial. Mr. James Costello was charged with maliciously attacking Mr. Peter William Sutcliffe with intent to cause grievous bodily harm.

James dismissed his lawyers taking the decision to defend himself. This if anything added to the spectacle with Costello and Sutcliffe verbally sparring throughout the proceedings. Christopher Leigh acting on behalf of Peter and leading the prosecution used the platform to ensure and underline the fact that Peter was involved in this case, it should not affect the jury's ability to deliver a fair and impartial verdict.
"All men are equal before the law, be they high or low, good or bad, and the rule of law extends to our prisons as much as it does to the streets or our homes. That man Sutcliffe is just as entitled to the protection of the law as you or I". (Forget all things Peter William Sutcliffe,

forget all things Yorkshire Ripper). During the trial, Peter's feigned concern for his attacker and fellow man was highlighted during the court case.
"You need all the help you can get from psychiatrists, not from the courts".

Tuesday the 1st of November 1983CE, presiding Judge Lewis McCreery halted the trial, discharging the jury and ordering a re-trial.

Wednesday the 2nd of November 1983CE, a new jury were sworn in and the case was re-heard.
Doctor Brian Cooper, the principal medical officer at Parkhurst prison when cross examined explained that Mr. James Costello could react in a violent way as part of a symptom of the fact that he was suffering from a personality disorder of a psychiatric type.

Monday the 7th of November 1983CE, and a verdict was returned on Mr. James Costello, he was found guilty by the jury by a ten to two margin, of wounding Peter Sutcliffe with intent to cause grievous bodily harm. James did not react well, kicking open the dock door and vacating the dock swearing and abusing at the jurors.
"How can anyone use too much violence against the Ripper?"

Tuesday the 8th of November 1983CE, and Mr. James Costello is finally sentenced to a further five years penal servitude. Judge McCreery in sentencing Costello stated in his 'final' address to the court room and Costello.
"You are one of the most dangerous and evil men it has been my misfortune to encounter".
Oh the irony that these words were not aimed at Peter, Peter the victim? Costello harangued, heckled, argued and badgered the Judge throughout.
Costello in exasperation told the judge.
"I don't understand how any man can get sentenced for using too much violence against a guy who has killed 13 people and had me by the throat. I know I am a violent man. I was not well at the time. I was on my way to Broadmoor". Costello was an anti-hero hero, serving rough justice on the elite criminal class.

Wednesday the 30th of November 1983 CE, Peter William Sutcliffe is declared bankrupt at Bradford County Court.

Chapter 43
Peter Meets Keith

Time passed and the Yorkshire Ripper was continually in the press, he was often linked with unsolved attacks and murders other than the ones he had been charged with. The 1981 CE Byford Report, which had certain parts withheld from public consumption highlighted thirteen cases that may have been attributed to Peter Sutcliffe. The 1982 CE Sampson Report expanded on these thirteen cases. West Yorkshire Metropolitan Police Force still reeling from the bad press that had been laid at their door, decided it would be best practice/damage limitation to question the Ripper whilst he was in custody and find out if he was responsible for these additional attacks. This meant that at least it would be the Yorkshire force that uncovered them, a sort of perverse damage limitation. Assistant Chief Constable Colin Sampson knew that Detective Superintendent Keith Hellawell had built up a rapport with Sonia, (he had been a shoulder to cry on, a confidante, a helping hand and guide through her continued troubles in coming to terms with the fact that her husband was the infamous Yorkshire Ripper), when he had been assigned the job of dealing with Sonia Sutcliffe's complaint on how she was dealt with during the investigation into her husband. Sampson therefore earmarked Hellawell for a very strange and protracted investigation/interview process with the Yorkshire Ripper.

A jump back in time, way back to January 1981 CE. *Sonia wasn't one to suffer in silence and made numerous complaints about the police, their actions, attitude and how they handled the investigation. Assistant Chief Constable Colin Sampson assigned Keith Hellawell a rising star within the force to conduct an inquiry into the allegations of damage to Sonia's property, house and garage when the police searched her home. It was during this period that Sonia Sutcliffe and Keith Hellawell developed a friendship of sorts. This relationship would prove significant for all things Yorkshire Ripper.*

Detective Superintendent Keith Hellawell was a thorough and dedicated officer, articulate and affable but also with a steely and resolute character and on receiving the order from Sampson began to make plans on how best to tackle the task in hand. Firstly he decided to enrol the services of

Detective Inspector John Boyle who was an old adversary of Sutcliffe, Boyle had dealings with Sutcliffe from his arrest and eventual confession. He was also an integral part of the hunt for the Yorkshire Ripper, he was a link to the past, offering continuity, inside knowledge and a fast track think tank to all things Ripper, a walking talking data base. Boyle's local knowledge and historical understanding would be vital to the success of this mission, a counter mission to Sutcliffe's theological divine mission to rid the world of prostitution, their mission was to provide justice for victims who had suffered at the hands of Sutcliffe. But more importantly to preserve and maintain the good name of their beloved West Yorkshire Metropolitan Police Force?

The team set about their task to investigate, re-investigate seventy-eight unsolved attacks that could be the work of the Yorkshire Ripper. The team systematically set about reducing the number to a more manageable number. They worked tirelessly reducing the number initially to sixty, then down to forty-seven and finally the team were left with twenty-two possibles. These related to twelve in West Yorkshire and ten elsewhere. After further short listing, the number was reduced to a more realistic and workable ten, probables. The team then decided to re-investigate the ten Yorkshire Ripper probables. The team graded them from one to ten, number one being most probable and ten the least likely.

1. Tracey Browne, Silsden, attacked 27/08/1975 CE = admission, (of sorts) 1992 CE.
2. Ann Rooney, Horsforth, attacked 02/03/1979 CE = admission, (of sorts) 1992 CE.
3. Yvonne Mysliwiec, Ilkley, attacked 11/10/1979 CE.
4. Maureen Lea, Leeds, attacked 25/10/1980 CE.
5. Debra Schlesinger, Leeds, murdered 21/04/1977 CE.
6. Gloria Wood, Bradford, attacked 11/11/1974 CE.
7. Sixteen-year-old student, Harrogate, attacked 17/02/1979 CE.
8. Rosemary Stead, Bradford, attacked 06/01/1976 CE.
9. Maureen Hogan, Bradford, attacked 29/08/1976 CE.
10. Bradford stone in the sock attack September 1969 CE.

As part of his plan Detective Superintendent Keith Hellawell approached Sonia and explained that he had been ordered to reinvestigate attacks and murders that Peter may have perpetrated. Sonia facilitated the visit and smoothed the way for Keith to meet her estranged husband, Sonia was certain that it was all a waste of time, but Keith explained it was a necessary evil. Sonia grudgingly agreed.

"Peter's done nothing else. He's told the police all he knows...You'll be wasting your time...I'll tell him to expect you". This gave him a foot in the door allowing some credibility to build up a rapport and attempt to get Peter to admit to his previous indiscretions. At least it was a plan.

So in late 1983 CE, the duo of Detective Superintendent Keith Hellawell and Detective Inspector John Boyle set off for Southampton, with plethora of information, names, dates, locations and theories. They took the ferry crossing to the Isle of Wight and headed towards the daunting façade of Parkhurst Prison. On their arrival they first met the Governor who offered help and support to the team. He provided background information into Peter's mental state, Peter was still refusing to admit he was suffering from mental health problems and was therefore on no medication. The Governor explained that Peter was a model prisoner and explained to his two guests that he had reserved the Roman Catholic Priest's office for their tryst with Peter, he had put a lot of thought and consideration into this and explained that he felt it was an appropriate room for the interviews to be located. The room offered privacy but was familiar to Peter who had often visited the priest, so hopefully it would reassure Peter and provide a neutral venue for the initial ice breaker meeting.

Inside the Priest's office the furnishings were sparse but functional, it consisted of three metal frame chairs a wooden desk that had seen better days and a filing cabinet. The two officers sat down and prepared themselves for the arrival of Sutcliffe. Eventually Peter was escorted into the room. John proffered his hand, Peter seemed taken aback, eventually he placed his clammy hand in Keith's and gave him a firm handshake. Keith introduced himself and John to Peter, Peter didn't seem to recognise John, his old sparring partner. Both police officers felt slightly unnerved by the dark staring eyes of Peter. Dark staring eyes that had now taken on mythological importance. Dark staring eyes now synonymous with the Yorkshire Ripper, a cloak of malevolent evil cast upon a working-class man from Bingley. A cloak of loathing, aversion, repulsion but also a strange attraction. A fixation. Then he spoke, his high-pitched Bingley accent ill at ease with the beast that was the Yorkshire Ripper.
"Sonia told me about you. She say's you're alreight".

And so it began, Peter took centre stage. Mints, (bribes), his favourite sweets. Ice breaker, head breaker, life taker. Reminisce about the good old days, his 'active' days where the plague of the Yorkshire Ripper cast a dark shadow across the north of England. Keith, Peter and John old adversaries, now all pretence, intense ingratiating, nauseating...wrong.
"You could have bumped into me when I was on my mission". Verbal jousting, banter and affability, an agreeable start, but a direct question about an attack was met with stony silence. Christmas cards and seasons greetings, newspaper scandals, teasing progress. Months became years, progress was slow, Parkhurst became Broadmoor. But still persistence wins the day.

Wednesday the 8th of February 1984 CE, Peter William Sutcliffe is granted an automatic discharge from bankruptcy this will happen in five years' time. The 8th of February 1989 CE. The only known asset that Peter has, his half share of 6 Garden Lane, however this had long since been transferred to Sonia in a maintenance settlement completed prior to his bankruptcy. This meant that Peter had nothing, therefore his victims could receive nothing.

Tuesday the 27th March 1984CE, Peter William Sutcliffe is finally transferred to Broadmoor Hospital, (under Section forty-seven of the Mental Health Act 1883) this is by order of the Conservative Home Secretary Leon Brittan. As with all things Ripper this cannot be done in a normal manner. A secret transfer saw two police cars escort a police van that contained Peter the seventy or so miles from the doors of HMP Parkhurst to the doors of Broadmoor Hospital. A little bit of over kill but Peter was used to that. One to the front, one to the rear, the Yorkshire Ripper in the van sandwiched in between. Inside the back of the van with Peter were six prison officers to ensure that nothing untoward happened, there was to be no escape for spring heeled Jack. Possibly an over exuberance on the part of the authorities, however they were probably still smarting from the humiliation this felon had caused their colleagues.

Chapter 44
Broadmoor Hospital

Broadmoor Hospital, Berkshire Peter Sutcliffe 7589
Broadmoor Hospital
Crowthorne, Berkshire
R611-7E6
United Kingdom

Peter thrived in his new environment, he settled in well to his new home. The daily sanctuary, solace from 21:00 hours through until 07:30 hours, eight and a half hours of refuge, asylum from the asylum, a haven from the rigours of daily madness. Free from harm, free from harassment, free?

07:30 and the patient's room is unlocked, an unwelcome intrusion the reality of the hospital regime impinges on the individual. The doors remain unlocked for a further five and a half hours, then at 13:00 hours the patient's doors are locked against them. This is Broadmoor policy to encourage socialising because it is deemed as therapeutically beneficial, although this is not always the case as Peter and Broadmoor found to their cost. Patients are forced together in various degrees during this eight-hour period, until 21:00 hours, when sanctuary is once again upon them. 21:00 hours the curfew of sanctuary.

Uncomfortable, out of control, disturbing, perturbing, noise annoys, disconcerting, upsetting and uncalled for.

Peter is the special one, he is tuned into a higher plain. He had a God given right to kill prostitutes. The voices are like a dog whistle inaudible to noncanine creatures. Like an extra sensory perception only available to selected individuals, the chosen few. Operating on a different frequency to the lesser mortals, they could tune into the Holy vibes of radio God transmitting to the susceptible, the ill and the unwell, or to the chosen ones. The voices soothe Peter, act as an ally. Their messages, their suggestions are fruitless, Peter's circumstances of confinement ensure that Peter is not influenced to act upon their promptings. Peter believed he had mastered the voices through self-control. Peter believed he could influence and control even God. Transmissions from God are now words of guidance and wisdom, no longer direct orders, no longer instructions, Parkhurst Prison had seen the end to the mission. Now his mission over Peter knew he would not kill again. Peter was a man of peace, he was no longer a threat. Peter was a man of peace.

Peter continued to refuse medication choosing to deny his illness, offer it no recognition, because Peter was in control. Peter only conformed to his captors on Peter's terms, when he was happy to do so, after all he was a personal friend of God. He would do what he wanted and was afraid of no man.

Art attack, old bed sheet canvas, paint, brushes, pallet original pictures or copies of old masters.

Control was intrinsic to him, order was control, control was deep-seated to his condition and he knew his rights. A highly controlled schizophrenic unravelling out of control into a fully-fledged paranoid schizophrenic.

The sparse bedside table on which Peter has placed his rubber plant, highlights Peter's minimalistic approach to room décor. Music cassettes, mineral water, books, a lockable photograph box which provides the myth of privacy and a storage place for his letters. In tandem with this Peter William Sutcliffe was a walking office, carrying personal papers, secrets safe from prying eyes. Private information free from institutional intervention.

Thursday the 18th of December 1986 CE, a Bradford County Court judge rules that 6 Garden Lane, Heaton is to be sold and Peter's half of the proceeds from the sale will be used to contribute towards repatriation damage claims made against Peter, by his victims and their surviving relations.

1992 CE press sensationalism, the great escape? Hacksaw blades not for decapitation purposes but allegedly for escape. Are found in Peter's room. A storm in a teacup, a teacup in a storm, a falsehood, a set up. Saturday the 23rd of May 1992 CE, Broadmoor Hospital release a press statement that says two hacksaw blades were found in Peter's room, these had been planted by another individual, an inept attempt at a tabloid scoop. The hospital was satisfied that this was not part of an escape plan and Peter denied any knowledge of the blades. Like he had repeatedly denied any knowledge of the murders and attacks he committed.

Thursday the 28th of April 1994 CE Sonia (nee Szurma) Sutcliffe is granted a divorce from Peter William Sutcliffe, this is granted at Reading County Court.

1994 CE was the year he said goodbye to the constant companion he'd carried in his head, well he hadn't said goodbye, because that would be mad and Peter wasn't mad. Peter decided to accept the medical help on offer. He now realised he had been ill during his missionary work. It had taken a long time for Peter to come to terms with the fact that he was ill. For long enough Peter refused any offer of help, denying the need, avoiding the diagnosis and rejecting treatment. Doctor Horne (Broadmoor's consultant psychiatrist) had spoken to Peter repeatedly, Doctor Horne had explained to Peter repeatedly, now Peter had decided to listen. Doctor Horne had promised to provide Peter with booklets and leaflets about his illness, allowing Peter to study and understand his condition, enabling Peter to come to terms with his illness.

Prescribed injections of Stellazine and Depixol ensured Peter was well and kept out unwelcome visitors inside his head. Late 2000 CE saw Peter's condition stabilise and improve drastically towards the end of the year. Doctor Horne became a constant, an oracle, a soothsayer to Peter. So much more than a Doctor, an advocate, a confidante, a teacher encouraging him to learn and understand his illness.

It could be deduced that such an acknowledgement would/could defer responsibility onto the illness and distance himself from the crimes, acknowledgement would/could lead to treatment, treatment would/could result in a cure, would/could result in a cure and then the possibility of release.

Chapter 45
Peter Meets Paul

Paul Wilson was a stocky man. Paul had been convicted of robbery, Paul had been diagnosed as suffering from mental illness. Paul did not like sex offenders, Paul had a pathological hatred of sex offenders, Paul disliked the fact that he had to share the same roof as 'these scum'. Paul, whose sanity was in question was fully aware that the Yorkshire Ripper was a sex attacker/offender. Paul knew that Peter William Sutcliffe was the Yorkshire Ripper. Paul was unhappy, he could not be held responsible for his actions. Paul believes he has been pushed into this particularly violent and uncomfortable course of action.

It was Friday evening on the 23rd of February 1996 CE when Paul headed onto the Henley Ward, where he targeted a private room in the Broadmoor Hospital where he knew Peter William Sutcliffe, the Yorkshire Ripper resided. Paul held a pair of headphones loosely in his hands. He tapped on the door and entered.

"Can I borrow a video Peter?" came his friendly enquiry. He closed the door behind him to ensure the pair had privacy. Then all hell was unleashed Paul punched Peter in the eye, the power of his thick set body and the shock of the unprovoked attack briefly incapacitating Peter. Paul jumped on top of Peter, forcing home the advantage of the surprise attack, hooking the flex around his victim's neck and tightening the grip.

Peter screamed, breaking the relative serenity of the ward, his scream alerted two fellow patients. Jamie Devitt, (aged thirty-six) convicted of murder in January 1982 CE and Kenneth Erskine AKA the Stockwell Strangler (aged thirty-five) a convicted serial killer, who was arrested in July 1986CE. The two 'heroes' reacted to the commotion raising the alarm, the pair then followed the noise to its source. Jamie and Kenneth entered Peter's humble abode, Paul was using the flex of the headphones to garrotte Peter. Paul was physically restrained by the hospital warders.

The scuffle was over, Paul was removed and taken into an isolation unit to calm down, throughout this period Paul protested vehemently about the sex offenders and his hatred for them.

No news from Broadmoor Hospital, no news from Alan Franey the general manager of Broadmoor, no police investigation requested. Was this an attempt to cover up the incident? Broadmoor sirens fell silent, news was sparse, and no news is good news? Well not for Peter. Broadmoor senior managers decided to order a cover up. A news blackout, staff members were discreetly reminded of their employer's code of conduct especially with regards to patient confidentiality and data protection, staff members were informed of the consequences if these rules were broken. The fact that the police were not invited to investigate the assault underlined the hospitals unwillingness to take the matter further. Alan Franey Broadmoor's general manager spoke only to dismiss.

"You know I cannot and will not comment on any incident which involves one of my patients, especially one who is of such high profile. It is hospital policy not to refer to individual patients and I have to respect that confidentially'.'

Excuses and cover ups were suggested, Thames Valley Police were eventually invited into Broadmoor to investigate the incident and ultimately Peter decided not to press charges.

Chapter 46
Peter Meets Ian

Monday the 10th of March 1997CE another day in Broadmoor maximum security hospital. Ian Kay (aged twenty-nine) was a petty thief with a fetish for Woolworths stores, he had first been jailed in Christmas 1991CE for sixteen robberies and attempting to kill a shop assistant. Released from Maidstone Prison on licence Ian was allowed home leave in August 1994 CE he duly absconded and went on to commit seven further store robberies, culminating in the murder of John Penfold an assistant manager at Woolworths Teddington store, Middlesex, on the 15th of November 1994 CE, where he stabbed his victim through the heart with a four inch blade, whilst attempting to steal one pound from the till. In his attempt to escape capture, Kay dropped the two fifty pence pieces. A senseless crime that provoked an outcry as to how this menace could have been allowed out of prison to reoffend.

July 1995 CE Kay was found guilty of murder and sentenced to a minimum of twenty-two years imprisonment, his defence lawyers used psychiatrists reports to argue that Kay was unable to control his violent impulses due to an abnormal personality disorder. This argument fell on deaf ears. Ian Kay became known as the 'Woolworths Killer' and Kay was subsequently transferred to Broadmoor Hospital when his mental health deteriorated even further. Ian had issues. Ian wanted to be top dog. Ian saw Peter as the way to gain that status. Ian was a man with a plan. Ian had only been at Broadmoor a short while when he hatched his plan to kill the Yorkshire Ripper.

March 1997 CE, Stephen Dorrell the Conservative Government Health Secretary had revealed his ministers were to undertake a review that would incorporate quality of care and security at Broadmoor Hospital. This may have been a result of repeated concerns raised by The Prison Officers Association highlighting staffing level and security issues at the maximum-security hospital, stating that some patients openly intimidated staff, this was exacerbated by problems of inexperienced nurses.

Ian Kay shared art therapy classes with Peter, they also shared the same mealtimes. Kay saw Peter as a way of cementing his 'top dog' status, Peter was a fast track ticket to achieving this status, gaining the respect of his fellow patients, ensuring that Ian would gain respect and 'carry' the fear factor. In the build up to his attack Ian initially attempted to conceal a razor blade, which he planned to implant into a toothbrush handle, but hospital staff discovered the razor blade and Ian hid his true intentions by claiming he'd procured the blade in an attempt to take his own life. Ian hid the truth, Ian hid his plan, Ian was going to cut Peter's jugular vein, right and left and then watch him bleed out and die. Ian had always wanted to kill Peter ever since he had been transferred to Broadmoor. Ian wanted to choke the life out of the Yorkshire Ripper, Ian was going to throttle the life out of the Yorkshire Ripper, Ian was going to provide justice for all his victims, Ian was going to become famous through his actions. Ian was to share top 'dog therapy' classes with Peter, whether or not he was compliant.

Ian had become more volatile his predilection for violence was out of control, he had attacked two other patients in the months leading to the attack on Peter. Ian is somewhat of a conundrum, outwardly he portrayed an impression of superiority, swanning around the ward like he owned the place, whilst inwardly he was insecure and scared, believing that he would become a victim. Ian therefore adhered to the motto, the best form of defence was attack and to prove himself he went on the offensive in the hope that the fear factor his reputation carried would ensure his safety. Ian was in a private room on the Henley Ward next door but one to Peter's and this upset him, he'd lost control, going crazy and protesting that it was wrong that the Yorkshire Ripper should be his neighbour.

Ian realised that he was soon to be moved again, this time to a different section of the hospital. Ian did not want to be robbed of his opportunity. Ian decided now was the time to put his plan into action. Ian Kay knocked on Peter's door, Ian was going to ask for an envelope and then Ian was going to attack Peter. Ian wanted his fifteen minutes of fame, fifteen minutes of frenzy. Andy Warhol was attributed with the phrase, *'In the future, everyone will be world famous for fifteen minutes',* his take on throw away media fashion and the cult of celebrity. Peter had become a creature of habit, he liked to stay on the ward and respond to his numerous pen-pals, and most of the other patients would have been attending courses or working so the ward was peaceful and calm without the hustle and bustle of most of the patients. Ian decided to seize the moment.

Ian asked a fellow patient to put on music, his plan was to use the music to mask his attack, music to attack serial killers by. First the trial run circa 14:00 hours. Ian knocks on Peter's room door.
"Can I borrow an envelope?"
Peter took one from his supplies and gave it to Ian and both men returned to the monotony of their day.

Circa 15:00 hours Ian found himself at Peter's door again, in his hand a Parker roller-ball pen, in his pocket an electrical flex, a make-shift garrotte perhaps. Peter walked to his door, opened it, Ian repeated his earlier request.
"Can I borrow an envelope?" Peter absent minded turned to get an envelope from his pile, Ian entered the room and closed the door behind himself. As Peter turned to face Ian and pass him another envelope, Kay attacked. Strike whilst the victim is unsuspecting, undefended, unaware, unready, a pale shadow of a Ripper-esque attack. The younger man

used his superior strength to pin Peter to the floor of his room, he then brought the pen towards Peter's left eye. The point, the tip of the pen found its mark one, two, three, four, five, six times. Blood spurted from Peter's face. Ian pushing it home deeper into the iris, the cornea, the pupil, deep into the dark sinister evil eyes. Deep into the disconcerting, unnerving eyes. The eyes are the gateway to the soul. Peter's eyes dark and sinister EVIL incarnate. Revenge, recognition. Ian the struggle won, Ian the stronger of the two men, Ian forced home his advantage. Squeals of pain muffled by Ian's hand and the loud music of a fellow patient. Partially blind was not good enough for Ian, Peter needed to pay for his sins, with his life. Ian drove the pen into Peter's right eye, one, two, three, four times. The shock of the attack had subsided as had Ian's initial fury, Peter finally managed to grapple the pen away from his eyes. The elder man's stamina finally showing through. In an attempt to complete his objective Ian clasped his hands around Peter's neck and attempted to choke the life out of him. His decision not to use the electrical flex may have saved Peter's life. Perhaps Ian was like Peter and didn't like the intimacy of the act of strangulation. Peter had tried it once on Marguerite Walls, when he tried again on Uphadya Bandaras he failed terribly. Ian later reflected boasting at his actions.
"I should have kneed him in the face a few times". Similar to Peter's hammer, stun technique. *"I should have straddled his body and throttled him with my bare hands".*
The bang of Peter's room door on the Henley ward as Ian exited the crime scene caught the attention of the nurse on duty, the nurse noticed that Ian's shirt was bloodstained. The nurse ran into Peter's room and discovered its occupier writhing, thrashing, squirming on the floor, his body wracked and distorted by pain, his hands covering his eyes, trying to stem the flow of blood.
"I can't see, I can't see".
Kay believing his mission complete left the prone Sutcliffe seemingly lifeless on the floor, he banged the room door shut and headed towards the roof. Hospital orderlies saw Kay who was covered in Sutcliffe's blood and restrained the assailant. Kay had blood on his face, his hands, he also had it on his clothes. Other hospital staff rushed into Peter's room, unsure what they would find. They were presented with Peter who stood distraught in the bathroom area, his back arched, clinging onto the wash hand basin.
"I can't see. I think I'm blind", he mumbled hysterically.
The Devil will find work for idol hands, Kay explained his action's.
"It was the Devil's work. He said God told him to kill thirteen women, and I say the Devil told me to kill him because of that. He killed thirteen women and deserved what happened to him".

Peter was initially seen by a doctor at Broadmoor, he was then taken to Frimley Park Hospital, Portsmouth Road, Frimley GU16; which had a specialist eye unit. Peter received emergency treatment from an eye specialist. Peter then returned to Broadmoor. Wednesday the 28th of January 1998 CE, Peter is taken the seven miles to the specialist eye unit, where he was assessed. As a result of Ian's attack Peter had lost the sight in his left eye, whilst the sight in his right eye was drastically diminished. The right eye also suffered reduced movement and impaired vision.

Tuesday the 27th of January 1998 CE Ian Kay appeared at Reading Crown Court, charged with the attempted murder of Peter William Sutcliffe, a charge that Ian openly admitted. Mr Justice Keene sentenced Ian to be detained without restriction, citing section 37 of the Mental Health Act 1983, in summing up he told Kay.
"You ought to be detained in hospital for medical treatment. You are in the best place at the moment".

March 1998 CE, the Sutcliffe family wrote a letter to Jack Straw, the Home Secretary. They made an appeal on compassionate grounds that Peter be transferred to Ashworth Hospital, Liverpool. They cited that the two-hundred-and-eighty-mile journey to Broadmoor from West Yorkshire was making visiting difficult as travel was getting increasingly difficult.

Regular visits from Sonia his ex-wife, break the monotony. Sonia was a driving force in Peter seeking compensation from his recent attack by Ian Kay in 1997 CE. Sonia cajoled, supported, worked, helped, aided and abetted Peter in completing the reams of paperwork in relation to his claim for damages following his injuries at the hand of his attacker.

Friday May the 2nd 1997 CE, Shipley, West Yorkshire Sonia is married to Michael Woodward a hairdresser.

Wednesday the 28th of January 1998CE, Ian Kay, AKA the 'Woolworths Killer', admitted to stabbing the 'Yorkshire Ripper' in both eyes with a pen in a prison hospital for the criminally insane. In no uncertain terms, Kay told the court he had meant to attack Peter with a razor embedded in a toothbrush handle.
"I was going to ... walk into the room and cut his jugular vein on both sides and wait there until he was dead... He said God told him to kill 13 women, and I say the devil told me to kill him because of that".

Chapter 47
Broadmoor Routine

Throughout his hospital stay Peter remained in contact with his father John, John posting his son phone cards to help facilitate this. Peter ever the dutiful son ringing him fortnightly, their Tuesday chats from 18:30 hours to 20:00 hours became a regular occurrence and proved good therapy for both parties. The pair last saw each other face to face in a 1993CE and when John's health deteriorated in early1999CE, unfortunately John Sutcliffe had been diagnosed with cancer of the bladder and this was compounded by chronic heart trouble. As a result both parties looked forward to their fortnightly chats even more than they had done previously.

1999CE, and Peter reflected upon his life. Maybe if he could have his time again, maybe if he'd have found religion earlier or maybe the brand delivered by the Jehovah's Witnesses things could have been different. Maybe? But you can't cry over spilt milk can you? Becoming a Jehovah's Witness had turned his life around, he contemplated and concluded that if he'd known what he knew at this moment in time back in 1974CE, it would have maybe all turned out differently. The world was after all on the cusp of a brave new world, a new millennium, a new hope. A tangible excitement was in the air and this atmosphere had seemingly rubbed off on Peter. A new kind of optimism.

Peter was a caring, sharing person anybody who really knew him could see through the lies printed in the papers and broadcast on the radio and television. Big hearted Peter, who aided and assisted a blind fellow patient, filling in his 'friends' menu list, how altruistic. Peter was a reformed character, Peter had gone through a reformation, and he refuted his past. However no remorse for his victims just sorrow for himself. Peter is there to listen, Peter is there to help, Peter is kind, Saint Peter?

Sutcliffe previously relaxed through his artistic bent attending classes in oil painting, however the anti-psychotic medication he was prescribed dried up his creative juices and left him uninspired. Formerly his paintings were of a reasonable quality and the subject matter was predominantly religious or historic figures. Although Sutcliffe is contrite in his enforced reflective state he realises that this is a price worth paying to be free from the voices, 1994 CE was the year he said goodbye to the constant companion and took his first steps to mental health.

On occasions Peter fell into the trap of self-pity, bemoaning his poor eyesight, I don't write as much as I'd like, I find it difficult after being blinded in one eye by another inmate. A constant victim, self-righteous, self-centred, self-effacing. The seriousness of his crime depreciating with every passing moment.

The fact that Peter had admitted his transgressions and accepted the medical help on offer ultimately projected his sins onto his illness thus metaphorically washing his hands of his actions to a degree that would enable him possibly to taste freedom once more.

Peter had served approximately two thirds of his prison tariff, there was hope, there was light at the end of the tunnel. Narcissistic, vain, self-absorbed, self-important, self-loving, self-admiring, self, selfish, selfless. Manipulative, self-motivated, freedom.

Peter knew he was right all along, why had they not listened to him when he told them about the voices, way back in 1981 CE. Why did they torture him so, bait and taunt him, why? Peter knew he was not mad, if anything they were momentary lapses of self-control. Temporary mental aberrations, his theological mission to rid the world of prostitution and make the world a better place for all. Peter would set the record straight, Peter wanted vindication, and Peter wanted justice. Forgotten was the inconvenient truth of DIY gimp pants, sexual intercourse, sexual mutilation and masturbation, hidden a false history that had become the one version of the truth.

The Broadmoor Hospital annual tribunal system enabled patients to be assessed, Peter petitioned for a transfer to Park Lane Hospital a high-security psychiatric hospital, Parkbourn, Liverpool L31 1HW. It was built as an overspill for Broadmoor in the 1970's CE and this was geographically more suited to Peter's free external support network of family and friends. This petition was unsuccessful.

There were thirty high risk patients on the Taunton Ward, Somerset House on the third floor, Peter held down a cleaning job, earning eight pounds a week cleaning the bathrooms and toilets on the Taunton Ward. This suited Peter's needs, allowing him more time to stay on the ward giving him more time for his bible studies and letter writing.

OCD, obsessive compulsive disorder, self-obsessed with personal hygiene, self-conscious. Jeans, trainers, black jumper or cardigan and/or tracksuit top was his attire and he was impeccable in his appearance. The arch manipulator, a user, devising personal tasks and quests for unsuspecting members of his entourage, family, friends and followers to fulfil for the sole gain of Peter Sutcliffe.

Peter had his heart set on being allowed out of the hospital, this was unrealistic due to his profile, the political mill stone of the Yorkshire Ripper. He had ideas that he would be able to have supervised/chaperoned outings and this was a goal to which he seriously aspired. In essence this highlighted his detachment from reality and contributed further to his hatred of the media if that was possible. His detachment became more polarised the longer he was incarcerated and exaggerated his inability to understand his predicament.

Peter struggled to come to terms with the common mentality, he was unable to tap into the common psyche and often showed open contempt upon people he considers to be mentally inferior. His intellectual snobbery is ill conceived and his dismissive demeanour sneering and almost taunting others for their supposed lack of refinement. His misconceived understanding and self-grandeur reflected poorly upon Peter. It showed he believed his own press, words and arguments portrayed about him by the media who were in his eyes always wrong and one of the root causes of the society he had set out to destroy.

Broadmoor Hospital was a more laissez faire regime than the prison environment, Peter would be allowed five two-hour weekday visits per month, along with weekly Saturday and Sunday visits. Peter would choose to vet his visitor roster to ensure that no unwelcome visitors came to deliver him a nasty surprise.

Pious, Christ like posing and posturing, crucifixes, Holy pictures, meditation, sanctimonious superior high Catholic Church ilk. Sunday service in Broadmoor Chapel, Peter remained detached aloof, deep in prayer a silent thinker, at one with God. An example a shining light for all to aspire to. For no matter how cruel and unscrupulous people have been to him over the past years, Peter is not bitter. He feels sorry for the ignoramuses with their misguided attitudes. He believed that the irresponsible press was directly a cause of the state of society. Oh what has happened to the moral majority, the great and the good? Are they smothered in a blanket of greed and self-pity? Hasn't anyone got any morals anymore?

Like a good Christian he has turned the other cheek, was this tongue in cheek lip service, for when did attacking defenceless women with hammers, knives, sharpened screwdrivers adhere to the Christian faith, deluded and confused or both.

Chapter 48
Yorkshire Ripper created 1967CE expired 2001CE

January 2001CE, the Yorkshire Ripper is dead, long live Peter William Sutcliffe, the fifty-four-year-old inmate of Broadmoor Hospital a high-security psychiatric hospital, believes he is cured. His psychiatrist Doctor Andrew Horne had worked with and assessed his patient and come to the conclusion in Sutcliffe's 'Mental Health Review Tribunal' that 'Sutcliffe could no longer be considered a danger'. Peter William Sutcliffe therefore informed his nearest and dearest that he was cured of his affliction, his alter ego, his doppelganger. This gave Peter hope, he had finally freed himself from the evil monster who had haunted his waking hours for over thirty years. Peter could now see a way out, a light at the end of the tunnel. He had accumulated twenty years of incarceration and had been sentenced to thirty years, with a recommendation that he served his full tariff.

Now cured he was two thirds of his way through his custodial sentence. He therefore possibly had only ten more years of penal servitude remaining. His cure had eradicated the voices in his head, the voices he believed came from God, the voices that instructed him to maim and murder a multitude of women in the name of his mission. Sutcliffe turned his back on his catholic beliefs and became interested in the Jehovah's Witnesses, receiving regular visits from their ministers in his secure hospital home, regularly participating and receiving bible classes, reading passages of the bible and praying together. The ministers call and see Sutcliffe on Tuesdays and Thursdays. Peter enjoys this pastime and prefers the Jehovah's Witness lessons to that of other denominations. He reflects that their teachings have helped contribute to his rehabilitation.
Sutcliffe reflected his past actions, he now viewed these as misdemeanours.
"I now realise how ill I was all those years ago". He confided with his visitors, that he also agreed with Doctor Horne's diagnosis.
"I'm so pleased as he is so right".

Doctor Horne, leading light in the field of psychiatry further elaborated his thoughts on his patient, stating that Sutcliffe had improved considerably and he regarded him as a model inmate. Living quietly in solitude, reading and studying the bible and listening to the radio. Sutcliffe is actively encouraged to participate in visits to ensure he maintains an understanding of the outside world, this can be achieved and promoted through face to face interaction with family and friends. Peter portrayed control he told the authorities, he was well, he told the authorities that he was sane, he was well and preferred prison life to that of what he might expect in hospital. His stoic endurance in the face of great adversity.

One day becomes the next, yesterday, today, tomorrow. Peter takes each day as it comes. Up and out of bed for 6:30 hours for his ablutions, then back to his room on the Dorchester ward to dress himself for the coming day. Once dressed he may lie on his bed and listen to the radio until breakfast which is served at 8:00 hours. After breakfast it's back to the confines of his room, where generally he'll set about reading any 'fan' mail, then he writes his replies, this is a difficult task for Sutcliffe who was blinded in one eye in a vicious attack in1998CE. His handwriting is neat and flowing unlike the scribble of Wearside Jack. He writes diligently with his left hand, the devil's hand, the hand that committed atrocious injuries to countless defenceless women. He may then study the bible, working to prepare for future lessons with the Jehovah's Witness ministers who regularly visit. This is something he seems to openly enjoy.

The Lord Chief Justice, Lord Woolf, further fuelled Sutcliffe's hopes of freedom when he claimed that sentence 'tariffs' should not be set by politicians. However doubt looms and the context of his crimes lead a Home Office spokesman to point out, if the inmate did apply for parole, it would take a very brave Home Secretary to agree that Sutcliffe was cured and should be freed.

Sonia Szurma/Sutcliffe/Woodhead visits on occasions, the former couple are still on good terms. Peter appreciates her loyalty (a trait he holds in high regard), he is reassured by it. Also the loyalty of his family and a few close friends, their steadfast support has helped his mental health improve.

August 2001 CE Peter changed his surname by deed poll from Sutcliffe to Coonan, his mother's maiden name. He explained that he had done this because he was struggling to get a bank account under his original moniker. Banks and Building Societies shied away from doing business with Peter, he alleged that they were in fear of breaching data security and confidentiality in light of over exuberant press scrutiny. He alleged that their concern was self-centred through concern that Sutcliffe/Coonan would sue at the first opportunity. The Bradford and Bingley Building Society would have been an ideal choice for Sutcliffe to become a customer. Which bank or building society was the lucky recipient of his custom, who knows? Changing his name was further distancing himself from the past, from the Yorkshire Ripper.

Peter explains how his surname is now redundant. Sutcliffe is possibly the final victim of the Yorkshire Ripper, Coonan is now the order of the day. Peter listens to Mozart, it calms and relaxes him. Peter likes to listen to classical music and watch films and recently procured a video cassette recorder from Argos. Peter is a reformed man, fat and bloated with inactivity.

Tuesday the 28th of May 2002 CE, the European Court of Human Rights ruled that sentencing of prisoners should not fall to politicians but to the judiciary. This gave Peter a chance of freedom, however slim this was. The Home Secretary could no longer set the minimum tariff and extend sentences to 'whole life' tariff, ensuring they would never see freedom. Peter was one of a group of a band of twenty prisoners that it was deemed must never be released.

Monday the 25th of November 2002 CE, the Law Lords supported the European Court of Human Rights and recommended that the Home Secretary should not be able to overrule/extend the sentencing of the judiciary.

In the case of Sutcliffe, and many others, it would be extremely unlikely they would ever be released. In an article in the Sunday Telegraph the previous day, it was reported that there was the possibility that police would lay new charges against some murderers to keep them from being considered for release after their original minimum sentencing was completed. It was reported that West Yorkshire detectives were confident they could bring new charges against Sutcliffe with regards to the 1977 CE murder of Debra Schlesinger and the 1980 CE attack on a Leeds art student, an open secret in the guise of Maureen Lea.

He was sentenced to life for each, with a recommendation that he serve at least 30 years.

2005 CE, uninterested in his past transgressions, Peter explains to his doctors.
"I'm weary of talking about the past and all that tragedy. It's constantly brought up by an army of doctors and psychiatrists".
Peter looks to the future in a positive frame of mind.
"There are hopes for the future". I have an appeal hearing against conviction and sentence".
Peter does not believe it when people tell him he will die in incarceration. Peter's future is bright. Peter is delusional, has Peter's mental illness really been resolved, or is he just in denial.

Long distance love affairs, personalised pen letters to a gaggle of female admirers, writing responses into the small hours. Once a postcard from Hell, a small village in Norway and Peter added in his prose. *'Not many people can say they've been to Hell and back! Tee Hee! Mind you I guess I have, with all the torment I went through during those horrible years'.* Self-centred, self-obsessed no remorse for his poor defenceless victims, just woe is me to the third degree.

Peter's neat and flowing handwriting mirrored how he wanted to be perceived. Fan mail, pen pals, love letters, he should set up a fan club. Julie, Sandra Olive, Diane and Pam. Pam Mills was from Leicester, and had cultivated a relationship with Peter.

Pam Mills Peter's prison pen pal, the Mills and Boon rose is the rose of romance, a rumour that romance was on the cards, in his letter, in her letters, in the air. Peter refuted claims of wedding bells. Pam Mills was a grandmother from Leicester and was thirty-nine when she started writing to Peter in 1990 CE. Pam felt sorry for prison inmates and after her divorce, she began to write to prisoners. Even though she knew they had done something wrong and deserved to be behind bars, an inner compulsion, and compassion ensured she struck up a number of correspondences, these were her prison pen pals. Pam had always been fascinated by the Yorkshire Ripper and had read various books about his crimes, she'd always found Peter a handsome man, once his identity had been revealed, a real head turner and saw no harm in contacting him. Over the years Pam has written to Peter over three-thousand times.

In 1995 CE Pam physically met Peter in the flesh, travelling to Broadmoor to meet him face to face. Once a week she would follow this ritual, leaving her Midlands home at 06:00 hours catching two trains and a taxi, to get down to Broadmoor Hospital. For love knows no boundaries. There she would spend five hours chatting with Peter locked in conversation. At one such visit Peter gave Pam a ring. Pam was so happy and contented, the pair made plans about the possibility of a wedding ceremony at the chapel in the hospital, they were targeting 2005 CE. Unfortunately the relationship was to fall on rocky times. Pam and Peter were engaged to be married, however circa 2005 CE Pam succumbed to pressure from her son Darren Platts, who had allegedly been forced out of his Ellesmere Road, Leicester home due to his mother's long distance love affair and association with the Yorkshire Ripper. The couple also shared numerous phone calls, Darren inadvertently answered one of these phone calls and was horrified to realise he was talking to the Yorkshire Ripper, horrified he begged his mother to end her relationship with Peter.

May 2004CE Peter requests a move to Wakefield High Security Prison in attempt to be closer to his dying father. Peter asked if there was a possibility of him being removed from hospital care and placed into a prison environment. Unfortunately Peter never got to see his father before he died. On Friday the 25th of June 2004CE John William Sutcliffe passed away at the age of eighty-one, he died at Manorlands Hospice in Oxenhope on the outskirts of Keighley; his funeral was held on Tuesday the 29th of June 2004CE at Oakworth Crematorium. Peter did not make a formal request to the Prison Service for compassionate leave to attend his father's funeral. The Prison Service possibly breathed a collective sigh of relief that Peter did not make the request, the potential logistic headache may have been refused due to the fact that Peter's presence at the funeral could constitute a security risk. Within the walls of Broadmoor Hospital, it was seen as a prudent move to place Peter on suicide watch, a purely precautionary measure, but better safe than sorry. This was due to the understandably depressed state Peter was in due to his father's death.

As a result of these events Labour Home Secretary David Blunkett began the planning for Sutcliffe's brief release, his party colleague and successor as Home Secretary Charles Clarke endorsed the plan of a day trip to the seaside.

Monday 17th January 2005 CE, early morning 5:30 hours, a small group of men embark on a very controversial journey, a journey that will hit the headlines when it is revealed. The seaside jaunt was prescribed by Broadmoor doctors, seeing the decline in their patient since his father's death and funeral back in June 2004 CE. This prescription was endorsed by the politicians who agreed that this visit would provide closure, this visit would hopefully prevent Peter from plunging into another episode of psychotic depression. It was planned that Peter was to visit the site where his father's ashes had been scattered.

Peter and a four strong hospital team arrive at the Cumbrian coastal village of Arnside at 10:00 hours, the five men disembark their vehicle, limbs stiff from the two-hundred- and sixty-mile journey. The vehicle a high security van looks out of place on the desolate sea front. The five men form a group at the side of the vehicle using the side of the van to shield from the elements. A brief discussion ensues and two of the men peel away from the group, a certain Mr Peter Coonan and a social worker, his social worker, they manoeuvre to a precise position, the place where Peter's late father, John William Sutcliffe's ashes were buried on the beach. Using photographs taken by his family at the time of the original scattering of the ashes to pinpoint the place his father's last earthly remains were scattered. The pair stand-alone, forlorn, the elder his head bowed in contemplation, the cold wind blows in from the sea. Guilt, sadness, hatred, love, fear, loathing, respect introspection, rejection, thirty minutes, one half hour, the social worker walks away leaving the mourning inmate to his soul searching. Unaccompanied, unfettered, undercover, covert, freedom of a sort, as the four men looked on. The beast is free? But the beast no longer exists, he is replaced by an old, sad and lonely man. The lone figure turns and walks to the group *"OK chaps, let's go back to the van"*. Another mission successfully completed another discussion with God. The five men walk back along the beach to the parked van, they climb into the vehicle and set off back to Broadmoor at 11:30 hours.

Peter had pledged that he would return to Arnside and pray at the place where his father's ashes were scattered. Peter forced the hand of the authorities warning that he would take his case to the European Court of Human Rights if it was necessary. A round trip of over five-hundred miles. A rite of passage, Peter returned to the safety of his room and the walls of Broadmoor Hospital, his duty done.

Freedom tasted for the first time in almost twenty-five years. Heady exhilaration restrained by his fifty-nine years. No handcuffs for Yorkie, the fat half blind beast of Bingley, no need. Ice cold winds sweep in from the Irish Sea and savage the desolate beach, savage the forlorn figures. Childhood memories, happy memories, memories. Camp sites, campfires, the great outdoors. Not Bradford, not Leeds, not Manchester, not Huddersfield, not Halifax, not industrialisation but agricultural. Heaven on Earth? Peter reminisced about the family caravan and all the holidays, Peter reminisced and in the distance he thought he heard an echoing ambiguous voice unclear, but near. The lone figure turns and walks to the group *"OK chaps, let's go back to the van"*.

2005CE clinically obese and a diabetic (a gift from God in 2003 CE) Peter needs to lose weight to ease his condition, to maintain his health. Peter even put his name down to join the gym housed within the walls of Broadmoor. Currently his diabetes is not under control and his blood sugar levels are menacingly high. Peter is a man with a plan, he knows the importance of exercise in combatting his illness and is keen to get into the gym and onto the weights, the rowing machine and the treadmill. He believes the doctors are too keen to administer insulin injections and has refused their best endeavours to do so, creating a little friction between himself and the health care professionals. But Peter is adamant, telling anybody that will listen of his plans.

"If I can lose some weight, my blood sugar levels should come down. If I can bring the B/S levels down I could avoid the insulin! I'm a man with a plan! Tee hee".

Peter the good Christian dismisses the 1997CE attack that left him blind in one eye, the support of his fellow Jehovah's Witnesses, his brothers allowing him to come to terms with the incident and proffer forgiveness on its perpetrator.

"I have forgiven the mentally ill person who did it as I am a Christian! It happened eight years ago so it's history". He also reflected on his present position and how life had treated him.

"Things could be worse! In fact lots of people are worse off in the world through poverty, disease, starvation, wars etc.!"

Chapter 49
The Devils Accomplice

2004CE, Detective Chief Superintendent Chris Gregg, of the West Yorkshire Police Force Homicide and Major Enquiry Team orders a cold case review the hoax letters or any remnants of theme were required, but first they needed to be located. Searches were undertaken in three UK forensic laboratories, Birmingham, London and Wetherby. Nothing was found in the Birmingham and Wetherby labs, conversely concealed in a corner of the London laboratory was three almost anonymous slivers of paper, (approximately 1cm by 1½ cm) originally it was part of the envelope that housed one of the hoax letters, *Pen-pal (Daily Mirror) Two Monday 13th March 1978CE*. These small scraps of paper 'housed' the gummed seal. DNA science had progressed massively in the intervening years and the police felt now was a golden opportunity. Sterile swab to sterile scalpel, one chance and one chance only. For the process would result in the destruction of the original sample.

The results were cross referenced with the National Police DNA Database holding profiles of all samples of convicted criminals since 2001CE, then came the breakthrough. A result of a database HIT. John Samuel Humble, 08-Jan-56, sample taken by Northumbria Police Force. Come in Wearside Jack your time is up. John was a petty criminal with a litany of minor misdemeanours to his name, he had gained a place on the register after being arrested for assault
In 2001CE, like the saliva that sealed the envelope way back in 1978CE the arrest and the collection of his DNA sealed his fate.

Tuesday the 18th of October 2005 CE, West Yorkshire Police officers arrested a forty-nine-year-old unemployed Sunderland man in relation to the hoax Ripper letters and tape, who was dubbed by the media 'Wearside Jack'. He was taken to a West Yorkshire police station for further investigations.

Wednesday the 19th of October 2005 CE,

The police leapt into action, attending 51 Flodden Road, Sunderland SR4. Their suspect incoherent in drink, shocked and stunned unable to comprehend his ruse of years gone by had come home to roost. It took the old soak a good time to sober up after years of alcoholism, the cause or cure of his earlier mister meaner? Sobriety and realisation begin to kick in but the suspect a non-descript individual, non-committal when quizzed on all things Yorkshire Ripper.

John Humble of Flodden Road, Ford Estate, Sunderland is named as the suspect in custody. John Humble is revealed/unveiled as 'Wearside Jack'. *'I see you are having no luck catching me?'* Words echo through time, travelling twenty-seven years, we be echo, for John is the devil's accomplice or is he? After hours of interviews John was refusing to talk, it was during a break in hostilities that the police informed John's solicitor that they had DNA evidence linking Humble to the crime, John was a billion-to-one match, John was 'Wearside Jack'. It seems that for John his luck as run out and the West Yorkshire Police Force don't need luck just DNA evidence. And then 19:46 hours and 13 seconds, it's been a long day for John, struggling to function without the crutch of alcohol to assist, high tension, high stakes, John decides to come clean, to clean up his act?

Detective Sergeant Stuart Smith, *"John this is your opportunity to tell your version of the story and your side of events what can you tell me about it John?"*

John Samuel Humble, *"I did send it".*

"Just repeat that for me what did you say?"

"I did send the letter?"

"Tell me all about it John".

"Later on June I sent a tape it's got me voice on it".

The devil's accomplice, but what is the back story to this man? John Samuel Humble born Sunday the 8th of January 1956CE, he grew up on the Hylton Lane Estate to the South East of Sunderland city centre. John Humble attended Hylton Road Primary School and then Havelock Secondary School, where he left little or no real impression. He lived with his mother and father Violet and Samuel, along with his two siblings Harry and Jean. Samuel died in 1964CE. John's working career was as unremarkable as his schooling, his various jobs included security guard, builder's labourer and window cleaner. He enjoyed watching football and playing darts. John visited Kayll Road library, Sunderland, SR4, where he gained inspiration for his hoax, the contents of a green-covered hard back book about Jack the Ripper was to prove fateful in the Yorkshire Ripper saga. John borrowed the book as early as 1974CE, copying transcripts and information from its pages, he became fascinated with the crimes and the killer. He also took great interest in newspaper articles and television and radio reports on the so-called Yorkshire Ripper. In 1990CE John married Anne Mason. The couple lived together for over fourteen years, however their relationship floundered when John lost his job and began to drink heavily, Anne left John. John then moved in with his brother Harry where his life spiralled further out of control. The pair became commonly known as the 'alkie brothers', John taking on another pseudo name 'John the Bag' on account of his many visits to HS Fairley off Licence with his rucksack to buy booze. All day drinking, despair and what ifs. Alcoholism to escape a humdrum life, to escape the guilt and nightmares.

No story, notoriety, publicity, hoax call, hoax life, free from the mundane half-life of unemployment, petty crime, existence and subsistence. A retched wraith like figure ravaged through drink, time had been unkind to John. John had been unkind at times.

Most notorious criminal hoaxer in history an investigation saboteur an accomplice of the beast of Bingley.

Thursday the 20th of October 2005 CE, John Humble appeared at Leeds Magistrates Court charged with attempting to pervert the course of justice. Nimble, humble, dressed from a jumble, drunken mumble, blood red hand, on remand.

Wednesday the 26th of October 2005 CE, the wonders of modern technology sees John Humble AKA Wearside Jack appear at Leeds Crown Court via 'live' video link up. The obligatory application for bail is rejected and he is remanded in custody at Armley Jail. Echoes of Peter, echoes of nearly twenty-five years past. A provisional trial date is set for his long overdue date with justice, February 2006 CE and Humble is ordered to appear before the court on Monday the 9th of January 2006 CE and make his plea.

Monday the 9th of January arrives and so too does his day in court. Humble, humbled but not bowed makes a live appearance where he entered a plea of not guilty to all charges in relation to Wearside Jack's letters and tapes. This time no application for police bail is made and Humble returns to Armley Jail to await his trial. The big day was set aside Monday the 20th March 2006CE.

In 2009 CE Humble was released under the pseudonym John Samuel Anderson.

Sonia Maree (McCann) Newlands

09:28 hours, Wednesday the 19th of December 2007CE, Sonia Newlands body is discovered by police in her Leeds flat. Sonia died aged thirty-nine; she had taken her own life. Sonia was the eldest daughter of Wilma McCann the first official murder victim of the Yorkshire Ripper.
Sonia had found life difficult to come to terms with especially after the violent and premature loss of her mother over thirty-two years ago. She had battled through life's difficulties compounded by health issues and alcohol addiction having attended a rehabilitation centre in her constant battle.

Another victim, a legacy of an indiscriminate, evil, twisted and sadistic murderer Peter William Sutcliffe/Coonan.

Sonia Marree Newlands, born the Tuesday the 1st of October 1968CE, died Tuesday the 18th of December 2007CE.

Chapter 50
Peter Meets Patrick

In 2000 CE Patrick was invited to his mother's Mitcham Park home, in Surrey, for a respite from the confines of Springfield Mental Hospital, where he was receiving treatment after being diagnosed as a paranoid schizophrenic. Whilst he was there an argument developed, this resulted in Patrick killing his sixty-nine-year-old mother, guilty of the murder of his mother. He strangled her believing that she was part of a New Labour government plot to assassinate him for his Conservative beliefs.

He appeared in court for sentencing on the 18th August 2001 CE, but was considered unfit to plea, in effect Sureda was not able to stand trial due to his mental frailty. As a result he was ordered to be detained indefinitely in a high security mental hospital, until he was fit for trial.

Saturday the 22nd of December 2007 CE, 13:00 hours in the Dorchester Ward at Broadmoor hospital. Peter Coonan sat eating his dinner, along with fellow patients, in the refectory. One such patient was Patrick Sureda. Most of the group were on second helpings but one man was not. Patrick was perturbed, troubled and distressed. Unable to focus on his food, incapable of concentrating on the task in hand. That of eating his dinner, he had cut it up with the stainless-steel table knife and was pushing it around his plate but was not actually eating it. Patrick saw Peter, Patrick saw the Yorkshire Ripper, Patrick identified his target. Patrick (then aged forty-one) pounced on his target, the man twenty years his senior. He then jumped up from the table and surged towards Peter who was sat with his back to him.
"I'll teach you, you bastard, for killing all those women".
Wielding the stainless-steel table knife, he aimed the blade at Peter's right eye. He screamed frothing with anger. *"You fucking raping, murdering bastard, I'll blind your fucking other one".*
The noise the fury, the vitriol alerted Peter of his assailant who had the advantage of stealth and surprise attacking from the rear. Patrick leapt onto Peter, he grabbed Peter around the neck, with his left arm. Half throttling, half holding, in his right hand seven inches of cold steel, pinning Peter to the chair he pushed the blade of the knife into his victim.

Peter struggled and forced himself and the chair backwards diverting the metal knifed blade away from his right eye, instead the steel blade cut the flesh on Peter's cheek, a centimetre below his eye. The blade penetrated his cheek, hitting the cheekbone and preventing further penetration. One, two, three, four times he stabbed and sliced at Peter's right eye. Thirteen patients and four nurses watched in stunned silence as the onslaught continued for about forty seconds, fast, furious, viscous and short lived. Roy Woodhouse a Health Care Assistant at Broadmoor was first to react, grappling Sureda away from his victim. Other hospital orderlies struggled to release the weapon from the attacker's grip.

The nurses quickly restrained Sureda, in total four of them overpowered him and placed him in a room on the isolation ward. The commotion over, the floor show finished, a restrained calm returned to the hospital floor. Peter was left with an inch-long scar just below his right eye.

Peter was taken to receive medical assistance, they deemed that Peter's injuries did not warrant a hospital appointment. Sureda eventually calmed down and later explained to the orderlies that he had intended to blind the patient formerly known as the Yorkshire Ripper. Thursday the 28th of February 2008 CE Patrick was charged with attempted wounding with intent, this charge was not made public for a further three months.

Monday the 2nd of June 2008 CE, it was decided that Patrick Sureda was declared still not fit to be tried for the murder of his mother some eight years previously, due to a relapse in his mental condition.

On Thursday the 5th of June 2008 CE it was revealed that the jury judged that Patrick Sureda had unlawfully killed his mother and he was remanded back to Broadmoor Hospital, until it was viewed he was fit for sentencing.

Leading up to the trial Patrick's mental condition continued to show signs for concern, he thought that his lawyers were in cahoots with MI6, the Royal Secret Intelligence Service; Dieu Et Mon Droit, God and my right, working globally to face and prevent threats and challenges to the United Kingdom's security, obtaining intelligence to counteract threats to the sovereign state. Working with the public to counter terrorism. Patrick refused to talk to his legal team, acting on the instructions of 'his' voices. He did not deny attacking the Yorkshire Ripper, in fact he openly admitted it. He also continually complained that he was in no fit state to be in court and his emotional and mental frailty impacted on his ability to function. He bemoaned the injustice from the courtroom dock at Reading Crown Court, the Forbury, Reading RG1 3EH.

Thursday 19th of November 2009 CE the jury returned a verdict on Patrick's alleged attack on Peter. They found Patrick Sureda guilty of attacking and wounding Peter Coonan with intent, in the dining room incident at Broadmoor, at Christmas almost two years previously.

Chapter 51
Regina versus Coonan

Monday the 1st of March 2010 CE, Peter William Coonan's legal team were requesting the High Court to set a finite minimum sentence on Coonan/Sutcliffe.

Thursday the 6th of May 2010 CE sees the High Court office announce a date of Friday the 16th of July 2010 CE for a tariff-setting hearing, this was done as a direct response to Peter Coonan's earlier application. This coincides with an upturn in Peter's demeanour, he is in an up-beat mood positive that one day he may yet be a free man. He views parole as a real possibility a target, a goal an objective to aim for. Peter knows he can now longer be viewed as a danger, his sixty-three years on the face of this world had taken its toll. But nevertheless Peter was happy his disposition enriched by the prospect of parole.

Friday the 16th of July 2010 CE, his day came, Sutcliffe's application for a minimum term to be set is heard at the High Court of Justice, the Strand, City of Westminster in London. Mr. Justice Mitting returned the ruling emphasising that the applicant must serve a whole life tariff, declaring that in the case of Sutcliffe/Coonan or more importantly the Yorkshire Ripper; *"An appropriate minimum term is a whole life term"*. Unless the law courts rule differently Peter Sutcliffe/Coonan will remain in Broadmoor Hospital for the rest of his life. Disheartened and downbeat, but still with some hope, Peter continued to place his faith in the judicial system, the judicial system that punished him and continued to punish him.

Wednesday the 4th of August 2010 CE the Judicial Communications Office confirm that Sutcliffe/Coonan as invoked his right to question the High Court of Justice's decision. Mr. Justice Whiting presides over a direction hearing to plan what evidence is submitted and how to plan the tariff setting hearing, Regina Versus Coonan. What could happen next? There are only one of two options. Mr. Justice Whiting could set a fixed term tariff that must be served prior to Sutcliffe/Coonan being eligible to apply for release. Or he could decide that Sutcliffe/Coonan must spend the rest of his years behind bars. Either way Sutcliffe/Coonan would not breath free air until the authorities were sure that he did not represent a danger to the general public.

High stakes indeed, Peter knew he was walking a knife edge. But he had nothing to lose. Peter knew all about knives, Stanley knives, screwdrivers, hammers, cord, broken glass, hacksaws, broken coffee jars, table knives and pens. For the pen is mightier than the sword, but it is now Peter's only hope. Another make or break meeting.

Tuesday the 30th of November 2010 CE, Sutcliffe's appeal hearing begins at the Court of Appeal, Royal Courts of Justice, in London.

Friday the 14th of January 2011 CE, Sutcliffe's appeal is rejected. His hopes shattered, a triumvirate of judges decree that considering Peter William Sutcliffe/Coonan heinous crimes a whole life tariff was the only viable recompense, the punishment had to fit the crime, it had to be proportionate to his hideous acts.

Wednesday the 9th of March 2011 CE, Sutcliffe's application to the Court of Appeal requesting the opportunity to appeal to the Supreme Court is rejected. In essence extinguishing any prospect of freedom.

June 2016 CE, a recent health tribunal considered that Peter was mentally well and no longer required treatment at Broadmoor. It is announced that plans are underway to reintroduce Peter back into the mainstream prison service. After over thirty-two years in Broadmoor. Uncertain, scared, afraid of the newfound ambiguity.

The former beast of Bingley, a timid, unhealthy and frail shadow of his former self. The Yorkshire Ripper had gone, all that remained was an empty vessel, inept and evil. Yet well. Unforgiven and unforgotten, Peter Sutcliffe/Coonan, once the Yorkshire Ripper born 1969 CE, died 2001 CE, aged thirty-two years old. Tainted by illness, touched by madness and evil to the core.

Saturday the 3rd of October 2015CE and Peter Coonan AKA Sutcliffe furthermore known as the Yorkshire Ripper roams free once more. 07:25 hours a strange cavalcade leaves Broadmoor Hospital, a dark blue transit van inconspicuous hiding its grim contents *"They came and got me up before seven. I don't like to get up at weekends until at least eight. They didn't give me any warning, just came and got me and told me I was going to hospital".*
Strolling, shuffling, joking
Crocs and socks unfashionable to the hilt, but a way of dealing with chronic smelly feet, bright red trousers, a beige overcoat hiding the bloated body of the wearer and a black baseball cap to disguise the features of the man beneath.

Their destination Frimley Park Hospital and the eye clinic for tests; 08:40 hours and the group left in the forlorn hope that nobody had witnessed their little outing, fifteen minutes later 08:55 hours they were back at Broadmoor make believing that none of this had ever happened. Peter settled down to his breakfast and although a little flustered and perturbed at the disruption to his routine, this was soon forgotten.

During November and December 2015 CE there were news reports that Sutcliffe was to face a Tribunal about being forced out of Broadmoor and back to Prison. Around the same time his former treatment expert of ten years went public and deemed that Sutcliffe was no longer mentally ill and should be treated in Prison for his Severe Personality Disorder.

Thursday the 24th of August 2016 CE, Peter William Sutcliffe/Coonan is moved from Broadmoor High Security Hospital to Her Majesty's Prison Frankland, Brasside, Durham DH1, not a million miles away from the stomping ground of Wearside Jack. Maybe 'Wearside Jack' may pay him a visit, or maybe not. Allegedly Peter crossed swords with his hapless accomplice. In 2006CE it was reported that Peter Sutcliffe/Coonan has written two letters to John Humble, or so the story goes. In one of the letters Sutcliffe/Coonan is said to have written:

"You have had your 15 minutes of fame and you have reopened old wounds again and put me back in the media spotlight. I do not need this now or ever again. The same thing will happen when you are released. You could have saved those three women, John. You have blood on your hands. I was under the influence of voices, what was your excuse, John? Drink and drugs, I hear".

During April and May 2017 CE it was leaked that he has been interviewed on two occasions for attacks and murders on a further seventeen victims. This left a chilling postscript to the sorry saga, opening up victims' false hopes of justice and closure. A cold case review probably instigated by Chris Clark's and Tim Tate's book Yorkshire Ripper, The Secret Murders, two plain clothed detectives had visited Coonan at Frankland Prison, possible victims were also contacted and asked to make new statements.

He also wrote:

"I want you to write back, John, so that we may exchange letters and maybe then organise a visit here. We have loads to talk about. I want you to say sorry for your crimes and interfering in the police investigation". Sutcliffe also inquires whether Humble was responsible for other killings at the time. His letter was signed: *"your friend Peter".* John Samuel Humble aka Anderson, died on Tuesday the 30th July 2019 CE, Peter never met John.

It was unfortunate however that his alter ego crossed paths with the various women documented in this book, and had an alleged Sutcliffe failed suicide attempt at Altar Rock, Bingley, in the early sixties been successful the Yorkshire Ripper would have never existed. A truly regrettable individual who reeked misery and mayhem on a generation.

References

The Yorkshire Ripper, The authorative study of the most vicious series of murders this century, Michael Nicholson, 1979, Star

I'm Jack, The police hunt for the Yorkshire Ripper, Peter Kinsley and Frank Smyth, 1980, Pan

The Yorkshire Ripper Story, John Beattie, 1981, Quarter/Star

The Yorkshire Ripper, The in-depth study of a amass killer and his methods, Roger Cross, 1981, Granada

Deliver Us From Evil, The harrowing story of the tracking and arrest of the Yorkshire Ripper, David A Yallop, 1982, Coward, McCann and Geoghegan

Somebody's Husband, Somebody's Son, The story of Peter Sutcliffe, Gordon Burn, 1984, Heinemann

The Streetcleaner, The Yorkshire Ripper case on trial, Nicole Ward Jouve, 1986, Marion Boyars

The Real Yorkshire Ripper, The evidence that was concealed. The deal for Sutcliffe's "Confessions" and the cover up, Noel O'Gara, 1995

Voices From An Evil God, The true story of the Yorkshire Ripper and the woman who loves him, Barbara Jones, 1992, Blake

Wearside Jack, The hunt for the hoaxer of the century, Patrick Lavelle, 1999, Northeast Press

Shadow of the Ripper, The secret story of the man who helped the Yorkshire Ripper to kill and kill again, Patrick Lavelle, 2003, Blake

Wicked Beyond Belief, The Hunt for the YorkshireRipper, michael Bilton, 2003, Harper Collins

Just A Boy, The true story of a stolen childhood, Richard McCann, 2004, Ebury Press

The Grim Ripper & Other UK Unsolved Crimes, Chris Clark (The Armchair Detective).

Yorkshire Ripper, The Secret Murders, Chris Clark and Tim Tate, 2015, Blake

Printed in Great Britain
by Amazon